Tobias
of the Amish

Tobias
of the Amish

*A true story of tangled strands in faith,
family and community*

Ervin R. Stutzman

Foreword by
Katie Funk Wiebe

Herald
Press

Scottdale, Pennsylvania
Waterloo, Ontario

Library of Congress Cataloging-in-Publication Data
Stutzman, Ervin R., 1953-
   Tobias of the Amish : a true story of tangled strands in faith, family, and
community / Ervin R. Stutzman ; foreword by Katie Funk Wiebe.
      p. cm.
   ISBN 0-8361-9170-6 (alk. paper)
      1. Stutzman, Tobias J., 1918-1956—Fiction. 2. Kansas—Fiction. 3. Amish—
Fiction. I. Title.

PS3619.T88 T63 2001
813'.6—dc21   2001024401

The paper used in this publication is recycled and meets the minimum require-
ments of American National Standard for Information Sciences—Permanence
of Paper for Printed Library Materials, ANSI Z39.48-1984.

TOBIAS OF THE AMISH
Copyright © 2001 by Herald Press, Scottdale, Pa. 15683
   Published simultaneously in Canada by Herald Press,
   Waterloo, Ont. N2L 6H7. All rights reserved
Published in association with DreamSeeker Books
Library of Congress Catalog Card Number: 2001024401
International Standard Book Numbers: 0-8361-9170-6 (paperback)
Printed in the United States of America
Book design by Michael A. King, Pandora Press U.S.,
   in consultation with Merrill R. Miller, Herald Press
Cover design by Merrill R. Miller
Cover art by Allan M. Burch

11 10 09 08 07 06 05   10 9 8 7 6

To order or request information, please call
1-800-759-4447 (individuals); 1-800-245-7894 (trade).
Website: www.mph.org

To my mother,
Emma L. Stutzman

Contents

Foreword

The search for one's father is age-old, going back to ancient Greek mythology. In this book, the author seeks a father he never knew. Tobe Stutzman died when the author was three, yet as the son grew up he heard legends of his father's accomplishments.

The book develops a number of significant themes. First, it offers closeups of the Amish people. The unity of the Amish family and community is striking. Husband/wife relationships show up as well, with respective roles in the family well-defined, rarely overlapping. The Ordnung (church expectations) and how it affects individual lives features large in the story.

Also apparent is the slow drift of the Amish toward less conservative churches under the influence of modernity. More education, revival movements, and use of cars, trucks, electricity, and phones are yearned for by some and vigorously rejected by others.

The third and strongest theme is the author's search for his father. Often today's public image of the Amish is of a serene, staid, and almost stodgy people. In Tobe Stutzman that mold was broken. The tug of creativity started young. He approached life in his own unique way even as a child. As an adult the drive to create furniture and metal equipment with his hands was strong. He knew what he wanted to make but always lacked sufficient venture capital to fund his projects. Another hindrance was his limited education, given that he had finished only the eighth grade. His great assets were physical strength, energy, and creativity.

With his hand-built goods and Amish ways of doing business, Tobe competed in a non-Amish commercial world. This meant a shop not hooked up to a public power system, no telephone, no car to solicit business, no trucks to transport products. Lacking an understanding of cost accounting, Tobe undercharged his customers. He had to hire vehicles and drivers to take him and his products to their destination. Advertising was a form of pride. He made up for the difference with hard work and long hours.

His business suffered several shop accidents because he lacked safety equipment. Sometimes his inventions flopped because they hadn't been thought through well enough to succeed in a world powered by electricity. He couldn't understand why people didn't trust him to pay his debts when he fell behind. He knew he would make good on his promises as long as he had health and strength.

In pursuit of his dream, he stretched the patience and good will of Amish church leaders by skirting the boundaries of Amish regulations. Eventually he got caught in the legal system, which demanded debt repayment. His investors, even from his church, finally forced him to declare bankruptcy. But that didn't deter him. He immediately started up again.

Ervin Stutzman writes with empathy and respect, acknowledging the strengths of the man he never knew. His depiction of his father is gentle, never demeaning. At the same time he doesn't turn away from what he found—a father's lack of good judgment in business decisions.

Well-known in American folklore is the poem (author unknown) telling of John Henry, a black steel driver for the railroad. His work is to pound a drill into rock to make a hole for explosives. Like Tobe Stutzman he is a large and strong man. One day he accepts a challenge to compete with a mechanical steel drill. Using a twelve-pound hammer, he outdoes the mechanical drill but dies of overexertion. Muscle power cannot defeat industrialization.

I see Tobe Stutzman as another John Henry, competing with modern industry and technology, primarily with creative genius and physical strength. It isn't enough. He can't win against the unfair odds. But if he died outdone in battle, he lives on in these pages. Read and enjoy.

—*Katie Funk Wiebe*
Wichita, Kansas

Author's Preface

Tobias of the Amish is an invitation to join me at a significant milestone in my life's journey. Death claimed my father, Tobias J. Stutzman, when I was a toddler. I have no memories of him. My mother rarely spoke of him. As a young man, I heard people say that my father was an ambitious Amish entrepreneur who ran into serious financial trouble. Until a few years ago, I was content to hear the sounds of silence that surrounded my father's death.

At that time I began searching for answers to my many persistent questions. What fueled my father's ambition? What prompted him to leave the traditional Amish practice of farming to pursue entrepreneurial business ventures? What gave him the tenacity to pursue his dreams in a church community that shuns progress and prizes tradition? What enabled him to rally support from conservative investors for his risky ventures? How did the church deal with his failures? I have rummaged through the corporate memories of his life, searching for clues in this quest.

While most events happened in the relative order in which they are presented here, this volume is not a strict chronology. Further, I have spared you the tedium of reading many dates. For the most part, I placed the events in a time frame by relating them to the seasons of the year or other events in the community or nation. I want you to experience the book as a story book, not a history book.

All three Amish communities—Thomas, Oklahoma; Hutchinson, Kansas; and Kalona, Iowa—portrayed in this volume used Pennsylvania German in everyday speech. They sang hymns in high German and used Martin Luther's translation of the Bible. For the reader's sake, this volume translates (or transliterates) both monologue and dialogue into English. The Pennsylvania German is written in italics, immediately followed by an English rendering. The reason for including German words is to remind the reader that the use of German functions as an important separator between the Amish and their more worldly friends and neighbors, usually called "the English." Language profoundly shapes one's reality and identity.

While *Tobias* is first of all a book about my father, it is much more. It is also the story of a family and faith community struggling with the challenges of a modern world. My father's story was vitally shaped by his participation in the three small Amish communities where he spent his life. None of these are widely recognized for their Amish population. Yet the story of the Amish and their contribution to American society is told most faithfully when it takes into account small communities scattered across the United States, including those that failed to thrive.

Finally, I trust that my story will prompt you to embark on a search for meaning in your own family history. How I wish I could hear your reflections as you hear mine. But that's enough talk *about* the journey. Let's get started.

—*Ervin Stutzman*
Harrisonburg, Virginia

Acknowledgments

This book is the culmination of many years of work, with much encouragement from people along the way. They deserve my sincere acknowledgment.

Most of all, I acknowledge the role that my oldest sister, Mary Edna (Stutzman) Yoder, played in the writing of this book. Just after Christmas in 1994, she was diagnosed with an advanced malignancy. In the spring of 1995, as she struggled with the prognosis that the cancer would take her life, she expressed a wish to read my manuscript before she died. Later, as she sorted through her personal belongings in preparation to die, she found personal diaries written in her childhood and teenage years. She shared them with me. Mary's involvement motivated me to concentrate on the project so that I could share it with her before her impending death. And her diaries filled in some informational gaps for the years 1953-56. She read the emerging manuscript a few weeks before she died and provided still further information.

Although I have chosen not to include reference notes in this text, I want to acknowledge some of the sources I used. I drew general information from many written sources, including legal records and published sources such as the *Hutchinson News; Pennsylvania Mennonite Heritage; American Mennonites and the Great War*, by Gerlof D. Homan; the *Herold der Wahrheit;* the *Sugarcreek Budget;* and the *Gospel Herald*. I drew much more specific information from the diaries of Walter

Beachy, Fannie Nisly, Mahon Wagler, Mary Yoder, and my mother, Emma Stutzman. These sources helped to provide depth and perspective, as well as a time frame for events.

As the manuscript grew to full length, I shared it with a number of readers, who provided both encouragement and counsel. My thanks go to Robert Baker, Janet Kreider, Elizabeth Kreider, Hubert Pellman, Carroll Yoder, and Paul Nisly for critiquing the work from a literary point of view. Their comments led to some extensive revisions.

David L. Miller and David Wagler, both of Partridge, Kansas, also read the manuscript. They each have extensive knowledge of the community life and history of the Amish, so they were able to critique the manuscript with an eye for nuances of fact as well as tone. Their comments and suggestions were very helpful.

Noah Good of Lancaster Mennonite Historical Society read the manuscript for the purpose of standardizing the Pennsylvania German script. Other staff at the Lancaster Mennonite Historical Society provided historical materials and other resources that broadened my perspective and lent greater historical depth to my work.

I am indebted to the many people who comprised the community of memory from which I drew this narrative. Dozens of family members, friends of my father, former employees, and other members of Amish communities in several states readily responded to my queries. Some shared their diaries or other written accounts with me. A number of them read the manuscript to insure its accuracy. Without the participation of these many informants, this project would not have been possible.

I am also indebted to Louise Stoltzfus as editor of the manuscript for Pandora Press U.S., which developed the book for Herald Press. Her skilled writing helped to make the book more readable. She also drew attention to possible errors of fact and matters of particular historical sensitivity. Any inaccuracies or indiscretions that remain, must of course, must be laid at my feet.

Last of all, I acknowledge the loving patience of my wife, Bonita, who accompanied me along the way in this journey. She has been a source of much encouragement.

Tobias
of the Amish

1

Prologue: Buried Dreams

Anna Stutzman sank into her rocking chair as the last rays of the midsummer sun dimmed on the Kansas horizon. Her bentwood hickory rocker soon moved in rhythm to the ticking of the Seth Thomas mantel clock. It had just turned dark outside when the Westminster chimes announced her bedtime—9:30 p.m.

Anna made no move to get out of her chair, glancing instead toward the bedroom where her son's body had lain for the funeral wake last night. These twenty-four hours later, he lay buried under the Kansas loam.

A caravan of mourners had threaded its way toward the Amish cemetery. The horse-drawn rig in front of her set the pace, pressed into Sunday service as a hearse. The early June sun beat down mercilessly on the carriages moving west on the sandy road. Waves of shimmering heat blurred the horizon under a cloudless prairie sky. Here and there in the procession a few cars with overheated radiators belched out steam. The fragrance of newly mown alfalfa hovered in the dry air, wafted on an occasional puff of the south wind. This scent blended with the rich aroma of nearly ripe grain in a nearby wheat field. It was occasionally spoiled by the odor of fresh dung, falling to the roadway in the wake of a flagging horse tail.

The lead wagon paused, then crossed Route 61, the hard-surfaced road that angled southwest out of Hutchinson through a grid of country roads. A mile away in the village of Partridge, a tall wheat elevator stood like a sentry on the horizon.

As they approached the burial ground, Anna looked beyond it to the next intersection. An old windmill stood among several ruined buildings surrounded by trees. It was the place where her son Tobe (one syllable, long "o") and his wife Emma had started housekeeping sixteen years earlier.

She glanced over at her daughter-in-law, whose face was etched with grief. The driver slowed and stopped the horse at the gate to the West Center Amish cemetery. White foam flecked the corners of the horse's bridle and dropped to the browning grass. An attendant slid off the wagon to open the gates. He uncoupled the short chain and swung open the two hinged gates made of woven wire that were stretched over metal-pipe frames. The horse stood still as the pallbearers slid the casket off the back of the wagon and carried it through the gate.

Dry prairie sod mixed with clay lay beside the yawning hole, hand-dug by volunteers the day before. A pair of garden spades angled out of the earthen pile. Three wooden boards spanned the top of the grave. The pallbearers gently laid the bier onto the boards as the family arrived at the grave. John D. Yoder, the white-bearded Old Order Amish bishop, motioned the family members toward one side of the hand-hewn vault. Anna stood silently alongside daughter-in-law Emma and her extended family.

Several dozen small grave markers lined the yard around them. Nearly all the monuments looked alike—round-topped slabs made of concrete. Some engravings were badly faded, the words rendered illegible by overexposure to the elements. A larger monument designated the place where sixteen bodies had been brought from nearby Ford County, Kansas. The Amish who abandoned that settlement for Hutchinson and

Partridge dug up the remains of their dead to bury them close at hand. A few gravestones kept vigil at the head of shrinking mounds, evidence of recent burials. Without the benefit of concrete vaults or waterproof caskets, the soil piled on the graves gradually sank until it was level with its surroundings.

Knotted ropes choked the rusty hitching rail that bordered the burial ground. The horses drew up quickly, eager to stand in the shade of the hedge trees planted by early settlers along the fence row. Buggies tipped sharply as passengers disembarked. Cars pulled off into the shallow ditches on both sides of the gravel road. Anna wrung her hands as the crowd of mourners swelled around her. Soon there were more than a hundred.

Anna watched as her three-year-old grandson, Ervin Ray, squirmed noisily in Cora Yoder's arms. As a minister's wife, Cora had special compassion for Emma's children. The young boy wiggled as he pointed toward the grave. Just then Noah Nisly, Emma's stepfather, admonished the woman, "*Du kannscht ihn annestellaeh, er kann selwert schteh.* You can let him down, he can stand by himself." Cora nodded and released the wiggling toddler. The young boy slipped out of her arms and onto the ground. He edged toward the wooden box that held his father's still body.

The assembly listened reverently as a small group raised their voices in song. Then the bishop stepped forward, perspiration beading his broad forehead. Dressed in black trousers, a long-sleeved white shirt, and a black suit coat fastened with small hooks and eyes, he opened a tiny black minister's manual and comforted the mourners with several passages of Scripture. Then came the familiar words of the committal:

> Forasmuch as it has pleased Almighty God, in his wise providence, to take out of this world the soul of the departed, we commit the body to the ground; earth to

earth, ashes to ashes, dust to dust, and commit the soul to God who gave it. . . .

The men removed their hats as the minister bowed his head to pray. A meadowlark sang from the fence at the edge of the yard. A whirlwind raised a flurry of dust on the road and flattened the grass in its path. Anna reached up to hold her bonnet as the dust devil swept through the crowd. The preacher's "Amen" was accented by the whistle of an approaching train on the tracks that ran along the highway.

Everyone stepped back as the attendants prepared for the burial. Grasping opposite ends of two braided hemp ropes, four men swung the loops under the wooden coffin. As they hoisted it off its wooden supports, two assistants drew away the boards that spanned the grave. The men lowered the coffin into the rough wooden box, releasing the ropes hand over hand. The bier sank unevenly into the rough box, then leveled as the ropes slackened against the bottom. On silent cue, the men on one side dropped their end of the ropes. The other pair tugged on the remaining ends, dragging the ropes out of the hole. Two-by-six-inch planks were laid over the box to keep out the soil, and several men picked up spades and began shoveling sod into the hole. Others stepped forward to relieve them. Soon a large mound marked Tobe Stutzman's resting place.

Anna walked away from the grave in silence. The pall of death pressed in like the summer heat.

Caught in her reverie, Anna paused her rocking as her husband John called from the bedroom. "Aren't you coming to bed?"

"Before long." She fanned herself vigorously with the newspaper that held her son's obituary. The clock struck ten as she picked up her glasses to read the obituary for the third time that evening.

Tobias J. Stutzman, son of John and Anna (Miller) Stutzman was born at Thomas, Oklahoma October 21, 1918 and died May 31, 1956 at the age of 37 years, 6 months and 10 days. He was married to Emma Nisly in Hutchinson, Kansas, October 10, 1940. Survivors included his widow, three daughters, and three sons: Mary, 14, Perry, 13, Glenn, 11, Edith, 8, and twins Ervin and Erma, 3. Also his parents and three brothers, Ervin, Clarence, and Perry, all of Hutchinson, Kansas.

Fresh tears coursed onto her cheeks as she again read the poem at the end:

The call was sudden, the shock severe
Little did we think his end so near,
Only those bereft can tell,
The sadness of parting without a farewell.

Anna had overheard a few people talking in hushed tones about the way her son had died. Was it God's punishment for breaking the church's rules about owning a car? There were whispered questions about other things too. Tobe worked fast and hard but couldn't always keep pace with his ambitious promises. To advance his innovative business ventures, he freely borrowed money from members of the church. Had they ever been repaid? What motivated him to act that way in the first place? What was he trying to accomplish?

Anna and John were unlikely to discuss these questions. What good would it do? It was time to pick up the pieces. To help Emma find a way to make a living for her family.

Anna put down the newspaper and began to hum a gospel tune. Then she sang the verses aloud: "What a friend we have in Jesus. . . . Are we weak and heavy laden, cumbered with a load of care? We should never be discouraged; take it to the Lord in prayer." As she finished the last notes of the song, she lifted herself out of the chair and went to bed.

Had anyone ventured to ask Anna, she would likely have had plenty to say about her son's ambitious dreams. She, more than anyone except Tobe himself, witnessed the tangled strands of Tobe's life, from the time of his birth to the awful moment when it was cut short by the grim reaper. Along with Tobe's father, John, Anna wove the first strands in Tobe's life.

2

Seeds of Ambition

It was just ten days before Halloween, October 1918. Anna Stutzman stood at the dry sink in their old farmhouse near Thomas, Oklahoma. The ground was white with frost.

Through the window, she watched an Indian family pass by on the road. A man with long black braids sat in the seat of the steel-wheeled wagon. A very large woman sat on the back, her feet dangling from the tailgate. The horse moseyed along, his ribs pressed hard against his gaunt sides. A greyhound dog trotted alongside. As the group passed the farm lane, the dog took off in hot pursuit of a jackrabbit. The hare ran through the farm yard and in front of the shed just as Anna's husband John stepped outside with his wheelbarrow.

Anna reached for a potato as she watched the dog pursue the rabbit into the field. A cock pheasant flew away with a startled cackle as the dog passed. She had just finished peeling the potato when she stepped to the door and shouted toward the shed, "John, go for the doctor. The baby's coming."

Anna's urgency propelled her phlegmatic husband into action. "I'll drop by to tell your folks," he said. "Then I'll go for the doctor." John hurried toward the barn to harness the horse. It was six miles to the doctor's office.

Anna watched John as he prepared to leave. Even when he was in a hurry, her husband of two years moved much more slowly than her own father, Ananias Miller. Known as a hard worker and an astute businessman, Ananias' reputation cast a long shadow over his son-in-law's path. In addition to his farming enterprise, Ananias bought and sold steers and had a large fruit orchard. His farm was a showcase of hard work. His sons talked often about ways to make money. But John seemed content with a small subsistence farm.

A few minutes after John left to fetch the doctor, Anna's mother Lizzie burst into the room. "So the baby's on the way. We'll need to get a few things ready before the doctor comes. You go lie down, I'll take care of everything."

Lizzie stirred up the ashes in the stove, added a few pieces of wood, then rushed outside to the water pump. A few vigorous thrusts of the handle brought water gushing into the kettle. It brimmed over the top and splashed onto the frozen ground. Lizzie put the kettle on the wood stove and stepped into the bedroom. By now Anna was in intermittent labor. "We'll need some old bed sheets," Lizzie said. Anna pointed toward the bottom shelf of the cupboard, then grimaced as a contraction gripped her body.

The doctor arrived in plenty of time. He glanced at Lizzie. "I can tell you've done this before. Everything is ready." A few minutes later, an infant boy slipped into the doctor's hands.

The doctor gazed into the baby's blue eyes. "He looks perfectly healthy."

Anna smiled through her pain, "Thank God."

John and Anna named their firstborn son Tobias. They'd likely call him Tobe or Tobie for short. It was a common Amish name. Anna's younger brother was named Tobias. So was the bishop who had performed their wedding ceremony.

• • • •

Bishop Tobias Yoder gave spiritual oversight to the little flock of Amish settlers who lived near the town of Thomas in Custer County, Oklahoma. The small settlement lay in the area known as Indian Territory.

Beginning in 1830, Native Americans from other parts of the country had been forcibly resettled to the Oklahoma Territory with the promise of land free to roam. The United States government promised them that the new land would be Indian territory "as long as the grass shall grow and the rivers run."

Then in 1889 the government broke its promise to the Indians and opened up some of the land for settlement by the white man. Soon the Indians' new domain was overrun by settlers who insisted on farming the land or mining its natural resources. A few Amish families staked claims in the famous April 19, 1892, land run. The new community that resulted extended hope to homesteaders with few resources. Cheap land and opportunities for farming drew Amish settlers from various parts of the country. John Stutzman's parents came in 1905. They bought a half-section of land for $3.50 an acre. Anna Miller's parents came in 1907 after they had participated in a failed attempt to establish a new Amish settlement in Gibson, Mississippi. They also lived briefly in Reno County, Kansas.

By the time John and Anna were married in December 1916, the Custer County, Oklahoma, settlement was large enough to form two congregations or church districts. Since the Amish worshiped in the homes of their members, the districts were kept small.

John Stutzman hoped marriage would stave off an impending call into military service. A war raged in Europe. Each day it appeared more likely that the United States would be drawn into the conflict. Some in Congress were calling for a military draft, the first since the Civil War.

Although President Wilson voiced opposition to conscription, the Defense Act of 1916 paved the way for a draft. By May 18, 1917, after various revisions in Congress, the President signed the Selective Service Act into law. All males twenty-one to thirty-one years of age were asked to register. By August the law was amended to include all males from eighteen to forty-six.

John was opposed to the war, but he registered along with about ten million other men across the country. Nearly three million were dispatched to military camps over the next eigh teen months. Along with their Mennonite kin, the Amish in Oklahoma were a peace-loving people. Their descendants, immigrants from Switzerland and Germany, had been drawn to the New World by the peaceful vision of Penn's Woods. They objected in principle to all wars, including skirmishes with Native Americans. Over several decades, they gradually spread out from the Pennsylvania heartland. Eventually, they settled from Canada to the Gulf of Mexico, from New York to Oregon.

The Amish carried on the simple faith of their sixteenth-century Anabaptist forebears in Europe. They often pointed to three verses that summarized their beliefs about war: "Thou shalt not kill" (Exod. 20:13), "Love your enemies" (Matt. 5:44), and "All they that take the sword shall perish with the sword" (Matt. 26:52).

In times of peace, few of their neighbors objected to their quaint beliefs. But when the Amish and their Mennonite kin quoted the Bible with a German accent in 1917, the scene changed. In the war against the seemingly irrepressible German Kaiser, Anabaptist beliefs appeared unpatriotic, even undemocratic. Most of the churches around them embraced war as an instrument for achieving God's will—democracy for all people. Some churchgoers enthusiastically mouthed President Wilson's war slogans. They called men to arms in their worship services "to make the world safe for democracy" through "the war to end all wars."

But the Anabaptists reiterated their beliefs in separation from the world and God's will for "peace among all men."

These differences introduced sharp tensions between the largely German-speaking Anabaptists and their English-speaking neighbors, whom the Amish usually called "the English." The war propaganda stirred up frenzy by demonizing the Germans and anything that smacked of German support. Conscientious objectors, or COs for short, were seen as supporters of the Germans.

German-speaking inhabitants in Oklahoma were relative newcomers. Unlike their kinsfolk in Pennsylvania, they had not yet established the credibility and trust of long association. By the time the United States officially entered the Great War on April 6, 1917, anti-German hysteria in Custer County ran high. A few months later in Mayes County, Oklahoma, patriots formed a Council of Defense. Like similar organizations across the country, the new council recruited soldiers and organized Liberty Loan drives. Some community organizations kept public records of contributors, threatening to punish anyone who was not "100 percent American." Over the next two years, they pressed their Amish and Mennonite neighbors to contribute to the war effort.

The federal government made no clear provision for conscientious objectors, so hundreds of Mennonites and Amish were drafted. Some refused to register and were sent to prisons. Others went to military camps but refused to follow orders or wear a military uniform. Some served as non-combatants, working as cooks, medics, or maintenance workers. A few served as soldiers on the European front.

Before Tobe was born, patriots burned two Mennonite church buildings in the towns of Inola and Chouteau in Mayes County. The local people were incensed that Mennonites refused to support the Red Cross and the YMCA. They could not understand why they refused to display a national flag in their houses of worship. Arguing that the "long-whiskered geezers" were pro-German, local patriots offered an Inola resident five dollars to burn down the General Conference Mennonite meetinghouse in town. The arsonist carried out their plan in June. Shortly afterward, the Mennonite Brethren congregation in Eden also found its meetinghouse in flames. When George Voth offered the use of his barn as a temporary place of worship, patriots burned it as well. The Amish, who worshiped in their homes, were less vulnerable to church-related arson.

The tension of the war days only intensified Amish convictions that God had called them to be a peculiar people. A separate tongue and unique customs helped define the boundaries between them and their English neighbors. The *Martyrs Mirror* and the *Ausbund* (their hymnal) reminded them of their martyr history. Yet they shunned controversy, preferring to be *die Stillen im Lande*, the quiet in the land.

The war ended in 1918, just three weeks after Tobe was born. Even so, the relationships between conscientious objectors and patriots continued to be strained. In a few Oklahoma communities, ill feelings and suspicions persisted for decades. Tobe grew up profoundly aware that he was different from his worldly neighbors.

Anna gave birth to a second son just a few days before Tobe's second birthday. But not all was well. The infant was born with a heart murmur. He lived only three days. John and Anna buried him nameless in the Amish graveyard near their farm home.

As Tobe approached his third birthday, Anna told her mother Lizzie he was no ordinary child. She gazed after him as he scurried to do her bidding, his rosy cheeks accenting a cheerful face and husky frame. In the winter, when it was time to get dinner, he'd say, *"Boombar hole,* fetch 'taters," bringing the spuds up from their storage place in the cellar.

Anna so depended on her young son to fetch her potatoes that she did not keep track of her inventory. One day unexpected company came for Sunday dinner. Off to the cellar Tobe went, entertaining her guests with his promise to "fetch taters." When he returned with only a few potatoes, she quietly chided him, "This isn't enough, you must bring more."

Tobe replied, "There's no more there." Anna said nothing, but the look on her face showed embarrassment with the scant serving of potatoes that marked the last of her supply.

Curious about everything, Tobe plied Anna with questions. "Mom, how come people can't fly like birds?"

"God didn't give us wings."

"Do birds get cold like people?"

"Sometimes. But they have feathers to keep them warm, like the ones in your pillow."

She answered the child's questions as best she could. Through it all, John watched from a distance. Child rearing was Anna's job.

Tobe loved his mother but longed for a playmate. He was nearly three years old when Anna gave birth to another child—a son. Apart from the large red birthmark on one cheek, he seemed perfectly normal. They named him Ervin.

Tobe quickly adapted to his baby brother. He worked and played with enthusiasm. As the boys grew, Anna was able to provide them with a few playthings. A small wooden box held wooden blocks, a little metal tractor, and a few stuffed toys. But the children often played at their grandparents home, not far away, where the box of toys was much larger.

The boys also spent lots of time outside on Grandpa's farm, watching their pre-teen and teenage uncles at work with the horses. When Tobe was only a year old, Grandpa Ananias was kicked by a horse. His leg was badly broken. It healed very slowly. Grandpa also had high blood pressure and hardening of the arteries. He spent large sums of money in search of relief from his persistent ailments. Tobe often heard his mother complain about her father's poor health.

Tobe was eight when Grandpa died of a paralytic stroke. Mother Anna often told the boys that she wished they could have worked alongside their Grandpa in the fields. In his prime Ananias had been industrious and productive. His plain clothes and gentle speech veiled a strong sense of ambition that drove him to take risks and expand his business interests. Ordained as a minister, he could drive a hard bargain, but he also showed compassion for those in need. On one occasion, Ananias offered a neighbor the opportunity to gather a wagon load of freshly raked hay from the alfalfa field. The neighbor piled the wagon so full that he had to come back to retrieve the hay that had fallen off as the wagon bumped through the field. Later, Ananias noted with some humor that the fellow got two loads out of the deal.

Although Tobe's life revolved around farm and family, he and his brother Ervin got to know their English neighbors, the Rainbolts. At first the Stutzman boys knew no English and the Rainbolt boys knew no Pennsylvania German. But the Rainbolts taught Tobe and Ervin to speak English and the Stutzmans taught their friends to speak German. From then on, they used either language when they were together.

Tobe delighted in watching the Rainbolt's Airedale chase after the occasional car that passed their home. The dog yipped as he ran alongside the vehicle, nipping at the wheels. A neighbor, Amos Bontrager, was determined to cure the dog of the habit. He fastened a gunny sack to one wheel and drove slowly by the house. Tobe watched as the dog latched onto the sack with his teeth. The twisting sack sent the dog rolling into the ditch. The stunned dog got up, shook his head, and gazed at the car as it disappeared in a cloud of dust. Amos repeated his trick more than once, but it never cured the dog. He still chased every car that came along.

As Tobe, Ervin, and their friends stood by the road, watching for cars as they approached, Tobe began dreaming of driving a car someday. As an Amish youngster, he had to be satisfied with horses and buggies for the time being.

During the school year, Tobe and Ervin attended the Jefferson School not far from the Stutzman farm. Tobe enjoyed the one-room school with its eight grades. It gave him ready opportunity to listen to the older pupils reciting their lessons. He often worked ahead with his lessons and delighted in memorizing his parts in the yearly Christmas program.

Tobe and Ervin especially looked forward to Christmas 1927, thinking about the upcoming gift exchange at school. They told Mother that they hoped one of the three Indian children would draw their names. The Heap-of-Birds family gave more expensive gifts than the others. Tobe wondered why his family didn't spend money on gifts. Anna explained that they didn't have much cash. Some of the Indian children had cash to spend because they got checks from the government.

A couple of days after Christmas, Tobe got a piece of mail from a friend. He ran into the house with his treasure. "Look, Mom, what I got." Grinning broadly, he handed her a postcard.

Anna took the card, then sank into a chair. She pulled her apron forward over the large bulge that announced the presence of another child. "Oh, this is a nice card." A village church stood nestled among snow-covered hills, surrounded by evergreens and barren trees.

Tobe read the caption aloud, "Ring out the old, ring in the new, Ring in a Happy New Year for you."

Anna smiled. "Yes, it's only two days away from the new year. Then it will be 1928." She turned the card over. "I see it's from your cousin Willie Yoder."

Tobe read the last sentence aloud, "Hope you had a Merry Christmas and I wish you a happy New Year."

Tobe grasped the card. "May I have it?"

"Yes."

"Good. I'm going to put it on the shelf by my bed."

Donning his coat and hat, Tobe walked around to a small outbuilding just thirty feet from the house. A blast of cold air hit him as he stepped outside into the snow. Entering the so-called washhouse, Tobe sank onto the *Schprausack*, the bag of straw and corn husks that served as his mattress. He looked at the card again, then set it upright against the bare wall on a shelf. Although the room was cold in the wintertime, Tobe didn't mind sleeping in the washhouse with Ervin.

Anna leaned back in her chair and rested. Her new baby was due in six weeks, but she would not have to wait. Two days later Anna felt the first twinges of birth pangs. After a short labor, she gave birth to another son on New Year's Eve. They named him Clarence.

The winter winds buffeted the drafty frame house and blew snow through the cracks. It seemed impossible to keep the house warm enough for the new baby. Sometimes, when it got too cold, Anna put little Clarence into the oven of the woodstove with a few embers burning. He was so small that Grandma Lizzie said he could have fit into a two-quart jar. At least he nursed well. Against what seemed to be great odds, he not only survived but thrived.

Each night after Clarence was asleep, Anna read stories to the older boys from *Egermeier's Bible Story Book*. She taught the boys a prayer for bedtime: "*Müde bin ich, geh' zur Ruh; Schliessi meine Äuglein zu; Vater lass die Augen dein, Über mir stets offen sein.* Tired I go to rest and close my eyes; Father let your eyes then, always be watching over mine."

Tobe worked with Anna around the house. He helped her with meals and learned how to do the family laundry. In the summertime, he helped her can vegetables from the garden and fruits from the small orchard. Anna told her mother that Tobe was as good as any girl. She also confided some worries about her precocious son to her mother.

"Tobe learns his school lessons so fast that I can hardly keep up."

Lizzie nodded. "He's a fast learner."

"Sometimes he's *unhendich schmaert,* unhandily smart."

"Does he talk back?"

"Not so much. But if he gets too much book learning, he might lose respect for his elders."

"Yes, that can happen. Maybe you should keep him at home more to work on the farm."

Anna nodded, but she never said anything to her husband about it. John already kept Tobe out of school whenever there was farm work to do. Tobe hated to miss classes. He begged his mother to let him go whenever possible. On one of the last days at school, Tobe's teacher, Mollie Bryan, rewarded his persistence.

"Tobe!"

He glanced up. He was surprised to hear his name.

"There's something here for you."

He strode to the front of the room.

"This is a certificate of attendance. You have only missed a couple of days this past year. Congratulations!"

Tobe glanced over the certificate's heading—Punctual and Regular Attendance. Just below the teacher had modified the printed notice of "having been neither absent nor tardy for three consecutive months," noting four *non*-consecutive months. Tobe nodded slowly. It was true that he had missed a couple of days. After school he raced home to show his mother and younger brothers, grinning with pride as he hung the certificate near his bed. He looked forward to the next year in school. Maybe he could have a whole year of perfect attendance. But Tobe knew that as he got older Dad would be even more likely to keep him out of school. And with Mother expecting yet another baby, there would be more and more housework for him to do.

3

Hope Deferred

Tobe hoped for a younger sister to help with the house-work. He didn't mind the household duties his classmates at school called women's work. Still a sister would be nice.

When Anna felt birth pangs in early April 1929, she sent Tobe, Ervin, and Clarence to Grandma's house. The boys could play with their uncles while Grandma assisted her with the birth.

After strenuous labor, Anna gave birth to another son. She held her breath as the doctor examined the child.

"Is something wrong?"

The doctor wrinkled his brow but said nothing. Anna and Lizzie watched as he palpitated the infant's small chest.

Then the doctor sighed, shook his head, and laid the lifeless infant on Anna's breast. "I'm sorry it went this way."

Anna stroked the child's wrinkled skin. Tears welled up in her eyes as she traced the curvature of its tiny ears with her finger.

The doctor packed up his bags to leave, then spoke in hushed tones to John, who had been waiting outside the room. John stepped up to the bed as the doctor made his way outside.

Clearing his throat, John Stutzman looked at his wife. "I guess I'll have to bury it."

She nodded. He turned and walked out of the room, heading for the barn.

Lizzie took a deep breath, then volunteered, half as a question, "I'll get it ready for burial?" Anna nodded and blinked her eyes. A tear splashed onto her cheek.

Lizzie spread the small birthing blanket on a nearby table. Tenderly, she took the baby from Anna's arms and laid it in the center of the blanket, folding the fabric over the tiny body and tucking the corners tight. She lowered herself into a chair, holding the child in her lap as she waited for John's return. When she heard the sound of John's footsteps at the door, she stood with the infant. "I'll go along to the cemetery," she said.

"You'll pick up one of John D's girls?" Anna asked. She would need assistance for a couple of weeks. John nodded and walked toward the buggy. Lizzie carried the small body and climbed in beside John as he took up the reins. They headed toward the cemetery. John tied the horse at the hitching post and picked up his spade. His mother-in-law watched silently as he walked to the grave where their last infant had been buried. He began to dig. The late afternoon sun slanted through the trees from the west, throwing shadows on his work. The black soil clung tenaciously to his spade, wet from the spring rains. He scraped off the mud with his four-buckle rubber boot.

Surveying the hole, now several feet square and sufficiently deep, John nodded to Lizzie, who knelt to place the blanketed body in the ground. She glanced toward the east then turned the body around. The dead, she knew, should be buried facing east so they could see Jesus at the second coming.

Lizzie watched in silence as John hastily covered the hole and headed for the buggy. Thirty minutes later, they were driving back to the Stutzman home accompanied by fourteen-year-old Clara Yoder. John had expected Clara's older sister Fannie to do the job. But Fannie was temporarily gone, and the family sent Clara. She could help John do the chores as well as help Anna with the housework.

John dropped off his mother-in-law at home, then with Tobe walking behind, briefly showed Clara her daily chores. She would take care of the chicks that had just arrived, milk several cows, and feed the calves. Tobe assured Clara he would help. Each would milk several cows.

Inside the house, Anna showed Clara how to do the house work. Clara watched with wide eyes as Anna explained how to use the iron, an unfamiliar gadget. She was used to heating an iron on top of the wood stove. Under Anna's careful eye, she unscrewed the cap on the can of white gasoline and gingerly poured it into the waiting spout on the new iron. Before long she was ironing the clothing that Tobe and Ervin had washed that morning.

The next day as Clara walked toward the garden to pick lettuce, she saw Tobe and Ervin gathered around a pipe that was sticking out of the ground. "What's that?" she asked.

"It's our bank," Tobe replied. "It's a worn-out pump that we buried in the ground."

"We put our pennies, nickels, and dimes in here," Ervin explained.

"Why don't you put your money in a piggy bank?" Clara asked.

"It's heavy," Tobe volunteered. "When we drop money in there, we can't get it out without digging up the pump. That way we won't spend our money on ice cream and gum."

"I see," Clara nodded, as she continued on her way to the garden.

Later that week, Clara glanced out the window as Tobe walked by with a garden spade. Ervin and Clarence followed close behind.

She watched as the boys walked to the site of their money bank. Tobe began to dig around the pipe.

When the boys came in for dinner, Clara commented, "I saw you dig up your money bank."

"Yeah," Tobe confessed. "Dad's going to the medicine show tonight, and he said we could come along. We needed to get some money out of our bank."

Clara smiled broadly. "I hope you have a good time."

John and the boys returned late that evening.

"Did you buy anything?" Clara asked.

"Just an ice cream cone," Tobe replied. "Dad doesn't usually buy medicine at the shows. He just goes to look around."

"Yeah," Ervin echoed, "Mom buys our medicine from the Watkins man."

"Or the Raleigh man," Tobe added. "They come around in a car."

"She likes to get Watkins liniment," Ervin remarked. "She uses it for her aches and pains like arthritis."

"And Disfusible Tonic," Tobe observed. "She gives it to us on a spoon. I'd rather be sick." He shivered. "Sometimes she gives us cod liver oil. I hate that stuff."

Clara laughed at the exaggerated expression on his face.

• • • •

Tobe liked having Clara around. She did okay with the cooking, especially the potato salad for the picnic on the last day at the Jefferson School. He ate three helpings.

The next Sunday, as Clara prepared to cook rice for dinner, she spilled it all over the floor. The tiny grains lodged in the wide cracks on the wooden floor. Tobe grinned as he watched her kneel on the floor, then stooped to help pick them out. It would have taken her a long time by herself.

Then there was the incident with the asparagus. At Dad's direction, Clara mixed fine sand with the feed for the chicks. It worked as grit. About that time, she picked the first asparagus of the season. Although she scrubbed it thoroughly, there were a few grains from the garden soil left in the asparagus dish. Dad asked, "Were you fixing this for the chickens?" He said it with his usual dry humor, but Clara felt hurt. She just blushed and quietly went on eating.

One day as Tobe and Clara milked the cows, she wondered aloud where John was. Tobe said he didn't know. He hadn't really thought about it, since Dad was often gone at chore time. Dad didn't talk about his whereabouts. But Clara's question got him thinking. Where was Dad at chore time? He remembered a scene he'd witnessed some months earlier.

Dad hitched up the horse and was about to leave the yard. He had not told Mom where he was going.

Mom pulled her hands out of the dishwater and stepped into the hot sunshine. "Where are you going?"

Dad set his jaw in protest, "*Muscht du alles wisse?* Must you know everything?"

Mother scowled, but remained silent. She wiped her hands on her apron and walked back into the house. Silence loomed large in the house for the next two days.

Tobe was almost sorry to see Clara pack up to go back home. But after three weeks, Mother was ready to manage on her own. Tobe waved good-bye to his newfound friend as she headed out the driveway with Dad at the reins.

As the buggy vanished, Tobe decided to walk to Grandpa's house. That day his uncles were in a teasing mood.

"Say Lookabay," said Dave as he pointed toward the nearby town. "*Glucke Beh*," Tobe replied. He was confusing the unfamiliar name of the town for the Pennsylvania German term meaning the legs of setting hens.

Dave and Henry laughed at his confusion. "Say it again."

"*Glucke Beh*." They laughed louder.

Tobe tried to join them in laughter as they slapped their thighs. He quickly responded by doing a somersault on the grass. That would distract them.

"That's a *Kommer-dumple*," Joe said, as he joined his brothers. It was a nonsensical expression they used for somersaults.

Tobe did another. He liked being the center of attention.

"Hey," Henry said, "We'll give you a quarter if you climb to the top of the supply pipe."

"Really?" He needed a quarter to replace the one he'd taken out of his buried bank.

"Yes, if you make it all the way to the top." Henry winked at his brothers.

Tobe rolled up his sleeves and grasped the pipe that carried fresh water from the windmill pump to the supply tank. The Aeromotor mechanism at the top of the derrick spun in the June breeze.

"Come on, let's see you do it," Joe said.

Tobe grasped the pipe and began to climb. His arms bulged as he hoisted himself up, his bare feet wrapped around the pipe. With each gain, he thought of all the gum and candy he could buy with twenty-five cents. But his uncles were determined to keep him from making it. When Tobe was about three-fourths of the way up, Joe yelled, "*Glucke Beh, Glucke Beh.*"

"*Kommer-dumple, Kommer-dumple,*" Henry echoed.

Tobe snickered and lost his strength. He slipped a bit as Joe and Henry let loose a stream of silly words. He snickered more and lost his grip, sliding all the way to the bottom.

"Come on, you can do it."

Tobe started up again.

More silly talk.

Finally, he gave up and walked home, his chin hanging against his chest. Anna dried his tears as he told her how hard he'd tried to earn that quarter. She consoled him, "Those brothers of mine can be so mean."

Tobe lay on his bed in the washhouse, remembering in detail how he'd failed on account of his uncles' *Glucke Beh* and *Kommer-dumple* talk. He determined he would grow up and show them he could climb any pipe on the property.

After the baby died, Tobe noticed that Mom talked less and sang more. Dad was quiet too, except when he complained that farm prices were very low. And everyone talked about the dry weather. In late October 1929, Dad brought home a newspaper that told about Black Thursday in New York City. The stock market plummeted, followed by a further fall in prices for farm goods.

The next year things got a little better. Clarence's third birthday was just around the corner when Mother had another baby. It was three days before Christmas. They called him Lester.

At the same time, Grandpa Miller's house bustled with preparations for a wedding. Tobe's uncle Dave was planning to be married to Lizzie Wingard on February 27, 1930.

Nine days before the wedding, Tobe's uncle Tobias got his right arm caught in a stationary baler. It crushed several bones in his arm and hand.

A few days later baby Lester took ill. Just two days before the planned wedding, the baby died of double pneumonia. Grandma said they must change the wedding date. On the day the wedding had been planned, people came to Tobe's home for Lester's funeral.

The following Tuesday, they all went to Dave and Lizzie's wedding. Everyone seemed a bit sober, especially Mom. Dad seemed even more on edge than before.

Tobe learned to tiptoe around his father when he was upset. Dad was quick to hit the animals if they didn't cooperate. He jabbed the hogs with a pitchfork or struck them with a board. He growled at the boys too, and sometimes hit them. Tobe was big enough to take care of himself, so Dad took it out on Ervin. He readily pounded him with his fist or whipped him with a branch he would rip from a tree.

In the fall of that year, Dad told Mom he was leaving to follow the corn harvest in Iowa. He handed her some cash and said, "This should take care of the family for awhile." She stared after him as he walked out of the house and down the road.

The next day John Stutzman steered a Model T Ford into his sister Gertie's driveway near Yoder, Kansas. He sidled up to the house and knocked on the door.

Gertie's eyes widened as she opened the door. "Are you here by yourself?"

"Yes. Can I park the car in the shed? And I'll need to borrow a rig. I want to visit the folks."

"Sure, go ahead." She stepped off the porch onto the sidewalk as her brother strode toward the car.

John climbed into the "T" and drove it into a corner of the shed. He led a horse out of the stall and hitched it to a buggy. Gertie watched as he headed out of the driveway toward their parents' home.

John's parents were puzzled at his appearance. "What brings you here?"

"I'm on my way to Iowa. I'm following the corn harvest."

"How will Anna make it while you're gone?"

"I left her $200 to take care of expenses. Tobe and Ervin can help her with the chores."

John didn't bother to tell his parents that he'd bought a car for the trip from Oklahoma to Iowa. They could think he was taking the train.

• • • •

When Tobe asked his mother where Dad was, she didn't know. Tobe hoped nobody at church would ask about Dad. If someone did, they'd just have to say he went to find work.

Although there was little money, the family had enough to eat. Mom had made sure of that by working hard in the garden the previous summer. Tobe especially remembered one morning. He watched Mom as she walked toward the garden, singing, "My heavenly home is bright and fair, Nor pain, nor death can enter there; Its glittering tow'rs the sun outshine; That heavenly mansion shall be mine. I'm going home . . . to die no more."

As she started picking tomatoes for canning, Tobe ran to help her. She sang as she filled the baskets with the ripe fruit. "We are going down the valley one by one, With our faces toward the setting of the sun; Down the valley where the mournful cypress grows, Where the stream of death in silence onward flows."

She stood and straightened her back before she launched into the second verse. "We are going down the valley one by one, When the labors of the weary day are done: One by one the cares of earth forever past, We shall stand upon the river bank at last."

It seemed Mother sang more songs about heaven after Lester died. Tobe saw the wall motto in their kitchen in a new way, "Only one life, 'twill soon be past. Only what's done for Christ will last."

Ervin was more sober too. One night in bed, he told Tobe he thought it was cruel to kill birds. With a homemade weapon Ervin had patterned after one he had seen at school, he would shoot turtledoves, mockingbirds, blue jays, and crows. The "pea shooter," as they called it, was made from a forked tree branch. Strips from an old inner tube and a piece of leather provided the thrust for propelling small rocks. But after watching Lester die, the fun went out of shooting birds. Tobe felt that way too. He didn't like to watch things die. The boys decided they would quit hunting birds.

Making kites was more fun, and Tobe and Ervin made lots of kites. Usually, they started by fashioning a large cross out of two long, narrow pieces of wood. Then, they ran a string through slits at the end. After cutting brown paper bags in the shape of a diamond, they mounted them on the cross with a flour and water paste. They pulled string out of an old carpet piece and tied the pieces together, before making a tail from a collection of Mom's old rags.

One evening after the sun had set, Anna watched as they prepared to fly one of their homemade kites.

"Why in the world would you want to fly a kite at night?"

Tobe tried to sound as reasonable as possible. "We're going to hang a lantern on it and watch it glow in the sky."

"What if it falls off and breaks?"

"We'll be careful. We did it twice before."

A few minutes later, Anna stepped outside to watch. She watched with wide open eyes as the kite rose in the sky with the lantern swinging underneath it. Tobe coached Ervin as he slowly unwound the string. The kite drifted over the Detweiler's pasture next door.

"Hey Mom, the last time we did this, the donkey saw it," Tobe shouted.

Just then the donkey began to bray. The lantern danced in the sky as the kite rose and fell in the night breeze. The donkey brayed incessantly.

"See what I said?" Tobe exulted. "This is fun." He gradually drew in the string and Ervin grabbed the lantern as the kite swooped toward the ground. Anna shook her head, and walked back into the kitchen.

Anna never quite got over all the inventions and gadgets her sons put together. One day she watched out the kitchen window as Tobe and Ervin played under the giant maple tree. She walked out to see what they were doing.

"Look what I made, Mom." Tobe was proud of his machine.

"It's a threshing machine," Ervin explained as he put some straw in the front. He turned the crank on their handmade tractor that ran a flat belt to the machine. Straw blew out the back.

"We used Dad's tin snips to cut out the tin," Tobe explained. "I cut out the wheels with a coping saw."

"I helped too," Ervin insisted. "There's a belt inside that runs the straw through."

"You made a nice machine," she said. "But don't forget that we have some weeds in the garden that need to be pulled." As she walked back to the house, the boys went on with their play.

• • • •

Dad eventually returned from the harvest in Iowa. Tobe overheard him tell Mom where he'd been, and life went back to the way it was before he left. If Dad and Mom ever discussed it further, Tobe didn't hear about it.

That fall Tobe heard that Grandma Lizzie Miller was getting married again to Bishop Jake Miller of Hutchinson, Kansas. The widowed leader had proposed earlier, but Grandma asked him to wait until her young sons, Joe and Henry, were a bit older. Now she was ready to be married and move to Kansas. Tobe would miss Grandma and his uncles. Mom promised that they could visit them in Kansas.

In November after four months of marriage, Grandma returned to Oklahoma to sell her household goods. Dad said the items sold cheaply because the country was in a depression. Tobe would have liked to buy a few things, but at the time, he didn't have enough money.

• • • •

Tobe and Ervin occasionally picked up a bit of cash through innovative means, and usually Dad let them keep the money. They bagged and hawked some of the peanuts that grew on the farm, walking through the crowd at auctions or medicine shows and selling peanuts for a dime a bag. Tobe couldn't resist helping himself from the bag. He loved peanuts.

During the spring plowing, the boys captured turtles that showed up on the freshly plowed ground. Collecting them in a barrel, they took them to the Indians who lived in shacks just two miles from the Stutzman farm. In exchange for fresh turtle meat, the Indians traded the boys watch fobs and other braided leather products.

Tobe wasn't afraid of the Indians like Grandma Lizzie Stutzman. Dad told Tobe that his mother used to hide her children under the bed whenever Indians came by in their covered wagons. Grandma always remembered the story of the Hochstedler massacre in 1757, when Indians had killed an Amish mother and two of her children in Pennsylvania. Rumor had it that the Amish mother had once spoken gruffly to the Indians when they came by for help. All four of Tobe's grandparents were descendants of that Hochstedler family.

Grandma Stutzman was so uncomfortable with the Indians that she insisted the family move from Oklahoma to Kansas. They moved the year that Tobe was born but occasionally came back to visit their son John and his family. Tobe's uncle Jerry Stutzman told him stories about growing up with the Indians in Oklahoma.

Once some Indians found a neighbor's cows, bloated from grazing too much alfalfa or kafir corn, outside the pasture fence. They butchered the cows and took the meat, leaving the skin and bones for the owners to discover when they got home. Tobe wondered how Jerry could be so sure it was Indians who had done it. Jerry said he knew because no one else would have done it that way.

Tobe liked the Indian children in his school, although he didn't understand their eating habits. His schoolmates told him that the women ate fat and entrails. The very thought made Tobe shiver.

Tobe attended his last day of school in June 1933. His face lit up as the superintendent called his name at the graduation ceremony for the small Jefferson School. He slid sideways out of his chair and strode to the front of the room.

"Congratulations!" The superintendent's face beamed as he handed Tobe his Certificate of Promotion.

"Thank you." Tobe eagerly received the envelope and returned to his seat in the back of the schoolhouse. He opened the flap and pulled out the contents, a thin sheet. He traced the edges with his fingers, savoring the words: "Admits the holder to any high school or accredited secondary school in the state of Oklahoma." Of course, Tobe knew he'd never go to high school. Dad needed him on the farm. Besides the Amish church discouraged higher education.

Tobe worked hard that summer. Along with Ervin, he hoed and thinned cotton on the home farm. The worst part though, was picking the cotton. The hulls cut his fingers. He tired of dragging the long canvas bag from his shoulders. The only part he enjoyed was stomping down the cotton in the tall wagon so it would make a tight bale. The gin in Thomas preferred the cotton as tight as possible. If he stomped hard enough, he could get a 400-500 pound bale out of a wagon load.

Tobe loved to work with the horses. Although they were used hard and were skinny, Tobe treated them with care. He dreamed of breaking his own horse when he was old enough. And he determined that when had his own farm, he'd buy draft horses for the field and save his drivers for the road. He wanted them to look sleek and healthy like Mose Mast's horses. The only time Dad's horses showed pep was when the boys tried to catch them in the pasture on a Sunday afternoon. They would run right past the gate into the barn.

Over the next year, Tobe grew so fast that Anna complained about how hard it was to keep him in decently fitting clothing. By his fifteenth year, Tobe stood taller than his dad. The hard work on the farm helped pad his frame with heavy muscle. Even the neighbors talked about Tobe's energy and ability to work.

As the wheat ripened the following summer, Enos Yoder asked the Stutzmans if Tobe could accompany his harvesters as a cook. He had heard that Tobe often cooked for Anna. Tobe was ecstatic. Enos was a big wheat farmer who owned land in the Oklahoma panhandle. Working for Enos would give him a chance to see how big operators worked.

John reluctantly agreed to release his son for the task, with the stipulation that Tobe had to cut enough wood for his mother to use in her kitchen stove during his absence. With more than his characteristic vigor, Tobe went out of his way to take care of all the details. He wasn't about to be held up by last-minute objections from his father. Tobe could tell that Ervin was wistful as Mom packed clothes and belongings for the trip. It was his first time away from home and family.

Tobe also went with some reluctance, knowing that Mom would really miss him. Arthritis had begun to cripple her hands, so it took more time than usual to get her meals together. And she was expecting another baby. They all hoped it would be a girl who could eventually help her in the house full time.

The time in the Panhandle went fast for Tobe. He could tell Enos liked his work. He began to dream of following the harvest like Dad. But for now, he'd have to work at home.

Soon after the school term started in the fall, Mother gave birth to another son. She seemed disappointed that it wasn't a girl. Everyone was relieved, though, that at least he was healthy. They named the baby Levi after Grandpa Stutzman. But they decided to call him by his middle name—Perry.

Several weeks after Perry's birth in September 1934, Tobe turned sixteen. Turning sixteen was a major milestone for an

Amish young person. Now Tobe could join "the crowd," as the youth gatherings were called. He began to attend the weekly Sunday evening "singing," a time to eat together in a home followed by a time of hymn singing.

Turning sixteen also gave young people the freedom to date and be out late at night. It was a time when many young men pushed against the boundaries of their faith community. They called it *rumschpringe*, "running around." Although some young people experimented with the ways of the world and never settled down to join the Amish Church, most came back to embrace the faith of their forebears for themselves. The elders reasoned that if young people were forced to join, they would not become good church members.

Tobe enjoyed being part of the youth group. He often found himself at the center of attention. The time with his friends provided relief from the tense environment at home. Tobe sometimes wondered if his family could stay on the farm. Although his parents were tight-lipped about finances, he knew they were having trouble with the mortgage. He'd once overheard his mother talking about her fear of losing the farm.

Tobe remembered his mother's comment as he worked the soil one hot day in July 1935. He slapped the reins on the work horses plodding in front of the rusty harrow. "Giddup Ribbon! Giddup Rowdy! Giddup Bert!" The tired horses quickened their pace for a few moments, then gradually slowed. Tobe let the reins slacken. It was just no use pushing the horses too hard on such a hot day. They'd never last till evening. Sweat beaded on Tobe's brow and rolled down, forming rivulets through the dust on his ruddy cheeks. The late afternoon sun bore down on his exposed forearms. His darkly tanned skin stood in bold contrast to the faded blue cotton shirt that draped over his wet chest and upper arms. His tanned and leathery bare feet contrasted with the light blue of his faded denim trousers.

Tobe wasn't convinced that harrowing would do much good. Yet he knew that some effort had to be made to keep the soil from blowing away. There had been so little rain that there was scarcely any moisture under the surface. By the time the horses made a pass around the field, Tobe could hardly tell where he'd harrowed on the last round. It was bad enough to work the fields when it made a difference, but this was ridiculous.

Tobe's thoughts drifted. *I don't really enjoy farming, I have no choice. Dad doesn't warm up well to suggestions for change. I wish Dad was more like Grandpa Ananias. Mom says that when-ever Grandpa made a business deal, he came out on top. She thinks Dad could benefit from following his business. But Dad hates it when she makes comparisons or talks about the way her father did things. He just gets more determined.*

As Tobe guided the horses around a corner facing a stub-bled field, he recalled with disgust a time when the whole fam-ily had insisted that it was time to harvest a field of oats. Rain was threatening for the weekend. It was imperative to get the oats bound into sheaves before the Sabbath. Dad resisted, not wanting to give in to their suggestions. He said he had other work planned. It rained that weekend as well as much of the next week. By the time they could get into the field, the oats were hardly worth harvesting.

I'd like to be on my own. I'll do things differently than Mom and Dad. I might not even live on a farm. Maybe I can do some-thing more prosperous, like starting a business.

Tobe's eyelids sagged as he rode along. After eight months of being with the youth group, he felt the affects of late nights out each Sunday. Working all day every Monday after a few hours of sleep wore him out. His head began to nod. He jerked suddenly to maintain his balance as the horses jostled each other. *Ich muss frieh ins Bett geh denowed.* I must get to bed early tonight.

He stifled a yawn as he looked up toward the sky. A movement high above him caught his eye. A hawk soared on the warm air that rose from the scorched earth. He watched as the bird circled on widespread wings, searching for prey. Abruptly it tucked in its wings, dropping soundlessly toward a target far below. Talons extended, the fierce creature plummeted to within a few feet of the ground, then spread its wings just in time to break the fall. Snatching up a scampering creature along with bits of dirt and straw, the raptor flapped toward the young farmer and his horses. As the hawk drew nearer, Tobe spotted a large field mouse quivering in the hunter's cold grip. The large bird landed nearby, picking at the captured rodent with its hooked beak. The mouse struggled valiantly, then lay still. After ripping its game to shreds, the hawk flew away, landing on a far corner of the field. Tobe swallowed. It was so cruel.

He turned his attention back to the task at hand. The passes around the field were shorter now as the team moved toward the center. The horses seemed to understand. They moved more quickly, anticipating the finish. Tobe made the final pass up the middle of the field and angled out across one corner. He paused at the gate to lift the teeth of the harrow out of the soil. The large levers screeched as he grasped the handles to release the catches. He mounted the seat and clucked to the horses. They lowered their heads and pulled through the open gate.

Tobe marveled at the large amount of sand piled up in the fence row. Stuffed with tumbleweeds and other vegetation, the fence served as a barrier to the blowing sand. The lower third of the fencepost and the bottom strand of barbed wire lay buried under the sand. The wind rose as Tobe drove the team toward home. Loose sand whipped upward from the earth, stinging Tobe's cheeks and face. He squinted his eyes to narrow slits. *Tseltz nimmie regere?* Will it never rain?

The horses quickened their pace as they pulled the harrow down the gravel road toward home. The shiny metal runners screeched against the surface, accenting the thud of plodding hooves.

Tobe unhitched the team and led them to the water tank. He slipped the bridle over Ribbon's large ears and pulled the bit out of her mouth, then did the same for Rowdy and Bert. The horses' throats rippled as they drank. The wheel on the windmill creaked, then spun as a gust of wind sent it whirling into a blur of metal. The pump shaft rose and fell briskly. Cool water surged from the supply pipe into the metal tank.

Satisfied, the horses lifted their heads. Tobe led them to their stalls. They moved eagerly, looking forward to a night of rest. Tobe thrust the metal feed scoop into the bin brimming with oats. Hearing the familiar sound of the scoop, the horses whiffed the air in anticipation. The oats sent up a puff of dust as they dropped into the wooden manger. The horses snorted as they hungrily munched the yellow grain. Tobe held the scoop in his hand as he watched the horses. He stroked the shiny edge of the metal. *I could make these. That would be more fun than farming.*

The hot summer finally gave way to autumn, bringing welcome relief from the heat. A sprouting crop of winter wheat spread a shaggy green carpet across the brown loam. Farmers worked mostly inside now, repairing implements and settling in for the long winter.

One chilly day in November, Tobe felt a change in the air. Dad was unusually quiet. He climbed the ladder to the barn loft and pitched some loose hay down the hay hole.

Inside the house, Anna looked at Ervin, who was reading the weekly newspaper. "You can ring the bell for supper."

Ervin hopped out of the chair and ran outside. He loved to ring the bell. He grasped the rope and yanked it twice. The bell sounded out loud and clear in the cold air.

As the last peals faded, Ervin thought of the time when a neighbor had died. He'd rung the bell for a long time, then mounted a horse to inform all of the neighbors.

Tobe heard the bell and climbed down from the hay mow. Mom was pumping air into the gas lantern as Ervin washed his hands in the porcelain bowl in the dry sink. She hung the lantern on the wall beside the table and called out, "Let's eat."

Everyone moved silently to their places. Mom lifted baby Perry into the wooden high chair. He banged his spoon as the family bowed their heads in silent grace. Anna gently clasped the offending spoon. Dad cleared his throat and the family raised their heads. They reached for the serving dishes in front of them.

Everyone seemed extremely quiet. Only the gas light's gentle hiss accompanied the babble of the baby and the noisy chewing of his brothers. The lantern's rays sent shadows beyond the table.

As Tobe wiped his plate clean with a scrap of homemade bread, Dad broke the silence: "*Mir ziehe veck von do.* We're going to move." Tobe paused with his bread crust in mid air. Mom cocked her head apprehensively. Clarence and Ervin looked at each other in alarm and asked, "Where to, Dad? Why are we moving?"

4

Nowata

John cleared his throat. "We can't stay here. We're too far behind on the payments for the farm. We'll have to give it up."

"Can't Harry be patient with us?" Tobe knew that Harry Miller, an English neighbor, carried the mortgage.

"Yes, we could pay if he would be patient. But farm land is hard to get around here and someone else wants this land. The bank won't lend us any more money."

Tobe swallowed hard. After a long silence he said, "Where are we going, Dad?"

"Nowata. There's a farm there we can rent from the Oklahoma School Land Commission. Quite a few people are doing that."

"When are we going?"

"Sometime in December."

Tobe wasn't surprised that his folks wanted to move. Others from the Thomas, Oklahoma, area had moved to Nowata. Anna's cousin, John D. Yoder, had moved with his family in January 1932. They went mostly because land was scarce in the Custer County area. Ever since, Tobe had been hearing snatches of conversation about the Nowata settlement. Russian Mennonites had once lived there, but moved away and sold their land to non-Mennonites. Now Bishop Eli Nisly of Reno County, Kansas, was buying farm land for his children. His oldest daughter Susie and her husband Andy

Miller moved first, followed by six of her brothers and sisters. Now Eli and his wife Fannie had moved there as well.

Of course, it was as dry in Nowata as in Thomas. The newspapers had dubbed the whole region a dust bowl. But people clung to the hope that it would rain again; that soon they would experience the kind of harvest Andy Miller reported in fall 1932. That year the corn grew so tall that he had to stretch to reach the ears. The soil in Nowata seemed promising for mixed crops. Back in Reno County, Kansas, people were paying $100 an acre for farm land. The farms in Nowata County, Oklahoma, were selling for $20 an acre.

Tobe realized farm concerns weren't the only reason his folks wanted to move. The budding Amish settlement would provide community for the Stutzman family, perhaps without the sense of competition Mom felt in Thomas. Mom and Dad were eager to move some distance away from her brothers and sisters, whose picture-perfect farms served as a painful reminder of their own financial state.

Even so, Tobe wasn't excited about moving. There couldn't be many young people, so there'd be few girls to date. He would miss the young folks in Thomas, especially his friend Ervin Miller. Living so far apart, they would hardly get to see each other. Two hundred and fifty miles was much too far to drive a horse and buggy.

Tobe choked back his objections. There was no use getting Dad upset. He longed to be twenty-one when he could make his own decisions.

Dad set the date for moving to Wednesday, December 4, 1935. Over the next month, the family sorted belongings and packed for the trip. They decided to sell some of their livestock. On the day of the sale, Tobe watched in disbelief at the low prices the animals brought on the auction block.

"What am I bid for the Jersey calf? Good lookin' little critter. She'll make a good cow some day. All right, who'll give me fifty cents? Fifty, fifty, fifty, fifty, fifty. All right then, let's make it forty. Forty, forty, forty, forty.

"Come on now," the auctioneer pleaded. "This is a good looking calf. Who'll bid me twenty cents?"

Two hands went up. "That's better. I got twenty. Who'll bid me twenty-five? Twenty-five, twenty-five, twenty-five. Sold for twenty-five cents!"

Tobe choked back tears. Dad said it cost fifty cents to sell a calf at the auction. You couldn't get ahead this way.

Moving day rolled around all too soon for Tobe. It was a cold day with a slight breeze. Weeds sparkled with heavy frost along the garden fence as the rented trucks pulled into the Stutzman yard. Dad had hoped to get all of their household goods and farm equipment into two large truckloads, but they soon discovered they would have to make a third load. It meant extra expense, but what were they to do? Another truck soon arrived.

The group started out with the family traveling in the truck cabs. Dad chose to ride on top of the first load. Some miles out of Thomas, the truck approached a railroad track at a sharp angle. Not seeing the oncoming train from his right, the driver slowed only slightly with the intent to cross the tracks. Seeing the danger from his vantage point on top, Dad grabbed a garden rake and banged on the roof of the cab. The driver braked to a halt just as the train roared by in front of them. Inside the cab, Tobe's heart throbbed as he imagined what might have happened.

The rest of the trip was uneventful. Nevertheless, Tobe was relieved to see the sign announcing the town limits of Nowata.

The little town of Nowata lay in Cherokee Indian country on the northwest edge of the large Oologah Lake. Twenty miles to the south lay the town of Oologah, the birthplace of Will Rogers who was of partial Cherokee descent. The famous comedian had died earlier in 1935 in a plane crash. Just north of Nowata was the town of Delaware, named after the Indians who had settled there.

Formerly called Metz, Nowata was the Record Town for District No. 3 in the so-called Indian Territory. In 1889, the post office had changed the name of the county seat. The new name came from the Delaware Indian word "no-we-ata," meaning "Welcome." The sign painter at the train station misspelled the word, and it remained "Nowata."

Nowata was surrounded by oil fields discovered before the Great War. In those boom days, the small town had boasted a half dozen hotels and boarding houses. The Tin Pan supplied a dance floor and plenty of girls. You could rent rooms by the hour. The opulent Savoy stood as a proud testimony to the vigor of the oil boom. Some of the richest oil people in the region had worked out their deals in the offices and lobby of this landmark hotel in the middle of town.

Following the Great Depression, a barrel of oil sold for as little as twenty-three cents. Still, Saturday night in Nowata was the busiest time of the week for shoppers. The H. C. Good furniture store stayed open until 10:00 p.m.

The oil dealers weren't the only ones who were suffering. Farmers in Nowata County were losing their crops due to the drought. Some folks joked that Nowata meant "no water." Government statisticians took notice that in 1930, crops had failed on 8,061 acres. By 1935 crops had failed on 28,971 acres. Land prices dropped from $26.20 to $14.60 per acre on the average. Farmers planted less corn each year, often planting oats instead. As the Stutzmans prepared to join the Amish farming settlement, they faced tougher times than they could have anticipated.

Tired from the five-hour trek, they drove toward the farmstead that would be their new home just five miles west and two miles south of Nowata near the tiny village of Watova.

As the driver approached and slowed, Tobe noticed a row of small cedars along the left-hand side of the road just beyond the lane. The trucks pulled into the driveway and parked near the barn. Tobe immediately headed for the water pump to get a drink. The water tasted rusty and full of iron.

After he quenched his thirst, Tobe eagerly surveyed the small plot with the four-room house. A cistern lay close to the southeast corner of the house. He cranked the mechanism on top that brought water to the surface. Nothing. Too little rain.

Ervin joined Tobe as he walked west from the house to a small cave. Tobe opened the folding door on top and stepped inside. It was damp and dark, but it would provide shelter in case of a tornado. Close to the cave stood the chicken house. Beyond that lay a small washhouse and smoke house.

The boys watched as one of the trucks backed up to the barn at the east end of the property. They ran to help the men unload the livestock.

The driver commented, "The barn looks a bit small."

John replied, "Yeah, but it'll have to do for now. We'll eventually need to build another barn for the cows." He led one of the horses down the ramp while Tobe and Ervin followed with the others.

Just then Anna hollered, "*Buwe, kummet un helfet uns mit die Sache.* Boys, come and help us carry things." The boys ran toward the trucks that were loaded with boxes and equipment. Each filled his arms and headed for the house. Tobe swung open the entrance door and stepped into the living room. He set down the box and walked into the small kitchen to the left. Anna explained that the room off the kitchen would serve as a bedroom for the three oldest boys. Perry would sleep in the living room. John and Anna would have their bedroom off the living room. A small extra bedroom left room for a hired house helper.

The next Sunday the family drove their buggy the two miles to the Sunday school held at the Diamond Point school house. To Ervin and Clarence, it was already becoming familiar territory. They had been attending school there the past several days. Clarence quickly ran to demonstrate the swings and merry-go-round in the front yard, while Ervin showed Tobe around the well-kept yard surrounded by a chain-link fence. They couldn't recall seeing a schoolhouse built of brick before. Even the outhouses and the utility shed were made of brick.

As they stepped into the building, Tobe looked over the new faces. Everyone seemed friendly. Although few Amish communities in the United States and Canada conducted Sunday schools, the Stutzmans were accustomed to the movement from their days in Custer County.

Designed to teach reading and knowledge of the German Scriptures to the young, Sunday school classes provided an opportunity for participation in open discussions about the Bible. First organized among the "English" churches, Sunday school seemed like a dangerous innovation to many Amish. Most Amish leaders reasoned that if young people gained more knowledge of the Scriptures than their elders, it would erode the authority of parents and elders. Furthermore, if lay persons, rather than ordained ministers, were given responsibility for teaching the Scriptures, it could lead to an attrition of ministerial authority in the church.

Nowata's Bishop Eli Nisly not only tolerated but actively promoted the Sunday school program. Along with others who had moved from the Reno County, Kansas, community, the bishop believed that salvation required more than simply joining the church.

The Stutzman family had just been seated when Ben Yoder, the Sunday school superintendent, opened the service with a welcome. Then the group sang several songs. One was the German version of "What a friend we have in Jesus." Tobe soon noticed that the group sang much faster than he was used to in the church service back in Thomas. Stranger still, the group sang a few songs with an English chorus between the German stanzas, and they didn't use the *Ausbund* he had known in Custer County. The *Ausbund* had served Amish communities for hundreds of years, containing many hymns that were penned at the height of Anabaptist persecution in the sixteenth century.

Anna sang with obvious abandon, her soprano voice standing out above that of the other women. Caught up in the spirit of the song, she scarcely noticed the questioning looks cast her way. The frustrations of an unhappy marriage, crippling effects of arthritis, and bleakness of subsistence farming found release as she sang the lyrics from her heart.

After the singing, Ben Yoder dismissed the congregation to break up into smaller groups. Children studied a German reader, concentrating on mastering the alphabet and a few simple sentences. The young people learned to read the Psalms in German. The adults studied passages of Scripture, women in one room and men in another. A man stood in front of each class to lead the discussion because Amish women did not teach classes. Tobe decided he would try to adjust to this new community of faith.

Over the next weeks, the family settled into their new home. Spring weather arrived early in 1936. The March sun coaxed fresh color out of the brown grass in the yard. The farm work loomed large for John and the boys as they faced the challenge of carving a living on the rented farm. Would the land give its fruit this year?

Tobe pondered the question as he watched the last drops of fresh warm milk drip off his bucket into the stainless steel tank of the cream separator. The separator began to hum as he cranked the cast iron handle. The steel ball inside the handle clanked with each turn until the handle turned with sufficient speed. Centrifugal force rendered it silent. Tobe opened the spigot from the tank and watched the milk flood over the spinning stack of disks. Soon milk and cream found their separate paths out of the spouts into waiting buckets below.

It paid to separate cream from the milk of their six cows since they could sell the cream for cash. Once a week, they took it to Nowata and sent it by trolley to the creamery at Coffeyville. Each week the creamery returned the milk cans filled with whey. The pigs squealed with delight at the treat.

Although he tried, Tobe wasn't very happy in Nowata. He attended the weekly singings because it gave him a chance to get to know the few young people better. All the single people from age sixteen up to middle adulthood were invited. A married couple always provided supper. Because the youth group was so small, the hosts usually joined in all the activities. After supper the group sang for thirty minutes in German, using the *Gingerich* book, then switched to English using the *Church and Sunday School Hymnal*.

The young people sang in unison, although the new books contained notes for singing parts. The Amish community stressed that singing in four-part harmony made too much allowance for individual expression and pride.

Several times a year the whole Nowata youth group traveled to the Amish community in Mayes County, Oklahoma, for fellowship. Tobe dated girls in Mayes County several times over the winter months. He thought it would be fun to go more often, but fifty miles was a long way.

Once when Bishop Mose Troyer of Mayes County was away from home, his children invited the Nowata group to join their youth group for a dance. Accompanied by mouth organ music, the young people danced until five o'clock in the morning. That kind of thing never happened among the Nowata Amish. They had a reputation for being strait-laced.

Tobe liked some of the young women, and he started thinking about having a date with Fannie Mast. The next Sunday evening at the singing, he trusted his friend Roy Miller with the mission and said, "Ask Fannie if she'll let me take her home this evening." Tobe wouldn't have minded asking Fannie himself, but decided to stick by the Amish custom of having someone else ask. It would be less embarrassing for both of them if she wanted to decline.

Tobe stole glances in Fannie's direction as Roy nonchalantly approached the trio of girls where she was standing. Tobe pretended not to notice when Roy and Fannie talked briefly. He saw Fannie nod her head. Shortly after Tobe sidled alongside Fannie and said, "I'll go hitch up the horse."

A few minutes later he guided the horse toward the house. Stopping near the front door, he drew the horse back at an angle so that the rim of the buggy wheel on Fannie's side provided plenty of clearance for mounting. When she saw Tobe, Fannie strode from the house and stepped into the carriage. He clucked to the horse and they were off to her home.

It was well beyond midnight when Tobe bid Fannie farewell on their first date. They had a few more dates, but after a month or two, Tobe lost interest. However, he started thinking more seriously about the future. How would he know whom to marry?

He began to watch his mother more closely. He admired her pluck. He felt sorry for her too, especially with her intensified struggle with arthritis. The stress of the move to Nowata seemed to aggravate her condition. She could hardly carry out her normal domestic duties. Nevertheless, she was quick to help others.

One stormy night, a knock came at the door. Tobe watched as Anna opened the door to a stranger.

"Ma'am, could I have a cup of hot water? I'm very thirsty."

"Yes, come in out of the weather," she said.

"Thank you, Ma'am."

Anna put a tea kettle on the wood stove and pointed to a chair. "Please sit down. What's your name?"

"Foxworthy. I've come all the way from Nebraska. I'm trying to collect the money for some horses I sold down here. I never got paid."

"That's too bad. It's awfully stormy and cold to be outside tonight. You can stay here."

"No, Ma'am. After a warm cup of water, I'll be on my way."

Tobe watched from his chair as the stranger drank the water and left. "I hope he gets his money," Tobe said. "He's trying hard enough."

Although the stranger hadn't accepted Mother's offer to stay overnight, Tobe admired her compassionate spirit. Dad wouldn't have offered to house the stranger. Tobe wished to marry someone like his mother.

Despite her arthritis, Anna was sometimes able to share in the work with the neighbors. One day Anna gathered with other women to help her neighbor Alma Nisly with a baby quilt. Quilting together gave Anna and Alma a chance to talk about their lives. By the end of the day, with the assistance of Alma's sisters-in-law, Saloma and Drusilla, the coverlet was almost finished. Anna said, "If the rest of you want to go, I can stay a little later to help Alma finish this."

"Well, it will be dark when I get home. Maybe it's time to go." Saloma moved toward the clothes tree in the hall.

Drusilla echoed, "I'll go too." They put on their coats and left. Only Alma and Anna remained at the task.

Anna took a deep breath and spoke as Alma reached for more thread. "John and I just can't seem to get along with each other."

Alma gave Anna full attention as Anna continued, "He's stubborn, determined to do the opposite of what I want."

Alma nodded in silence.

"He has such a temper. Sometimes I'm afraid of what he'll do."

The younger woman paused. "Oh?"

"He takes out his anger on the animals. And the farm equipment. One time he got so mad at one of our sows that he almost starved her to death."

Alma looked puzzled. "That doesn't make much sense."

Anna continued. "I'm afraid of what he might do to himself." Her needle stopped in the middle of a stitch. Her voiced quivered, "I'm afraid I'll come home one of these days to find him hanging in the barn."

Alma's eyes widened as she listened in silence.

"I don't know what I can do. I've often prayed for help. I guess I'll just need to let God do whatever his will is."

Alma nodded. "There's nothing more you can do."

Anna sighed deeply. Several tears splashed on her hand and onto the quilt. She brushed them away and went back to stitching.

Alma noticed that Anna's thread was getting very short. "Let me get you more thread for your needle. With your arthritis, it's too hard for you."

Alma reached for the spool of white thread lying on the quilt. She measured off about a yard with her outstretched arm, then ripped it with her fingers. She twisted the frayed end of the thread between her wet lips, then deftly pushed it through the eye of the small needle. "Here you are."

"Thank you. It seems I have a hard time with these fingers. I'm thankful that I can still quilt."

Alma stood up. "It's getting too dark to see." She lit the lantern and hung it on the hook in the ceiling.

Anna rose to leave as Alma finished the last few stitches. "*Danki shea fer das Esse.* Thanks for the meal."

"You're welcome. Thanks for helping with the quilt."

The next day Anna was clearly in pain as she prepared the evening meal. She grasped a potato with her gnarled fingers and began to peel it. Soon she winced, put down the potato, and dabbed at tears with a handkerchief pulled from underneath her cape. She made her way to the ice box and pulled out a bottle of whiskey. She poured the contents into a cup, watching as the last drops from the empty bottle rose to half the height of the glass. Then she poured an equal amount of lemon juice into the glass and sat down on the rocking chair. Just as she finished drinking the concoction she heard the sound of tin cans being loaded onto the wagon. Tobe and John were leaving for town.

She rose and spoke through the screen door. "John."

"Yes." He looked up.

"I'll need some things in town."

"Write them down."

She moved to the roll top desk and pulled out a reddish Eversharp pencil. On the back of a used envelope, she scrawled out a list: "Salt, 5 lb. sugar, 10 lb. bleached flour." She hesitated, twirling the pencil between her gnarled fingers. She finished with a scribble, "Black thread, whiskey."

She called Tobe to the front door. "You can get everything but the whiskey at the General Store. And don't let anyone from church see you with it."

"Okay." Tobe knew she wouldn't be caught dead drinking whiskey if the doctor hadn't ordered it. Maybe Dad, but not Mom.

Mom sometimes went to the hot springs for her arthritis. The mineral water at the clinic near Claremore, some thirty miles south, drew people with many ailments from surrounding states. Some of their Amish friends spent time there too. But the treatment provided only temporary relief for Mom's pain. Despite her reluctance, the doctor advised her to drink some whiskey on occasion.

• • • •

John and Tobe pulled up to the Nowata trolley station just as the station master announced the arrival of the trolley from Coffeyville. The two men quickly swung their metal cans of cream out of the wagon and onto the wooden platform. The porter rolled the cans up to the steps and hoisted them into the car, exchanging the cream for cans of whey. Tobe lifted the whey into their wagon, and in a few minutes, the trolley was on its way to the next stop.

Tobe made the necessary purchases at the General Store and loaded them into the front of the wagon as John waited. Then they headed toward the liquor store.

Tobe sat back as John stepped out of the wagon and tied the horse. He watched as his father glanced up and down the street. Some folks from church were hitching their horse just up the street. John lingered at the horse's bridle. Tobe stole a glance toward the open buggy up the street. The occupant was looking in their direction. What was Dad going to do?

Just then John spied a gentleman walking up the sidewalk. John intercepted the stranger. "Could you do me a favor?"

"Perhaps."

"Buy me a bottle of liquor. My wife needs it for her arthritis. The doctor says so." He pressed a bill into the man's hand.

The coarse-shaven man glanced up at John's face, then down at the bill. He looked at Tobe sitting in the wagon, then nodded. "Sure. I'll do that for you." He walked into the store.

Tobe breathed a sigh of relief. Mother would be embarrassed to have others at church know about the whiskey, even if the doctors prescribed it.

5

Joining Church

The next morning as Tobe got out of bed and dressed, he thought about the folks from church who'd been watching them in front of the liquor store. Had they noticed Dad's purchase? The Nowata congregation was small, and everyone seemed to know everyone else's business. Still, Tobe was thinking about joining the church with the next instruction class.

Tobe rubbed his three-day-old whiskers with his hands. It was time to shave again. He picked up the galvanized bucket in the kitchen and stepped outside to the cistern pump. The frost glistened on the slab rock under his feet as he hung the bucket on the pump. After a few fast turns of the crank, the bucket was full.

He stepped back into the kitchen, poured a little water into a granite pan, and set it in the kitchen dry sink. He took the tea kettle off the wood stove and added its steaming contents to the water in the pan until it felt right to his finger. Then he dipped his shaving brush into the water, swished it in his soap cup, and slathered the soapy substance onto his whiskers. He flipped open the single-edged razor and began to shave, viewing himself in the small round mirror on the wall above the sink. He swept the razor from ear to chin. The razor grated against his skin. Reaching for the leather strop, he sharpened the blade by whisking it briskly against the strop.

Tobe's mind went back to church membership. Fannie Mast and two girls from Mayes County were going to join the upcoming class. Was this the time for him to join? He would soon be eighteen. Tobe pondered the question as he finished shaving and made his way to the barn to do the chores.

That Saturday night as Tobe prepared for his weekly bath, he thought again about possibly joining church. The last rays of the evening sun shone through the small window of the wash house as he poured hot water into the galvanized tub. He pulled off his clothes and threw them onto the floor. Squatting in the round tub, he lathered himself with the soap Anna purchased at the store in Nowata. It sure beat home-made soap. He laid the bar on the wooden shelf and scrubbed all over with a washcloth. Then using the granite dipper, he poured warm water over his thick brown hair. It was time to get a haircut again. Maybe one of the boys at church could do it this time. Mom didn't cut it short enough. Again he dipped water from the tub and poured it over himself. If he decided to be baptized, the bishop would pour water on his head. Tobe shivered in the cool evening as the rivulets ran down his body.

He stepped out of the tub and rubbed himself dry with the bath towel. The door scraped open as Tobe pulled on his trousers. Ervin walked in, "Are you soon done?" he asked. He set a bucket of hot water on the floor.

"Yep," Tobe answered and emptied the tub outside the washhouse as Ervin began undressing. Then he walked to the well and pumped half a tub of cold water. Well water wasn't fit for drinking, but it would do for bathing. Tobe shoved the cold water through the doorway to Ervin and walked toward the house. His mind was made up. He would join the church.

The next morning Tobe went to the Sunday morning church service, held every other week in the homes of people in the Amish community. The worshipers began singing the first song as the ministers went upstairs for pre-service prayer and planning. A few minutes later, Tobe joined the three young women who had declared their interest in joining the church. Together, they walked up the steps to meet with the ministers. It would be the first of nine sessions of instruction.

Bishop Eli Nisly led the session, drawing the other minister into the discussion as he saw fit. Then he dismissed the young applicants for membership as the congregation concluded the singing of the *Loblied,* a praise hymn always used as the second hymn in each service. Sung in a slow chant, it took about twenty minutes to sing through the four stanzas.

After only two sessions of instruction class, the two girls from Mayes County left the community, leaving Tobe and Fannie as the only applicants for membership. In the last session, both he and Fannie promised that they would be faithful members of the church for the rest of their lives. Then the minister asked Tobe if he would be willing to serve as a minister if he were called to do so. Tobe agreed that he would, knowing that this commitment was required of all young men who joined the church.

Two weeks before the scheduled baptism, the ministers took counsel of all the church members regarding their willingness to receive Tobe and Fannie as members. After the benediction in the morning worship service, the bishop asked all members to remain seated while children and non-members left the room. Then the leaders took counsel from each person, wending their way among the benches where the congregants were sitting. To Tobe's relief, there was an *eenich Rot,* a unanimous voice.

The baptism was scheduled to be held in the morning service on May 16, 1936, at the home of John and Lizzie Nisly. John was one of Bishop Eli's sons.

When Tobe arrived at the Nisly home for the baptism, he joined the men who stood in the customary circle near the barn. The women had their own circle near the house. The perimeter of each circle expanded as churchgoers unhitched their horses and joined the group.

Bishop Eli Nisly glanced at the watch he had pulled from his pocket. It was time for the service to begin. He stepped toward the farmhouse. The other men followed. Each paused to lay his hat on the bench just inside the porch. Then they filed silently to their seats on the backless wooden benches in the living room. The women made their way to the adjoining room as the ministers took their places on the bench near the front of the room. They faced the congregation.

A number of men strode forward to greet the ministers. They greeted each one with a holy kiss, lightly joining their lips according to the custom of their ancestors. Then they took their seats. Tobe didn't go up front but took his seat near the back of the room.

Soon one of the men called out a hymn number from the *Ausbund*. The congregation turned to the lyrics, preparing to sing the hymn without the benefit of printed musical notes. The *Vorsinger*, or song leader, led the song from his seat in the third row. He sang the first note clearly, holding the first syllable for a time. The group joined in with the second note, savoring each syllable in the style of Gregorian chant. They continued this way, the song leader starting each line with the congregation following after the first syllable. Halfway through the song, a group of teenage boys entered the room and sat in the back row. Generally the last to arrive and the first to leave, the young men who had not yet joined the church seemed least eager to participate in the long service.

When the singing ended, Preacher Andy Miller stood up to give the *Anfang*, the first sermon of the morning. Without benefit of written sermon notes, he exhorted the congregation in German. His message was laced with a few words of English as well as the more colloquial Pennsylvania German. Drawing on biblical illustrations and allusions, he urged the faithful to follow God's will. In typical Amish fashion, he concluded with the words, *"Auch ich will die Zeit net lang verbrauche in mein grosse Armut und Schwachheit und die Zeit wegnehmen von dem Bruder wo es mehre Deel hat.* I don't want to consume more time with my great unworthiness and weakness; it takes time away from the brother who has the main message." Then he called the people to prayer.

All turned and knelt facing the benches on which they had been seated. The minister opened the German prayer book, knelt in the same direction as the congregants, and commenced to read a lengthy supplication. The young boys in the rear of the room stirred restlessly on their knees.

At the sound of the "Amen," the congregation turned and rose to their feet. The minister stepped forward to read the assigned chapter from the New Testament. In keeping with tradition, the men faced the minister as he read; the women in the next room faced away.

An hour had passed in the service when Bishop Eli Nisly stepped forward to preach the main sermon. He stood in the doorway between the two rooms, his deep blue eyes surveying the congregation. He was short and slender with a disproportionately long torso. Unlike most of the men under his charge, he did not wear suspenders. Regular men's trouser belts were forbidden by the church discipline so Bishop Eli kept his broadfall trousers in place by wearing them tightly around his waist.

The bishop turned his attention from one room to the other as he exhorted the people concerning the necessity of faith in Christ. Unlike some bishops who emphasized church traditions in their sermons, Eli pled for heart conversion. He recounted the story of Philip the evangelist in the book of Acts, who baptized an Ethiopian eunuch upon confession of faith in Jesus. Relying on memory, he cited various passages of Scripture that dealt with baptism. Then he drew on accounts from the *Martyrs Mirror*, reminding the worshipers of their Anabaptist forebears who had been persecuted for refusing to baptize their babies.

Tobe listened with full attention as Bishop Eli exhorted the congregation to forsake the world and its lust. The bishop's wide forehead and balding crown glistened with perspiration as he concluded his hour-long sermon. After he sat down, Eli invited several men to testify that they were in unity with the thrust of the message. Each added a brief exhortation of his own for the baptismal candidates. Then the bishop closed his remarks and called for the people to pray. Everyone turned and knelt, facing the bench on which they had been seated. The bishop read a prayer from the prayer book.

After the prayer, everyone was seated. The bishop called out Tobe's and Fannie's names and asked them to come to the front. Both knelt at the bishop's feet, their backs to the congregation. The bishop opened his book and asked several questions.

Both answered the questions in the affirmative, pledging faithfulness to God and the church. Then the bishop cupped his hands over Tobe's head and intoned, "*Auf deinen Glauben das du bekennt hast vor Gott und viele Zeugen wirst du getauft in Namen des Vaters, des Sohnes, und des Heiligen Geistes. Amen.* Upon your faith, which you have confessed before God and these many witnesses, you are baptized in the name of the Father, the Son, and the Holy Ghost. Amen."

At each mention of a person of the Trinity, the minister who was assisting Eli poured a small amount of water into the bishop's cupped hands. Then Eli emptied his cupped hands over Tobe's head. The water ran down onto his clothing and dripped onto the wooden floor.

After baptizing Fannie in a similar manner, the bishop reached for Tobe's hand with the words: "*In Namen des Herrn und die Gemein wollen wir die Hand geboten, so steh auf.* In the name of the Lord and the church, we extend to you the hand of fellowship, rise up." He helped Tobe to his feet and greeted him with a holy kiss. Likewise, he grasped Fannie's hand as she stood. The bishop's wife stepped forward to greet Fannie with this solemn kiss of fellowship.

The assembly stood as the bishop read a benediction from the prayer book. Then he announced the place of the next meeting and the congregation joined in a final song. The people sat quietly for a few moments before the children and young people began to file out of the house. Then all ages stood, and the visiting began.

Several men readied the room for the noon meal. Under the direction of the host, they rearranged the benches into tables, using stands especially made for this purpose. Within a few minutes, the tables were set and ready for the first shift of people eating the noon meal. Men gathered around one set of tables, women and children at another. Together, they bowed their heads for prayer. After a time of silence, the man at the head of the table cleared his throat. Hearing this cue, everyone raised their heads.

The meal was standard Amish church fare. Mothers reached for bread, spreading butter or a special peanut butter and molasses mixture on slices for their children. They plunged their forks into jars, pulling out pickles and red beets. All these were spread on the oilcloth that covered the tabletop. There was no need for plates. People concluded the meal by licking their fingers and wiping the oilcloth clean with a damp rag. The second shift could now be served using the same silverware. Folks lingered for a time after the meal ended, then left for home.

As Tobe rode home, he thought about his new status as a church member. He couldn't really say he felt any different except for a quiet sense of assurance that he had done the right thing. Unlike some of the young men who joined, it was not a major adjustment for Tobe to become a member. He had no car, camera, radio, or other worldly entertainment that would need to be surrendered. Of course, he would now be expected to keep the *Ordnung*, or church discipline. But he could also give and receive counsel, particularly at the special meeting called two weeks before each semi-annual communion service. At this meeting, the bishop and ministers reviewed all of the rules from memory. Those who were willing to indicate their support for the rules could take communion.

Although the rules remained unwritten, they were well understood. If a rule was no longer in force, the ministers simply did not mention it. This way of dealing with change was easier than changing a written code although some issues addressed by the *Ordnung* seemed nearly unresolvable. Like the matter of tractor ownership.

Ever since 1928, when Joe Stutzman of Hutchinson was required to make a confession for hiring a tractor to till his soil, the tractor issue threatened the unity of the church. Some farmers claimed that tractors would unduly compact the soil, making it less tillable and productive. Others asserted that the use of tractors would break the intimate connection between animals and the land.

Bishops Jake Miller of Hutchinson and Eli Nisly of Nowata both worried that tractors would lead to bigger farms. Larger farms would lead to larger investments, increased wealth, and less dependence on fellow church members in times of need. Tractors, many church leaders feared, would also lead to trucks. Motorized vehicles could then take members away from their homes and lead them to rely on resources outside the Amish community.

Bishop Eli's children pressed for the acceptance of both tractors and combines, believing that they made the difference between failure and success on the farm. Another church member's landlord upped the ante by informing him that if he wanted to keep farming his land, he would have to use a tractor. The bishops hesitated, realizing that it could bring reproach from other Amish communities who still banned the tractor in the *Ordnung*.

The matter became so heated that three bishops from the eastern states were called in to settle the dispute. The visiting bishops concluded that tractors should not be permitted. One church member quietly protested the decision by posting a chart labeled "Methods of Progress" on the wall of his barn. It showed the steps in development from a crooked stick to a tractor and plow. When his family hosted the church service, the men crowded around the large poster. Handwritten on the chart near the tractor were the words, "If this is wrong, why don't we go back to the crooked stick?" It seemed to be a direct challenge to the bishops' logic. Other church members, including Bishop Eli's children, put on pressure as well. The issue came to a boil.

In the summer of 1935, the year before Tobe joined the church, the bishops and ministers changed their minds. They announced their decision to allow tractors and combines, albeit with steel wheels only. A few weeks later the first tractor showed up in Nowata.

Tobe's father didn't buy a tractor until the spring of 1937, then he bought a Model D John Deere. Tobe was the first of the boys to use it. He was captivated by its staying power. Unlike horses, who needed time to rest on hot days, the tractor didn't tire. And unlike horses, tractors didn't need to be fed when they weren't working.

The drought conditions in Nowata often left grain and hay in short supply. In the August 1936 issue of the *Herold der Wahrheit,* Susie Miller explained the situation to readers in other parts of the country:

> We are having dry weather, and grasshoppers, and chinch bugs eat our harvest such as corn, kaffir, etc. (row

crops), but I feel we shouldn't complain and place our whole trust in our Savior, Jesus Christ. We have good oats and pretty good wheat and some barley. If we get a good rain we might yet have good kaffir, etc. So we have enough to be thankful for.

The rains didn't come on time, either in the fall or the next spring of 1937. The summer continued hot and mostly dry, although the oat crop seemed to defy the predictions that there would be a scant harvest. Tobe looked at his neighbor Eli F. Nisly's oats with some envy. Someone estimated that they would make sixty bushels to the acre, a yield that provided lucrative profits. When harvested, the oats produced only half of that projection. It seemed that the land in Nowata promised a lot and delivered little. There were many loads of straw but little grain.

That summer Tobe helped Noah Mast harvest his oats east of Nowata. Together, Tobe and Vernon Pearsall unloaded dozens of wagons of short-stemmed oats as fast as several men could bring them in. Tobe was eighteen years old, and he stood over six feet in height, much taller than his father. As he worked, his biceps swelled against the sleeves of his faded cotton shirt. He often worked alongside older men, determined to outshine them. Young Johnny J. K. Yoder's mouth stood open in awe as he watched Tobe feed the sheaves into the mouth of the twenty-two-inch threshing machine powered by an F30 International Farmall tractor. Johnny was sure none of the other men in the congregation could have kept up with Tobe that day.

Tobe was proud that his father trusted him to tie hay bales for the neighborhood. John owned a stationary baler, and neighboring farmers brought their loose hay on wagons and fed it into the baler. Tobe enjoyed tying the bales, a job his father wouldn't have readily given to others. If the bales were too long, the wires needed to be spliced. If they were too short, buyers didn't want to pay a good price. Tobe enjoyed the challenge of getting them just right.

• • • •

The summer of 1937 wore on, hot and dry, with little rain to bring relief. One Sunday afternoon it was especially relentless, too hot to stay in the house and too hot to play outdoor games.

"Let's go swimming at Levi Stutzman's pond," Tobe suggested.

"Great idea," Ervin agreed. "Let's invite some others to go with us."

"*Ich will aa mitgeh!* I wanna go too," chimed in nine-year-old Clarence.

"*Du kannscht net! Du bischt zu yung!* You can't go. You're too young." Tobe didn't want to be bothered.

"I'm going to tell Dad. He won't let you go if you don't let me go along," Clarence countered. He wasn't about to be pushed aside.

Tobe stepped into the house to inform their parents of their plans. Mom sat on a rocking chair, the *Sugarcreek Budget* lying askew on her lap. Her mouth hung slightly open, her head tilting sideways in sleep. The boys crept quietly past her to their parents' bedroom. Dad lay asleep. He stirred as the door creaked, "Yes, what do you want?"

"We're going to the neighbors. We'll be back by supper time." Dad grunted out an okay, and the boys were off.

Tobe was glad Mom was asleep. She didn't usually approve of recreation on the Lord's Day.

After stopping by to pick up their friends, the boys raced to the swimming hole, five in all. It was a quiet pond, fed by a small stream. Several large elms cast shade over the water. Everyone quickly stripped to their bare skin and dove in. Straw hats, trousers, and shirts lay strewn on the bank of the pond.

Tobe dove into the water, plunging to the bottom of the deepest part. Shielded from the sun's rays, the water was cold and dark. Tobe fingered the muddy bottom, burying his hands in the slippery silt. He came to the top, spluttering away the bits of moss that caught on his lips as he broke the surface. The other boys splashed and yelled as the activity increased.

Tobe swam toward the far side, his head barely out of the water behind his hands in a lazy doggy-paddle stroke. He spied a turtle near the bank just ahead of him. Seeing Tobe, it dropped quickly out of sight. Tobe veered off toward the right because he'd once heard there were snappers in this pond. No use challenging a snapper in its native territory. He swam to the edge and climbed onto the bank, sitting on a rock with his feet dangling in the water. A pair of catfish nibbled at his toes. He picked up a stone and skipped it across the water. *Eight skips. Pretty good.*

Watching a swallow swoop down to snatch a mosquito off the surface of the pond, Tobe shivered as the breeze stirred the leaves in the large elm. The water would feel warm now. He trotted to the deep end and dove in. Holding his nose, he determined to stay under water for at least one minute. He counted off the seconds—*fifty-eight, fifty-nine, sixty*—then burst to the surface, gasping for air to fill his starved lungs.

Soon his companions were at each other, splashing water with sharply cupped palms in waist-high water. Tobe ran around the end of the pond. He didn't want to miss the action. Grabbing a bucket at water's edge, he joined the fun. It soon became a free-for-all contest to see who could move the most water. Even Clarence held his own, although with some care not to get drawn into the deeper part. Once before he had gotten in a bit too deep. The other boys had needed to rescue him.

It was glorious. With no thought of the burning sun, the boys romped in and out of the pool, their white skin smudged with mud. Tobe had a large dark stain on one leg, evidence of the muddy bank where he sat with his legs barely submerged.

The water battle past, Johnny J. K. paddled around the pond on an inflated inner tube. He couldn't swim, so he depended on the tube for life support in the deeper part of the pond. A farm dog paddled toward Johnny. The mutt clawed at the rubber tube, straining to get on top.

Johnny shooed him away. The dog swam off to friendlier quarters. Suddenly, Johnny noticed his tube was deflating. He cried out in panic, but no one heard. He screamed louder.

Tobe came to his senses. *Johnny is drowning.* He dove into the water and swam rapidly toward his desperate friend. Seizing the flattened tube, Tobe pulled it toward the shore, his flailing friend in tow. When they got to the edge, Tobe dragged Johnny onto the grassy bank.

Johnny sat on the side of the pond, gasping for air. His face was pale and he said he felt sick in his stomach. The boys gathered around with sober faces. What would they have done if Johnny had drowned?

Tobe noticed that the sun had dropped quite low in the western sky. His mind jerked him back to reality and his promise to Dad. *It must be past supper time, and we haven't chored yet.* They hastily stepped into the sun and vigorously shook their heads, spraying water from their long hair. After wiping the excess water off their dripping bodies with their hands, they pulled on their clothing and headed for home. *Dad will be upset.*

John met them as they arrived. "*Buwe, Zeit fah chorah.* Boys, it's time to chore." They moved wordlessly, each grabbing a milk bucket. No use making things worse with excuses.

The next day the sun blazed overhead as Anna made her way to the garden. "Clarence!"

"Yes?" The boy yelled from the corner of the shop.

"Bring the wheelbarrow. We have red beets to pull."

"I'm helping Dad."

John turned. "Go help your mother."

"Okay." Clarence scampered toward the barn and pushed the steel-rimmed wheelbarrow toward the garden.

Anna looked up from the beets. "When the bucket is full, dump it in the wheelbarrow. It will only take a few minutes, then we'll cut off the tops in the shade."

Despite the small amount of rain that summer, Anna had been able to raise vegetables in the garden. The boys sometimes watered the thirsty soil with well water.

In August of that dry, hot summer, Lovina Yoder, the live-in maid at Tobe's home, reported that the cistern was dry. There was no water for drinking, cooking, or washing.

Anna summoned the boys. "Go over to the Carr Ranch and get us some water so we can wash today." Anna refused to use well water for doing laundry. The minerals in the water stained the clothing.

Clarence harnessed the horse while Ervin and Tobe loaded metal barrels onto the wagon. They drove to the ranch just two miles away. The Carr's pond had been built by the Civilian Conservation Corps. The federal government, concerned about the drought in the area, had dug ponds for landowners interested in designating land for such use. Because they were cattle ranchers, the Carrs had benefited from this offer. They didn't mind sharing with the Stutzmans and other neighbors who ran out of water during the dry season.

The boys returned with several barrels of water. Lovina helped dip the water out of the barrels into the wash tubs. They splashed playfully as they worked. It was fun to get wet on those unbearably hot days.

Anna asked the boys to clean out the cistern. There was no better time than when it was empty. Tobe lowered a ladder into the square concrete vault and took off his work shoes.

Carrying a bucket, he lowered himself into the hole and stood in the sludge at the bottom. Frogs hopped against his legs as his eyes adjusted to the darkness. Mud oozed between his toes and tickled his ankles.

Tobe bent down to scoop up the sludge. Ervin descended partway into the cavern. They exchanged buckets. They encountered more frogs, some dead, some alive, as they scraped up the sludge. Tobe tried not to think too much about the fact that the family drank water occupied by frogs. But drinking the bad tasting well water would be even worse. Soon the hole was clean, ready for the next rain that would fall from the roof gutter into the concrete cavern.

The frogs reminded Tobe that it had been a while since they'd had frog legs to eat. "Clarence, let's hunt bullfrogs at the Carrs!"

"Okay, I'll get the .22." Clarence felt comfortable hunting on the Carr ranch. The Carrs had given him his first job—hoeing cockle burrs.

It wasn't long before the two boys had bagged three of the huge jumpers. They fried the legs for lunch.

"Man, these are good eating."

"Sure are. Let's go get some more."

Before long they'd gotten another half dozen. An afternoon snack!

The hoped-for rain did not come in time to save the summer hay crops. Nor was there any corn at all. Then in fall 1937, the weather patterns changed dramatically. From September 16 to November 1, twenty inches of rain fell on the Nowata community. The ground was so wet that Tobe's family was barely able to plant the next year's winter grain crop.

As winter approached and the farm work wrapped up for the season, Tobe and Clarence picked up a bit of cash by hunting cottontail rabbits in the slough just east of their farm.

They dressed the rabbits and sold them at Nowata for fifteen cents apiece.

Frost blanketed the ground as John and his neighbor, Eli Nisly Jr., walked together toward the small stream that flowed through the slough. As they approached, a young filly raised her head. John pointed to the young mare. "Would you be interested in buying her?" he asked.

Eli sized up the horse. She looked healthy and sleek. "Why do you want to sell her?"

John pointed to the filly. "See that crease just across the top of her withers? It's like a groove that runs all the way across. I guess it's a birth defect."

Eli wasn't sure he was interested. "Don't you think it will keep her from pulling when she grows up?"

"No, it doesn't seem to affect her at all, it just looks a bit strange. My family's been poking fun at me ever since I bought her. I just want to get rid of her."

John walked toward the filly, who leapt away. Eli watched as she jumped over the small stream. It didn't seem that the young mare was handicapped in any way. "How much do you want for her?" he asked.

"Eight dollars."

"It's a deal."

"Good, you can pick her up anytime."

The abundant fall rains did not continue into the spring season. In March the Nowata area had a terrific dust storm. The air was yellow all day with a strong south wind. By the time the wind dropped, Tobe couldn't see the neighbor's house a fourth of a mile away.

Tobe began to wonder about the family's future in Nowata. Two years without a decent crop was almost more than they could stand. Others had to be thinking about it too. The trickle of settlers into the settlement had stopped as early as 1936. Now families were starting to move away. The

Overholts moved to Virginia, the Millers to Reno County, Kansas, and another family to McMinnville, Oregon. Two newly married couples, Raymond and Fannie Headings and Jerry and Clara Miller, also chose to move away rather than farm alongside their parents. The settlement was shrinking fast.

Tobe didn't dare say it, but he hoped to join those who were leaving. His future in farming wasn't his main concern. He was worried about the prospects for marriage.

The next Sunday evening Tobe rode home from the singing by himself. A slight breeze made the hot July night a little more bearable. Fireflies dotted the meadow and danced around the buggy. With a quick swipe of his hand, he captured one in his hand. Watching in fascination as the light flashed through the spaces between his fingers, Tobe slowly opened his hand as the insect crawled out and flew away.

As the buggy rounded a corner, Tobe faced the full moon. He wished for a girl with him in the buggy. But there were only a few girls, and he had already dated most of them at least once. With people leaving the settlement rather than moving to the settlement , the chances of finding an eligible young woman seemed as rare as the summer rains.

He found himself wishing that he could pay a visit to another community, like the one in Hutchinson, Kansas. There were some very nice girls there. He spent lots of time thinking about Preacher Levi Nisly's daughters. Ever since he'd first met them last summer, he wished he'd live in Kansas so he could get to know them better.

6

Emma Nisly

On July 2, 1937, a car pulled into the Stutzman driveway. Clarence raced outside to see who had come. A gentleman stepped out and handed an envelope to Clarence who gave it to his mother. Tobe watched her face wrinkle with grief as she read the telegram. Grandma Lizzie Miller had died of a burst appendix that morning. The family scrambled to make arrangements for traveling to Hutchinson. A Mennonite man from the nearby town of Pryor agreed to take them in his car.

Hundreds of mourners came by to convey condolences to Lizzie's second husband, their beloved Bishop Jake Miller. On Independence Day, they crowded into the two houses on the Miller farm for the funeral. At the meal following the service, Tobe sat with his uncle Joe Miller and a large group of young men. Tobe took the opportunity to notice the young women who were seated nearby. Several caught his eye. He whispered to Joe: "*Wer sin selli Maed as datt driwwehocke?* Who are those girls sitting over there?"

Joe glanced at the young women, then back to Tobe, "They're Levi Nisly's daughters. The one at the end is Emma. She's very popular with the boys. The other one is her sister Barbara."

"How old is Emma?"

"She's older than you. I think she just turned twenty-one."

"How about Barbara?"

"She just turned sixteen."

Tobe straightened his hair as he stole occasional glances in Barbara's direction. Afterward, he asked her for a date. She refused. Maybe she wasn't eager to date when she was only sixteen. Perhaps her older sister would make a better match. He'd ask her the next time.

The trip to Hutchinson increased Tobe's desire to get away from Nowata. That summer the main crops failed for the third year in a row. Some meadow hay even died for lack of moisture.

In August Tobe returned to Hutchinson. The Stutzman family visited his uncle Henry to congratulate him and his wife Mary on the birth of their firstborn, Eldon. They stayed for the worship service the next Sunday.

After the singing on Sunday evening, Tobe asked Emma for a date. She accepted. They spent an enjoyable evening together.

Tobe was thrilled when Emma sent him a letter the next week, but he said little to his family about his interest. Anna noticed that Tobe spent more time at his writing desk. She noticed too that he was always eager to collect the family's daily mail.

One day when Tobe was gone, John and Anna both went out to pick up the mail. Her leather shoes crunched the frost-laden grass ringing the post of the mailbox. Anna opened the rusty lid. She held it up for John to see: "A letter for Tobe from my brother Joe. I wonder if Joe is getting married. He might be asking Tobe to help in the wedding."

That evening when Tobe came home, he eagerly tore open the envelope. "Hey, Mom, Uncle Joe is getting married to Catherine Yoder on December 9. He's inviting me to be one of the 'extras' in his wedding! He says that I can pick my own partner."

"I suspected that's what the letter might be about. Who will you ask to be your partner?"

"I guess I'll have to think about that." Tobe was pretty sure it would be Emma Nisly, but he didn't want to say it.

That evening Tobe wrote Emma a letter using the quill pen and some nice stationery his mother kept in the writing desk. He told Emma about the invitation and asked her to serve as his partner. He sealed the envelope and walked to the mailbox.

Tobe was delighted when Emma responded with a letter accepting his invitation. The weeks seemed to drag by as Tobe looked forward to seeing her again. His anticipation grew as the family drove to Hutchinson together for the big event.

Tobe's brother Ervin watched as Tobe and Emma stood side by side. Tobe caught Ervin's eyes then winked as he stole a sideways look at Emma. Ervin winked in return. This was the girl Tobe had been telling him about.

After the wedding ceremony, Tobe and three other young men served as hostlers at the event and as chauffeurs from the wedding ceremony to the reception. There they joined their partners as food servers. After serving at the tables for several hours that afternoon, Tobe and Emma returned the next day to help clean up the home. They washed hundreds of dishes, but Tobe didn't mind. The honor of being asked to serve made the hard work worthwhile.

Tobe liked Emma. She was pleasant and laughed a lot, particularly at his jokes. The two of them enjoyed talking. He wished Dad and Mom would do more talking. Mom did plenty of talking, but Dad just kept quiet. It was hard to tell what was going on in Dad's mind, and it seemed useless to try to pry it out of him. Tobe promised himself that when he got married, he'd be sure to talk things out.

• • • •

Back home in Nowata several weeks later, Tobe joined the rest of the family for the annual butchering event. Together, they rode along the slough toward Eli Nisly Jr.'s farm. To distinguish him from his father, Bishop Eli, most church folks called him *gleene Eli* (little Eli) or Eli F.

The Stutzmans and the Nislys helped each other on the farm with hay baling, butchering, and other farm tasks. Because the weather had turned cold enough to store meat without refrigeration, it was a good time to butcher for the season.

John Stutzman guided the team of horses into Eli F.'s yard. Tobe watched with interest as the flame flickered on the pipe that rose above the gas well. He wished Dad could have a well on his property.

As the family unloaded their butchering supplies near the corral, Tobe noticed the filly Dad sold to Eli the year before. "How's the filly doing?" Tobe asked Eli.

"I've started using her. She'll soon be broke. She's really going to make a good horse. Your dad gave me a good deal."

Tobe was disgusted. Why had Dad sold her so cheap? It just didn't make sense.

Eli F. stepped into the corral to round up the steer they'd be butchering. Eli raised Shorthorn cattle, a breed that produced milk as well as meat. He was proud of the herd, declaring that they had beef to the hocks. They thrived on the native grass in the rolling hills around Nowata. With the drought turning farmland into grassland, raising beef made sense.

Tobe wished Dad would raise beef, but he didn't seem interested. It wasn't that Mom didn't show interest. She often reminded Dad that her father had done well with beef cattle. But Dad wasn't interested in beef farming. He seemed more interested in raising hogs although he never had a large herd. He said Grandpa Stutzman taught him you should always have a fat hog on hand, either to butcher or to sell.

Butchering season was a time of celebration. Even though the crops did not do well, there was always enough to eat.

Fresh meat brought a sense of cheer. That evening Tobe wolfed down several fresh hamburgers.

Christmas was a time of celebration too. It was a good reason for Tobe to make another visit to Hutchinson. This time Ervin went along. He was now sixteen and dating. They stopped for the night with relatives at Yoder, Kansas. Then on Christmas Day 1938, they headed for the church service near Partridge. Tobe felt a bit self-conscious as he walked into the Jake Yoder residence. Through the doorway, he spied Emma, sitting with the other young women. Emma smiled, flushing slightly. She whispered to her sister Barbara, "Should we invite the young folks from Oklahoma to our house after the singing tonight?" Besides the Stutzman brothers, there were other visitors—two girls and a boy. Barbara agreed to the idea.

That evening after the singing, Emma stood in the knot of young people around Tobe and his younger brother Ervin. "Do you have a place to stay overnight?"

Tobe turned, "We thought we'd probably stay at Jake Miller's."

"You can all stay at my house." Emma turned slightly red as she spoke.

The visitors glanced at each other. "Sure, why not?"

As Amish boys are wont to do when they handle the reins in crowded buggies, Tobe sat on Emma's lap as the group rode home in the crisp December air. When they arrived at the Levi Nisly farm, Tobe helped Emma step down. For several hours that evening, the house rang with laughter and excitement. Finally well after midnight, the guests were shown their beds. The house was quiet. Tobe lay awake after the girls retired to their room. He wished he and Emma could slip off somewhere together. Perhaps some other time.

The Lord's Day dawned bright and clear. Because it was a Sunday school Sunday, it was a day to relax. Emma's folks went to Sunday school, but the young people opted to stay home.

In the evening Emma and others took Tobe and Ervin to Amos Yoders, where the two brothers spent the night. The next morning they headed back home to Nowata, and Emma went back to the home of Ed and Lizzie Nisly where she served as a live-in maid. Ed was her uncle, a brother to her father Levi.

When Emma arrived, Ed and Lizzie decided to go shopping in town for Christmas bargains, leaving their six young children with Emma. She washed the Sunday clothing and cleaned the house before noon. In the afternoon she made a pair of trousers. When Ed and Lizzie came home, Lizzie expressed delight with Emma's work.

After supper Lizzie stepped away from the table while the rest lingered. She went to her bedroom and came back with a glass dish in her hands. Holding it out to Emma, she said, "Merry Christmas."

Emma took it, turning it upside down and around, feeling the raised designs. "It's really pretty. Thank you."

"You're welcome. We thought you might want to put it in your hope chest."

Emma smiled, her face flushing just a bit. "I think I'll take it to my room."

• • • •

Back in Nowata, life for Tobe seemed to move at a very slow pace. He gazed out the window as the snow fluttered against his north bedroom window. It felt good to be inside, but he would have preferred company. It was too quiet for comfort. The chores were all done so he wouldn't need to go outside again until late afternoon.

Tobe pulled out his French harp and began to play. Although the church frowned on the public use of musical instruments, Tobe and Ervin played them at home. Tobe played the French harp and a Jews harp, as well as a guitar he had made. His folks didn't seem to mind, as long as he kept the instruments at home.

Tobe laid down the harp and picked up his homemade guitar. The gentle music buoyed his spirit. Suddenly, Clarence burst in. "Tobe, let's go sledding! The snow is just right!"

"Sure, why not?" Tobe, Ervin, and Clarence bundled up into layered clothes and headed for the long hill west of the house. The snow soon packed into slippery ice, making for fast sledding. The three young men joked and tussled as they spent the afternoon sliding down the slope.

In Hutchinson where Emma was, snow fell often that winter and early spring. Emma watched with interest as it covered the ground one Sunday morning during the second week of April 1939. The wheat was already several inches tall, and wet snow clung to the tiny blades, bowing them to the ground. As Emma and her brother Henry headed for the evening singing at Ray Heading's home, flakes fell on the horse, forming ice on the flowing mane.

After the singing, the young people stepped outside into the magical whiteness. It was perfect for packing. A snowball flew toward the knot of young women standing on the porch. It hit Emma, splotching the front of her coat. Soon the missiles were flying thick and fast.

Laughing, the young women jumped off the porch and ran toward a mound of snow that had been scraped from the sidewalk. Soon it was boys against girls. Snow mixed with laughter and yelling from both directions.

Soon almost everyone was snow-covered. The girls dashed in the house and held the door closed behind them. The boys pushed at the door. Relenting, the girls let the door open while the boys piled inside. They all huddled around the stove, puddles forming on the wooden floor.

Later that evening, scattered flakes fell from the gray sky as Henry and Emma rode home in the open buggy. A crust of snow formed on the horse's back, dripping down his steaming sides. Emma's ears were cold inside her bonnet.

Henry dropped her off at the front gate of Uncle Ed's house, then he headed on home to their parents. Emma walked through the darkness toward the house, pausing on the step to brush the snow off her bonnet. It felt good to be in for the night.

Tobe made his next trip to Kansas to see Emma just as the cherries were beginning to ripen on the trees. On Saturday afternoon, Emma's mother invited him to a meal along with eight other young people. Tobe sat beside Emma at the family table. As they conversed, he kept his eye on Emma's mother. Mary was pleasant and hospitable. Tobe enjoyed her ready smile and jovial manner.

The visitors played games all evening and long into the night. Then they spread out on spare beds and sofas for the night. A few slept on the floor. Just before she dropped off to sleep, Emma penciled a note in her blue daily diary, "Did the Saturday work, finished Lester's shirt and pants, dark blue. Went home in eve. had visitors overnight namely Ira Y. and Emma K., Henry Y., and Lizzie P., Lizzie Fry, Ralph K., Tobe, and Levi Miller and Elizabeth Y." By this time, Tobe's name didn't need a last initial. He was special. She tucked the diary back into her dresser drawer, blew out the lamp, and hopped into bed.

There was no church service the next morning, so the young people played games and talked. The day passed quickly, ending with the singing at Alvin Millers. Afterward, Tobe took Emma home for a date.

An occasional cloud obscured the light of the moon as they rode the buggy toward her home. Tobe reached into his pocket and pulled out a piece of gum. "Want some gum?"

"Thank you." She seemed pleased.

They rode in silence at first, listening to cicadas in the locust trees along the fence rows. Fireflies danced in the meadow.

Tobe held the reins in one hand. With the other, he tapped out a rhythm on his leg in time with the horse's gait.

"Do you like horses?" Tobe asked.

"Sorta. Do you?"

"Yes. I occasionally break them."

"Really? How did you learn to do that?"

"We bought a training course from Professor Berry. You can really teach a horse a lot if you know how. It's cheaper to buy a horse that's not broke and train him yourself."

"Yes, I can believe that." She motioned with her hand. "The driveway is here to the right."

Tobe steered the horse up to the hitching post, then laid down the reins and tied the horse. Emma stepped down from the buggy. Tobe's hand reached for hers. Their fingers intertwined as they walked toward the frame house.

They stepped onto the porch and swung open the door. Tobe held the door against its spring, then let it rest gently against the doorstop. They moved into the house, their eyes well-adjusted to the darkness. She led the way to the sofa where they sat down next to each other.

Tobe broke the silence. "Have you ever ridden a horse?"

"Once when I was a little girl."

"Did you like it?"

"Not really. I almost got bucked off. I guess the horse was a little spooked."

"I like riding bareback. You don't have to take time to saddle them that way."

"Aren't you afraid you'll fall off?"

"Nope. I hold onto the mane."

They talked quietly, aware of the faint sound of snoring from the bedroom where Emma's parents slept. Tobe's arm stole ever so slowly around Emma's shoulders. She leaned against his shoulder, then reached up to remove the pins from her covering. Removing her organdy cap, she laid it on the library table at the end of the sofa. She relaxed against his arm, her head resting on Tobe's shoulder. The fragrance of her perfume filled his nostrils. They lay down on the sofa.

Hours passed with bits of conversation interspersed with long periods of silence. Tobe wriggled. His right arm felt numb. Emma lifted her head as he adjusted his arm. More silence.

The clock struck one. "I guess I should be going." He hated to leave.

They sat up together. As they walked to the door, he picked up his hat from the table.

They stood at the door momentarily, then Tobe took her into his arms and kissed her in the moonlight.

"Good-bye."

"Bye."

Tobe's mind raced as he rode home to the place where he was staying. Emma was fun to be with. No wonder she was so popular. The boys enjoyed talking to each other about the girls.

Some of Tobe's friends said they liked sitting in rocking chairs on their dates. They told their dates they could either sit on their laps or in the rocking chairs beside them. Both gave the opportunity to be close, but Tobe thought he preferred the sofa.

He'd heard that Emma's younger sisters spoke up against the practice of courting in the dark. They and like-minded young people were soon called *"die Lichtbrenne,* those who burn lights." Unlike *"die Annelege,* those who lie down," these young people sat up for dates in the light of a lantern. This new practice cast a shadow of judgment on the way the Amish had dated for years. Tobe resisted the change. Hadn't most young people successfully chosen marriage partners while dating the old way? Not many young people went too far. Why change now? It appeared that Emma felt the same way. She liked being close to Tobe on the sofa.

The next night after the trip back to Nowata, Tobe lay awake with his brother Ervin in the double bed. The sound of Clarence's rhythmic breathing rose from the single bed nearby.

"How did you like Kansas this time?" Ervin asked.

"I really liked it." Tobe's enthusiasm pushed his voice beyond a whisper. "I spent time with Emma."

"Which Emma?" Ervin whispered.

"Emma Nisly, of course."

"Which Emma Nisly?"

"You know. Levi's Emma."

Tobe knew that his younger brother was teasing. Ervin had his eyes on a different Emma Nisly, Sam and Delilah's daughter. They lived not far from Levi and Mary's place.

Tobe heard Clarence stir. Was he listening?

"It's time to go to sleep now," Tobe said. "I have a big day tomorrow." He rolled over and soon fell asleep.

Two weeks later Tobe got a letter from Emma. He tore open the envelope and took the letter to his room. His mouth dropped with envy at the last few sentences. "I have an invitation from Lizzie Bontrager to travel out west with a group of young people. I talked it over with my folks. They say it's okay to go. Will plan to leave on July 21 at five o'clock in the morning. Chit will be driving. Perhaps I'll send you a card along the way."

Tobe was jealous. What if she developed an interest in one of the young men who traveled along with the group?

Anna watched as he sat down at the writing desk to respond. "I see you're writing someone again," Anna said. "Is it a letter to Emma?"

"Yes. She's the prettiest girl in the church in Hutch. She's going on a trip out west."

"Remember, beauty is only skin deep. I don't want you to be going with a girl who has low standards."

"Mom! She's a preacher's daughter. She's really nice."

"I know. But sometimes young people get into the wrong crowd. I'm not sure it's a good idea to go on a sight-seeing trip. They could get involved in activities that are out of the *Ordnung*."

Emma wrote Tobe twice about the upcoming trip. She also told about riding home from the singing in the back of a truck. Tobe smiled. He knew that such behavior pushed hard against the *Ordnung*. Riding in a motorized vehicle for pleasure might even require a public confession in church.

• • • •

Emma and her friends left for their Western trip at 5:00 a.m. on July 21, 1939. Through regular mail, Tobe learned about their progress. They stopped at many of the major tourist sites near Denver: Cripple Creek, Pikes Peak, Seven Falls, Cave of the Winds, and Garden of the Gods. Then they stopped to see some relatives before heading for Cheyenne, Wyoming, where they picked up tickets for the rodeo. Tobe wondered what Emma's father would say. Fairs, rodeos, and farm shows were clearly forbidden by the church.

After a visit to Yellowstone National Park, Emma and the others moved on to North Dakota. There they stayed for a time with Amish acquaintances. The three boys fanned out to find work in the neighborhood. So did Emma. She told about it in a letter.

"We were in church at Jerry Yoders. It wasn't a very big *gmee* [church service]. I went home with Mary again. The boys came there then and took our clothing to our places. We were at Coblentzes for supper. Last Monday, I started to work for Dave Yoders. This week, I made pickles, picked beans, picked June berries, washed and ironed, patched a little, washed the house and porch, baked bread and rolls, made jelly, and worked in the garden pulling weeds. On Sunday, we went to the Mennonite Church in the morning. In the afternoon, we had a picnic. In the evening we went to the singing at Ezra G. It wasn't much of a singing."

Tobe grimaced. It sounded a lot like Nowata.

He continued to read: "We picked sweet corn to sell. . . . The menfolk plan to start threshing on Thursday. I'm helping with the cooking. We'll probably stay here till September then go on out West. . . . Must go if I want to get this in today's mail. Love, Emma."

Tobe folded the letter and put it back into the envelope. Perhaps some day he'd get a chance to travel.

The next weeks dragged by with scant news from North Dakota. In mid-August the monotony on the farm was broken when Mary Miller, Anna's live-in helper, turned ill after a hard day of work. Mary had been with the Stutzman family only a month. A widow with adult children, she preferred to live with others, and Anna enjoyed having her as a maid.

Anna hovered over Mary in the intense August heat. She wet a cloth in the porcelain bowl next to the bed and wiped Mary's brow. She suspected a stroke.

"How are you feeling now?"

"My head hurts." Mary's speech was slurred.

As the evening passed, Anna watched helplessly as Mary moaned in pain. Anna sat by the bed throughout parts of the night, at times drifting off to sleep. At four o'clock she wiped the sweat from her friend's brow.

"Mary? Mary?" Anna leaned over the bed. "Mary?"

No reply.

Anna lifted Mary's wrist, seeking for a pulse. None. She sighed with grief. With the August sun beginning to tint the horizon, they would need to move quickly to preserve the body. She called Tobe.

"Yes."

"Get up right away. Mary has just died. We'll need to let Preacher Andy and the others know."

"Okay." Tobe jumped into his clothing and headed for the stable to harness the horse. In a few minutes he was on his way to spread the sad news. Andy notified Mary's home community in Hutchinson that the body would be sent there that evening.

With the help of neighbor women, Anna bathed and dressed Mary's lifeless form and placed it into a wooden coffin made by John D. Yoder. Clarence hovered around the body.

By mid-afternoon people began to assemble at the Stutzman house for the funeral, the first for the small Amish community. After the solemn ceremony, all paid their last respects by filing past the coffin. The congregation dispersed as the coffin was hoisted into the back of a utility buggy for the trip to Nowata. It was imperative to catch the evening train for Hutchinson where family members had arranged a second funeral. The next day Mary's body was laid to rest in the West Center Amish Cemetery near Partridge.

Tobe was helping Anna with tomato canning when he learned that Emma's travel group was preparing to move on from their summer stay in North Dakota. Emma wrote about a short trek into Canada and their return to North Dakota, with plans to head further west in a day or so. He looked forward to hearing news from Oregon.

The next letter told about a change of plans. Emma wrote, "On Tuesday, I shelled beans from the garden. Barbara and Edith went into the field to get wheat that got wasted and brought it up for the chickens. On Wednesday, it was foggy so we were inside most of the day. Chit came by to tell us that they planned to go back home instead of taking us further west. Today, I was feeling lonely and blue."

Tobe reread the letter. *So they didn't get off after all. I'd be glad to take Chit's place if I had a car. I wonder why he and Anna decided to go back? What are the others supposed to do?*

It wasn't long before Emma's traveling group made new plans. Hank Beachy from Iowa came by with a car and volunteered to drive, so they left North Dakota only a week after Chit's disappointing announcement. Over the next few weeks, Emma and her friends toured many of the well-known sites in the west. Passing through Yellowstone National Park for the second time, they journeyed on to Yakima, Washington, and down the Oregon coast. On their way south through California, they drove through the trunk of a 300-foot-high redwood. They continued through the mountains of San Francisco and on to the orange groves outside Los Angeles.

Heading back east, they took the long desert drive to Boulder Dam and continued through the cotton fields of Phoenix, Arizona. They stopped briefly at Carlsbad Caverns, then made their way over bad roads and through wastelands to El Paso, Texas. Another long day's drive and the group ended up in Thomas, Oklahoma. After a couple of days of visiting in Custer and Mayes Counties, the weary young adults headed north. Tobe was quite disappointed when they didn't stop by Nowata on the way.

When they returned to Hutchinson late on a Saturday evening, everyone decided to spend the night at Emma's home, telling Emma's family about the many things that had happened on the eleven-week trip. After a Sunday packed with activities, Emma bid the rest farewell at 3:00 a.m. on Monday morning.

The butchering season had just started in Oklahoma as Tobe rode toward the mailbox after dinner on a chilly October day. It was his birthday. Would anyone send him anything?

He flipped open the lid and quickly glanced at the two letters. Good! A letter from Emma!

"Happy birthday!" The words in Emma's letter leapt off the page as Tobe walked into the house and plopped into a rocking chair. He kept reading.

"The last few days have been busy with housework at home. I helped clean the upstairs this past week. . . . Was in church at Menno Yoders. They had the church for Mennys. Will's Mary, Menno's Mary and I waited the table. Then we went to Mennys for the singing.

"Uncle Dans and Eds are coming for supper on Thursday night. I will tell about my trip."

Tobe glanced at the calendar. Thursday night, that was this evening. It was nice to know what Emma was doing.

As Tobe cleaned out the barn the next day, his mind kept drifting to thoughts of Kansas. *I wish I could just move up there. I sure wouldn't want to bring Emma down here to live. I don't see how this settlement is going to make it. The drought and crop failure make this twenty-dollar-an-acre farmland look like a poor investment. And Bishop Eli is seventy-six. How much longer will he be able to carry on? Who will take his place?*

Tobe plunged his manure fork into the heap and heaved it onto the waiting spreader. The fields were frozen, so it was a good time to spread manure.

As his father approached from the side of the barn, Tobe paused, "Dad, I'd like to move to Kansas."

"You're not twenty-one yet."

"I know. But I could send you my wages. I could earn real good up there."

"What if we need you here?"

"Ervin is sixteen now. And Clarence can manage the horses real well."

"What makes you think you need to move?"

"There's not many girls around here I can date."

"How about Mayes County? There are young people there."

"I like the Kansas young people better."

John stroked his long full beard. "I'll think about it." He walked away.

Tobe watched his father walk toward the house. The prospects of moving to Kansas didn't seem good. He rammed the fork into the pile and flung a large heap of manure into the wooden spreader. A few minutes later, the spreader was full. Tobe vaulted up onto the seat and clucked to the horses.

The next day Tobe received a letter from Will Miller of Partridge, Kansas. It was an invitation to work for him as a hired hand. Tobe's heart skipped a beat as he read about the farm work. The family milked thirteen cows by hand. Will rented some ground in addition to his own and used a steam engine to do custom farm work—threshing wheat and oats, binding corn, and filling silo. He also did custom grinding with a stationary hammer mill. Tobe could see why Will needed a hired hand. Would Dad let him go? Maybe now that he had a definite offer. He would ask him tomorrow.

7

Kansas

Tobe was ecstatic. "I did it! I did it! Dad's going to let me go!" Of course he'd need to send his paycheck back home, but the freedom to choose his place of work tasted as sweet as honey. He immediately wrote a letter of acceptance, hoping to start soon.

Meanwhile, his parents' fortune turned. One day when Tobe picked up the mail at the box, he saw an envelope with an attorney's office return address. It was addressed to Mother. What could it be?

He held his breath as Anna opened it.

"Oh, it's the check."

"What check?"

"The settlement check from Grandma's estate."

Tobe's father stepped into the house. His wife handed him the check. "It's the settlement for the estate," she said.

John looked at the check and read the accompanying letter. "This is a good amount of money. Since it's written in your name, you'll need to endorse it." Anna walked to the desk and reached for his fountain pen. She scrawled her signature on the back of the check and handed it back to John. She sighed. "I hope we can use it to buy some land."

"There's a piece over near Tobe Yoder's for sale."

"How many acres is it?"

"About eighty."

"Is it good soil?"

"Good enough."

"Some of the land around here isn't so good for farming. Maybe we should buy cattle like Eli F.'s did."

John turned away without comment. He put the check into the desk and went back outside to the barn.

• • • •

Within a few weeks, Tobe had word from Will Miller that he should come as soon as possible. He took the train to Kansas.

His short, bowlegged boss walked fast, talked fast, and worked fast. Tobe quickly learned that work on the Miller farm was demanding. Will Miller expected an all-out effort from his farm hands, and he wasted no compliments. It seemed that no one could work fast enough to please him. It was hard for Will to keep hired hands.

Tobe rose to the challenge. He was determined to prove to his boss and other Kansas people that he could work as hard as any of them, and Tobe soon won Will's grudging re-spect. On most tasks, he could outpace the smaller, older man. Not that Will didn't voice an expectation that Tobe do even more.

Tobe countered by bargaining for some side benefits. It wasn't long before he conflicted with Will regarding the use of his oats. Tobe liked to reward his horse with high-quality oats when he came home late on Sunday night. From the start of his employment, he'd given his horse a bucket of oats from Will's bin. Will thought it unnecessary to feed a horse late at night. He suggested that if Tobe must feed his horse, he should use the less expensive feed from the bull's feed bin.

Tobe persisted despite Will's jabs at his practice. He was sure he had more than paid for the oats with the extra work he put in on the farm. As the months went by, Will lapsed into silence on the matter. Maybe his boss had given up.

Not so. One evening when Tobe arrived home late at night, he chanced to shine his flashlight into the feed bin before filling his scoop with oats. At the front of the bin were two buckets, filled to the brim and carefully smoothed on top. Tobe immediately saw the ruse. Will had set a trap to see if Tobe was still feeding his oats. Tobe rubbed his chin. He couldn't get oats without disturbing the buckets. He remembered that there was another opening in back of the bin, so he left the two buckets undisturbed and got his oats at the alternate opening.

The next morning as Tobe was getting dressed, he stepped to the window and glanced toward the barn. He watched as Will opened the door, looked into the feed bin, and jerked back his head. Tobe burst out laughing. Will didn't mention the matter again, so Tobe kept feeding oats to his horse.

Will's wife Rebecca was Emma's aunt. Soft-spoken and kind, she was careful not to impose on others. Sometimes it seemed to Tobe that she was trying to compensate for her husband's brusque manner.

Perhaps because Tobe had no sisters, he reveled in his daily interaction with the girls in the Miller family. He took special interest in Mary, only six months younger than he. Tobe's friend, John C. Yoder was dating her, but Tobe didn't mind making him worry a little about losing her hand to Tobe. Meanwhile, Tobe watched jealously when any other young man spoke to Emma Nisly.

Tobe enjoyed being with Emma but wasn't ready to be tied down in marriage. There were lots of other young women in the youth group, and Tobe was often the center of attention. His ability to imitate the voice and motions of others provided lively entertainment. Although Tobe sometimes felt like an outsider, he also felt the admiration of his peers. And more than once, he heard Will's daughters say that their dad was proud of all the work he got done.

Part of Tobe's reward for his work was permission to use Will's shop for his own projects. Having made a few items in Oklahoma, he developed some bigger projects. Since there was little cash for the purchase of new lumber, he bought used oak dining tables as a source of hardwood.

Tobe built his first large piece of furniture for his boss. It was a sink cabinet that replaced the dry sink. Will and Rebecca were so pleased that Tobe was encouraged to build a dresser bureau. Will's daughter Emma bought it for $16.00. Not long after, her sister Mary followed suit with a similar piece.

Tobe sent his farm wages to his father but pocketed the money from his budding spare-time enterprise. Didn't he deserve the money he'd earned after hours? He might even start up his own woodworking business.

Will had very few woodworking tools, so Tobe designed and made some of his own tools. He supplemented his handmade collection with some he bought with the cash from his sales. In a year's time, Tobe accumulated a set of woodworking tools more complete than his father had ever had.

Tobe's projects drew attention from the whole Miller family. Eight-year-old Edna, youngest of the Miller children, often hung around the shop admiring Tobe's work. She watched as Tobe traced a pattern and cut out the pieces for a guitar.

"Have you ever made a guitar before?" she asked.

"Yes."

"How do you know how to do it?"

"I just do it."

Tobe grinned as she stood bright-eyed while he glued the pieces together.

"How long do you need to leave the clamps on there?"

"Overnight," Tobe told her.

A few days later, after he bought the strings, Tobe played the guitar in his bedroom. Edna knocked softly on the door. "May I come in?"

"Sure."

Edna sat at the foot of Tobe's bed, listening to him strum the new instrument. Tobe's strong tenor voice echoed off the ceilings and walls of the small room. Soon her small voice joined in, at first timidly then with more confidence.

When Tobe paused between songs, Edna asked, "How did you learn to play the guitar?"

"I just play it by ear."

"Is that how you learned to play the mouth harp?"

"Yes, and the accordion too."

Tobe read the admiration in Edna's eyes, so he went out of his way to impress the young girl. One day at noon as the men came toward the house for dinner, she ran up to Tobe. He swooped her up and swung her over the picket fence, then set her down gently. He grinned as her eyes grew wide. It was something her father wouldn't have done.

Because Edna enjoyed being with Tobe, he invited her to help sand one of his woodworking projects. She seemed delighted so he put her to work on other projects as well. In return for her help, he bought her a covered dish with a ruby red lid and a clear glass bottom. She displayed her treasure on a shelf.

Just after Valentine's Day, Bishop Jake Miller, who had been married to Tobe's grandmother Lizzie, had a farm sale. People came from far and wide, pulled in like nails to a magnet. Were they seeking bargains? Or were they just wanting to see what Bishop Jake had accumulated? Tobe was particularly eager to attend because some of the things to be auctioned had belonged to his grandmother. He might even be able to buy an old table to use for hardwood.

Tobe's mother Anna came up from Nowata, hoping to buy something that had belonged to her mother. To Tobe's delight, Emma was there too. The two young people spent time walking among the goods for sale.

A few weeks later, Emma moved in as a house helper for her Aunt Lizzie Yoder, who was expecting a child. Lizzie was married to Menno Yoder Jr. Emma and other Amish around Hutchinson referred to the family as Mennys to distinguish them from the family of Menno Yoder Sr.

It was early summer, and the wheat was ripening when Lizzie Yoder gave birth to a son, whom they named Edwin. Emma took care of the small boy and did the household chores. She was still living with the Yoders when tragedy struck on her parents' farm. Emma told Tobe all the details the next Sunday night.

• • • •

There was no sign of trouble until after the whole family was asleep. The night was unbearably warm. Emma's mother Mary awoke, her senses aroused by a crackling sound through the open east window. She sniffed the air. Smoke! She hopped out of bed to investigate. Orange flames flickered through the cracks in the barn siding. She shook Levi awake, then shouted up the stairs, "*Die Scheier iss am Brenne!* The barn is on fire!"

In moments the household was alive with activity. Levi barked out orders: "Lizzie, run to the neighbors to call the fire department. Boys, get the horses out of the barn. Let's get the buckets lined up."

Lizzie slipped into her clothing and sped up the gravel road toward the Schlutzbaum's home, the closest neighbors with a phone. Her bare feet pounded the worn track on the right side of the road, her path lit only by the moon.

By the time Lizzie got to the neighbors, Roy Miller had already alerted the fire department. He had been plowing Dick Kauffman's land just a quarter of a mile north of the Nisly farm. As was common, he worked at night for relief from the intense summer heat. About midnight he noticed a light in the Nisly barn. Before long he detected flames. He drove his tractor, with plow trailing, to Merle Kent's house. They put out a general call on the Hutchinson phone exchange, notifying all who had a phone. Then he drove quickly to Roy Terrill's place, a quarter mile west. They put out a general call on the Partridge exchange. Within minutes people from a ten-mile radius were coming to the fire. They honked their horns to wake the Amish as they passed their homes.

Emma's younger brother, Raymond, approached the barn stable, hoping to lead the horses to safety. It was impossible. The heat was too intense. Soon the roaring flames burst through the barn roof, the fresh hay in the loft blazing like an inferno. The pony screamed in agony, and Raymond stepped back. At least the driving horses were outside. Two of the other boys, Henry and Fred, shooed the milk cows out of the corral into the pasture and locked the gate.

The gathering crowd soon realized they couldn't save the barn. They turned their efforts toward the outbuildings. Fortunately, the night breeze pushed the flames away from the chicken house and the nearby shed. A buggy was parked in front of the chicken house. Levi grabbed the buggy shafts, hoping to pull it to safety. He quickly dropped the shafts, his hands blistered by the heat.

Levi glanced up and saw the flames licking at the east end of the chicken house. Since it was impossible to approach the building from the outside, Levi quickly decided to pour water against the wall from the inside to cool it down. Volunteers joined the family to form a line, passing buckets of water from the spring house toward the fire. Levi worked at the dangerous end of the line, pouring the water at the most vulnerable spots.

The stock tank, which was the closest source of water, was too close to the roaring fire to be of any use, so the volunteers had to settle for a bucket brigade from the two water tanks in the spring house. People dashed here and there to douse the flying embers that lighted on the vulnerable wooden shingles of the nearby outbuildings.

About the time they feared the buildings would be lost, the family heard sirens. Soon fire engines roared into the barnyard and trained hoses on the outbuildings. Neighbors stood in clusters, faces lit by the flames from the barn. There was little to do but watch as the barn collapsed on itself. No section was left standing. The town firefighters advised them to let it burn itself out. No use having to clean up charred wood.

By the time the sun rose, only a pile of smoking embers remained. The putrid odor of burned flesh filled the air. Levi examined the carcasses of the horses lying in the rubble. "I thought the horses were put outside last night."

"I thought so too," his son Fred replied. "They were supposed to be put out to pasture."

"Well, they weren't. We've lost four draft horses, the pony, a buggy and all the harnesses," Levi said quietly. "In the hay loft, we lost the first cutting of alfalfa and a little straw and hay left over from last year."

In the afternoon Emma came home from Mennys to survey the damage. Barbara accompanied her as she walked around the ruins. Emma spied the charred remains of the horses. "It's a pity that the horses were inside."

"Yes, I'll say. We thought the heavy horses were outside. Someone forgot to let them out last night."

"How did you do the milking?"

"We tied the cows to stakes and trees this morning. That's how we'll have to do it till they get the new barn built."

The afternoon and evening passed by quickly. The family huddled at the supper table, discussing the next steps for dealing with the loss.

"I'll ask Oliver Troyer to boss the work crew," Levi suggested. "He did a good job sixteen years ago when we first built the barn. We can just build on the same foundation."

"It looks like part of the foundation will need to be rebuilt," Henry offered. "It's pretty crumbly in a couple of places. I guess the heat was too much for it."

Fred agreed. "It looked like the concrete just exploded. That happens when you get heat and moisture together."

Emma pushed back her chair. "I would love to stay here and help, Mom, but Mennys are really depending on me."

Mary agreed. "Yes, you must go back there. We'll have plenty of help here."

Over the next few days, neighbors streamed to the Nisly farm, offering assistance or bringing food for the workers. In a few days, the site was cleaned up and plans were laid for rebuilding. Oliver Troyer guided the work with full-time help from John Helmuth and John B. Yoder. Tobe got a release from Will Miller, and he chipped in a couple of days as well. Two weeks after the fire, a new barn stood on the same site. All it needed was paint.

One Sunday evening after the singing, Tobe took Emma home to Mennys. As they sat together on the sofa, Tobe said, "I guess your folks have got hay back in the hay mow again. We're working on the second cutting of alfalfa over at Will Miller's."

"Yes, Dad said they put several loads in yesterday. They made sure the hay was pretty dry."

"Did they think that wet hay caused the fire the last time?"

"We don't know for sure, but that's what they're suspecting."

"I can see why they'd want to be sure they got it plenty dry. You sure wouldn't want to have combustion and start another fire."

"No." Emma wrung her hands and sighed.

There was a long silence.

Tobe continued. "Today after church we were talking about how barn fires sometimes get started by lightning.

That's why some of the English people put lightning rods on their barns."

Emma responded. "My dad always said we can just trust God. We don't need lightning rods."

"That's true," Tobe nodded. "But Willie Wagler told us about the time that lightning struck after church at John Helmuth's place."

Emma's frame straightened. "I'll never forget that day."

"So you were there?" Tobe's eyes widened.

Emma nodded. "It was June 1, just four years ago. The weather was unsettled during the whole church service. It looked like it could rain. The lightning came when the church service had just let out and the boys had gone out to the barn. We girls were standing on the porch when it hit."

"Willie said the lighting struck the windmill twice and hit the barn too. He said it struck Alma Nisly and several others. Do you remember who all got hit?" Tobe asked.

"It knocked some people to the ground—my cousins Barbara Nisly and her older sister Clara, my grandma Katie Nisly, and my aunt Anna Mast, who was expecting a baby. It hit Enos Nisly pretty hard too. He was walking to the barn with his dad and a couple of others, John C. and Abe Yoder."

"Was anybody hurt bad?"

"Clara and Barbara were hurt the worst. We were afraid Barbara was dead. The lightning tore her underclothing to shreds. It tore the sleeves on her dress, too. She was unconscious. They laid her on a bed and called the doctor. It took the doctor a long time to come. By the time he got there, she had come to."

"Did it do any damage to the house?"

"Yes, the lightning ruined the cooling tank in the wash house. We had some food in the tank to keep it cool. The lightning went through the reinforcing rods into the tank. Pieces of concrete ended up in the food."

"Willie said Ed Nisly saw the lightning coming from the north. When it hit, it went like a ball of fire after the dog."

"Yes, he went yipping toward the barn. About that time, the lightning knocked the window out of the top of the barn onto the floor."

"Where were you when the lightning hit?"

"I was standing right there with Barbara and Clara. In fact, I was closer to the windmill than Barbara. She was barefoot that day. I had shoes on. Some people thought that maybe the people with bare feet were more likely to get hit."

Tobe put his arm around her shoulder. "I'm glad you didn't get hit."

Emma sighed. "Me, too. It was such an awful day. Like Orpha Wagler said, 'It felt like God's judgment.'"

Tobe nodded. "God's ways are higher than our ways."

Emma added, "It was so hard on Barbara and Clara's parents. You know lightning earlier killed their son Roman?"

"No, I didn't know they had a boy named Roman."

"He was my first cousin. When he was six years old, he was in the wash house one Saturday night about five o'clock. Lightning struck the windmill and followed the control wire into the wash house. He was killed instantly."

For the next several weeks, Tobe's mind kept returning to the incidents of lightning in the neighborhood. Was it wrong to have lightning rods? He knew the church's answer, but he wasn't sure he agreed.

The summer of 1939 passed by quickly at the Will Miller farm. One day at the church dinner, Tobe watched the older men's heads shake in amazement as Will rehearsed their accomplishments for the week.

By fall Tobe and Emma were seeing each other nearly every week. Tobe was quite sure he would not return to live in Oklahoma. At least not to Nowata. The news that his mother shared in her regular letters was rarely inspiring.

During the first week in November, Tobe's dad was taken to the Nowata hospital for an emergency operation. Tobe's grandmother, Lizzie Stutzman, spent a week in Nowata, helping Anna. When Lizzie returned to Kansas, Tobe stopped by her home to hear how his family was coping with the illness.

An early December letter from his mother brought mixed news. "Dad is doing as well as expected. He sat up in his chair for the first time on November 30. We are grateful to the Lord for his mercy."

In this letter, Anna shared another bit of news that distressed her. "Andy Mast went to Mayes and signed up for the Navy for six years. His grandpa Eli Nislys are very sad to see him go. It's not the way of our people."

Tobe couldn't imagine himself going off to war. It just wasn't right.

The pace on the Miller farm slowed during the winter months. Tobe devoted his extra time to his woodworking projects. One day Emma came by to see her cousins and visit Tobe. She told of butchering four hogs up at the home farm. "We canned sixty-eight quarts of meat. That should be enough pork to last us most of the winter."

"Would you like to see what I'm making in the shop?" Tobe asked Emma and Will's daughter, Mary, hoping to impress the young women.

"Sure," they both echoed.

The threesome trudged through the snow. With a hint of pride in his voice, Tobe showed Emma and Mary a bureau he was making.

"Who's it for?" Mary inquired.

"Whoever decides to buy it. I usually make one or two ahead." Tobe didn't say it, but he was thinking about making one for Emma.

February 1940 brought blizzards, foggy weather, and a leap year. Lying on the sofa with Tobe after the singing one night, Emma reflected on the recent weather. "That was a real blizzard we had last Sunday. It was hard to get to church."

Tobe laughed. "Yeah, Wills didn't have far to go, but they decided to stay home. The snow was really blowing."

"Yes, the drifts got pretty high. The buggy was scraping bottom and the horse could hardly pull through."

Tobe shifted the conversation to his new hobby. "Since I've had more time this winter, I've done more woodworking. Maybe some day I'll start my own woodworking business. I can do woodworking in the winter and farm the rest of the year."

In the spring Tobe and Emma both attended the Kuepfer farm and household sale. Since the Kuepfers were moving to Canada, the family put most of its belongings up for sale. At the last minute, Tobe bid on one of the horses. It was a fast horse but reputed to be somewhat balky. Tobe was confident he could train it.

The auctioneer glanced back and forth between bidders. Tobe couldn't see who else was bidding. He just kept nodding his head when the auctioneer looked his way.

Sold! The auctioneer pointed to Tobe.

Tobe strode forward to claim his horse, the first one he could call his own.

• • • •

By the summer of 1940, Tobe and Emma were seriously dating. He joined Emma at her home one Sunday when her grandparents were there. Sitting with the men as they conversed in the living room after dinner, Tobe posed a question: "Where did the Nisly clan come from?"

The Nisly men enjoyed talking about genealogy, so Levi started the story. "Christian Nisly was the first of our ancestors to come across from the Old Country. When he was seventeen years old, he came from Germany to this new land.

He landed in Philadelphia on October 12, 1804. Since he didn't have enough money to pay his fare, he worked for Christel Zug, who agreed to pay his debt in return for his help on the farm.

Grandpa Dan stepped into the conversation. "At first, Mrs. Zug was disgusted that her husband had brought home *ein deutscher Lump* (a n'er-do-well) to be a farmhand. But after Christian lived there four days, he churned such perfect butter that she changed her attitude toward him." The group laughed.

Levi continued, "After working off his debt for the ship passage, he moved to Somerset County, Pennsylvania. He got married and was ordained to the ministry in the Amish church in Holmes County. He had fourteen children."

Grandpa broke in, "Christian's son Abraham was my father. He was one of the first Amish settler here in Hutchinson. My mother was his second wife. We moved to Shelbyville, Illinois, from Indiana when I was only two years old. You know my oldest brother Eli. He's the bishop in Nowata."

Tobe nodded. "Oh yes. I forgot that he was your brother."

Dan continued. "Our ancestors used to spell their last name, 'Nisley,' with an 'e.' But my father said it was prideful to have more letters than were needed, so he started spelling it the way we do now.

"Dad had intended to move his family from Illinois to Grand Island, Nebraska. They came west on the train looking for land. But when they got to Kansas City, they changed their plans. There was flooding in the city, so they couldn't cross the river.

"While they were waiting for the water to drop, a land agent heard about their interest in good affordable land. He offered to sell them inexpensive land in Hutchinson, and they decided to investigate. They ended up buying farm land for five dollars an acre. My father was the first Amish settler in this area. They came to Hutchinson in July 1883, when the town was only twelve years old. They had five railroad cars full of belongings."

Dan interrupted, "That was for *two* families. The Christel Borntrager family came with them."

Levi stroked his long untrimmed beard, "That's right. They traveled together. When they got to Hutchinson, they spent two nights at a hotel, getting ready for the trip across the prairie to their new home. First, they put the wheels on the wagons. Then they had to transfer all their belongings from the freight cars onto the wagons. The railroad didn't go to Partridge at the time. It went up to Nickerson then to Great Bend. The Atchison, Topeka, and Santa Fe railroad wasn't built until the next year.

"They took the Sun City Trail, about where Route 61 is now, toward Partridge, which was then called Reno Center. They settled on the farm where Dan Millers live now, just west of Henry Miller's place. There was native bluestem grass growing six feet tall on the prairie in those days."

Levi looked at Dan. "It's right, isn't it, Dad, that the Borntragers lived with your family in a two-room shack until the Borntragers could move into their own house?"

"Yes, some of us children used to sleep under the table. There just wasn't enough room for everyone to sleep otherwise. One of the children was Barbara. We call her Bevly. She's married to Noah Yoder."

Tobe grinned. He liked Noah. Although the older man used coarse language, the two of them got along well. Noah always spoke his mind. Tobe flinched as he remembered one of the stories he'd heard about Noah. Once Noah nearly cut off his finger. He took a quick look at it then took out his pocket knife and severed it for good. Tobe figured Noah dealt with the pain by taking a swig of whiskey. His son John B. told him that the family kept plenty on hand. As a young boy,

John had accompanied his father on occasional trips to Kansas City to buy it by the barrel.

Tobe's mind was jerked back to reality as Levi went on with his story. "Christel Bontrager was a bishop. He's the one who donated the acre of land for the West Center Cemetery."

Dan broke in again, "In the early days, they had church services back and forth between Yoder and Partridge. They met every other week the way we do now, only they didn't have Sunday school in between. They had to drive all the way to Yoder for church once a month or every other time they met. It was fifteen or twenty miles, depending who had services that day. It was very cold in the winter time. They had to use twisted grass or cow chips to heat the houses during that first winter because there were no trees. The second winter, they burned corn cobs. They raised corn like they were used to doing in Illinois, but there was no market for it here. So they burned it for fuel."

Dan lowered his voice, "My father-in-law, Dawdy Mast, used to say that Bishop Borntrager wanted the church to be 'extreme Amish.' He overemphasized rules and traditions. But Dawdy Mast had four reasons why he moved here." He counted them off. "To avoid smoking, drinking, *unehelich Beischlof* (bed courtship), and to establish Sunday schools. He was glad that Kansas was a dry state, because he didn't think the Amish should be drinking."

Levi stepped in. "As time went on, the younger people wanted Sunday schools. Some of the early advocates were ministers, Jake Miller, Eli Nisly, and Dawdy Mast for instance. Since the older bishop and others were opposed, they had to go slowly."

Tobe cocked his head. "But we have Sunday school now."

Dan nodded. "Yes, the first Sunday school was held at our place in a building just north of our house. Bishop Eli supported the Sunday school effort, but he didn't attend. He knew that as bishop he needed to be more neutral. But he sometimes gave his counsel about the way the meetings should be conducted. After a few more funerals, he felt free to join."

"When were you ordained as ministers?" Tobe asked the two men.

Dan spoke up first. "I was ordained in October 1907. We had communion at church that morning, but I stayed home because my wife was expecting a baby. When they took nominations at church, I was named for the lot. Someone came for me in a buggy. I was chosen that day and they ordained me. Then I walked home. I was in the lot for bishop the next year, but the lot fell on my brother Eli instead."

Levi leaned forward. "And I should say that Bishop Borntrager wasn't very happy about the way it turned out. From then on until he died he didn't often come to church. It was about five years. He thought the church was going in the wrong direction. But things got better when some of his children moved away."

"And when were you ordained?" Tobe asked Levi.

"I was ordained for the west district in 1932."

As the conversation turned to other topics, Tobe sat back in reflection. He couldn't imagine his father being a preacher. The Nisly family was very different from the Stutzmans.

That evening Tobe dropped Emma off at the Harry Yoder home where she was working. "I guess you learned my family history today," Emma laughed. "They seemed eager to tell you all about it."

"Yes, I enjoyed it. I was glad to hear how this area first got settled."

The sand plums were in season when Emma left the Yoders to work at the Billy Williams home. It was some distance from hers, so it took much longer for Tobe to drive her there. As they headed out in the buggy one Sunday evening, Tobe asked, "How does it feel to work in an English home?"

Emma shrugged. "Oh, it's not that much different than working for Harrys. Of course, they have electricity and an inside toilet. That's nice. But I have many of the same things to do, like washing, patching, ironing, cleaning, and working in the garden. Last week, I butchered a few chickens."

"I thought you were going to stay at Harrys for another month or two."

"I was planning to, but Mrs. Williams is not feeling well. She just got home from the hospital not long ago. They needed somebody right away, and they wanted an Amish girl. I'll still help Harrys sometimes."

Tobe switched the conversation. "That was quite a car that John Overholt had at the singing tonight." The young visitor had served as the driver for another group of young people who had taken a western trip.

Emma grinned. "Yeah, it sounds like the bunch really enjoyed their trip out west."

"I heard about his car when he went through here in June. It's a 40-model Ford with a V-8 engine. I wouldn't mind having a car like that."

"It probably takes a lot of gas," Emma suggested. "I wonder what he charged his passengers for the trip."

"I heard him tell Mahlon Wagler he charged each person a penny per mile."

"That's more than we paid on our trip," Emma noted.

"If I ever get a car," Tobe laughed, "I'll take you along for free. For now you can have free buggy rides whenever you like."

They laughed as Tobe draped his arm around Emma's shoulder. They lapsed into silence as the moonlight peeked through the open window.

Much later that night, Tobe began the long trek back to Will Millers. He fell asleep only to awaken with a start as his buggy pulled into Will Miller's driveway. Grateful for a well trained and careful horse, Tobe fed him some oats before walking wearily toward the house. These late Sunday nights were wearing him out. It was time to settle down and get married. Surely Emma would say "yes" if he asked her.

Upstairs in his bedroom, he tossed his clothes onto a nearby chair and slipped between the sheets. When should he ask her? Perhaps next Sunday. As he started to frame the words for a proposal, he fell asleep.

8

Making Covenant

Tobe was thrilled when Emma said "Yes." And he was pleased to learn that her parents approved of their plans. They set the date for that fall, October 10, 1940, and Tobe planned a trip to Oklahoma to tell his parents.

Together, Tobe and Emma began to dream about where they'd live. "There's an old place near Partridge where nobody lives now," Tobe said. "I think Dr. Brownlee owns it. Maybe we could fix it up and live there cheap."

Emma went shopping for fabric to make a wedding dress. She brought it home and laid the royal blue fabric on the dining room table. With only about a month till the wedding, she was eager to get started. She called her sister, "Lizzie, come here for a minute."

Lizzie stepped in from the kitchen, a paring knife in her hand. "Yes."

"Are you watching to see if anyone is coming?"

"Yes and so is Barbara. We'll warn you in plenty of time if someone drives in."

In keeping with Amish custom, Emma was determined that her engagement would be secret until the public announcement two weeks before the wedding. Neighbors could be very nosy.

She carefully arranged the dress pattern, cut from discarded newspaper, on top of the cloth. After rearranging the pieces a couple of times, she was satisfied that she wasn't wasting any material. She pinned the pattern pieces to the fabric and began cutting.

"How's it coming?" Barbara asked, stepping up to the table after Emma had worked for a while.

"Real well. I just have the cape to do yet. I'll be able to start sewing this afternoon."

"As soon as you're done, we'll want to set the table for dinner."

"Okay." After Emma finished cutting out the last piece, she gathered up her fabric and took it to the sewing room.

The next morning the Singer sewing machine hummed as Emma guided the fabric underneath the bobbing needle.

"Mom," Emma called, "can you help me for a minute? I can't seem to get the pleats right."

"I can help for a few minutes," Mary replied, "but I'm expecting Dawdys to come help with the butchering."

The two of them soon had the pleats pinned neatly in place. Emma gathered up the material and moved to the machine. Mary watched as Emma flipped down the presser foot, spun the wheel, and slowly pumped the treadle.

"This wool is heavy," Emma commented, "the needle doesn't go through very easily."

"Yes, you have to be careful."

By the end of the day, both Emma's wedding dress and the butchering were finished. Then they heard the sound of buggy wheels in the yard. Barbara went to the window. "It's Menny Yoder."

Menny climbed out of the buggy and came to the front door. "I'm wondering if Emma can help us. We had a new baby girl this morning."

"Oh," the girls crowded around. "Now Mary Ellen will have a sister again. What's her name?"

"Clara Mae."

"Oh, that's nice. I guess she's named after Aunt Clara."

"Yes."

"I'll get my things together," Emma volunteered. "It will only take a minute." Soon Emma had her things together and climbed into the buggy with Menny. Barbara and Lizzie waved good-bye as Menny clucked to the horse.

The next Sunday church was held at the home of Menny's father, Menno Yoder Sr. Following the service and the noon meal, the young people gathered outside in small groups to chat. Emma chatted with Amanda Beachy, a friend from another state. Everyone looked up with interest as a young man walked up with a camera.

"*Ich will en Gleichnis nemme.* I'm going to take a picture," he announced. "Who would like to be in it?" Group members eyed each other nervously. Cameras and photographs were forbidden by the church. The leaders sometimes warned that pictures nurtured a spirit of vanity, admonishing people to heed the words in one of the Ten Commandments, "Thou shalt not make onto thee any graven images."

Nevertheless, some nonmembers owned cameras, knowing they would need to put them away once they joined the church. Tobe stepped forward. "I'll be in the picture. Come on, Emma and Amanda. You can be in it too." Tobe beckoned the reluctant young women with his hand. Emma giggled nervously and looked at her friend. They stepped forward, followed by several young men.

Tobe wished that Emma could stand next to him, but he didn't say anything. It would only invite suspicion that they were engaged.

The breeze pushed one ribbon of Emma's covering forward as she edged toward Tobe, her hands clasped behind her back. Willis Miller stepped back a bit to keep from being wedged between them. They all grinned widely as they waited for the click of the box camera. Didn't the book of Proverbs say that forbidden fruit tasted sweet?

As the day of their wedding drew closer, Tobe and Emma worked feverishly to prepare everything, especially since Emma's brother Henry was getting married a week before she was.

"It sure is a lot of work to get ready for a wedding," Barbara observed as she scrubbed the floor in the girls' room.

"Yes, it's always a lot of work for the women. The men-folk get by pretty easy," Lizzie said.

Emma agreed. "Henry does have it pretty easy compared to me."

Emma's younger brother, Rufus, objected from the next room. "But you women forget that the men have all the out-side work. Henry's busy fixing up their new place so they can move in."

"And Tobe is going to have a lot of work to get the Brownlee place ready for us to live," Emma commented.

"When is he coming back from his parents?" Barbara asked, dusting the bureau with a few quick swipes. She knew that Tobe had gone home to Nowata to be with his family and pick up some things.

"This evening. I'm going to the train station to pick him up."

The Nowata train arrived on schedule at the Hutchinson terminal. Emma stepped forward as Tobe got off the train, holding his suitcase with one hand and balancing some boxes with the other. Tobe watched with envy as a couple in front of him kissed each other. Then again, he thought to himself, English people showed too much affection in public.

He shook Emma's hand and put on his jacket as they walked toward the hitching post. "It was hot on the train," he said. He paused to toss his suitcase and the boxes into the buggy. Emma climbed in as Tobe untied the horse. She held the reins until Tobe settled in beside her. Tobe steered the horse sharply to the left, and they were off.

"What did your folks say when you told them we're getting married?" Emma asked.

"They were expecting it," Tobe grinned. He clucked to the horse. *"Die Memme gleicht dich. Se sagt du machst an gute Frah.* Mom likes you. She says you'll make a good wife."

Emma responded, "My mom wants you to come over to our house for dinner after church tomorrow. As soon as we're published, we can go straight to our house."

"Good," Tobe said. He shivered with anticipation.

The next morning overcast skies hid the sun from view during the worship service at the Dan Miller residence. After the benediction, the deacon announced: *"Was Brieder and Schweshdre sin, solle wennich schtill sitze bleiwe.* Those who are brothers and sisters shall remain seated for a time." At these words, the children and others who were not church members filed out. Only full members could participate in council meeting, held in preparation for the fall communion service scheduled for two weeks later.

As was the custom, the ministers took the counsel of each church member. The ministers made their way through the congregations, receiving each member's answer to the "counsel questions." All were given opportunity to give testimony that they had peace with God and their fellow believers. In addition each was to give individual consent to the *Ordnung.*

Tobe overheard the man behind him give the standard response, *"Ich binn ainich mit dem Foreschtellah und die Apschtella. Ich hab Frieda mit. . . .* I'm in agreement with that which is required and that which is forbidden. I have peace with. . . ." Tobe wished he could turn the hands forward on the mantel clock. It would soon be time for the deacon to announce the wedding date.

When all had given their counsel, Bishop Jake Miller stood and cleared his throat. "Two weeks from today, we will be meeting at Levi Nislys for our communion service. On the

Thursday before the communion service, Tobe Stutzman will be married to Emma Nisly. The wedding will take place here at the Dan Miller place."

Tobe felt every eye on him as he stood and made his way outside. Emma stood waiting at the door as Tobe hurriedly hitched his horse. He was glad to be able to leave the service a few minutes early. Otherwise, the guys would tease him. As it was, the young people were filing out of the house by the time Tobe pulled up to the front door.

Emma eagerly stepped into the buggy and settled into the seat. Tobe clucked to the horse and slapped the reins. The horse balked. Irritated, Tobe slapped the reins again, harder this time. Nothing. The bemused crowd grew in size, watching as Tobe tried in vain to get his horse to move. Noah Nisly stepped forward to help but to no avail. Tobe cracked his whip, with no better result.

Finally he got out and gripped the horse's bridle. He stepped forward, tugging gently on the bridle. Suddenly the horse leapt forward. Tobe vaulted over the back of the buggy seat as the buggy flew by. He heard laughter as they sped out the lane, the horse's tail streaming over the dashboard of the open buggy.

Tobe laughed. "Now that's more like it. This horse was made for racing, not standing around." A few drops of rain settled the dust on the road as the rig sped along. A jackrabbit zigzagged in front of the buggy then darted into the ditch. In a matter of minutes, Tobe guided the horse into the Nisly farm yard. "Well, we have eleven more days till the wedding."

"Yes. I can hardly wait."

The rest of the Nisly family drifted in over the next hour.

"I heard the horse balked," Emma's father joked as they sat in the living room.

"Yes, he does that sometimes. But this wasn't a very good time to do it."

Emma's brother John laughed, "That's the way it goes sometimes."

The afternoon passed by quickly. Henry and Elizabeth joined Tobe and Emma at the supper table along with the rest of the Nisly family. Anticipation filled the air as the two couples talked about their upcoming weddings.

They discussed their plans for the coming week. "Tobe and I are planning to make a trip to town tomorrow to buy some supplies for our wedding," Emma ventured.

"We'll need to help over at Perry Yoder's house on Wednesday," Barbara reminded them. "We promised to help Elizabeth's family get the house ready."

Emma's brother Fred spoke up, "They have meetings on nonresistance at the Yoder Mennonite Church on Tuesday night. I heard that Mahlon Wagler and some others are going down there. All the boys have to register for the draft by the sixteenth, so the ministers want to help the COs. The government is going to draw draft numbers on the 29th."

"I don't think I'll have time to go to the meeting," Tobe declared. He hoped against hope that he wouldn't be drafted. But the new war in Europe threatened to draw the United States into the conflict just as the Great War had around the time his parents were married. During that war, life had been hard for conscientious objectors. Tobe hoped they would have an easier time getting exemptions from the military.

The next two weeks were jammed with activity: laundry, cleaning, butchering, and baking. On Tuesday and Wednesday before the wedding, many neighbors came by to help because Emma's mother lay in bed with a bad toothache. When they finished, they had butchered twenty-five chickens, baked twenty-six apple pies, twenty butterscotch pies, and a dozen cakes. They had made applesauce, carrot salad, and tapioca.

By Wednesday evening when Tobe's family arrived, the Nisly farm and house stood ready for the wedding reception.

Henry Kroeker brought Tobe's family in his car. They pulled into the Nisly drive, a livestock trailer in tow. Tobe walked out to meet them with enthusiasm, since it was his cow in the trailer. He directed the driver toward the corral where they unloaded the young cow named Rose. It was the wedding gift he had been promised by his father. Tobe looked with some concern at her hips, rubbed raw by the tail gate. "Looks like the trailer's not quite long enough," he commented.

"Yeah," Tobe's brother Clarence agreed, "it's too tight for comfort. But I think that will heal up with no problem."

Tobe turned to his mother, who was watching the proceedings. "Dad didn't come along?"

Anna cleared her throat. "No." She looked away.

Tobe swallowed hard. What was wrong with Dad? Was he so embarrassed about his own marriage that he wouldn't come to his son's wedding? Was he upset at Mother? Whatever the reason, there was no use discussing it.

The next morning Tobe and Emma rode to their wedding service together. They laughed as they remembered the difficulty they'd had with the horse the last time they'd been at the Miller place. Today, they'd be escorted by the hostlers back to Emma's home for the reception.

The service began at 9:30 a.m. The congregation sang while Tobe and Emma met the ministers in an upstairs bedroom. Bishop Jacob Miller instructed them regarding marriage. The other ministers chimed in from time to time, sharing insights regarding the proper relationship between husband and wife. They also reviewed the obligations of church membership.

Marriage in the church strengthened the covenant bond that began with baptism. Married folks were to serve as an example to others, particularly their children. Before heading down the stairs to the waiting congregation, the ministers gave final instructions regarding the plans for the ceremony.

Because the church rarely deviated from the pattern of the forebears, Emma and Tobe knew the order of service well.

They came down the stairs first and sat in the main room. There they were joined by the two couples designated as witnesses. The bridal party of six sat on chairs. The three men sat together with Tobe in the middle. Emma sat opposite Tobe with one woman on each side. Only the couples in the wedding party could sit together as men and women in a worship service. The rest of the attenders sat on benches. All ages were present, from young babies to elderly grandparents.

The church service proceeded in the manner of Sunday worship except that the sermon focused on marriage. The preacher drew illustrations on marriage from the Bible, mostly from the Old Testament. He also made favorable reference to a man named Tobias in the Apocrypha, noting that he was blessed because he married one of his own tribe. Similarly, it was good for young Amish men to marry one of the members of the Amish church.

The minister also emphasized the doctrine of the apostle Paul regarding the submission of women to their husbands. He stressed that a man should leave his father and mother and be joined to his wife. The two should become one flesh—the very essence of marriage. Marriage was a union that could be broken only by death. Separation or divorce were cause for excommunication from the church.

The preacher ended his sermon just as the mantel clock struck half past eleven. At that moment, the "extras" arrived. They quietly made their way to the row of seats reserved for them. As table waiters, they had helped with food preparation at the Nisly house all forenoon. Along with the mother of the bride, they couldn't afford the luxury of two hours in the worship service while the task of feeding two hundred people stared them in the face. If they came at half past eleven, they would be just in time to witness the vows.

Bishop Jacob Miller stepped forward and asked the bridal couple to rise and come forward for the exchange of vows. In keeping with custom, Tobe rose and walked forward with Emma following. They stood side by side before the bishop. Their witnesses remained seated.

With a sober expression the bishop intoned, "You have now heard the ordinance of Christian wedlock presented. Are you now willing to enter wedlock together as God in the beginning ordained and commanded?"

"Yes." Both assented. Tobe nodded slightly for emphasis.

Looking at Tobe, the bishop asked, "Are you confident that this, our sister, is ordained of God to be your wedded wife?"

"Yes."

Fixing his gaze on Emma, he asked, "Are you confident that this, our brother, is ordained of God to be your wedded husband?"

"Yes."

The bishop's eyes went back to Tobe: "Do you promise your wedded wife, before the Lord and his church, that you will nevermore depart from her, but will care for her and cherish her, if bodily illness comes to her, or in any circumstance which a Christian husband is responsible to care for, until God will again separate you from each other?"

"Yes," Tobe nodded.

The bishop faced Emma. "Do you also promise your wedded husband, before the Lord and his church, that you will nevermore depart from him, but will care for him and cherish him, if bodily illness comes to him, or in any circumstance which a Christian wife is responsible to care for, until God will again separate you from each other?"

"Yes." Emma was sober.

"Clasp the right hands." Tobe reached for Emma's hand. The bishop continued with a reference to the apocryphal book of Tobit, "So then I may say with Raguel, the God of Abraham, the God of Isaac, and the God of Jacob be with you and help you together and fulfill his blessing abundantly upon you, through Jesus Christ. Amen. I now pronounce you husband and wife."

At this pronouncement the table waiters silently filed out and got into their waiting buggies. Riding two per buggy, they drove to the Nisly farm to serve at the reception. Although any members of the church could attend the wedding, only those "called" would come to the reception that followed.

The stretch of road to the Nisly farm had been graded just a few days earlier. With recent rains wetting the new dirt and gravel mixture, the road was a sea of mud. Only with difficulty were the couples able to negotiate their way.

After dropping off their partners, the hostlers returned with a buggy each to take the bridal party to the reception. Each hostler rode on the lap of one couple of the bridal party with reins in hand. Driving the first buggy in the procession, Emma's brother Henry escorted Tobe's friend John Yoder and Emma's aunt Katie Bontrager. Emma's brother John followed with the bridal couple, who always rode in the middle buggy. Trailing them came Tobe's cousin Edwin Schrock with Ervin Stutzman and Barbara Nisly. They laughed and talked over the sound of hoof beats as they headed for the wedding feast. Soon a stream of buggies made their way through the thick mud to the Nisly home.

At the appointed time, the bridal couple and their attendants took their places at the *Eck*, the corner table reserved for them at the reception. Tobe and Emma sat in the center with a pair of witnesses on each side. A decorated cake and two large glass bowls of fresh fruit pointed to the special nature of the event. A stem glass stood in front of each of the witnesses. Inside each glass was a folded handkerchief, a candy bar and other sweets, along with an artificial flower.

No one wore special garb. Aside from the wrapping on the wedding gifts that were piled on a nearby table, the decorations at the *Eck* were the only unusual adornment in the house.

The farmhouse and yard bulged with its 175 guests. Many stood outside or scattered to various rooms. When all were seated at tables for the first shift, the bishop called out: *"Wann der Disch voll iss, welle mir bede.* If the table is full, let us pray." It was the signal for silent prayer.

As the prayer ended, three couples assigned to wait on the bridal party moved quickly into action. They carried serving dishes to each table piled high with hot steaming food—baked chicken, mashed potatoes with gravy and dressing, and peas. Then came cole slaw, bread served with butter and jelly, followed later with fruit, cake, and pie. In addition to the main menu, the bridal party had peanuts, candies, and other snacks on their table.

When the first shift finished, the helpers cleared the tables and a second group of guests was seated. Some helpers served while others washed dishes. According to custom, the boys from the youth group ate in the last shift. As people finished eating, the wedding couple passed out candy bars. The wedding cake would be eaten at a later date.

As the afternoon wore on, some of the adults went home to do farm chores or tend to other duties. The young folks remained for the evening service.

When everyone had eaten, Emma went upstairs to her room. The unmarried women followed. They crowded around her as she took off her black covering and put on a white one. Only married women wore white coverings.

The young men scattered to the barn and other outbuildings to explore the Nisly farm. The young men razzed Tobe about his new state of matrimony. Some threatened to shivaree after the evening meal. Tobe took it in stride. Weddings were often a time for mischief, but Tobe wasn't worried. They only wanted to have fun.

As evening approached, the Nisly boys went about their chores. The other young men watched as they milked the cows and fed the horses.

The sun was touching the horizon when Tobe heard Barbara call from the house. "Supper is ready. Call everybody in."

The young men made their way back to the house. Each climbed the stairs to pick a partner for the evening meal. The bridal party again took their places at the *Eck* for the evening meal. After supper they handed out more candy bars to the guests.

After the supper table was cleared, the group sang together in English as well as German. By 9:00 buggies began to leave, lamps glowing through the darkness.

The mantel clock struck ten as Tobe and Emma made their way up the stairs to their room for the night. Tobe sat down on the edge of the bed and took off his shoes. Emma sat down beside him. The flickering kerosene lamp cast shadows on the bed behind them as he they talked softly about the day. Then Tobe got up and blew out the lantern. A sliver of moonlight slipped between the window shade and sill onto the wooden floor as the pair undressed in silence.

Tobe hopped into bed, the cold sheets chilling his bare skin. He heard Emma click the latch on the door before she joined him in bed. He pulled her close with his strong arms. They lay quietly in each other's arms, their combined warmth staving off the autumn chill. They could hear the rattle of dishes and the banter of conversation in the kitchen.

Tobe wondered what Emma's parents were thinking in the bedroom right below them. Before meeting Tobe, Emma sometimes ran around with a rowdy group of young people. Her parents didn't say much, but they couldn't have been too happy to know that Emma and her date were often alone in the dark living room until the wee hours of the morning. Emma's younger sisters, Barbara and Lizzie, were far more careful. Ever since they'd read an article on courtship in the *Herold der Wahrheit*, they'd been very conscientious. Some of the other young people in the youth group refused to date in the dark. It seemed to Tobe like they were going a bit overboard.

Tobe liked Emma's mother. She couldn't have approved of everything her children were doing, but she didn't complain about it or scold them like his mother. She tried to look on the positive side of things. It would be good to be part of the Nisly family.

9

Partners

Streaks of sunlight tinged the eastern sky as Tobe awoke the next morning. Emma stirred as he swung his legs out of bed and pulled on his trousers. He fastened them up with "police suspenders," wide green elastic straps with yellow stripes. He ran a comb through his hair and went downstairs. Emma followed soon after. There was much work to be done. Cleanup from the wedding and preparation for the upcoming communion service would consume the next two days.

Tobe walked quickly to the barn to milk his new cow. Emma went to the kitchen to help her mother with breakfast preparation. As the family finished an early breakfast, they heard the sound of a buggy coming in the lane.

Rufus ran to the window. "*Die Hilfer sin do.* The helpers are here." Yesterday's table waiters were coming back to help with the cleanup.

Mary was on her feet in an instant. "We better carry in some water and get it heated up. We'll need a lot of hot water for all the dishes. Raymond and Rufus, you can do that."

Mary appointed each to their tasks—washing mounds of dishes, stacking benches, churning butter, and mopping floors. By late afternoon, the follow-up work from the wedding was nearly done. As the last of the helpers drove out the lane, Emma turned to her mother.

"Tobe and I are leaving to go with his mom to see our new place. Then we're going to Dawdy Stutzmans for supper.

We'll probably stay there overnight since it's so far to go." Tobe's grandparents lived near the town of Yoder, about thirteen miles away.

"That's fine. We'll see you sometime tomorrow then."

Now that the events of the wedding were behind them, Tobe was ready to work on their new place in earnest. Together with his mother and brothers, Tobe and Emma crowded into Henry Kroeker's car and headed south on the rutted road. As they approached the shelterbelt bordering the south end of the Nisly farm, the driver spoke up. "Those trees look like they were planted recently."

"Just last year," Emma replied. "The WPA planted them."

"What kind are they?"

Emma pointed to each row as they passed by. "Osage orange or hedge apple, cottonwood, American elm, black locust, hackberry, mulberry, pine, cedar, and Russian olive. There are some fruit trees too, planted in a couple of different places in the rows."

Anna was fascinated, "I heard that the government was trying to get people to plant trees. What good are they supposed to do?"

Emma turned toward the back seat. "Dad says they're hoping that shelterbelts will help stop some of the dust storms so they're giving away free trees. All we have to do is weed them. It also gives jobs to people who lost their work during the Depression. Eleanor Roosevelt was the one who helped this to happen."

As they came toward the first intersection, Emma pointed ahead to another shelterbelt. "Harry Yoders own those trees. I helped with the hoeing when I worked for them earlier this year. It's a lot of work." She motioned with her hand. "We'll turn right here."

Henry steered the car toward the west. Tobe turned to his mother as he pointed to his right. "They say the first Amish settlers came to that place over there where Dan Millers live now."

"We go left here at the corner." Tobe motioned with his hand.

Henry made the turn, heading south. As they came to the next intersection, Tobe said to the driver, "That's Will Miller's farm, where I used to work."

Less than a mile further on, Emma said, "My dad owns this place. My brother Henry lives here now. He got married just last week."

"Our place is just ahead to the right after you pass this next intersection," Tobe directed. As the driver slowed down and turned into the yard, Anna asked, "*Wer eegnet daer Blatz? Who owns this place?*"

"Dr. Brownlee. He lives in Hutch."

"How much is he charging you for rent?"

"Nothing for now. He's just glad if someone can fix up and use these buildings. No one has lived here for years. He said he'd pay for the materials if we do the work."

"That sounds like a good deal."

"Hensley Hill rents the ground. He'd like to tear down the buildings, but Dr. Brownlee would rather have someone get some good out of them."

Anna agreed. "It would be a shame to tear them down."

The driver pulled up to the house and shut off the engine. Everyone got out, and Tobe pointed out the various buildings. The two-story frame house with a small porch stood to the right of the driveway. Beyond the house was the wash house and windmill. An outdoor toilet stood nearby, easily accessible from the house. Opposite the wash house stood a long, low chicken house. Straight ahead, the drive ended between a small barn and a shed. Several elm trees shaded the house and yard. A wide row of elm and locust trees grew along the fence row bordering the property on the north and east.

Together the group walked toward the house, flattening the tall weeds in the front yard as they went. The front door scraped against the wooden floor as Tobe opened it. The rooms echoed as they walked through the dilapidated structure. The window sashes and sills begged for repair and paint. The wallpaper was torn and stained. In one room, large pieces sagged from the ceiling. The wooden floor was mostly bare, with paint remaining only in the grooves.

They moved into the bare kitchen. Tobe motioned with his hands, "Along this wall, I'm going to build cabinets."

Emma's eyes brightened. She had never worked in a kitchen with cabinets. After they had walked through both floors of the house, Tobe led the group outside. They looked into all the outbuildings, chatting about the best place to locate the animals, tools, and equipment. As Emma talked with her mother-in-law about the best place for a garden, Tobe was visualizing a new shop where he could launch a woodworking business. The best location seemed to be across the driveway from the house. He stepped off an imaginary foundation, checking to see how it would fit in the available space.

Tobe glanced at the setting sun. If they were to get to their supper appointment in good time, it was nearly time to leave. They all got into the car for the trip to Yoder. As his mother shut the door, Tobe felt a knot welling up in his throat. It would have been great for Dad to see their new place. He pushed those thoughts aside and turned to his mother. "*Well, Memm, was denkscht?* Well, Mom, what do you think?" So far, she hadn't said much.

Anna nodded her head as she spoke. "Oh, I think with some hard work it will make a nice place for you. I'm glad that you can get it rent free."

"Yes, we're glad, too," Tobe replied. "Emma's family will help us fix it up. We hope to move in about three weeks from now. Until then, we'll live with Emma's folks."

The next day the group was back at the Nislys to help the family prepare to host the bi-annual communion service. They called it *gross Gmee*, the big church. It was the most solemn event of the church year.

All went as planned and the family farm was ready for the 9:30 service on Sunday morning. Deacon Peter Wagler stood at the door with a stack of *Ausbund* hymnals on his left arm. As worshipers entered the room, he handed them a hymnal from the top of the stack with his right hand. From time to time, he replenished his stack from a box behind him.

The ministers made their way up the stairs as a song leader started the first song. Then they sang the Lob Lied. When the ministers returned, they sang a song of blessing and invocation reserved for the communion service. Bishop Jake Miller gave Christian greetings and an orientation to the service. "We are grateful to be gathered here on this special occasion to celebrate the suffering of our Lord. Today we will share in the bread and the cup. If there is anything that is not right among us or anything that would interfere with this fellowship, you may make it known now. If so, we will not continue until all is made right." He paused for a moment and looked around the room.

Tobe wondered if anyone would speak up. He'd never seen it happen, but Mother said she'd been present at times when someone brought up a matter that had been missed in the council meeting. There may have been unresolved conflict, bitterness, or someone who disregarded the *Ordnung*.

Hearing only silence, Bishop Miller led in prayer. Everyone bowed their heads. It was shortly after 10 o'clock when Emma's father stood to give the *Anfang*. Following long custom, he recounted the story of God's redemption, using the first few chapters of the book of Genesis. He spoke rapidly, his head bobbing with emphasis as he told about the creation of the world, the judgment of the worldwide flood, and the faithfulness of Noah in building an ark. He ended his message by rehearsing how Noah built an altar and prayed to the Lord.

Then Emma's grandfather stood to weave the next strands into the story of God's redemption. He first read a passage of Scripture from 1 Corinthians 10. Then he recounted how God had sealed his covenant with Noah by the sign of the rainbow in the sky. He spoke of Abraham and the patriarchs, calling to mind the children of Israel and their long sojourn in Egypt. He recalled their great deliverance by the hand of Moses and described the forty years when they wandered in the wilderness. Finally, he showed how Moses brought the children of Israel to the very edge of the Jordan, only to be denied entrance by an act of disobedience. He spoke almost as rapidly as Levi, his vigorous gestures accenting his staccato voice.

Dan was just finishing his message when Bishop Miller got up from his seat and walked out of the room at 11:30 a.m. Tobe watched him leave, knowing that the bishop would eat a bit early, then preach through the lunch hour. The rest of the people would eat in short shifts, starting at noon.

By the time the bishop returned ten minutes later, a guest preacher had begun the third sermon of the morning. He expounded on other themes from the Old Testament: the inheritance of the Promised Land, the time of the judges, the disobedience followed by exile, and the coming of the prophets. He paused as the mantel clock struck 12:00 noon, then concluded with a short exhortation to obedience.

Tobe shifted wearily in his seat. His stomach growled as Bishop Miller rose to deliver the main sermon of the day. The bishop began by quoting the prophecies in Isaiah regarding the coming Messiah. Then he told the story of Christ's birth from the Gospel of Luke before turning to make his way through an exposition of the Gospel of Matthew.

Tobe's eyes drooped as Jake recounted the story of Jesus' temptation in the wilderness. His head jerked up as the man beside him stood to leave for a short lunch break. Tobe followed him to the kitchen. With a few others, he stood at the table eating open-faced sandwiches, pickles, and red beets. Tobe didn't mind missing a piece of the sermon. He had heard the same texts expounded at communion for many years. He watched with just a bit of envy as a few young men slipped outside through the kitchen door. He wouldn't have minded having some fresh air himself.

Tobe went back to his seat. He tried to listen, but was distracted by the young men behind him. They were chewing gum. Tobe wished they'd chew more quietly. It seemed irreverent to make such noises as the bishop spoke about the passion of Jesus Christ.

Tobe was exhausted from the long week of activities. The backless bench gave little support, and he tried to ignore the growing ache in his back. The air in the crowded room was stale. He leaned forward with his head in his hands, his elbows on his knees. He heard the quiet, steady, breathing of the man beside him. It was hard to stay awake.

Tobe awoke to hear Jake tell about the time Jesus found his disciples sleeping in the Garden of Gethsemane. Jesus told them, "Could you not watch with me one hour? Watch and pray, that ye enter not into temptation: the spirit is willing but the flesh is weak."

Tobe rested his head in his hands. "The spirit is willing but the flesh is weak." He could hardly blame the disciples for falling asleep. He dozed off again. Raymond Wagler, who was sitting beside him, gently poked him in his ribs. Tobe shook himself awake. Jake was about to finish. It was almost three o'clock. Jake concluded his sermon by telling about the ascension of Jesus Christ and his promise to the disciples that they would be filled with power from on high. Finally, the bishop announced that it was time to share in the service of communion.

Deacon Wagler stepped into the kitchen and returned with the communion emblems. There were two loaves of bread, fresh-baked and sliced by the deacon. There was a glass jug filled with grape juice. The practice of using wine had been discontinued some years earlier since it tempted the young men. Beside it stood the coffee cup from Mary's kitchen that would be used to serve the juice. The deacon placed the emblems on a small table at the front of the room and covered them with a white cloth.

After reading a passage of Scripture, the bishop lifted the cloth and took a slice of bread into his hands. He invited the congregation to stand as he bowed his head for a prayer of thanks and blessing. All stood. When he had finished praying, the members remained standing while others were seated. Children and other nonmembers were free to observe, but only members would receive communion.

Bishop Miller broke off a chunk of the bread and ate it, gave a piece to Levi and the other ministers in turn, then to the deacon. He served the men in the congregation, breaking off a piece of bread for each one. He first served the elderly men in the front benches, beginning with the oldest. He went from bench to bench, handing a chunk of bread to each member. Each man sat down when he received his portion. The bishop worked his way through each row, moving toward the back where the boys were seated. Deacon Wagler stood at attention with a fresh supply of bread. Whenever a slice of bread had been served, he handed the bishop another slice.

As the bishop made his way through the narrow rows, each man scooted back in his seat to let him through. Tobe received the bread with open palm, then bowed slightly at the knee before placing it his mouth. He chewed it slowly, savoring the taste of fresh bread. Then he sat down.

After he finished serving the men's side, the bishop moved to the next room where the women were seated. He served the older women at the front of the room first. Then he moved toward the back of the room where the young girls were. When he was finished, he put the remaining bread back on the table and spread the cloth over it. Tobe anticipated that Mary would serve it to the family for the noon meal. It would not go to waste.

The bishop then turned to bless the fruit of the vine. The deacon picked up the jug and poured juice into the cup, handing it to the bishop. Bishop Miller held it up and invited the congregation to stand for the prayer of blessing. Again, those who expected to receive the cup remained standing while others sat down.

The bishop stepped toward the men in the front benches. He handed the cup to each communicant in turn, extending it to them with the handle exposed. When his turn came, Tobe took a small sip and handed it back to the bishop. He noticed that some turned the cup to choose a fresh spot to drink. By the time he received it, there were no unstained edges. Each time the cup was empty, Deacon Wagler stepped forward to fill it from the glass jug.

When all the men were served, the bishop made his way through the roomful of women until all were served. Bishop Miller gave the half-empty cup to Deacon Wagler. He put it back under the white table cloth at the front of the room.

Emma's grandfather, Preacher Dan Nisly, then read a passage from the thirteenth chapter of the Gospel of John. The Scripture told the story of Jesus washing the feet of his disciples. The minister read the last several verses with emphasis, "If I then, your Lord and Master, have washed your feet; ye also ought to wash one another's feet. For I have given you an example, that ye should do as I have done to you. If ye know these things, happy are ye if you do them."

The congregation waited as the ministers and the deacon left the room to prepare water for the ritual. Mary had a kettle on the stove with hot water which the ministers used to warm the cold water in the galvanized tubs.

Through the open door, Tobe watched as the minister placed two tubs for the women. The ministers sat down on the front bench and removed their shoes and socks. The bishop and Preacher Levi washed each other's feet first, then the other two ministers took their place. The deacon joined an elderly man by the first tub. So on it went, each man pairing with someone who sat near him. The women followed suit in the adjoining room.

Tobe was next to Raymond Wagler, so they would wash each other's feet. Tobe stooped down in front of the white porcelain tub and took Raymond's foot in one hand. With his other hand, he splashed a bit of water on the foot then rubbed it dry with a terry cloth towel. He repeated the ritual with the other foot. Then they changed places.

When Raymond had finished washing Tobe's feet, they greeted each other with a robust handshake and the kiss of fellowship. Then they returned to their seats to put on their shoes, socks, and coat. Tobe sat quietly till all had finished washing their feet.

The clock struck four p.m. as the ministers collected the tubs and carried them out of the room. Deacon Wagler took his place at the door with a small bag to collect *Almosegeld* or alms. As the worshipers left the room, many placed money into the deacon's bag. The ministers used it to help those in need, those members who had suffered loss of health, finances, or property. It could also be used for some mission projects.

A stream of buggies was leaving the farm when Tobe walked toward the barn to milk his cow and help his in-laws with the evening chores. When the chores were finished, Tobe and Emma joined the supper and singing for the young folks.

Married couples generally kept attending the singings for six months after their wedding. It was considered stuck-up for them to quit sooner.

As the young people dispersed into the night, Tobe and Emma retired to their room. Tobe looked at Emma and said, "I'm getting to bed earlier tonight than I have for years on a Sunday night. I think now that I'm married, I'm going to get more sleep."

"Good night." Emma chuckled. She soon dozed off to the sound of Tobe's measured breathing.

A week passed and it was Tobe's twenty-second birthday. Emma smiled as she prepared the ice cream mixture, breaking several eggs into the rich cream scooped off the top of milk from their own cow. After tossing in a few other ingredients, she put them into a canister in the hand-cranked freezer. Then she took chunks of ice she had been saving in the ice box and put them into a sack. Wielding a sixteen-pound sledge hammer, she smashed the hunks of ice that bulged the sides of the bag. Then she dumped the pieces out of the bag into the ice cream freezer, packing them tightly against the canister. Last of all, she poured a cup of salt onto the top of the ice.

Emma sat down on a small stool and began to crank the handle of the freezer. She hummed to herself as the pieces of ice swished around in the wooden bucket. After twenty minutes of steady cranking, the handle turned much harder. She lifted the lid to check the creamy mixture. *"Baut faddich.* Almost done. " She replaced the lid. Another few turns of the crank and she declared it finished.

By the time Tobe arrived at the Nisly home, several invited guests had arrived. Tobe's brother Ervin and the newly-wed Henry and Elizabeth came for the evening. As Tobe opened the door, Emma's brother Raymond led out in a traditional tune. Emma's family and the guests joined in, finishing off with "Happy Birthday dear Tobie, Happy Birthday to you."

Tobe's face looked different now. Ten days of beard marked his move into the state of matrimony. The hard brown stubble was beginning to turn into softer whiskers.

Everyone gathered around as Emma pulled the agitator out of the ice cream freezer bucket. Deftly, she slid a bowl under the dripping beater. The creamy mixture collected into a rich puddle.

"Who wants to lick the paddle?"

"I'll take it," Tobe volunteered. He spooned off the larger chunks, then licked off the remainder with his tongue. His beard hairs shone with droplets of ice cream. He reached into his pocket for his large red handkerchief. Wiping his stubbly beard, he commented, "I'm going to need to get used to having food in my beard."

Emma giggled and nodded. She spooned the creamy mixture out of the four-quart container into individual dishes. Everyone seated themselves around the table. Soon the men had cleaned their dishes. At a prearranged signal, one of them grabbed Tobe's legs and the other his shoulders. The Nisly family had a tradition of forcing the person with a birthday under the table. The men finally wrestled Tobe to the floor, but they couldn't move him toward the table. The girls grabbed the table and lifted it over the three men. Cheering, they declared, "We did it!"

Emma noticed that her mother had not taken any ice cream. "Mom, don't you want any?"

Mary replied. "No, the cold hurts my teeth. They are really bothering me. I'm getting them all pulled tomorrow. They've been bothering me so much that I'm glad to get rid of them."

"Mom, you'll look funny with all your teeth missing," Raymond commented.

"You'll hardly be able to chew," Lizzie empathized. "Maybe you can eat lots of ice cream then."

Mary laughed. Ice cream was reserved for special occasions.

It was fall harvest season so Tobe earned extra cash by helping several farmers shock fodder. Each evening, he worked to get the Brownlee place ready for moving in. Emma helped her mother with household tasks—cleaning, sewing and canning. They also quilted several comforters, and because it stayed unseasonably warm that fall, Emma was able to can tomatoes near the end of October. With the work of harvest, preparation for winter, and remodeling the Brownlee place, Tobe and Emma were very busy.

As October turned to November, Emma realized Tobe had been too optimistic about how long it would take to make the Brownlee place livable. She spoke to Tobe about it after a long evening of work by lantern light at the new place.

"How long will it be till we move?"

"Oh, I suppose about another two weeks. Are you worried about it?" Tobe's voice reflected a bit of annoyance.

"No."

A few moments passed before Tobe spoke. "We could move in before it's completely finished. It will be easier to work on it while we live here rather than have to drive back and forth to your folks' house."

"Can we move in by the middle of November?"

"Yes, that would give us about two more weeks."

Things moved along well over the next few weeks as they finished different parts of the house. The worktable came last, since it took the most time for Tobe to build. Emma finished staining it the day before they moved in. It was the third week in November.

• • • •

Emma's father occasionally asked Tobe to help with various farm and harvesting projects. One day that fall they were cutting heads off milo plants for grain. The rest of the plant would be used for cattle feed. Tobe loaded huge bundles while Emma's brother Fred operated a long knife on the side of the rack. The sharp guillotine cut the heads off an entire bundle in one whack. While chopping vigorously with the knife, Fred didn't see that Tobe was repositioning the bundle under the blade.

Tobe yelled, "Wait!" as the knife came down.

Fred stopped the knife just as the blade touched Tobe's arm. The color drained from Fred's face.

"I'm sorry."

Tobe's knees suddenly felt weak, but he shrugged it off. "Let's just be glad nobody got hurt." He grabbed another bundle and put it in place.

That evening at the table after Tobe had gone home, Fred reported the incident to the Nisly family. Raymond spoke up. "Did you hear that Tobe and Emma got some free feed from Uncle Ed?"

"No." Levi leaned forward to hear the story.

Raymond explained. "Uncle Ed had some tall feed he didn't really need for the cattle. He told Tobe and Emma they could have the feed if they topped it. They went in and harvested the whole field in one afternoon. Ed just couldn't believe they were done. He doesn't know how fast they can work."

"Tobe is a strong worker," Levi admitted.

"I think he's put on weight since he got married," Raymond asserted. "He's getting bigger muscles too. Emma must be feeding him pretty good."

Mary nodded. "He's a big eater, that's for sure."

When the harvest was finished, Tobe directed his energies to woodworking projects. Emma worked with him to build several pieces of furniture. One evening as they worked together, Tobe asked Emma, "What would you say if we went full-time into a woodworking business?"

He saw Emma catch her breath. "Could we make a living?"

"Well, we can hardly keep up with all the orders we have now. I'm sure we'd have a lot more business if we'd advertise."

"Where would we have our business?" she asked.

"I could build a shop right here. There's plenty of room on the other side of the driveway."

"I guess it's okay. But I don't see how we could afford it."

Tobe shrugged. "We'd need to borrow the money, but I think we could soon pay it back. Let's do it this summer, okay?"

Emma nodded. "Okay, we can try it and see what happens."

Tobe began to design his new shop just after spring communion. He drew a rough draft at the kitchen table, trying to visualize the placement of his equipment. Looking out the door toward the garden, he saw Emma and watched as she stooped over to transplant young tomatoes. *I married a hard worker,* he thought to himself. *She's the best in the whole community. She keeps the house and garden going and still helps me with the business. She even cleaned the manure out of the hen house without complaining!*

Tobe saw Emma as an essential part of his budding woodworking business. While Tobe always did the design and assembly work, he depended on Emma to do most of the finishing. He didn't really enjoy sanding, filling gaps with wood filler, or staining, varnishing and painting. In woodworking as he had done when farming, he took the broad strokes while others came along to fill in the details.

Before Tobe got his new shop built, he made an improvement to allow himself to work at night. When he finished it, he called to Emma from the roof. She looked up from her hoeing. "Look at this," Tobe said. "I hooked up a generator to this windmill. It will run some lights in my shop." Emma walked toward the shed and shielded her eyes from the morning sun as Tobe slid toward the edge of the roof. He swung his legs onto the ladder and made his way to the ground. "Here, let me show you." Emma followed him into the darkened shop.

"I found this generator on an engine at the junk yard. I'll run the wires from it down to this battery." Picking up two light bulbs, he moved toward the center of the room. "I'll mount these lights right over here so we can see to work at night.

Emma stood amazed. "I guess it will save kerosene."

"Sure. Wind is free."

"Will the preachers mind?"

"I don't know. I'm not going to ask them."

Soon Tobe had the electric lights running every night. He liked them better than a kerosene lantern.

••••

That spring of 1941, Tobe and Emma decided to visit his parents in Oklahoma. They left Hutchinson on the 4:10 a.m. train and arrived at 1:30 p.m. Ervin met them with the buggy. They spent the evening and the next day in the Stutzman household. Emma worked alongside her mother-in-law, helping in the garden and cleaning around the house.

"It's nice to have your help with the Saturday work," Anna said.

Emma smiled. "I'm just glad to help."

At the dinner table that day, Anna commented, "It sure is good to see all of my boys around the table again." She nodded at Emma. "And now we have a daughter as well." Emma smiled.

Perry piped up. "*Mir hen en Diener gemacht in die Gmee letscht Sunndaag.* We made a preacher in church last Sunday."

Tobe looked at his six-year-old brother. "Who is it?"

"John D. Yoder."

"Oh, I like John. He's a good carpenter."

Clarence broke in. "What are you saying? Does that mean he'll be a good preacher?"

Tobe retorted. "Jesus was a carpenter. He was a good preacher."

"*Well, Buwe! So wie der schwetzet!* Boys! What a way to talk!" Anna's voice signaled disapproval of their lightheartedness.

Tobe's voice softened, "Well, I think John D. will make a good preacher. He's easy going and won't be too strict with the discipline. But he's not young any more. How old is he?"

"Fifty-four," Tobe's mother answered. "John was in the lot before, back in Custer County. He felt the call of God then, but he wasn't obedient."

"How was that?" Clarence sounded perplexed.

"Well, he confessed afterward that God showed him which book the lot was in. He didn't want it, so he took a different book."

Perry's face wrinkled into a frown. "How could God show him? Did God point to it with his finger?"

Tobe's father sat silent as Anna's face registered her continuing discomfort with the conversation. "God has his way. I guess you just don't understand it until it happens to you. Then somehow, God shows you."

The table talk soon drifted to Tobe's woodworking business back home. Hoping to catch some sense of his father's reaction to the project, Tobe described his plans to build a new shop. But Tobe couldn't tell what he was thinking. Should he ask him directly? No, Dad could speak for himself if he had something to say. Although Tobe tried, most of the time it felt like he would never understand his father.

••••

The day after Tobe and Emma returned from their trip to Oklahoma, Tobe received an official-looking envelope in the mail. The stamped message—*Official U.S. Mail*—prompted him to open it right away. He scanned the letter quickly, then turned toward Emma, "I'll need to go to Hutch for registration. I guess they're wanting to keep track of all the COs."

Would he need to go into service? It would mean putting off building the new shop which he hoped to do as soon as he had sufficient funds in hand. Fortunately, spring and summer provided many opportunities to earn some cash.

The Murphy family nearby was leaving for vacation so Tobe agreed to chore for them. They brought their cows to the Brownlee place to make milking more convenient. He helped Sim Moore and others bale hay. At night he worked on shop projects. He welcomed the light from his roof generator as he finished a wagon box for Abe Garver just in time for the wheat harvest.

Emma helped with Tobe's projects whenever she could. Even though the beans were begging to be picked, she sanded and painted Enos Knepp's cupboard. Otherwise, Tobe wouldn't have finished it by the time he had promised. Even with their joint effort, Enos watched as they put on the finishing touches when he came to pick it up.

With that project finished, Tobe shocked oats for Barney Koestal until late one evening. Emma was waiting up for him, ready to prepare cold milk soup. Tobe gulped down the food, making small talk between bites.

As he scraped the bottom of his dish, he commented. "Something funny happened today at Koestels."

"Oh?"

Tobe laughed. "I was shocking oats along with Barney. He's not the fastest worker. I was hoping to get the field done today so I was pushing it pretty hard. Well, he told me to slow down. He said it's not good for oats to be shocked so fast." Emma joined Tobe in laughter. What difference did it make to the oats?

About the middle of June, Tobe ordered most of the materials for his new shop. Before the wheat harvest was over, Tobe pulled in a number of men to help pour the footer for the new building. Emma helped when she wasn't cooking for the harvesters or working in the garden. The twelve bushels of potatoes from mid-July came in handy for the large dinners needed for the threshing crew.

It was the third week in July when Tobe hammered the last nail into the shingles on the roof of his new shop. He climbed down from the roof and surveyed the structure from the shade of an elm tree. Hard as it was for him to wait until the harvest was over, Tobe waited until the last week in July to pour the floor.

Then as soon as the concrete had set, he moved in the equipment he'd been collecting over the past several months. Then he rigged a line shaft along one wall, connecting it to a gas-powered Wisconsin V-4 engine. By the time he finished, flat belts ran from pulleys to a large band saw, a lathe, a table saw, a planer, and a jointer. By starting one motor, he could run any of these pieces of equipment simply by tightening the belt that powered that tool. Tobe felt ready to go into major production.

With all Tobe's excitement about the new shop, he hadn't noticed Emma's own excitement about another development. She told him about it as they lay in bed together one night.

10

In the Family Way

Tobe was exhausted as he crawled under the sheets beside Emma. He lay quietly and watched the moon through the south window. The cord dangling from the half-open shade swayed slightly in the breeze, its shadow dancing on the bed sheet. A cricket in the far corner of the room echoed the crickets outside.

Tobe was thinking about his new work space. "I'm really going to like the new shop. It's so much more roomy than the space we had in the shed."

"Uh huh." Emma adjusted her pillow and straightened her nightcap.

"If we go into production, I'll need to hire some people," Tobe's mind was racing. A sliver of moonlight shone on Emma's face as she turned toward him.

"I could just start with a few part-time people and put out a lot more stuff. Like those swing horses I designed." Tobe sensed her silence. "What do you think? Should we be hiring someone to help us in the shop?"

Emma cleared her throat. "After next spring, I won't be able to help as much any more."

Tobe turned toward her, trying to read the expression on her face in the moonlight. "Why, what's the matter? Don't you like working in the shop?"

"I don't mind helping, but I'll need to take care of the baby." Emma's voice quivered slightly.

"The baby? You mean we're going to have a baby?"

"I'm pretty sure."

Tobe shivered with anticipation. "When will the baby come?"

"The first of April."

"*Oh es iss heftich*. That's incredible. Who should we tell first?"

"Let's wait for another week to make sure. Then we'll tell the folks."

Tobe squeezed her hand. "I can hardly wait."

The next morning Tobe whistled as he went about his work. He was going to be a father! Maybe he'd have a son who would grow up to be a partner in the business.

He had just shut off the table saw when he heard a horse and buggy on the driveway. He looked out the window to see a rig pull up to the hitching post. A young boy hopped out, followed by his mother. It was Emma's aunt Lizzie Nisly. She turned to follow the boy toward the shop.

Tobe stepped to the entrance. "Hello, Lizzie!"

"Is it all right if Samuel looks around the shop? He's interested in woodworking."

"Sure, I'll show him around." He tousled the young boy's hair. "*Ich waar aa mol en Wunnernaas*. I was once a curious little boy myself."

Lizzie smiled. "I'll be inside with Emma. You can send Samuel in when you're tired of him."

Tobe grinned. "He's the one who will get tired. I'll put him to work."

Samuel's eyes grew wide as he surveyed the layout of the workshop. Tobe motioned with his hand. "Come over here, and I'll show you how the big equipment works."

After showing Samuel the various tools, Tobe led him over to the corner of the shop. "Let me show you this swing." The wooden swing was suspended from the ceiling by a board that swiveled and a set of ropes. Tobe pointed toward the seat. "You're a little big but it will hold you just fine. Try it."

Samuel hopped onto the swing. By pushing his legs against a set of wooden pegs, he soon had the swing moving rapidly in a defined arc. A big grin lit his face.

Tobe smiled. "You like it, huh? You can swing on it while I get back to work. When you're done swinging, you can watch me work. If you like, I'll let you help me with something."

Tobe moved toward the furniture project he had started two days earlier. For the next hour, Samuel watched as Tobe cut the pieces for a chest of drawers. Then, at Tobe's suggestion, the young boy swept the floor and straightened out the scrap pile. He was just finishing up when Lizzie came to the door.

"It's time to go home. I hope he wasn't a bother."

"Not at all. I was glad to have him. He was a good helper."

Tobe watched them go, then turned back to his work. He'd love to have a boy like that.

Two weeks later, Emma told Tobe she was sure she was pregnant. She shared the secret with her mother. It would be Mary's second grandchild. Henry and Elizabeth were expecting their first child within the next two months.

Juggling his time with a few farm jobs, Tobe gave most of his attention to production in the shop. Soon people were asking for a range of wooden furniture: tables, cabinets, dresser bureaus, cedar chests, and magazine racks. Tobe even began building custom-built buggies. Then he struck up a deal with a Nebraska dealer to make wooden wagon boxes that ranged from eighty to two hundred bushels in capacity.

But Tobe had broader visions. He dreamed of making wooden truck beds. He could manufacture them and market them to farmers in the surrounding community.

That fall after council meeting, the weather turned very dry so there was no farm work to do. It reminded Tobe of the dust bowl days in Oklahoma. Dust devils swirled in the air. After two days of high winds, huge clouds of dust blocked out the sun. Fine, mist-like sand hung in the air, pressing its way through cracks in doors and windows and depositing a thin layer on Emma's furniture.

Relief finally came in the form of autumn rains. By early October, Tobe had forgotten about the dry weather. He was busy thinking about projects for the winter.

• • • •

One morning while visiting with a neighbor, Tobe learned that Bishop Eli Nisly of Nowata had succumbed to cancer. As Tobe rode home, he wondered whether he should go to the funeral.

He stepped into the house to ask Emma about it. Together, they decided it was best for Tobe to stay home. Tobe thought aloud, "I guess Eli never did get another bishop ordained down there. I doubt the settlement will survive. I'll probably be hearing from my folks one of these days. They'll be moving away from Nowata."

"Do you think so? It's not so dry down there this year."

Tobe kept thinking about it all day. Would the folks be moving back to Kansas? Could he convince his father to help him with his shop projects?

By the time the fall butchering season started, Emma could feel the unborn life moving inside her womb. The days were turning cold now so Tobe put the stove in the living room. There were plenty of wood scraps from the shop to keep it going.

Emma's dad helped butcher a beef. She canned some and prepared the rest for cold storage in Hutch. When she and Tobe dropped the meat off in town, they took some time to look at the Christmas lights on the houses. Emma's family always celebrated Christmas with their own traditions. They exchanged gifts in Christmas boxes filled with fruit and other goodies. Then they ate ice cream.

The young people generally exchanged gifts a few days after Christmas in a New Year's box. Some celebrated "Old Christmas" or Epiphany, as Protestant neighbors called it.

On Christmas Day 1941, Tobe and Emma entertained visitors from Oklahoma, Tobe's brother Ervin and Johnny J. K. Yoder. After the prayer of blessing, Tobe gestured at the dishes Emma had prepared, "Just reach and help yourselves."

The table was small so each reached in to serve themselves without passing the food. They were soon engrossed in conversation. Ervin was finishing up the last of his beef when he asked Tobe, "Did you hear that Uncle Jerry is thinking about joining the military?"

Tobe's face fell. "That's too bad. When Uncle Johnny joined the Army up in Nebraska, Mom was so disappointed."

The group lapsed into silence. It was a serious matter to join the army.

Finally, Johnny J. K. broke the silence, "We heard about the Pearl Harbor attack on the radio. Your folks had the singing that evening. An English man and his wife got stuck in the mud trying to go up on the west side of the hill. He came to the door to get help while we were singing. Your dad told us to hitch the horse. When we were pulling out the car, the woman in the car heard about the Pearl Harbor attack on the radio. She told us we were going to war with Japan."

"I hope we don't get drafted," Ervin said.

Tobe changed the subject. "I'm sorry I couldn't get to Bishop Nisly's funeral."

"Oh," Ervin replied, "The weather was terrible for a funeral. It rained something awful."

Johnny chimed in, "It was so wet and cold. Had it been snow instead of rain, we would have had a blizzard. It rained so hard that the grave kept getting water in it."

"But the cemetery is on a hill. How could you get so much water in the grave up on a hill?" asked Tobe.

"It must have come in from the sides. The men said the rough box had six inches of water in it just before they let the coffin down. It came in faster than they could dip it out."

Johnny leaned back in his chair. "It's too bad that he died but it was his time to go. He couldn't really eat anything for the last while. The cancer just took over his body."

Ervin agreed. "Even Fannie said it was a blessing that he could go. For the last few days, he lingered. Some of the men from church helped out by sitting with him at night. Dad took his turn along with the others."

"The doctor came out several times to give him shots," Johnny said. "He had terrible pain."

"How is Fannie taking all this? Is she going to stay in Nowata?"

Ervin replied, "The way she talked, she'd like to stay. This past year wasn't as bad for farming as it was for several years there. We had more rain at the time we needed it."

Tobe mused, "I wonder if people will stay there or move away?"

"I don't know, some have already moved away."

After dinner Tobe took the two men out to the shop. "Want to see the equipment running?"

By late afternoon the demonstration was over and Tobe's guests left to visit other friends and relatives. As they waved to their departing friends, Tobe grinned and turned to Emma. "Did I ever tell you about the time Johnny J. K. almost drove over his own plow in the field?"

"I don't remember."

Tobe laughed. "He was plowing a big field with their new Minneapolis Moline KTA. One time when he came around the field, there was the plow in front of him in the furrow! He had stepped on the automatic hitch release when he got on the tractor and never realized it until he came around." Emma chuckled along with Tobe as they walked back to the house.

• • • •

As usual the Nisly family butchered a hog in January. Emma joined in with the work. In turn her mother helped butcher for Tobe and Emma. Emma canned both meat and broth. The larder was starting to fill up.

She was cooking sausage when Tobe came in from the shop. He stamped the snow off his shoes near the entry then stepped inside. "Someone said yesterday that the government just passed a new law that changes the time. They're calling it War Time. We're supposed to turn the clock forward an hour."

Emma groaned, "That means it'll be darker in the morning. We'll have to use the lanterns to chore. Why do they have to change the time?"

"They say it'll save electricity," Tobe explained. "Maybe we Amish should just keep the old time since we don't use electricity."

Emma nodded vigorously. "I don't see why the government should interfere with the time."

Tobe opened the glass face of the mantel clock and swept the hour hand clockwise, pausing to let the mechanism chime at each quarter hour. "It'll take me some time to get used to it," he said. "I'm sure the cows will notice the change too."

Emma nodded, "So will the chickens."

Tobe's mind turned to the day's events. "I guess we'll be going up home tonight?"

"Yes. We're surprising Lizzie and Barbara for their birthdays. Are the cedar chests ready?" Tobe thought for a moment. "Except for the hinges. I'll put them on before dinner."

"I think they'll really like the chests. The inlaid star pattern is so nice."

"I thought it turned out pretty good. I'll have to make you one."

"I'd like that," Emma said, rubbing her jaw. She winced. "My tooth hurts. I think I better have it pulled."

"I've got a bad one too. We could both have it done at the same time. Do you mind going to town when you're showing so much?"

"No, if it needs to be. I can wear my heavy coat so it doesn't show so much."

"Are you going to church this Sunday?" Tobe asked, knowing the services were scheduled to be held at Emma's folks.

"I don't believe so. I don't want all the people looking at me."

"Then I'll just stay home with you," Tobe promised.

Early in the week, they made the trip to town and got their teeth pulled. They also made a few purchases. When they arrived home, Tobe guided the horse into the yard and pulled the rig up to the chicken house.

Emma stepped down from the wagon. "If you unload the chicken crate and carry it into the chicken house, I'll take the chicks out. I need to go get an apron."

"Okay, but hold the horse first, okay?"

Emma held the horse's bridle while Tobe swung the crate over the side of the wagon. He lugged it into the small building and set it on the wooden floor. Emma handed the reins to Tobe and went in the house. Slipping an apron over her head, she went back to the chicken house. As she pulled the chicks out of the crate, they scattered. Dust floated in the air.

Early the next morning, Tobe finished the chores as Emma started the gas motor to run the water pump. She filled a nearby rinse tub and the washing machine with water. Then she put in a load of clothing.

Next she yanked on the cord of the machine's Briggs and Stratton motor. On the second pull, it roared to life. The sound reverberated against the walls of the wash house. She flipped the lever, and the agitator began to swish the load of clothing. She opened the lid and dropped a bag of lye soap into the water. When there were sufficient suds, she fished out the soap with her hand and laid it back on the wall shelf. Tobe walked out of the shop as Emma carried the basket of wash toward the wash line.

"I'm hitchhiking to town. I need to order some supplies at Davis Lumber. I should be back before noon."

"Good. Can you get me some sandpaper? I'm going to try to get the kitchen floor sanded before the baby comes."

"Sure, I'll get plenty." Tobe was eager to see the floor get done.

Emma went back to her wash as Tobe strode out the lane toward the highway. She seized a pair of wet rags and walked the distance of the clothesline, wiping two side-by-side lines clean and dry. When she came to the end, she reversed and came back on the other two lines. Watching as Tobe crossed the railroad tracks, she hung the clothing in straight rows.

Emma was reading the mail in the dimming light of evening when Tobe came home. "What did we get?"

"A letter from your folks. And here's one from Mary Burkholder. Must be the circle letter."

"What's Mom have to say?"

"Quite a few things. This is a long letter. She says she's still improving after the operation. She says Mrs. Noah Nisly is staying at Daniel Yoder's house while she's down for treatments at the mineral springs. It's not too far to drive that way.

"Oh, and here she says they're planning to move away from Nowata around the 29th of March. They're coming to Yoder, and they will live with your Dad's folks. The 29th? That's only two weeks away."

Tobe broke in. "That will never work. Dad will not get along with Dawdy."

Emma glanced up from the letter. "Why not?"

"He's too stubborn. He won't do things the way Dawdy will want to see them done. It won't go long until they'll need to move again."

Emma sighed. "Well, those are the main things. You can read it." She pushed the letter across the table to Tobe.

True to their plans, Tobe's parents moved to the Yoder, Kansas, community on March 30, 1942. Tobe and Emma went to meet them. Although the birth of her baby seemed imminent, Emma spent part of an afternoon helping his folks get settled. She was particularly self-conscious around her mother-in-law.

Three days later, Emma felt a contraction. Tobe had just gone to work in the shop. She felt excitement rising within her. *Is the baby coming?*

She tried to go about her work. *There's no use being in a hurry. Mother says it often takes a long time for the first one.* She finished washing the dishes and packed some clothing for her hospital stay. As she went to close the suitcase, she felt a similar contraction, only stronger. She trembled with excitement. After another thirty minutes of anxious waiting, she was sure it was time to head for the hospital. She walked toward the shop to tell Tobe.

11

Settling In

On the second day of April 1942, Emma gave birth to a baby girl. They named her Mary Edna to honor both Emma's mother and a favorite aunt.

After a week in the hospital, Emma came home. With help from Tobe, she walked into the house and went straight to bed. Mother Nisly said she shouldn't be up until the baby was two weeks old. Emma's sister Barbara moved in to take care of household routines. Having just turned 21, Barbara was allowed to keep her own wages, and Tobe agreed to pay her three dollars a week.

It wasn't long before the Will Miller family came to see the new baby. Tobe welcomed his former employer with a wide smile. He invited ten-year-old Edna to sit in a small chair he had made for the baby. As her parents admired the infant, Tobe pointed to the baby and asked Edna, "*Gell, hot sie net en sheener Naame*? Doesn't she have a pretty name?"

"*Yah*. Yes. She has two names. One is the same as mine."

"I noticed you gave her a middle name," Becky Miller observed. Few people in her generation had been given a middle name. To some of the Amish, a middle name seemed worldly. If someone needed a middle initial, they could use the first letter of their father's first name.

"Yes," Tobe replied. "We thought it would help to keep some of the names straight. There are so many Marys. Henrys gave Dorothy a middle name too."

As the women chatted about the baby, Tobe and Will talked about the crops and the upcoming harvest. "The oats are looking pretty good," Will said. "They're a little bit ahead of the wheat."

"That reminds me," Tobe said, looking a bit embarrassed. "Remember when you used to tell me that I shouldn't feed my horse oats?"

"Yes, I was glad when you quit doing it."

"Well, actually, I didn't quit. I just got them from the back of the bin."

Will jerked forward in his chair. "*Well du alter Ding, du!* Well, you old thing, you!" Was it a word of rebuke? Or affirmation for Tobe's shrewdness? Tobe wasn't sure so he laughed it off, "I thought I'd better tell you sometime."

Then to change the subject, Tobe went to the bedroom and returned with his guitar. "Edna, shall we sing a few songs together?"

"Sure!"

They had only sung one song when they heard buggy wheels in the driveway. Will rose from his seat. "Someone else is coming. I guess we should be going."

"You don't need to rush off," Emma objected.

Will put on his hat as a knock came on the door. Tobe opened it to see his brother Ervin.

"Come right on in."

Ervin stepped inside. "I see you have company."

"No," Will said, "we're just ready to leave." He walked toward the door with his family close behind. Tobe waved a good-bye as they headed for their buggy.

"Come again."

Tobe stepped back inside to see Ervin leaning over the baby's cradle. Ervin was grinning broadly.

Tobe walked over to the cradle and affectionately shook the baby.

"Oh, don't shake the baby that way," Ervin objected.

Tobe straightened up and looked Ervin right in the eye. "This is *my* baby," he declared.

Ervin swallowed the words that rose in his throat.

Tobe relaxed. "How about having some peanuts?" He reached for the jar on the shelf.

"That sounds good," Ervin replied as he held out his hand.

The two brothers chatted for an hour before Ervin rose to leave.

Tobe yawned as he closed the door behind his brother. He was tired. The new baby brought extra work even though Barbara was helping.

When Mary Edna was just over a month old, Emma stood at the kitchen window peeling onions for supper. She looked up to see Tobe coming in the lane. He had gone to do some grocery shopping. Tobe carried two bags from the back of the buggy. The spring breeze ruffled his shirt as Emma opened the screen door for him. He set the bags on the table. "I didn't get all the sugar you asked for. I think I got everything else though."

"Were they out of sugar?" Emma's brow knit with the question.

"No, they're starting to ration it. I guess there's a shortage because of the war."

"I wish I would have known ahead of time. I would have tried to save some. I'll need a lot for canning this summer."

"Maybe they won't ration it that long." Tobe reached into his pocket. "They gave me some ration coupons. This lets us know how much we can get." He handed Emma the slips of paper.

She examined the coupons. "We'll have to be very careful how much sugar we use."

"I guess so," Tobe said, heading for the door. "I'm going to start on the wagon box order. I'm running a bit behind."

On the second Sunday in May, Tobe and Emma took Mary Edna to church for the first time. As Emma walked toward the buggy, she pulled the blanket over the infant's eyes to protect her face from the morning sun. Handing her up to Tobe, Emma climbed in and put the child onto her lap.

"I guess we'll see John today." Tobe sensed that Emma was eager to see her younger brother again. They were invited to Emma's parents for Sunday evening supper. Young John Nisly had been drafted and was serving in Civilian Public Service. CPS provided a place for young conscientious objectors to do civilian task in lieu of military service.

Tobe spoke softly. "I wonder what your folks think, now that John left the church and bought a car. It seems when he moved to Iowa to work for Uncle Fred in '39, he decided he didn't want to be Amish any more. He worked with all those English people in the turkey processing plant. That's when he decided to join the Mennonite Church at East Union."

"Mom doesn't say much about it, but I wish Dad wouldn't take it so hard."

Later that day Tobe and Emma headed for home just as the sun was setting.

"That's a beautiful sunset," Tobe declared. "Look how the clouds are lit up, way up into the sky."

Emma agreed. She shifted her sleeping baby to the other arm. "It should be a nice day tomorrow. Mom always says, 'Evening red and morning gray, sends the traveler on his way. Evening gray and morning red, brings down rain upon his head.'"

"I hope it's a nice day. I want to paint some wagon boxes tomorrow."

"I'd like to get out into the garden. We have some weeds that need to be pulled."

"Did you hear John say they're getting ready to shut down the CPS camp there in Henry, Illinois?"

"No, that must have been when I was putting Mary Edna to sleep."

"He says it'll probably close down by September. The people there are really patriotic. The COs were warned not to go to town."

"I hope he'll be all right."

"I'm sure he will be. They just have to be a little cautious."

• • • •

After Mary Edna was born, Emma spent much less time in the shop. Tobe often worked long after supper as he tried to stay caught up with the work.

One evening in late spring, it was raining hard when he came inside. Emma looked up from the rocker where she sat patching a pair of socks in the dim light of the kerosene lantern. Tobe poured water into the granite pan at the small sink and pulled up his sleeves. "We haven't had this much rain in years. I'm glad I got my painting done on Monday."

"It sure is wet," Emma agreed. "It keeps me out of the garden."

"Things are bad in Hutch. The river is flooding." Tobe splashed water on his face and arms. "They say the dike might break. If it did, most of the town would be under water."

Tobe ran a comb through his hair, then sat down and thumbed through the *Budget*. "There sure are a lot of ads for scrap iron in the *Budget*. It must be part of the war effort. This would be a good time to be in the scrap iron business."

"I don't think that's such a good idea," Emma said. "We're having enough trouble keeping up with the business we have."

"That's true," Tobe admitted. "I think I'm going to hire some part-time workers."

Over the next few months, Tobe hired a few workers. Most like Orie Schrock were farm hands looking for a little work on the side.

"The wagon box orders keep coming in," Tobe told Emma one August evening. "When everyone pays up, we'll have some extra cash on hand."

Emma's face brightened. "That's good. I thought you said you still owe money to the lumber company."

"That's true. But that'll change before long."

"I hope so. We'll need some cash to pay for the hospital when the next baby comes."

"That won't be until next April."

"Maybe March."

"I'm sure we'll have it when we need it. By the way, I saw my dad at the lumber yard today. He said they're moving over to the old hatchery place."

"Why? I thought they were buying Dawdy Stutzman's place."

"They wanted to, but Dawdy decided to sell it to Sam Schrock. Dawdys are moving back to Indiana. Now Dads have to move. When they moved to Yoder from Nowata, I figured this might happen. Dawdy never did trust my dad with his things."

"That's too bad. At least they'll be closer to our place."

"But they won't be able to make a living by farming there. Clarence and Perry will probably hire themselves out."

Tobe's prediction proved true. After only a short time at the hatchery place, his folks moved again. This time they rented a farm that lay at the far western edge of the Amish community. For the first time since Tobe had moved from Oklahoma to Kansas, he was back in the same church district with his parents.

That winter an epidemic of whooping cough found its way into the community. Some families were quarantined.

Emma expressed her concern. "Do you think I should stay home from church so Mary Edna doesn't get it? It's hard on babies."

Tobe didn't seem worried as she rocked back in her chair. "Can you put a stool under my feet?" she asked. "They feel all swollen. I'll be glad when this baby finally comes."

"It should be any day now, shouldn't it? March will soon be past."

"I hope it's soon. I'm tired of carrying it."

Perry Lee was born on March 28, 1943, just a few days before Mary Edna's first birthday. This time Emma's sister Elizabeth came to help with the baby and the housework. Because she wasn't 21 and couldn't keep her own money, Elizabeth worked out an agreement with her sister Barbara. Barbara agreed to work at home in exchange for Elizabeth's wages.

When Emma no longer needed Elizabeth in the house, she moved into the shop to work for Tobe. One day Elizabeth confided to Tobe and Orie Schrock that she enjoyed shop work better than house work.

When Elizabeth went home for a weekend, Barbara asked how she liked working for Tobe. "Pretty good. You know I like working with wood. The customers aren't always happy though. We have a hard time meeting the deadlines."

"Maybe he figures that his helpers can work as fast as he can," Barbara suggested.

Elizabeth groaned. "That's probably true."

"The other thing is, Tobe figures his deadlines as though he were always working. He doesn't figure the time it takes to talk to the customers. When he starts talking to a customer, he loses track of time."

Barbara laughed. "He is quite a talker."

• • • •

Later that summer, Tobe rolled up his sleeves and splashed water onto his face and arms. Then he scrubbed them with Life Buoy soup. He ran a comb through his hair as he walked to where Perry Lee lay in the bassinet. "Ooh, pretty boy," he cooed. He stroked the child's tiny palm with his finger.

Emma put the last of the serving dishes on the table. "Dinner's ready."

Tobe scooted up to the table. "The baby seems real content."

"Yes," Emma said. "He sleeps a lot."

After silent grace, Tobe reached for the potato dish. After serving himself, he poured a generous helping of gravy on top. Handing the gravy to Emma, he said, "I wish my brother Ervin could work for me. He's 21 and doesn't have a farm. We could go into a partnership as Stutzman Brothers. What would you think of that?"

"Doesn't he have to stay with Fritz Warnken as long as he has a farm deferment? He can't just work anywhere until the war is over, right?"

"I'm not sure. Maybe we'll have to wait until the war is over. I do know that Fritz really likes Ervin's work. He even pays Ervin extra money for keeping the equipment in perfect shape."

That afternoon as Emma was working in the garden, she noticed dark clouds coming up from the western horizon. "I think it's going to storm," she told Tobe, who was working in the shop. "Maybe we need to get those wagon boxes inside. The paint is still wet."

"Let's wait and see," Tobe said.

An hour later as Tobe went toward the house for supper, he surveyed the sky with alarm. Low-hanging clouds churned and boiled overhead. An eerie green tinted the dark blue clouds.

The wind picked up as Tobe pulled the wagon boxes into the shop. The air turned much cooler as a few small hailstones began to fall. Soon the hail fell in earnest, white balls of ice peppering the ground. Tobe glanced out the open doorway toward the garden. The balls grew in size, crashing on the tin roof and rattling against the window panes.

Tobe noticed the chicken coop. Why didn't those chickens have the good sense to go inside when it was hailing? The ground was white with balls of ice, some as large as golf balls. Then just as quickly as it had started, the hail stopped. On the western horizon, the sun peeked through a thin spot in the cloud layer. In the east a rainbow began to form.

The next morning, Orie came to work a bit later then usual. Tobe was putting the finishing touches on a truck bed.

Tobe looked up as he stepped into the shop. "That was some storm last night," Tobe said.

"It sure was," Orie replied. "Did you have hail?"

"Yes, we did. It's lucky that most of the farmers had their wheat cut. Otherwise, they'd have lost the whole crop."

"We had hail at our place too. But north of Hutch is where they really got hit. Someone said they found hail thirteen inches in circumference."

"*Oh, es iss hesslich!* That's terrible! That would put a knot on your head." Tobe shuddered just to think about it.

Tobe watched as Orie worked. He wished Orie would move faster. If he could speed up a little, it'd be easier to stay on schedule. It was enough to make Tobe long for Ervin.

A few weeks later, Ervin let Tobe in on a secret. There would be another Emma Nisly in their family as he had asked Sam and Delilah Nisly's Emma to marry him.

As they were getting into bed that evening, Tobe told his Emma about Ervin's plans. She wasn't surprised. "I'm glad for them. But it's so sad that Sam can't be here for the wedding."

Sam Nisly's death earlier that summer had shocked the community. After shaving over a pimple on his lip, Sam had mysteriously contracted erysipelas, a form of hemolytic streptococcus related to strep throat. "I feel so sorry for Delilah. How old was he? Do you remember?"

"Only forty-seven, I think," Tobe said as he adjusted the thin sheet. "I guess there's nothing anyone could do. At least that's what the doctor said."

Emma pulled back the bed sheet. "At the quilting the other day, someone was telling a story about how Noah Nisly went over to Sam's to do some healing with his hands. I guess it didn't help. They were saying Sam and Delilah asked Noah to come when one of their children was sick. Noah measured a string around the child's stomach then wrapped it around an egg and put it in on the hot coals on the base burner. If the egg burst open, it was supposed to mean something."

"That's pow wowing. We never believed in that," Tobe said. "My mother wouldn't hear of it. They say that Dawdy Mast used to teach against it too. He didn't believe in superstition."

Emma turned to lie on her side. "My Dad teaches against it too. By the way, did I tell you that Mom has to go to the hospital?"

"No. What's the matter?"

"Female problems. They're going to operate."

• • • •

Several weeks later the sun shone brightly as Tobe got up from the breakfast table one morning. Emma dried her hands on the pink hand towel. "I'm planning to go up home today. I want to see how Mom is doing. She came home from the hospital last night."

"Did the operation go well?" Tobe asked.

"The doctor thought so."

"She'll probably be in bed for awhile," Tobe ventured.

"Probably. I'll fix you some sandwiches for lunch. You can slice some of those fresh tomatoes."

"Good." Tobe often ate fresh bread with tomatoes and lettuce from the garden.

"There's some cantaloupe too. I just picked it yesterday."

"Thanks. Are you sure it'll be enough for both of us?" Tobe laughed when Emma made a face. She never ate cantaloupe. It was one of the few foods she didn't like.

"I'll hitch up the horse when you're ready," Tobe volunteered. "You'll have your hands full with the babies." He picked up his hat and headed for the door.

"Thank you."

That evening Emma told Tobe that her Mother was gaining strength. After she put the children to bed, Emma read the *Budget* in the soft light of a gas lantern while Tobe worked on his account book. He looked at Emma, "Did I tell you what Dan Headings told me today?" The Headings family was involved with a Mennonite mission outreach on Pershing Street in Hutchinson. "He said they can't pick up the local children any more because of gas rationing."

Because Tobe and Emma didn't have a car, they didn't worry much about gas rationing. But Tobe sympathized with his Mennonite neighbors, and he wished the Amish church would change its rule against car ownership.

• • • •

Some weeks later when Bishop Jacob Miller announced that the church was intending to ordain another preacher, Tobe couldn't help hoping that a progressive young man would be chosen.

Although some were much more likely than others to be nominated for the task, all of the adult men in the congregation were potential candidates. The date for the ordination was set for October 10, the same day as the semi-annual communion service. Bishop Miller entreated church members to pray and fast in preparation for the event.

Tobe thought about the ordination as he went about his work. He recalled his baptism and how he had agreed to serve as a minister if asked. What if he were named? What would happen to his business? The ministers did all their church work without pay.

Emma sometimes talked about what it was like to be a minister's daughter so he shared his concerns with her. "How old was your dad when he was ordained?"

"I think he was about thirty-nine."

"I wonder what it would be like to be ordained," Tobe asked.

Emma remembered how it was for her father. "After Dad was chosen, he got up an hour earlier every morning to meditate on the Scriptures. He got up at five o'clock and let the boys sleep until six. Then they went to chore together."

"It's a lot of work to memorize so many Bible verses," Tobe sighed. Since the use of notes was frowned upon, Amish preachers usually spoke from memory at the pulpit.

"I remember the first time my dad preached he happened to misquote some passage from the Bible. When Dawdy Nisly gave *Zeugnis* (testimony), he corrected him."

Tobe grimaced. "I'm sure I'd make mistakes too. Especially if I preached as fast as your Dad."

Emma laughed. "Both Dawdy and Dad preach pretty fast, don't they? But people understand if you make mistakes. And if you can't think what to say, you can always sit down and let one of the older ministers finish the sermon. Even Bishop Jake did that one time."

Tobe shrugged his shoulders. "We'll just have to wait and see what happens."

Tobe felt the weight of the matter, particularly as they drove to the service on Sunday morning. The first part of the service proceeded as usual, but during the second sermon of the morning, a visiting bishop spoke on the duties of preachers and deacons. He exhorted the members of the congregation to obey their leaders as God intended. He told the story of the rebellious Israelites who died in the wilderness because they grumbled against Moses. He rehearsed how Ananias and Sapphira lied to the Holy Spirit and to the apostle Peter, resulting in death. He reminded the congregation that God alone knows the human heart.

When the preacher sat down, the whole congregation was quiet. The sense of God's sovereignty weighed like a blanket over the assembly.

Bishop Jake Miller gave brief instructions, then retired to a side room. Several ministers accompanied him. It was the time for nominations to be taken. All members, both men and women, were eligible to present a name for consideration. One at a time, a number of persons stood and made their way to the room where the bishop and ministers sat. In the presence of the one giving the nomination, the bishop and a ministerial assistant recorded the nomination on a sheet of paper. After a lull, the bishop stepped from the side room and announced that they would wait only a few more minutes. Five more minutes passed while all sat in silence. No one left the room, and the time for nominations was closed.

The bishop and his assistants returned with solemn faces to announce the names of the persons who would participate in the lot: John Helmuth, Levi Helmuth, Joe Miller, Levi Miller, Raymond Wagler, Peter Wagler, Willie Wagler, John B. Yoder, and John C. Yoder. Tobe breathed a deep sigh of relief that his name had not been called.

The bishop invited all of the nominees to sit on a bench at the front of the men's side of the congregation. Then he took a slip of paper on which was written a verse from the Book of Acts. He gave it to two minsters who retired to a separate room.

The first minister placed the slip out of sight within the pages of one of nine books, then put the book back into the stack. The second minister mixed the order of the books until neither knew the placement of the slip. Together they returned the stack of books to the bishop.

Again, the congregation sat quietly until the two men returned with the books. Bishop Miller fastened an elastic band around the outside of each book. The bands held the pages tightly closed so that the pages wouldn't open even slightly to reveal the location of the slip.

The bishop stood the books on a table in front for all the men to see. Then he led in prayer, asking for the Lord to guide the right man to choose the book with the slip in it. The nominees were seated in order from the oldest to the youngest. The oldest, deacon Peter Wagler, rose first and chose one of the books. The others followed in order, returning to their seats with the books in their hands.

There was hardly a sound in the room as the bishop stepped up to Peter and took the book from Peter's hand. He opened the book. No slip. He took the book from the second man and opened it. No slip. The suspense grew as he continued with the next seven books. No slip. When he opened the ninth book, held by Willie Wagler, he paused briefly, then looked up and intoned, "The lot has been found in Brother Willie's book." Willie was Peter Wagler's son.

Willie's wife Alma, who was seated in the adjoining room, could not see the proceedings. But when the bishop made the announcement that Willie had been chosen, she sank to the floor in a faint. A woman nearby fanned her vigorously, but she didn't come to. Several women quietly lifted Alma off the floor and carried her into a downstairs bedroom.

Meanwhile, the bishop proceeded to ordain Willie. First he asked several questions about the young candidate's commitment. Willie answered each in the affirmative. Then he stood to receive the charge of ordination. Following the giving of the charge, he knelt for a prayer of consecration. All of the ordained men who were present gathered around him.

They laid their hands on him as the bishop prepared to pray. Tobe heard subdued weeping on the women's side of the congregation. The calling to preach was a heavy burden.

• • • •

The Sunday after Willie Wagler's ordination, Tobe and Emma relaxed with some popcorn at the end of the day. Emma reminded Tobe that her brother John was getting married on Tuesday. John was between assignments in Civilian Public Service, having just completed a stint with the fire fighting unit at Glacier National Park. While on break, he and his girlfriend, Mary Plank, had decided to have a quick wedding.

Tobe dipped his hand into the bowl of popcorn. "I guess we won't be going."

Emma shook her head. "I wish we could, but it seems like it would be hard for us to get away. And besides, it will be a Mennonite wedding."

• • • •

Two months after John and Mary's son David was born, Emma realized that she was pregnant again. She waited to tell Tobe until the week before Christmas, just to be certain.

Tobe was happy. "Perhaps we'll have another little boy to help in the shop."

Christmas 1943 passed quickly with little time for rest or celebration at the Stutzman house. Tobe worked on New Year's Day. Not until he was hanging the new calendar did he remember his brother Clarence's birthday. He had turned sixteen so he'd be joining the young folks.

The next week, Tobe was tossing scraps of wood into the wood stove when he heard a buggy outside the shop. He glanced outside to see his brother Ervin in the driveway. Swinging open the door as Ervin approached the shop, Tobe greeted him warmly. Ervin surveyed the piece of furniture Tobe was making. "Who's it for?"

"A lady in town."

Ervin paused and cleared his throat. "Well, did you hear what happened to Clarence last night?"

"No." Tobe raised his eyebrows.

"He's in the hospital with a broken ankle."

"What happened?"

Ervin warmed his hands by the stove. "Well, he was cutting up with the young folks." Tobe paused for a moment to hear what had happened.

12

Setbacks

Ervin stroked the edge of the workbench as he told Tobe the story, "Last night Clarence went to the singing for the first time. Mom told him to come home right afterward. Well, you know how dumb those young simmies can be sometimes."

Tobe had been busy hammering nails into a truck bed. Straightening up to give Ervin his full attention when he heard the word *simmies*, Tobe remembered what it was like to be young and foolish.

"The singing was at Felt Headings. After the singing, Amos Nisly had a date with Mary Yoder. It was a double date with Mary's sister Bertha and Elvin Helmuth. Your Emma's brother Raymond has his eyes on Mary so he was jealous and decided to make trouble. He convinced Clarence and a couple other boys to go with him. The couples were at Dan Yoder's place. The boys sneaked into the house and shone their flashlights around the kitchen. The two couples had gone upstairs, but Raymond discovered a half-filled container of ice cream in the freezer. After finding spoons in the cupboard, the guys ate the ice cream right out of the container."

Tobe shifted impatiently on his feet. "So what happened to Clarence?"

"They decided to go upstairs to find the two couples. They crawled out a window onto the roof and around to the outside of the bedroom window where they thought Amos and Mary and Bertha and Elvin were hiding. Raymond's buddy

Melvin lost his grip on the eaves and fell down on the roof. I guess the frost made it slippery. He grabbed for a hold and got Clarence's legs. Then Clarence lost his grip. They both rolled off the edge. Melvin knew where the steps were so he kinda rolled to one side and dropped beside them. Clarence fell right on the steps. His ankle started to swell almost right away."

Tobe whistled. "*Oh, es iss hesslich!* Whew!"

Ervin continued, "Mary's dad heard the noise and came out to investigate. They decided Clarence should see a doctor, so they drove a buggy over to the Headings place where Fred Nisly was having a date with Mary Headings. They knew he had access to a truck. Fred took Clarence home to pick up Dad, and they went to the hospital. The doctor said the ankle was broken, but it was so swollen they couldn't set it last night. They hope to do it today."

"That's what happens to simmies," Tobe said with exasperation. "They're just lucky Dan didn't get mad at them. It reminds me of what happened out at Benedict Yoder's place."

Ervin shook his head, "I didn't hear about it. What happened there?"

"Well, you know that Benedict Yoders have a couple good-looking daughters, and they've been having lots of dates. Benedict was tired of always having these young guys show up to make trouble so he started getting out of bed and asking them to leave. Finally, he got so tired of the carousing that he decided to do something about it. He figured that if Jesus chased the moneychangers out of the temple with a whip, he could chase the boys out of his house.

"He crawled out his bedroom window while the boys were in another part of the house with their flashlights. He strung a strand of wire across the sidewalk about fourteen inches above the ground from one gatepost to another. Then he crawled back into his bedroom window. He took his razor strop and ran out of the bedroom, yelling at the guys to get out of the house. The boys ran out with the exception of one who hid under the table. Of course as they ran out, they tripped over the wire at the gate and fell on the ground in their Sunday trousers.

"After the boys were gone, Benedict was in bed thinking about what he had done. He started feeling guilty for chasing them with his strap, so he decided to see if they were still around. Listening from behind a tree, he heard them talking about getting revenge. One of the young men said, 'Boy, you should see what I would do if I got hold of him.' So Benedict stepped out from behind the tree and said, 'Here I am. What do you want to do to me?'"

Ervin laughed. "I bet that surprised them."

Tobe grinned. "It sure did. They both apologized for what had happened. After that the boys quit bothering the house when the girls had dates."

"Maybe that's a lesson to remember when Mary Edna grows up," Ervin suggested. "You have to be careful what you do to the boys who come around. Otherwise, you'll just have more trouble."

Tobe stroked his beard. "I suppose so. But for now I've got too much work to do to think about mischievous boys. We have a truck bed I have to finish by tomorrow. We just shipped off the last of those fifty wagon boxes to that new dealer in Nebraska. That's going to be a real good money maker for us. I'm looking for a big check in the mail soon."

"That's good. Is Eddie Conkling still working for you?"

"Yeah, he should be here before long. He doesn't usually get around too early in the morning. I need a good worker like you here. Would you consider it?"

Ervin put on his gloves as he prepared to leave. "Emma and I want to have our own farm. But maybe I could work part time when my farm deferment ends."

"I hope you'll give that some more thought. And when you see Clarence, tell him I hope his ankle gets better soon." Tobe turned back to his work as Ervin walked out the door to his buggy.

Later that day, Tobe heard the snort of a horse outside the shop. He looked up to see his mother walking toward the shop. Anna Stutzman paused at the door, looking again at the new sign Tobe had mounted outside the door: "IF IT IS MADE OF WOOD, WE CAN DO IT."

Tobe stepped out to greet her. "What do you think of my sign?"

"I don't like it."

"What don't you like about it?

"*Es laut wie Hochmut.* It sounds like pride."

"If it's true, it's not bragging," Tobe insisted. Because she hadn't been in the shop for quite awhile, Tobe took his mother for a tour, showing her how he built the truck and wagon beds that were keeping him busy.

He pointed to his helper, crouched underneath one of the finished truck beds. "This is Eddie Conkling. He often does the wiring for me. He drives for me too."

Ed scrambled out from underneath his project and offered his hand. "Hello, Ma'am." He flashed a wide smile.

"Hello, I'm Tobe's mother."

"Very pleased to meet you. You have a wonderful son. I enjoy working for him."

• • • •

For the next few days, Tobe waited eagerly for the mailman to come by. The check for the large order of wagon boxes should come any day now. When the letter did arrive, Tobe was deeply disappointed.

"What's the matter?" Emma asked, seeing his glum countenance.

"You know those fifty wagon boxes we sold through that dealer in Nebraska?"

"Yes."

Tobe spoke softly as he sensed the anxiety in Emma's voice. "Well, as it turns out, he's rejecting the whole lot. He says we had an agreement to assemble them with screws. That's how he advertised them to the public. We put them together with nails because they go together a lot faster that way."

Emma let out a long, deep sigh. "What are we going to do?"

Tobe tried to sound optimistic. "I guess we'll sell them to someone else. I'm sure we can still make a little money on them."

Emma bit her lip as Tobe went back out to the shop. Tobe worked later than usual that night.

The next morning, Emma heard the lid rattle on the chamber pot while the nearly full moon was still suspended above the western horizon. She tucked her head under the covers as Tobe dressed and went outside. It was much too early to get up.

When Tobe came in from milking, he told Emma he'd decided to sell the wagon boxes to another dealer at cost. It would be too much hassle to have them shipped back to the shop.

Emma sighed.

As they ate breakfast, Tobe said, "I've been thinking. What if I asked Ervin Miller to get into the business with me?"

"You could ask him to see what he'd say." Emma knew that Tobe would probably get along well with Ervin. They had both grown up in Thomas, Oklahoma, and married girls from Hutchinson. Ervin and Mary's wedding came less than a year after Tobe and Emma's. Ervin's hard-working manner reflected quiet ambition.

"I'm going to invite him over to look around," Tobe declared.

At Tobe's invitation, Ervin came by the next day. Tobe walked through the shop with him, showing him the various projects in development.

Tobe popped the question as they paused to warm their hands by the wood stove. "Ervin, I think you'd be just the right person to work with me to expand this business. Why don't you go into partnership with me? There's no limit to how big this company could grow. You could be the manager and I could work with production and sales."

Ervin's eyebrows crinkled. "Well, I'd have to think about it and talk it over with Mary. She likes the farm."

"You could still farm on the side. This would keep you busy in the winter."

Ervin squinted his eyes and stroked his thin beard. "I'll have to give it some thought."

"Sure, take your time." Tobe sensed that Ervin would decline if he was pushed any harder.

When Ervin left, Tobe worked on the accounts. He had been planning for the big check from the wagon boxes. Now he had to find some way to pay an overdue lumber bill. When he headed back to the shop, he saw Eddie relaxing in a chair. Tobe motioned toward him with his hand. "*Dapper schwind.* Quick, hurry! Your time is my time. If you're not working, you're stealing my money."

Eddie jumped to his feet. He pointed toward the truck bed. "Well, this one's almost finished. After I get the lights hooked up, all she needs is the pin striping. I guess you'll do that." He crawled under the truck bed and resumed his work.

Tobe gripped the striping bottle and unscrewed the lid to find only a little paint. He poured in some white paint, added a bit of paint thinner, and shook the bottle well. Then, using an edge guide, he ran the striping roller along the stakes and

187

frame of the truck. The thin white stripes stood in contrast to the red body paint.

Eddie watched as Tobe finished. "It looks real good."

"Thanks. They're going to pick it up tonight. By the way, can you drive me out west of town tomorrow? I have some work to do on cabinets there."

"Sure can. What time?"

"How about seven o'clock in the morning? It'll take the whole day."

"Will do."

The next morning, Tobe wrote out instructions for his helpers as he waited for Eddie to arrive. He glanced up as Eddie's 1937 Ford truck pulled into the yard. The black half-ton pickup glistened in the morning sun. Tobe grabbed a box of tools and swung them into the back of the truck. Eddie's son, Dale, scooted to the middle as Tobe jumped in. "The truck's looking good."

"Yep. I waxed her last evening."

"Where'd you get those numbers on your front grill?" Tobe asked as Eddie pulled out of the driveway.

"I took them off an old telephone pole. Don't they look good shined up?"

"Sure do."

They had traveled about half an hour when Tobe pulled a bunch of celery out of a paper bag. He held a stalk out to Eddie. "Want some?" Tobe often brought stalks of celery to eat along with peanuts.

"Sure, thanks." Eddie broke off a piece.

• • • •

The sun had set by the time they finished the day's work and started for home. About halfway through the trip, Eddie looked over at Tobe, "You tell Emma I liked those homemade sandwiches and orange juice we had for lunch." When Tobe

188

didn't respond, Eddie glanced over. He squinted for a better look, then asked, "Where's Dale?"

He reached over to shake Tobe awake and sighed with relief. Dale was there all right. He was leaning on Tobe's chest, his face hidden under Tobe's long beard as both of them slept.

Eddie dropped off Tobe at the shop. As Tobe turned to get out, he said, "How about coming by with the stock racks in the morning?"

"Okay, I'll be here," Eddie said.

The next morning Tobe was assembling materials for a new truck bed when Eddie pulled into the yard, stock racks securely fastened to his pickup. Eddie parked the truck and got out.

Tobe pointed toward the barn and said, "Just back her up to the corral there."

"What for? What are you hauling?"

"My cow. I'm going to sell her at the sale today."

"How come?"

"I need some cash. I'm getting too far behind on my payments to you."

"Heck, no. No way are you going to sell that cow. Your children need the milk to drink. I'm not worried about getting the money."

Tobe hesitated. He started to reply, then paused as a small fighter plane roared overhead on its way to the Yoder air base. "Well, okay, if you can wait for the money."

"I can wait. No problem."

The next day Tobe pondered his debt situation as he and Eddie worked side by side on a truck bed. "Eddie?"

"Yeah."

"How about if we work out a trade for what I owe you? I could make you a set of kitchen cabinets."

"That sounds good. I'd have to ask my wife though."

"You ask her. If she says 'yes,' we'll make a deal."

The next morning Eddie came beaming into the shop. "Margaret says she'd be happy to get new cabinets."

It was several months before Tobe had time to build the cabinets at Eddie's home. Margaret Conkling watched with fascination as Tobe fastened the last of the doors onto the fronts of the cabinets. He stepped back to examine his work.

"Will those shelves hold the weight of all my dishes?" Doubt was evident in her voice.

Tobe reached up and hung on the cabinet with his feet dangling. "How's that?"

"That's good." Margaret grinned widely.

The months slipped by as Tobe looked for shop workers. With two young children and a third on the way, Emma was too busy to help in the shop. Both Ervin Miller and Emma's brother John had turned down Tobe's invitation to partnership, so Tobe began looking for someone to run day-to-day operations. Should he ask Clarence? But their mother's rheumatism was so bad she depended on Clarence to help with the housework. Would he be responsible enough?

Clarence loved practical jokes. Along with Emma's brother Raymond and some other boys, Clarence had gotten involved in more mischief, this time around Halloween at Will Yutzy's expense. Or at least that was their plan. It began when one of the boys suggested that they push over the outhouse. "Let's run and hit it high. We'll be able to push it right over."

Another yelled, "One, two, three, go." The group ran toward the outdoor toilet, their eyes well accustomed to the darkness. But they failed to see that Will had prepared for pranksters by moving his outhouse three feet off its base. The boys ran headlong into the hole, carefully covered with a thin layer of brush.

Cursing their luck, they tried to wipe the muck off their boots. "We'll get him back," one of them threatened. "Let's take the wheels off his manure spreader."

It wasn't the first time this sort of thing happened at Halloween in the Kansas Amish community. A favorite trick was taking the wheels off a buggy and remounting them after sticking the shafts through a fence. After their outhouse experience, Clarence and his friends decided to remove the wheels from Will Yutzy's manure spreader. High on their success, they plotted more mischief.

"How about doing something at Noah Nisly's place?"

"Yeah, let's go."

They rode their horses through the darkness to the Nisly farmstead. There they pulled pieces of farm equipment from the shed and set them in the driveway until it was thoroughly blocked.

"Let's put a buggy up on top of the barn," someone suggested. "I'll go up there and help pull." A couple of boys tied their lariats together and tossed them over the roof of the barn. Two others scrambled onto the roof. With help from below, they drew a buggy up to the peak and left it there with a pair of wheels on each side of the ridge.

Still not satisfied, they explored the inside of the barn with their flashlights. "Hey, let's put these saddles on the cows."

"I wish I could see Noah's face when he sees these cows."

"Yeah, I wish I could see it when he finds the buggy on top of the barn."

"He'll never know who did it," someone said as the group sauntered out the farm lane on their horses.

Tobe and his workers heard about the pranks the next day. Such stories always made their way around the rural neighborhood, but Tobe was surprised several weeks later when Clarence confessed his wrongdoing to the church at a council meeting preceding the communion service. Clarence, it seemed to Tobe, was committed to living with a clear conscience. That might make him a good shop manager someday. Meanwhile, he kept looking for part-time workers.

Many of his potential helpers were restricted by farm deferments. Conscientious objectors were not required to go off to war, but they were limited to farm jobs. The ongoing conflict in Europe and the Pacific meant that Tobe's brother Ervin was still not available, nor was Emma's brother Fred.

The war also meant that some shop supplies were difficult to come by, particularly metal parts. And Emma complained that food was being rationed.

"Sugar rations got cut by twenty-five percent," Emma fretted one day in early spring, 1945.

"There must be a very short supply," Tobe reasoned.

"I'm just worried we won't have enough sugar for canning this summer," Emma countered.

"Well, we've always made it so far."

Emma was so frugal government rationing rarely affected her buying habits, but the limits on sugar, shoes, and even meat and cheese bothered her. Rationing was a constant reminder that the nation was at war.

Differences of opinion about the war sometimes brought tensions to the shop. Eddie Conkling wasn't about to become a conscientious objector so he stood at odds with Tobe's convictions. Eddie celebrated July 4 with enthusiasm while Tobe harbored deep reservations about such nationalistic displays. Mostly, they avoided talking about it.

One morning soon after the Fourth, Eddie brought bad news. With uncharacteristically long strides, he headed for the shop door and looked for Tobe.

"Did you hear Willie Wagler got hurt? He's in critical condition in the hospital."

"No!" Tobe looked up. "What happened?" Besides being the new preacher, Willie was a nearby neighbor.

"He got hit in the face with the crank on his tractor. It smashed his cheekbone and tore out his eye."

"Oh my! It must have kicked back."

"Yeah. He stalled the tractor when he was pulling a combine. He got off to crank the tractor and bent over a little too far. When the crank kicked back, it caught him in the face."

"That's too bad. I hope he makes it."

A week later during Sunday morning church services, news came that Willie was worse. Bishop Miller paused in his sermon to lead the congregation in a time of prayer. Tobe swallowed hard as he watched a stream of relatives leave for the hospital to say their "good-byes." A pall settled over the service.

Tobe thought about Willie often as he went about his work the next week. What would it be like to die? What would it be like to be the family who was left behind?

In a miracle of blessing and grace, Willie Wagler defied the doctor's predictions. He rallied and came home less than two weeks after the accident. Within another week, he was back in church. Tobe told Eddie about it. He thought he could see Eddie squirm at bit at the news. Eddie wasn't a committed church member.

The drama of Willie's accident was dwarfed a few weeks later by the news of the U.S. bombing of the Japanese city of Hiroshima followed by a similar story about a bombing in Nagasaki. Although the war seemed far way, Tobe despaired. Would the war ever end?

Then just a week later, Eddie flung open the door to the shop to announce, "The war's over!"

Tobe came from the back room. "What are you yelling about?"

Eddie was wide-eyed. "The war's over. Japan has surrendered!"

Tobe's face lighted up as Eddie continued, "We finally got back at the Japs for Pearl Harbor. Those two atomic bombs did the trick. They realized right then that it wasn't worth fighting any more."

Tobe breathed a deep sigh of relief. He looked forward to the end of rationing and the constant call for new soldiers. Now Ervin and the others could be released from their farm deferments. Maybe life would go back to normal.

• • • •

A few months after the war was over, Tobe's brother Clarence learned that young men were needed as livestock handlers on ships going to Europe. The United Nations Rehabilitation and Reconstruction effort (UNRAR) was trying to replace the livestock killed in the war. Heifer Project supplied UNRAR with cattle and horses for Poland and other nations. The Brethren Service Committee supplied the manpower to care for the livestock en route. Since Clarence had worked with cattle and horses ever since he was a young boy, he longed to travel on one of the ships. He sent in an application then begged his parents to let him go. Tobe couldn't believe his ears. Clarence was only seventeen! Who did he think he was?

Tobe's folks had just moved closer to the center of the settlement into the Claude Park place. They were tired of living at the western margins of the community, too far from others in their church district. The move put them at the north end of the district, just a half mile north and east of Emma's folks. It gave opportunity for the Nisly and Stutzman families to spend time together. Since Emma's brothers and sisters occasionally worked at the shop, the two families came to know each other well.

As new neighbors, Anna watched Emma's two youngest brothers, Raymond and Rufus, till the ground across the road. Raymond sometimes worked without a shirt. Anna told her sons it was shameful to go without a shirt in public. The boys knew it bothered Raymond's mother too. But Mary was philosophical about it. "He'll probably quit it on his own one of these days. It doesn't seem to do much good to say anything about it."

While Anna readily admonished her sons for their misbehavior and youthful experimentation, Mary more often chuckled at hers. Anna confided to Mary that Clarence was talking about sailing to Europe. She and John hadn't said much about the matter, but they were sure that Clarence was both too young and too small to be accepted for the task. At seventeen he weighed only 125 pounds.

A few weeks later, Clarence got a reply to his application from the Brethren Service Committee. He waved the telegram in Anna's face, "Please report to the relief center in New Windsor, Maryland, by December 14. The ship will leave port on January 1." What had seemed almost unthinkable was about to happen.

John and Anna reluctantly agreed to let Clarence go. Tobe figured it must have been the official-looking telegram that convinced them. What would the people at the relief center have said if Clarence's parents had decided he couldn't go? Who would take his place?

Two weeks before Christmas, the Stutzman family stood in the lobby of the train station. John pulled $70 in cash out of his pocket and gave it to Clarence. Clarence's eyes widened. He walked to the ticket counter and told them his destination.

"That will be $35." The ticket agent seemed to be in a hurry.

Clarence handed the man four ten-dollar bills. The agent returned a wrinkled five dollar bill along with the ticket.

Just as Anna was exhorting Clarence to remember his vows to the church, the announcer shouted the arrival of the Santa Fe Express. People surged toward the track. Clarence mounted the train and took his seat. He waved to his parents as the train pulled out of the station then settled back into his seat and reviewed the travel route through Chicago, Baltimore, and on to Hagerstown, Maryland.

Tobe wondered what would happen to his brother. Would Clarence be content to stay in the Amish Church after seeing the world? Would he ever return to work at the shop?

13

Capital Strengths

The next Sunday at church, Tobe overheard some folks gossiping about Clarence. "Did you hear that Clarence Stutzman is going on the cattle boat? Why, he's not even eighteen years old. And he's so small. It's a wonder John and Anna let him go."

Tobe smiled on the inside. It *was* a wonder that Dad let Clarence go. He must have been in a good mood at the time.

On the way home from church, Tobe declared to Emma, "When I was Clarence's age, I wouldn't have had the nerve to ask Dad to go on such a long trip. I was just glad he let me go for several weeks cooking for harvesters in the Panhandle."

"The younger ones often get their way," Emma observed.

Tobe agreed, "Dad only let me go with the harvesters after I'd worked extra hard chopping firewood. On top of that, I gave him all the money I earned."

Emma nodded as she wiped baby Glenn's chin with a washcloth. "That's the way we did it in our family too. Dad kept the money we earned till we turned twenty-one. He did let the boys keep some of the money when they worked on holidays, though."

Clarence returned in the spring, full of stories from his adventure. He told about his experience one evening at Tobe and Emma's dining room table.

"First of all," Clarence explained, "when I got to the Brethren Service headquarters in Maryland, I found out I wasn't old enough to get the Merchant Marine card I needed to board the ship. I had to wait till I was eighteen, the day before the ship left!"

Tobe grinned as he dipped his hand into a bowl of popcorn. "I'd say that was cutting it a little close."

Clarence chuckled. "Yeah it was. But they put me to work in the warehouse, sorting clothing and other odd jobs. I got my card on my birthday, and we left Baltimore the next day— New Year's Day, 1946. We went down the Chesapeake and then into the Atlantic. I declare, I never saw so much water!"

Emma nodded. "I saw the Pacific Ocean when I was out west."

Clarence continued, "Two days out we had a big storm. I got really sick. The captain told me I could take some whiskey or eat some lemons. I took the lemons. That helped. That captain was tough as nails. If he'd told us to jump into the ocean, we'd have done it. Even when I was sick, he made me drag 100-pound feed bags from the lower deck to the third deck. My muscles got so sore."

Tobe looked over Clarence's small frame. "He must have been a slave driver. But it looks like you grew."

"I did," Clarence said. "But I think it comes from leaning so far over the rail to vomit."

They all laughed.

"What unusual things did you see in Europe?" Tobe asked.

"One of the scariest things we saw was a floating mine, the kind that blows up ships. It was left over from the war. We steered way around it.

"The other thing was the concentration camps and the battlefields. We got to ride around in an old Army truck with a canvas on the back. We drove through military dumps and concentration camps. We saw some of the ovens where the Nazis burned human bodies."

Tobe shivered.

"We drove around one of the battlefields," Clarence said. "Dead bodies of German soldiers were still lying frozen on the ground. There were huge piles of spent shell casings nearby."

Clarence reached into his pocket and laid a belt buckle onto the table. "I cut this off one of the bodies." Tobe picked it up and rubbed it with his finger. The words engraved on the buckle were familiar, *"Gott mit uns,* God is with us."

"That's what it says on our wall motto at home," Clarence explained. "I guess the Germans thought God was on their side. We thought God was on ours. It makes you wonder."

Tobe agreed. "It does make you wonder."

"Anyhow," Clarence said, "I'm keeping the buckle as a souvenir. I picked up some other things too. I found a helmet with bullet holes on both sides. I could see that a bullet had gone in one side and out the other. I pity the poor guy who was wearing it. I took it and a big shell casing with me. I thought they would look interesting on the shelf in my room. But when I got back to the ship, the cattlemen said I better leave them there. So I left them on the dock.

"But when we got back to Danzig where we first landed, I bought a couple of things from an old peddler. One was a hymnal from the Danzig Mennonite Church. There was also a plate from the church. I figured it would keep the peddler alive for another few days. Those people had a tough time of it. I'm glad to be here instead of there."

"Did you get paid for your work?" Tobe asked.

"Yeah, the cattlemen all got $110 for the trip. But I volunteered two weeks working at the Church of the Brethren headquarters. Then we went on a tour of Washington, D.C. We visited the Capitol building, the Lincoln Memorial, and the White House. Other places too. It was fun."

"I'm glad you're home again," Tobe said. "I need your help in the shop."

"I'll be glad to help," Clarence said. "I'll come in tomorrow morning if Dad lets me."

Tobe was relieved. It would help to have Clarence around when things got busy at the shop. It seemed that it was either feast or famine. At times, orders came pouring in. At other times, not much seemed to be happening.

When things were slow, Tobe looked for other ways to earn money. He was pleased when he got a request to enlarge a basement for some folks in Hutchinson. The next time Eddie Conkling dropped by the shop, Tobe talked to him about it.

"Hey, Eddie, how about helping me do a job in Hutch? There's some folks who want me to enlarge their basement."

"How would you do that? Is there a house on top?"

"Yeah, but we'll just knock out a basement wall and start digging. We'll put a new foundation under that part of the house."

"You want me to haul the dirt with my pickup?"

"No, I know this guy who owns a dump truck and a dirt elevator. We'd make a place for the elevator to come down into the basement. All we have to do is get the dirt onto the elevator. He'll take it from there."

"Sure, I'll help you out. You can ride to town with me in my truck."

"Good. Let's start next Monday."

A couple of weeks later, the basement job stood complete. Tobe talked to Emma about it as she was wiping the lids on the thirty quarts of tomatoes she was canning. "These people were really pleased with the job. I think I might look for more work like that."

"Did you make any money?" Emma asked.

"I think so. And it's not as dirty as shoveling coal."

"A customer was here today wanting to know when his wagon box was going to get done."

"I know. I'll get on it this afternoon. But I wanted to get the basement done first."

Tobe walked toward the shop as Emma carried the tomato jars to the pantry. If he hurried, he could finish the wagon box by the next day.

He had just started the saw when Emma's sister Barbara walked past the double doors of the shop. Her face looked drawn. Was there bad news? Tobe watched as Barbara knocked on the screen door of the house. He saw Emma come to the door with Mary Edna and Perry Lee close behind. The women looked serious as they talked.

Tobe turned off the saw and walked toward the house.

Emma stepped out. "Mom and Dad were in a car accident," she said.

"Oh no! Was anybody hurt?"

"Mom and Dad weren't hurt bad. But Hans Bontrager was killed. He was driving."

Tobe sighed deeply, "Oh no."

"There were six people in the car," Barbara said. "They were coming home from a trip when a tire blew out. Three people were thrown out of the car. They were about a half mile from Clements, Kansas."

"Where are Mom and Dad now?"

"They're home. Both of them are pretty well shaken up."

"I hope we can go to the funeral," Emma said. "It'll be at the Mennonite Church."

Tobe nodded. "We'll go." The Bontragers were Emma's relatives.

Tobe was able to get a couple of wagon boxes finished before the funeral. As he sat waiting for the service to begin, he thought about the many tasks waiting to be done at the shop. It seemed there was never enough time for everything he had planned. Too many interruptions like funerals. Would he ever feel like he was caught up? Or would life always be like this?

He listened as the minister talked about the uncertainty and brevity of life. It reminded him of the motto displayed in Mom's kitchen, "Only one life, 'twill soon be past, only what's done for Christ will last."

Was manufacturing the best thing for him to do for a living? Did it glorify God like farming? Emma was partial to farming as the best way to make a living, but Tobe thought she might change her mind once the shop made good money. Thinking about the shop reminded him that he'd promised to make some cabinets for a neighbor. He'd need to order some supplies the next morning.

Tobe shook his head to rid himself of thoughts about the shop. Why was it so hard to concentrate on the service? It was the same way at church. His mind was often busy with new ideas or the pressures of the past week. Sometimes, he was just too tired to pay attention. It was hard to stay awake. At least he didn't chew gum or clip his fingernails in the service like some of the young people.

It was easier to stay awake when Willie Wagler preached. For one thing, Willie expected people to pay attention. He spoke out against the practice of chewing gum in church. But mostly, he preached interesting sermons. More than the other preachers, Willie used modern-day illustrations to cast light on the biblical text.

Along with his older brother Raymond, Willie had traveled in Europe before World War II. In 1938 they wrote about their experiences in a series of articles for the *Herold der Wahrheit*, a Mennonite church paper. Occasionally, Raymond wrote for the *Sugarcreek Budget*, an Amish newspaper, as well. Raymond Wagler spoke with a breadth of ideas that made Tobe envious.

Tobe often talked to Raymond Wagler about business. He looked up to the native Kansan as a man of integrity who cared deeply about the welfare of others. Tobe listened more readily to Raymond's counsel than that of anyone else in the church.

It wasn't long before Tobe lost another day of work at the shop. Emma's brother Fred married Mary Headings. A few weeks later, Tobe and Emma stopped by to visit the newlyweds. Fred showed them the hutch they had been given for a wedding gift.

Tobe rubbed his hand on the varnished surface, then stepped back to look it over. "That piece isn't put on straight," he said, pointing toward the decorative wooden piece at the top and center of the hutch.

Fred stood back and took a careful look. "I guess you're right. No one noticed that before. You have a good eye."

The next few weeks ushered in another new year. The Stutzman family watched from the breakfast table as Emma put up the new 1947 wall calendar from the Hutchinson lumber company.

Emma told Tobe that she was expecting another baby. Tobe was happy. Maybe they would have another girl. Mary Edna would be five years old in April.

By springtime enough orders were coming in for truck beds that Tobe hired Melvin Yoder to work in the shop. He showed the young man how to use the shop equipment, particularly the large table saw. Tobe started up the big saw and laid a piece of oak on the table.

"Watch this," he said, as he stepped on the foot pedal. A large blade emerged from the table and sliced off the end of the oak piece.

"Boy, that thing really cuts," Melvin said as he took a step back.

"Yep, and you can lock the blade to rip lumber." Tobe pointed to the pile. "You can see we have 6 x 10s, 6 x 6s, 6 x 8s, and so on. Most of it is oak. We use oak for truck bed stakes and fir for the sides and floor. The best floors are made of grain-edged, tongue-and-groove fir. It doesn't splinter as easily. Sometimes we use yellow pine. It's cheaper.

"Now let me show you how we fasten the stakes to the side boards." Tobe fired up the Briggs and Stratton engine that was hooked to a flexible drill shaft. "It sure beats using a hand drill when you have dozens of holes to drill for one wagon box or truck bed."

Melvin nodded and drilled a couple of holes while Tobe watched. Tobe looked over Melvin's shoulder several times that day; Melvin seemed to catch on very quickly.

A few days later, Tobe watched as one of his creditors talked to Melvin about his work. Should he interrupt? He stepped closer so he could overhear what was being said.

"You should countersink the bolts so they won't stick out past the stake," Jake was saying.

Melvin objected. "That isn't the way I was told to do it. Besides, that would take a lot of extra work."

Tobe caught Melvin's eye and winked. Melvin took a deep breath. Soon Jake stepped outside to look at a finished bed that had just been painted. Melvin stepped up to Tobe.

"What right does that guy have to tell us how to make truck beds?" Melvin asked. "He wants the bolts countersunk. That would take a lot of extra time."

Tobe knew they had to take Jake seriously. "He's financing these so we need to go along with it. Just do what he says for now."

Melvin shrugged and went back to work.

Tobe moved toward the door. "I'll be back in a little while," he told Melvin. "I'm heading for town. I need to order some supplies."

Tobe walked to the highway and put up his thumb. A truck driver soon stopped. "Where you heading?"

"Hutch."

"Hop in. I'm going that way."

The driver dropped him off at the White Lumber Company. Tobe placed an order before following the yard worker to the warehouse.

"Let's see. You ordered a ten-foot 2 x 12," the yard worker said. "We only have fourteen-footers. I'll need to cut it to length. You'll have to wait while I get my carpenter's square back at the office."

"I'll cut it square," Tobe said.

"Oh no, we'll need to use a square so the next customer will have a good end left."

"If you let me have that saw, I can cut it square without using a square."

"No," the worker said, "I'll get the square." He laid down the handsaw and walked toward the office.

Tobe watched him go. Should he do it? Yes, he'd cut the board himself. If the man gave him too much trouble, he'd buy the whole board. He laid the board up to an edge and picked up the saw. He carefully sighted across then with a few quick strokes he cut off four feet.

The yard worker returned shortly and looked for his pencil mark on the board. "Oh, I see you've already cut it." He laid the square against the edge. "Well, it looks like you got it square."

The man picked up the board and walked toward the office without a word. Tobe grinned to himself. People just didn't realize how accurately he could cut a board.

Tobe told Melvin about it when he got back. Melvin laughed. "You can't really blame the man," he said. "Not many people who can cut a board as straight as you can. Most of us need tools. We can't just eyeball it the way you do."

Emma's brother Raymond happened to be in the shop, and he stepped into the conversation. "Hey Melvin, did you hear about the time when Tobe told Kenneth Tuxhorn his shed wasn't straight?"

"No," Melvin said.

"He had just built a new shed up the road from where Tobe's folks lived," Raymond said. "Tobe came to see it. When Tobe looked over the end wall, he said, 'It's not plumb.'"

"Kenneth said, 'Of course it's plumb. It was just built.'"

"So what did you do?" Melvin asked Tobe.

"I asked for a level and laid it against the wall. It wasn't plumb. Kenneth looked at it and just said, 'Huh?' I let it go at that."

Raymond continued. "That's like the time when you built kitchen cabinets for Carl Balyer in Hutchinson." He paused. "You tell it," he said to Tobe.

"You know how we do it," Tobe said to Melvin. "We built the cabinets at the shop then hauled them to the house. The final fitting took some trim work around the edges. At the end of the day, I was short one board, that wide piece that connects the cabinets on opposite sides of the kitchen sink.

"I came to work the next morning with the trim board ready to cut to length. Carl was watching me, since he was eager to see the job get done. I got my saw from the tool box, looked at the width of the opening from where I was standing, then cut the board to length without a tape measure. It fit perfectly. You should have seen Carl's face. His mouth was hanging open the whole time I nailed the board into place."

Melvin nodded. "I'll bet it was. There aren't many carpenters who can get by without measuring." He turned to Raymond. "I had to check up on Tobe a couple of times after he put the handles on cabinet doors and drawers. They were centered just right so I don't bother checking any more."

Tobe shrugged his shoulders as Raymond nodded his head in agreement. "Well," Tobe said, "We'll have to stop talking and get back to work. Eldo will be here first thing in the morning to take wagon boxes to Nebraska. We'll need to have this one ready to go."

"I made good progress this morning," Melvin said. "I just have the end gate to finish yet." The false end gates were made to drop down so farmers could shovel corn out the back.

The next morning Eldo Stucky of the Partridge Mill pulled into the driveway as the sun rose above the trees. He had recently bought a tractor trailer to haul corn down from Nebraska for milling so Tobe hired him to deliver wagon boxes on the way up. In a matter of minutes, Tobe and he had the wagon boxes loaded and ready for the trip. Emma bid Tobe good-bye as she handed him the lunch she had prepared.

"Are you finding good help in the shop these days?" Eldo asked.

"Yeah, the Yoder brothers are doing real good. Melvin worked for me first. Now I've hired his brother Mervin too. You've probably seen their bicycles out front. They ride them to work."

"The wagon boxes look good," Eldo said. "I'm glad they're selling well."

They had gone just a little further when Tobe broke out a bag of peanuts. "Want some?" He offered a handful to his friend.

"Nope. I love 'em, but they don't agree with me health-wise."

"Too bad."

Tobe snacked on the nuts most of the way. By the time they arrived at their destination, Tobe had consumed a pound.

When they returned from the short delivery trip, Emma had good news, "The sugar rationing has ended." Tobe was relieved. It was nearly a year since the War had ended in the Pacific. Emma would need lots of sugar to can fruits and pickles for their growing family. The baby was due to come in September.

Edith Ann was born on schedule. But Tobe knew that something was wrong by the doctor's tone of voice when he came to the fathers' waiting room, "Your wife had some difficulty this time."

"What's wrong?"

The doctor looked grave. "It's a problem we call *placenta previa*. It means she delivered the afterbirth before the baby. We tried to push it back in but couldn't. We ended up hurrying the birth with forceps. I'm afraid your little girl didn't get enough oxygen. Her skin was quite blue when she was born."

Tobe swallowed hard. "Will she be normal?"

The doctor paused. "That's hard to predict. We'll have to wait and see."

During the first few months after Edith's birth, Tobe didn't notice much that was different except that one eye seemed out of focus. Edith was a beautiful child.

Tobe didn't see too much need to be concerned although he sensed that Emma was worried. She didn't say much but seemed to be lost in thought at times.

It didn't seem right to complain. There were so many things to be thankful for. The war was over. The rationing had ended. And Tobe was benefiting from some of the nation's war castaways.

The Air Force barracks at Salina was slated for demolition so Tobe's neighbor, Fred Williams, bought a couple of them to use for lumber on a new dairy barn. He contracted with Tobe to help him take them down in exchange for free lumber. Tobe worked with a crew of Amish men to tear down the barracks. Later, he told his children about the job.

"Dad, what are barracks?" Mary Edna asked.

"They're big long houses where soldiers live."

"Did the soldiers move to another house?"

"Yes, the soldiers all went home to their own houses. Now that the war is over, they don't need the barracks anymore."

Tobe hired Eddie Conkling to provide transportation to and from the demolition site. On the way up one morning,

Eddie asked Tobe in his jovial manner, "Well, Tobe, how are things goin'?"

Tobe laughed. "My two boys were busy yesterday. While we were up here, they were working at home. I got home last night to find out they had painted my whole workbench red!"

"How old are they?"

"Perry Lee's four. Glenn Wayne's three."

Eddie whistled. "They're startin' young, ain't they?"

"Yeah, they'll soon be taking your painting job, Eddie," Tobe quipped.

Tobe salvaged nearly a tractor-trailer load of lumber from the demolition project. Most of the pieces were 2 x 4s that were three to four feet long. Back at the shop, he converted them into pickets by sawing the boards into four pieces and rounding one end of each piece with a band saw. Why waste usable material?

When the salvage work was done, Tobe asked Eddie to take him on a couple of short sales trips. One morning they struck out west on Route 61 to market a pickup load of wooden hobby horses. As they drove through small towns in western Kansas, Tobe watched for prospective buyers.

Spying a large hardware store, Tobe asked Eddie to pull up to the front of the building. He went inside to introduce himself while Eddie stayed in the truck. The proprietor said he wasn't interested in wooden products, but he finally agreed to come look at them. Tobe offered him a good price for buying in quantity, and the guy bought the whole lot.

Tobe was exultant. "It's not hard to sell these things if you just get out and do it."

Several weeks later, Tobe and Eddie took another marketing trip. Looking for a repeat sale, Tobe headed back to the store where he had made the hobby horse deal. Eagerly, he walked into the large hardware supply store. One look at the proprietor told him something was wrong.

"I'm Tobe Stutzman."

"I remember you."

"How have the hobby horses sold?"

"I've not sold a single one."

"That's too bad. You must not be a very good salesman."

When the proprietor's face turned dark, Tobe dismissed himself and left. Back in the truck, he told Eddie, "I think we better not come back here for awhile. He's not too happy with us."

"Gotcha."

They passed most of the day making new sales or checking up on previous accounts. As they rode home, Tobe felt a weariness creep over his frame. He lapsed into silence. Eddie glanced over to see him sleeping, his head leaning against the door frame. Tobe didn't wake up until they bounced over the railroad tracks near his home. He looked up. "Oh, we're here already?"

"Yep."

Tobe grabbed his lunch box and stepped out of the truck then waved to Eddie as he went out the driveway. He took a quick look around the shop, then went to the house to tell Emma about his day.

• • • •

As the fall of 1947 turned into winter, Tobe dreamed of building a bigger shop to expand. The Brownlee Place was not for sale. Where could he get land or buildings that fit his needs? The shop really should be along a main road.

Eventually, Tobe's eyes lit on a place that seemed to fit the bill perfectly. Menny Yoder owned a farm that bordered Route 61, just two miles east of the Brownlee Place. He could move his current shop to that location. In fact, they could build a house there as well. All Tobe had to do was convince Menny to sell.

14

Gaining Ground

One cold morning early that winter, Tobe approached Menny about selling some land bordering Highway 61. Menny was reluctant at first. But several weeks later, Tobe's persistence paid off, and Menny agreed to sell two acres. Tobe was exuberant as he reported the news to Emma.

"*Mir tsele unser eegner Blatz hawwa!* We're going to have our own place! Now we can build a decent house and have a good business right next to the highway!"

Emma did not look happy.

Tobe's face turned sober. "Don't you think it will help the business?"

She pursed her lips. "I suppose so. But how can we afford it?"

"We'll do it somehow. I can shovel coal or dig out basements for some quick cash. Let's plan to move sometime next summer."

In Tobe's mind, that was the end of the conversation. He went out to the shop where Mervin Yoder was rebuilding the gas engine. "How's it going?"

"I'll be done with this by late afternoon. I had trouble getting the new rings on these pistons yesterday. But Bus Oberg saw the trouble I was having. He brought me this ring compressor. That did the trick. The pistons went in slick."

"Good. We'll need that engine running soon. We have work lined up."

"I'll do my best."

Tobe watched as Mervin tightened a bolt on the engine head. Should he tell him the news about the property agreement? Why not?

"I'm going to be moving my business," Tobe told Mervin.

Mervin's eyes widened. "Where to?"

"I'm buying some ground from your uncle Menny two miles east of here, on the south side of the 61 highway."

"When will you move?"

"Sometime next summer."

"That should be a good place to have the business," Mervin said, as he tightened a bolt on the engine.

Over the next few weeks, Tobe was consumed with thoughts about the new shop. Being along the main road would make the shop much more visible. The business could really grow and expand. He could even set up a lighted sign if the church would allow it. Having electricity in the shop would really help the business. It just didn't seem right that he needed to get rid of his wind generator for the sake of peace in the church.

Tobe hoped some of these rules would change. There were rumors floating around the neighborhood about plans to start a more progressive church sometime next summer. Maybe he could join the new church. But what would Emma say?

The rumors ran wild when guest preachers Raymond Byler and Nevin Bender visited the area in mid January. Both were leaders in the Conservative Amish Mennonite Conference. They explained that they had come to Kansas at the request of several young families in the church. They met with Bishop Harry Diener at the Yoder Mennonite Church and Bishops Jake Miller, Levi Helmuth, and John D. Yoder of the Old Order churches.

News soon spread that the ministers were indeed exploring the possibility of starting a new congregation in the

Hutchinson community. It would offer a more progressive alternative to the Amish Church. The new fellowship would likely have services in English, require less traditional dress patterns, and permit modern conveniences such as cars and electricity, not to mention the use of rubber tires on tractors.

Talk about the new church heightened the tensions between the two Amish church districts. Those in the west district pressed for change. The east district held back. Tobe couldn't help wondering if the new church would have been formed if the two districts could have agreed on the *Ordnung*.

Tobe talked to Emma about the possibility of joining the new church.

Emma looked pained. "What would our folks think? You know they aren't happy that John left."

Tobe knew Emma was worried about what her parents thought so he dropped the discussion for the time being. There would be plenty of time to decide later on. Now was the time to concentrate on getting together the money to purchase the new property. He had just agreed to enlarge another basement.

Tobe was thinking about the down payment as he squeezed his muscular frame through the small opening he had made in the foundation. He pulled his pick and shovel in after him. Crammed for elbow room, he plied his pick at the hard dirt. Soon there was enough room for the head of a dirt elevator to protrude through the opening. Tobe scooped the loosened dirt into the elevator which lifted it to a waiting truck. Before long, there was enough room for Tobe to stand up. Melvin Yoder joined him as the space expanded to make room to swing two shovels.

Eddie Conkling stepped outside to watch as dirt clods emptied into the dump truck.

After an hour of hard shoveling, all of the workers paused for a bit of rest. Tobe poked around at some stubborn dirt clods. Melvin shook his head as he watched Tobe work. "You can really work fast."

"Yep," Eddie said, "Nobody can move dirt like Tobe."

"No wonder Will Miller liked you as a worker," Melvin commented.

Tobe leaned on his shovel and wiped his forehead. "Yeah, I don't think he realized how lucky he was."

"How's that?"

"I worked really hard for him. But regardless how much I got done, it wasn't enough. I remember one morning when he planned to go to town. He talked about the farm work we had to do and mentioned something that needed to get fixed. I worked like two people to get all of it done while he was in town. When he came home, he said it was too bad more work didn't get done."

Melvin shook his head.

Tobe continued. "Will was a pusher. One time we were riding in a wagon with a team of horses. A train was coming so he pushed them to beat it. We got over the tracks just in time. When I looked back, the conductor was shaking his head at us. He tipped his head back and put his hand up like he had a bottle. I think he was telling Will he must have been drinking."

The men all shook their heads as Tobe continued, "He was always in a hurry. If someone came to visit, he wouldn't take much time to talk. He'd say, 'I'm not getting my work done and I'm just taking your time.' People got the hint."

Tobe reached for a jug of water. "I'm thirsty."

"It's too bad we have to do this basement now," Melvin said. "We have work back in the shop that should be done."

"That's true," Tobe said. "But this is a way to make some quick cash."

"Did you give him a price on this, or are we doing this by the hour?"

"I gave him a price. It was probably a little low. But people are afraid to pay by the hour. They think we'll poke around instead of working. That means the harder we work, the more money we make. So, let's get back to work," Tobe said, as he picked up his shovel and began flailing dirt into the elevator.

They finished the basement at the end of the week. On Monday he was back in the shop trying to catch up with orders. He had just opened the doors for business when a stranger walked in. When he went to pay for a small item, he pulled a huge roll of cash from his pocket. Tobe's eyes bulged. After the man left, he walked to where Melvin was working.

"Did you see that huge roll of cash?"

"Yeah, he was really showing it off."

"There must be something we could sell to that man. There's no reason he needs all that cash in his pocket."

Tobe could have used that cash to pay his workers. As it was, he couldn't always pay the Yoder brothers on time. But they seemed content to wait for their pay until after a truck bed was sold. They were convinced that eventually he would pay them.

The winter wheat was just forming heads when a number of large-scale farmers from the nearby town of Inman ordered truck beds. Of course, they wanted them in time for the harvest, just a few weeks away.

Tobe couldn't turn down such a good offer even if the time frame seemed unrealistic. If he got the job, he could pay all his workers right up to date. But just as they started on the big order, Melvin sprained his ankle so badly that he couldn't work. How were they to get these truck beds finished?

Tobe kept his eye on the ripening wheat crop. Would they make it in time? The buyers were so impatient that they offered to help finish making the beds. Tobe said they could help if Melvin gave direction. So Melvin stood on crutches and showed the men how to put the beds together. Tobe breathed a deep sigh of relief when the last of the beds was finished in the nick of time. The wheat was ready for harvest.

During the harvest season, Tobe made preparations to move his business to the new property. He moved back and forth between the old and new sites, finishing up projects at the Brownlee Place while preparing the new place for the move.

It was a hot morning in July when Tobe poured the concrete slab for the new shop. He waited impatiently for Melvin and Mervin to arrive. Since they were late, Tobe started the work by himself, mixing and pouring concrete from the portable mixer. The temperature rose along with the sun, and Tobe noticed with some consternation that the concrete was setting up very quickly in the heat.

"Perhaps a bit of water will slow it down," Tobe said aloud to himself. He splashed water on the uneven surface and stroked his trowel across the lumps and ridges. Tobe was working frantically to smooth out the surface when the two Yoder brothers rode their bicycles up to the site. "It looks like you're having trouble," Melvin offered.

Tobe was upset. "I think it got away from me."

"What are you going to do?"

"Nothing for now. I guess later on, if we think it's too bad, we can pour more concrete on top to smooth it out."

The men were finishing up the job when Tobe's mother stopped by.

"Hi, Mom," Tobe said. "I hear you bought a place in Whiteside." His parents would live only two miles northeast.

"Yes. We'll be moving in a few weeks."

Tobe nodded his approval. "It'll be nice to have you so close by." His face brightened. "Maybe Dad could work for me in the new shop now that he won't be farming any more."

"Maybe he could." She paused. "When will you start building the house?"

"As soon as I get the shop moved and into production."

Later that week, Tobe borrowed his next-door neighbor's tractor for the moving job. They drove the green Oliver into the center of the empty shop early in the morning. To get the building off its foundation, Tobe used a number of house jacks. Soon the whole building was suspended on the jacks. By that time, several men had arrived to help. They inserted four full-length telephone poles under the building that reached from one end to the other. The tractor stood in between the two sets of poles. Then they put jacks under the poles. The whole assembly creaked upward.

When the poles were high enough, the men pushed a wagon running gear under each end of the poles. They hitched the tractor to the running gears and started to pull. The tractor and its carriage lurched forward.

Tobe guided the tractor slowly around to the sharply pitched driveway. Just as he was beginning to turn onto the road, one corner of the building scraped the ground. Tobe stopped. He would need to make an adjustment or risk having the building slide off the running gear.

He was pondering the situation when the Yoder brothers arrived at 8 a.m., their usual starting time. "You must have gotten up before the sun this morning," they quipped.

"Yeah, I wanted to get an early start."

"Looks like you're having a bit of a problem."

"Yeah, why don't you get a jack under that end over there? As soon as the wagon wheel gets out of that low place, we'll be on our way."

Thirty minutes later the team of men had made the turn out of the driveway and headed south. Interested onlookers gathered to watch. Only the lower part of the tractor wheels were visible under the sides of the raised building. The lugs pounded the hardened road surface as the building moved south toward the main highway.

As they crossed over the railroad tracks, the load shifted to one side and got stuck on the tracks. Eddie Conkling immediately yelled at Tobe. "Did you tell the railroad that you'll be crossing here?"

"No, if a train comes, we'll just have to try to get out of the way." Tobe wasn't worried. From years of observation, he knew that no train was due for another hour and a half. It took about an hour to get the building off the track. Then they crossed the angle highway and continued on the gravel road. Mervin went ahead to redirect oncoming traffic because the shop took up the whole width of the road. All went well as they traveled south to the intersection, took a wide turn, then headed east.

The last leg took them back north. Just south of their destination, they came to a narrow bridge. The crew worked quickly to remove the bridge's side barriers so they could get through. It was afternoon by the time they pulled onto the new site. After some careful maneuvering, they got the building onto the concrete slab. Most of the men went home while Tobe anchored the shop to the concrete slab. High winds could move a building if it wasn't anchored properly.

A few days later, Tobe borrowed a tractor and a slip to dig the hole for his basement house. Then he started building the wooden forms for the walls. To speed up the project, he decided to finish building the forms while others poured concrete. He sent the two Yoder brothers to borrow another concrete mixer from Will Miller and to recruit help in the neighborhood. By evening they had two mixers and several helpers lined up to work. The gasoline-powered mixers could mix about a wheelbarrow load of concrete at a time.

Will usually charged five cents per mix to loan out his mixer, but Tobe wasn't about to pay for the use of it. Will had told him the mixer was paid for. Why should he charge people to use it? It just wasn't right.

John B. Yoder and John Helmuth finished building the wooden forms while Tobe supervised the concrete work. By late evening, they had finished the concrete. Tobe surveyed the project with satisfaction. "We did a lot of work today."

Tobe was driving back to the Brownlee place when he noticed that the wind was rising from the southwest. A long low front was approaching. Tobe clucked to the horse and pulled down his hat. As Tobe turned into the driveway, he heard thunder in the distance. Glancing toward the west, he saw dark blue clouds accented by flashes of lightning. Up to five different bolts snaked out of the sky at the same time. A fresh breeze stirred up dust as clouds swirled overhead.

The breeze turned to a gale as Tobe went about his chores. Tumbleweeds scurried along in the wind. Fine dust filled the air. The tall weeds along the road were bent down almost double, their tips nearly brushing the ground. The windmill ran at a dizzy speed.

Tobe and Emma had just latched the windows when rain began to pour. It came in a deluge, sheets of rain pounding the windows. The panes rattled noisily.

Tobe flinched as he heard tin ripping off the shed roof. A ragged piece crashed against the side of the barn. A tree creaked, then ripped apart as a huge branch crashed to the ground. The house shuddered on its foundation as the storm unleashed its full fury. Tobe listened anxiously as the skies dumped rain. Would it hurt the concrete?

In the morning he pulled on his clothing and checked the rain gauge. Four inches! He milked the cow and gulped down his breakfast, then headed for the new place. Water and mud had poured down the slope into the hole, pressing hard against the new concrete. Tobe was moping over the scene when Melvin arrived to help take off the forms. Melvin was sympathetic. "*Mir hen zu viel Rege ghat letscht Nacht.* We had too much rain last night."

"We sure did," Tobe replied. "It looks like the mud pushed the wall in here on the south side."

Melvin sighted the wall. "Can we straighten it out?"

"I'm afraid not. The concrete's set up now." Tobe spoke in a low voice. "We should have put more reinforcement in the wall or more bracing on the inside. But how could we have known that it was going to rain like this?"

"There's water in the basement too. I wonder how deep it is?"

Tobe grabbed a 2 x 4 and plunged it into the water. He drew it out and looked at the water mark. "About two feet. We'll need to get it out of there. I'll find a pump and let you start pumping it out. It'll take a while."

They found a small pump and started emptying the basement. As the gasoline engine chugged away, Tobe grumbled to himself. Of all the times to get a big rain. Why did it have to come when the basement walls were just poured?

Later that morning, Tobe's Uncle Henry Stutzman came by in his buggy. Henry was the youngest of John Stutzman's brothers. He lived just up the road from John's new place in Whiteside. "The storm was bad up our way. It took the roof off your parents' house, and our basement has five feet of water. Do you think you can come help?"

"I'll get up there as soon as we're finished here. Is everyone okay?" Henry assured Tobe that no one was hurt, and by early afternoon Tobe loaded up the pump and drove to the scene. Henry's wife Lydia met him. Tobe started the pump and showed Henry how to keep it going.

As water spewed out of the basement, Lydia told of the terror they had experienced the evening before. "Henry had just come home with the tractor when that big cloud came in from the west. It was pouring heavy rain when we heard a knock at the door. It was one of the workers on the railroad, looking for a phone. The railroad cars where the workers live had blown off the side track onto the main track. We were all worried that a train would come along and hit them. We told him we didn't have a phone. The neighbor's phone was knocked out by the storm. Some Amish boys brought flashlights to stop the train. It was going pretty slow because of the storm. The train was stuck there until 4:00 o'clock this morning."

"It's good they got it stopped. Otherwise it might have derailed."

"Yes, we thanked God for his protection through the whole storm. The wind was so strong that we thought the whole house was going to lift off the foundation. The boys and I knelt and prayed in the kitchen, asking God to protect us. We heard a big bang. The north door blew in and hit the other side of the room. The windows in that room all broke out, as well as in our east bedroom. Our curtains ended up in the trees and out by the railroad. The kitchen was the only safe place. The Lord answered our prayer."

Lydia paused to get her breath. "When we finally went to bed, we heard the canning jars gurgling as they sank into the water in the basement. I'm so glad you can clean it out today. But you better get on up to your folks."

Tobe and his father surveyed the damage. It seemed so unfair to lose part of the roof before they had even moved into the house.

The storm was the main topic of conversation at the shop that week. Eddie sympathized with Tobe, "Your folks really took a beating. Their roof blew off before they ever got to move into their house. The storm really didn't affect us much in Partridge. I heard it was only about three miles wide—one mile west of Whiteside and two miles east. The radio reported lots of storm damage. Trees, roofs, and outbuildings are down. Because it rained so hard, they're calling it a 'hurricane on land.'"

"The *Hutchinson News-Herald* said it was the worst storm in Hutch's history," Melvin chimed in. "And Nickerson was hard hit."

Over the next weeks, Tobe helped with clean-up at a couple of neighboring homes. He also worked on the new basement house between shop projects. The shop workers helped when he needed a carpenter's hand.

Tobe's brother Perry dropped by one afternoon to see the progress on the basement house. He watched as Tobe was setting the rafters into place. "*Tselft es Dach soll flach sei?* Is the roof going to be flat?"

"*Ya.* Yes."

"Flat roofs leak water."

"If the roof is totally flat, it won't leak. The water will run off the edges." Tobe didn't care for his youngest brother's advice. He pointed toward the wall. "Hold the rafters on edge by the pencil mark and I'll nail them on the middle beam." Perry moved to the task and helped for several hours that day.

The house was nearly finished when Tobe built a small pole barn for the livestock. Quickly stepping off distances, he calculated the span for each side by the number of steps and scratched a mark into the dirt for each post. His shop helpers did most of the construction work. After the walls were up, Tobe walked into the shop one morning. He looked upset.

"What's wrong?" Melvin asked.

"I just discovered that one side of the barn is a foot longer than the other!"

Melvin laughed. "How did that happen? You never miss on measurements."

Tobe was angry. "If you knew what all I had on my mind when I stepped it off, you'd understand."

Already he was several hundred dollars behind in paying Melvin's wages so Melvin suspected what was going on. He tried not to complain.

What Melvin didn't know was how many other unpaid bills there were. One of the creditors threatened Tobe by saying if he didn't pay by a certain date, he would lose his new buildings.

It bothered Tobe when people came around to collect on debts. He tried not to get upset, or at least not to show it.

Soon after the new shop got into full production, Tobe invited Emma's brother Raymond to join the work crew. Raymond shivered as he watched Tobe rip oak boards on his table saw. The four-horsepower Wisconsin engine lugged down as Tobe shoved the boards through, his fingers barely clearing the wicked 14-inch blade.

"You'll cut your fingers some day," Raymond warned. "You should have a guard on the saw."

Tobe laughed. "Nah. Guards on power tools are a nuisance. They get in the way and slow things down."

Raymond shook his head, "You get your hand too close to the blade."

Tobe waved Raymond back to work. Raymond was too cautious. Besides, he didn't have much experience in woodworking.

• • • •

When Tobe and Emma moved into their new basement house, Raymond moved in with them. He was nearly twenty-two years old and planning to join the new Conservative Mennonite church so it seemed best to move away from home.

Late one evening by lantern light, Raymond told Tobe and Emma about the new group. They were going to have worship services every Sunday rather than every other Sunday like the Old Order churches did. To be more effective in missionary work, the group was saying, they needed to allow some modern conveniences. So far, that meant a church building, automobiles, electricity, and telephones. It wasn't clear whether the group would be officially shunned by the Old Orders. Tobe and Emma hoped not. They didn't want to see that kind of tension in their family.

"Who all comes to your meetings?" Tobe asked, wondering whether any other relatives were planning to join.

"Right now it's John Helmuths, Elvon Helmuths, Sol Yoders, William Millers, Melvin Beachys, and David M. Millers. They're pretty much committed. We heard Harry Yoders, Jonas Yoders, and Henry Millers might start coming. Then there are some young folks—Eli Helmuth and Katie Nisly, along with Mary and me."

"What does Dad say about it?" Emma asked.

"Not much. I guess he thinks as long as I'm not married it's not so serious if I leave."

"Who will be your bishop?" Tobe asked. Tobe suspected that Raymond and his steady girlfriend, Mary Yoder, would soon be announcing their engagement. They would need a bishop to perform the wedding ceremony.

"From what I'm hearing, it'll be Nevin Bender until we can ordain someone here. He's going to baptize the young people when he comes in January."

The clock struck 10:30 p.m. "Well, it's past our bedtime," Tobe said as he stretched and rose from the table.

Tobe and Emma retired to their room. They lay in bed, quietly conversing about the new church.

"So Uncle Henry is joining," Tobe said. "Maybe we could join too. It would be nice to have electricity and a telephone in the shop. And a car would really help me in my business."

"But Dad's a preacher. He would be really disappointed in us. We might even be excommunicated and shunned. You know what happened to Abe Nislys."

"Yes, I know."

The Nislys lived near Abbyville on the far western edge of the Amish community. For ten years, they had worked as tenant farmers on ground owned by Howard Carey, the owner of Carey Salt in Hutchinson. Because someone else owned their home, they were allowed to use electricity in both the house and barn.

When Carey put the farm up for sale in early 1948, Abe and Sarah bought it. Over the next weeks, they converted all their electrical systems to other energy sources. For the first time on that farm, the family adjusted to kerosene lanterns for lighting. Abe replaced the milking machine and other electric motors with gasoline units, knowing the replacement units were less efficient and took more maintenance.

After making all of these changes, Abe took some time to replace the electric water pump in the basement. Six months passed after the farm purchase, and he had not yet made the change.

Just before fall communion, Bishop Jake Miller and Emma's father, Preacher Levi Nisly, went to visit Abe and Sarah. Levi was Abe's cousin, and Jake was Sarah's older brother. The preachers informed the Nislys that they were out of the *Ordnung*. They recommended that Abe and Sarah withhold from taking communion the next Sunday. Abe protested, explaining that they would make the change as soon as possible, but the ministers persisted. On communion day, the Nislys were barred from participation.

The punishment seemed severe to Tobe, even though Emma's father had helped the bishop to administer it. It seemed the church leaders were trying to impress on members the seriousness of their church vows. Some people were even saying that those who left the church were going to hell because they'd forsaken their vow to be loyal to the church. They said children of the members were safe because they'd never joined.

"We should have the Nislys over for Sunday dinner tomorrow," Tobe suggested.

"Oh, Tobe, Abes always keep their house in such good order. Things aren't fixed up well enough around here. Our house isn't even finished."

"Well, if we can live in it all the time, they can probably stand to be here for an afternoon," Tobe countered.

A few moments of silence passed. "Okay, we can have them," Emma agreed.

Now back in good standing with the Amish church, the Nisly family accepted Tobe's invitation to dinner. They told Tobe and Emma of their intention to remain loyal to the church even though their daughter Dorothy and her husband were joining with the new church.

Over the next months, Raymond often talked about his participation in the new group. Tobe listened with interest and some caution as Raymond shared his enthusiasm. The emerging group seemed eager to recruit new members. Should he talk to Emma about it again?

That evening he brought it up after they were in bed. "Raymond was talking about the new church today. He really likes that the worship services are in English. It makes it easier to invite people who can't speak German."

Tobe paused. "I've been thinking more about joining. What do you think?"

Emma lay quietly for a very long time. Finally, she whispered, "I hate to disappoint my parents."

"Well, let's sleep over it," Tobe said. "We don't need to decide now."

Emma didn't say much for the next two days. Tobe was concerned. Was she worried that he would decide to join the new church against her will?

Finally, he turned to her one evening and said, "I've decided we won't join the new church."

Emma sighed. "Good." Relief was evident in her voice.

"We don't want our parents to be upset," Tobe said.

"Besides, we've borrowed money from people in the church. We don't want to offend them. It would be nice if people didn't get so upset, but that's the way it is. We'll just have to live with it." The moon shone through the small window in their basement bedroom as Tobe spoke.

"Anyway," Tobe added, "I want the children to learn how to read German. If we join the Conservatives, I'm afraid they won't learn it. Now that Mary Edna is in school, she's learning English really fast."

Mary Edna walked to Elmhirst, a small one-room school house, just a mile and a half away. She quickly adapted from speaking Pennsylvania German at home to English at school.

"Yes, Mary Edna learns very fast," Emma replied. She paused. "I'm a little worried about Edith, though. She's a year old now, and she still doesn't crawl. Mary Edna was walking by this age."

"But the boys didn't walk so early," Tobe reminded her. "Maybe Edith is just a little slower." He yawned, took a few deep breaths, and soon fell asleep.

Several months later on the first Sunday of November, Tobe and Emma attended Raymond and Mary's wedding. Nevin Bender performed the ceremony. That same fall, Emma's sister Barbara married Alvin Yoder in a traditional Amish wedding. Of Emma's seven siblings, only Rufus and Elizabeth remained unmarried. Would they join the Conservative Church?

From conversations at the shop, Tobe knew that his brother Clarence was thinking of joining. The midweek meetings and the mission emphasis evidently appealed to Clarence. Along with his friend, David L. Miller, he planned to start Bible study events for some of the Amish young people.

Bishop Levi Helmuth gave cautious support to the new venture in spite of strong objection from some older members. But Levi encouraged Clarence and David to wait until after the fall communion to avoid trouble. They did. Under their leadership, a group of young people began midweek meetings just before Thanksgiving. Young men joined older men in taking turns presenting essays or topics for discussion.

Although young women weren't allowed to share topics, they felt free to join in the discussion. Willie Wagler's sister Orpha was especially eager to study the Scripture. In a bold move, she registered for the six-week Bible term at Hesston College, a Mennonite school some forty miles away. None of her male peers had entered the college world so she was taking a risk in a church where the leaders frowned on education beyond the eighth grade.

The Thanksgiving and Christmas holidays slipped by quickly in the Stutzman household. It was after lunch on New Year's Day when Tobe realized that it was a banner day for his brother. He looked over at Emma, who was stirring up gravy for dinner. "Clarence is of age now. He turned 21 yesterday."

Emma nodded. "Yes, we should have them over for his birthday."

Tobe continued, "Remember how Mom and Dad gave Ervin and me each a cow when we got married? Well, they're not going to do that for Clarence because he went on that ship before he was twenty-one. Mom reminded him that there's plenty of service to do around home."

Clarence wasn't the only Kansas Amish fellow to give time to voluntary service. Other young men from the youth group had also joined with Mennonite Central Committee's efforts in Puerto Rico, France, and Germany. When the young men came home with a growing vision for mission and relief, it was contagious.

"Will Clarence keep working for us now that he's of age?" Emma wondered aloud.

"Yeah, I think so, at least for a while. Since Melvin quit, I really need his help."

"Did you ever get Melvin paid up?" Emma asked. "You were $600 behind."

"Not quite. He probably thinks he won't get the money. But he'll get it soon."

"Would your brother Ervin be able to help more at the shop?"

"I wish he could. But he and Emma are spending a lot of time getting the farm and dairy going. He'd like to build a herd of Ayrshires."

"Thing's seem to be going well for them," Emma observed with a tinge of envy.

"Yes, Ervin will be a lot better farmer than Dad ever was."

"Probably so," Emma replied. "But your Dad had some bad luck through the years."

Ervin and Emma would soon face their own stroke of misfortune. Tobe learned about it on the first Sunday in April. He was hitching the horse to leave for church when his brother Perry came racing into the yard with the buggy. Tobe watched as Perry sprang out of the buggy and threw the halter rope around a tree. Why was he here on a Sunday morning? One look at his brother's countenance told Tobe that something was very wrong.

15

Raising the Stakes

The words tumbled out of Perry's mouth. "Ervin Emma is in the hospital! She was badly burned this morning."

"Oh no! What happened?" Tobe asked.

Perry told the story. Emma and Ervin had gone out early to do the milking as they always did. When they were nearly done, she hurried to the house to start breakfast. It was chilly so she decided to light the heater. Because the wood was still quite green, Emma tried to pep up her fire with coal oil.

In her rush, she poured coal oil from a two-gallon can that was almost empty. The can exploded, setting Emma's clothes on fire. She went for water but there wasn't very much in the house so she ran onto the porch and screamed for Ervin. He raced in from the barn and tried to tear her burning clothes off, but of course he couldn't do it.

By the time Ervin ran to the pump house for water, Emma had managed to wrap a throw rug around her. That smothered the fire so Ervin used the water to put out the fire in the room.

"She's burned from her hips to below the knees. They took her to the emergency room at Grace Hospital. Mom says be sure to go visit her."

"We'll go today," Tobe promised.

Less than two weeks after Emma's injury, Tobe suffered his own injury. The shop crew had just come to work when a customer stalked through the door. Visibly upset, he walked to where Tobe was standing. "I thought you said my truck bed would be finished yesterday. Your men say you haven't even started on it."

Tobe puckered his lips. "When must you have it?"

"Early next week."

"We'll have it for you on Tuesday. We've been running just a bit behind."

"Okay. I'll expect to see it finished out front when I get here on Tuesday noon." He clearly meant business.

"We'll do it."

Tobe turned to his workers as the irate customer walked toward his car. "Well, we've got our work cut out for us." He yanked the starter cord on the Wisconsin engine. Grabbing a handful of oak planks, he dumped them beside the large saw. The engine pulled down as he pushed the saw to maximum capacity with the thick boards. He gave the saw little rest as he settled into a quick rhythm—pushing, reaching over, pushing again, reaching again.

As Tobe was reaching to grab the end of a board he had pushed through the saw, the wood bound tightly against the spinning blade, yanking his hand into the circular teeth. The flesh of his palm screamed pain as the blade sliced toward the bone. Tobe winced and yelled as blood spurted from his hand.

Eddie Conkling and Raymond Yutzy came running with towels. They hastily wrapped the injured palm. Eddie exclaimed, "We gotta get him to the hospital!"

Bill Schrock, who had just happened by, volunteered his car. Eddie looked at Raymond, "You drive."

"No, you have a license. You drive."

"All right." Eddie's voice was quivering.

One of the other workers ran to the neighbor's house to call the police. Perhaps they could provide an escort.

Tobe got into the passenger seat. He held up his injured hand to keep it from pounding. Raymond hopped into the back seat behind Tobe. Eddie pulled onto Route 61 and floored the accelerator in the '37 Ford sedan.

Eddie had dreamed of being an ambulance driver but this scared him. What if Tobe lost too much blood? He glanced at Tobe then back to the road. Raymond looked at the speedometer. When the needle was pushing past ninety, he shouted, "Ain't this a runnin' Jesse?"

"Sure is, " Raymond replied.

As they passed the intersection at Broadacres Road, Tobe laid back the towel just enough to look at the cut. He fainted. Raymond leaned forward to hold his boss's shoulders.

In another minute, they came to the main intersection in South Hutch. Eddie ignored the stop sign and screeched left onto Route 17. Tobe slumped forward again. Blood dripped onto the floor mat as Eddie raced toward the bridge over the Arkansas River. Then he spotted the escort. "Hey, there's two police cars at the entrance to Carey Park."

Raymond waved wildly at the officer that was standing outside the car. Alerted by the emergency call, the officer was waiting for them. He turned on his lights and siren, then headed for the hospital. Eddie followed with the second police car in tow. The small caravan roared through the traffic lights on Main Street. Eddie glanced at his speedometer. Seventy five miles per hour!

Soon the caravan slowed and pulled into the entrance at Grace Hospital. Raymond hopped out and yanked open the door for Tobe.

Eddie shook hands with the policemen. "Thanks," he said gratefully, "you saved us a lot of time."

Tobe's face looked washed out as he walked up to the double glass doors. He hesitated at the door. "I hate to drip blood onto this nice linoleum floor."

"Come on, this is an emergency." Eddie was impatient. They pressed forward.

A nurse directed Tobe to a chair. "What did you do to your hand?"

"Cut it with a saw."

"A hand saw?"

"No, if I'd used a hand saw, I'd have stopped before this happened," Tobe was annoyed. The nurse applied a tourniquet to stop the bleeding.

A doctor stepped up and gently lifted Tobe's hand. He shook his head as he examined the damage. He cleared his throat, "We'll need to take the hand."

Tobe shook his head, his eyes pleading. "Please let me keep it. Can't you try to stitch it?"

The doctor puckered his lips. "The cut is very deep. You came very near to severing the main nerves in your thumb." He paused again. "I suppose we can try to stitch it. But if the wound develops gangrene or other infection, the hand will need to come off."

"Good, I'll take very good care of it."

Tobe left the emergency room somber-faced. What if he lost his hand? Could he stay in business?

Tobe went back to ripping boards the next day. With his bandaged hand elevated to keep it from throbbing, Tobe pushed the boards through the saw with one hand.

Raymond Nisly watched as Tobe grabbed and flipped the boards with one hand. "I believe you can saw as fast with one hand as the rest of us can with two," he said to Tobe.

The rest of the work crew worked harder on the promised truck bed and got it done on time. When the customer came to pick it up, Tobe explained what had happened. The chagrined buyer apologized for his anger. Tobe said there was no need to apologize; the injury had been his own fault. He would be more careful in the future.

Tobe's injured hand healed slowly—much too slowly for his liking. For months afterward, he squeezed a rubber ball to build up the strength in his hand. Gradually the sinews to his fingers regained their strength. The nerves again pulsed with feeling, but his hand never fully recovered. His fingers would not cooperate to button the cuff on the right sleeve of his shirts so Emma always buttoned that side for him.

Although orders for truck beds kept coming in, it was difficult for Tobe to turn a profit. He found it difficult to charge enough for his products. Besides, the capital expenses for the new property drained the cash from his enterprise. To find cash, he turned to well-to-do members of the church. One was Emma's Uncle Ed Nisly.

Tobe approached Ed one summer afternoon. Ed's daughter Vera Mae sat at the dining room table as Ed welcomed Tobe onto an enclosed porch at the front of their house. They chatted a few minutes before Tobe turned the conversation to the matter of finances. He asked, "Will you loan me money to help carry the business forward for the time being?"

Tobe saw Vera Mae lean slightly forward as her father framed his reply. Ed's wife Lizzie looked up from the stove. Were they listening? Lizzie seemed to catch Ed's eye. Ed spoke so softly that they might not have caught his response. "Well, Tobe I don't know that I have the money to loan to you just now."

Tobe was disappointed. He replied: "*Oh, Ed, waan ich so viel Geld hett wie du hoscht, dann waer ich ganz froh fer dir Geld lehne.* Oh, Ed, if I had as much money as you have, then I'd be very glad to loan you money."

Ed held firm. After a few strained pleasantries, Tobe dismissed himself and went home.

Back at the shop, Tobe found himself pushing boards through the jointer faster than usual. "There's no use getting upset," he reminded himself. "Probably Ed was just in a bad mood. I'll stop by to see him again one of these times." Almost by second nature, he reached for the can to oil the babbitt bearing on the machine. He barely glanced at the can as he squirted a generous dose of the used crankcase oil into the bearing holes.

Tobe set down the can and turned his attention back to planing boards. Some thirty minutes later, he grabbed the can to oil the bearing as usual. But this time the oil steamed into his face and ran down his beard. Tobe quickly looked around. Who had turned the spout? He saw one of the shop workers mischievously watching through the doorway. Tobe decided to take it in stride. There was no use fussing about small things. But he wouldn't give the prankster the pleasure of watching him look into a mirror. He walked to the workbench and wiped his face with a rag. Then he readjusted the spout on the can. From then on, he glanced directly at the spout before squeezing the handle on the oil can.

The next few weeks, Tobe put up a hog shed. It was late on Friday evening when he got home, and he was famished. Emma moved quickly to prepare the usual late-night summer meal for him. She pulled out several slices of homemade bread and broke them into a large soup bowl. After slicing canned peaches and fresh strawberries over the bread, she sprinkled white sugar on top. Then she went to the refrigerator for cold milk and set the pitcher next to the bowl, "Your supper's ready," she said.

Tobe stepped from the washroom, arms still partly wet. He paused a moment for silent grace, then poured milk over the bread and fruit. Unlike the Nisly family, he hadn't grown up with cold milk soup, but he thoroughly enjoyed it. It was a good meal for a warm summer night.

"We got the hog shed done over at the Tuxhorn Place," he said. "It went up pretty fast."

"Did you get paid?"

"No, but he'll pay soon."

"Will we make any money on the deal?"

Tobe admitted that they probably wouldn't make much. He had to pay Raymond for helping.

• • • •

In addition to the regular workers, young Edwin Yoder, the son of Tobe's next-door neighbor, Menny, started hanging around Tobe's shop. Tobe liked when Edwin picked up the nuts and washers that fell to the floor. He also enjoyed it when Edwin started a row of nails for him.

Tapping the 12-penny nails lightly on their heads, Edwin would make sure the points penetrated slightly into the hardwood board of the truck bed. It was like a game. The tall nails formed a large grid. When Edwin was finished, it looked like a giant string art project awaiting the connecting strands. Then he would call out, "Tobe, they're ready!"

Each time, Tobe would stride over with a large hammer and scoot onto the wooden floor. Edwin stood back to watch. Wham! The first nail went in with one blow. Wham, wham, wham. Three more nails were in. Wham, wham, wham, echoes ricocheted off the walls of the shop.

Tobe looked at young Edwin and said. "Maybe you can do that when you're grown up,"

Edwin scratched his head. "I hope so."

• • • •

Tobe kept looking for loans among church members, especially after the local banker became extremely conservative. On one visit, Virgil Teeter, the Partridge banker, admonished Tobe, "The small man has to do things in a small way."

Tobe was very frustrated. Without good loans, how was he ever going to become a large operator? Ed Nisly and several others had said no. Where was he to go? Maybe Menny Yoder would consider making a loan. His farm seemed to be doing well. It couldn't hurt to ask.

Tobe walked to Menny's farm early one morning. The compressor was running near the barn so he knew Menny was milking. He peeked into the milking parlor. Menny was changing the milkers from one cow to another.

"*Wie geht's?* How's it going?" Tobe's tone was cheerful.

"*So zimmlich gut.* Fine." Menny's mellow bass voice answered in return.

The sound of the milkers pulsed in Tobe's ears as they conversed. After a few minutes, Tobe got around to the reason for his visit. "Menny, I'm wondering if you could loan me some money. I have a lot of projects going and need a little cash to carry me through until I get some products sold. There'll be a good bit coming in over the next few months but I need some cash now."

Menny stroked his thin beard and pushed back the brim of his hat. "Tobe, I wish I could loan you some but I really don't have any to spare just now. I'm sorry."

Tobe's face fell. "Well, if you don't have it, I guess you can't loan it. I understand." He headed for the door. "I'll see you later."

Tobe wasn't so sure that Menny didn't have the money. Maybe he was afraid he wouldn't get it back. Where else could he go? He thought of Willie Wagler.

The next day Tobe drove his buggy to the Wagler farm. The preacher was walking from the barn to the house as Tobe guided the horse up to the hitching post. They exchanged greetings.

Willie gestured toward the house. "Please come inside." Tobe hesitated. He would have preferred to speak to Willie alone. His wife Alma might upset the balance. Alma was a second cousin to Emma.

Tobe followed Willie to the door. They both stepped inside the frame house. Willie took off his hat and put it on a shelf. "Excuse me while I wash my hands."

Tobe stood with his hat in his hand. Alma greeted him with a warm smile. "Hello, Tobe. Have a chair."

Tobe sank into the soft armchair. He surveyed the room. Things were always in perfect order at the Wagler home. He heard the pump splash water into a basin in the wash house.

Soon Willie joined him in the living room. They exchanged pleasantries, then Tobe put forth his request. "Willie, I came to see if you might loan me some money. With the moving of the shop and all, we ended up being over-committed. But we have a lot of projects going so we'll recover before too long. I just need some cash to keep my employees paid until I sell more truck beds."

Willie pulled out his handkerchief and wiped the eye injured in the tractor accident. "Can you pay interest?"

"I'll pay ten percent interest. That's much better than you can get at the bank right now."

Willie glanced at Alma, then back at Tobe. "Ten percent is pretty high. Can you afford that?"

"It is high, but I won't need the money for very long." Tobe sensed that Willie was weakening.

A few minutes later, Willie pulled the checkbook from his roll-top desk and wrote a check for a thousand dollars.

Tobe thanked him and stood to leave. "Thank you very much. Emma will be happy to know that you're helping us out." He picked his hat off the shelf and walked out the door.

• • • •

The summer of 1949 slowly turned to fall. Tobe heard the wind whipping up as he woke from his Sunday afternoon nap. He walked up the stairs to look outside. There was one thing he didn't like about the basement house—you couldn't see much through the small, high windows.

He stepped outside. The temperature was dropping. They'd had the first frost only two weeks before, but this felt much colder. He went back down and sat in the rocker to read the *Budget* as Emma awoke from her snooze on the sofa. Tobe commented, "I'm surprised Delilah doesn't have anything in the *Budget* about their barn being hit by high winds last week. They had quite a bit of damage."

"I'm surprised too. She usually tells about things like that." Emma sat up. "Shall I make you some popcorn?"

"Yes, I'd like that," Tobe replied.

Emma pulled out the popcorn popper. "I heard that Clarence has been attending the Conservative Church. Do you think he's going to join?"

"Yes, he's buying a car before long. It seems that more and more people are joining the new church. Mom and Dad aren't very happy about it."

The next day Tobe asked Eddie to drive him past the new meetinghouse the Conservatives were building along the Partridge Road. He was eager to see the progress for himself. They approached the new frame facility from the west and pulled into the parking lot.

"Looks like it's almost finished," Eddie commented.

"Yes," Tobe replied, "Raymond says there's just a little painting to be done."

Eddie's face lit up. "I like Raymond. He helped me clean up my life."

Tobe nodded. "Raymond said something about it. What happened?"

"Well, you know I used to cuss a lot."

Tobe nodded. "Yes."

Eddie shut off the truck and faced Tobe. "Back a few weeks ago, we were working on a truck bed together. My bad language was bothering both him and Raymond Yutzy. Raymond Nisly told me that God could change my life and help me stop my cussin'. He told me what Jesus had done for him. I asked what I should do. He said I should pray and ask Jesus to come into my heart. We knelt down right there by the truck bed and prayed. Then Raymond grabbed my hand and helped me get up. He said I should 'rise and walk in newness of life,' or something like that. He told me they were the same words Nevin Bender used when he received Raymond and Mary into the Conservative Church. Ever since that time, I quit my drinkin' and swearin'."

Tobe nodded. "That's good." But what good was it to pray without joining the church? Would Eddie join the Conservatives? What about his wife? Would she be willing to dress plain?

Tobe kept his thoughts to himself as Eddie started the truck and steered it onto the paved road heading toward Hutchinson. As they drove up Main Street in South Hutch, Tobe asked Eddie to stop by the nearest pay phone. He put a dime into the phone to call a customer.

When Tobe returned, Eddie commented, "You use a lot of dimes in those pay phones."

"Yeah, it gets a little expensive."

"It would probably be cheaper to have your own phone."

"That may be true, but our people can't have phones," Tobe said.

"If you joined Raymond's church, you could have your own phone," Eddie suggested. "That would sure make things a lot easier."

Tobe looked at Eddie and with a twinge of regret, said, "Emma's not ready to join."

"Clarence is joining. He bought a car. A 1947 Dodge."

"I know. He wrecked it too."

"He did?! I didn't know that."

"Yeah," Tobe explained. "Clarence and some other young people were on their way to a wedding in Iowa. Somewhere in Missouri they hit a patch of ice and slid off the road. The car landed on its roof. The top of the car was smashed down to the level of the windows. Somehow everyone got out without being hurt."

Tobe also knew that Clarence had just taken out State Farm insurance on the car the day before. The young people never made it to the wedding, spending Saturday and Sunday at a motel. But the damage was paid by the insurance company, and a repair shop just off the highway in Missouri jacked up the roof and sent them back home.

"They was lucky they didn't get killed when the car rolled over," Eddie said.

"Yeah," Tobe agreed. "Mom just about had a fit when she heard about it. She wasn't happy about him having a car in the first place. She's not happy about him being in Voluntary Service down in Mississippi either."

• • • •

Christmas Day 1949 dawned clear and cold. Tobe came to the breakfast table with good news. "Ervin says Emma won't need to see the doctor for her burns any more. She can take care of them herself."

Emma sighed. "It's so nice that she's finished with the treatment. It's been a lot of expense, and she got so tired of being in the hospital."

"She's looking forward to helping more on the farm again," Tobe added. "Ervin has been doing a lot of extra work. Now he might be able to help me more at the shop."

"Have you paid him back for the loan he gave us?" Emma asked.

"Not yet," Tobe answered. "I've got a few others I need to pay back first. But I've got some truck beds going out soon, and I'll be able to pay off a number of people."

Tobe would be glad to see that money. Some of his creditors had been talking to each other. They had gone so far as to put together a committee to help him manage his debt. To

241

Tobe's great relief, his brothers, Clarence and Ervin, worked it out so that the creditors agreed to give Tobe another chance. Tobe wasn't interested in having other people stick their noses in his business.

The day after Christmas, Tobe looked out the open doorway to see Abe Miller pulling his car into the driveway. Tobe pulled Raymond Yutzy aside as the man parked his car and walked across the yard.

"I'm guessing that he came to collect his money," Tobe confided. "I owe him quite a bit of money. I don't have the money, so I'll have to talk him into letting me have it for a little while longer."

16

Expanding the Business

Tobe reached out his calloused hand to greet the visitor with a warm handshake. "It's good to see you, Abe. How about taking a little walk back into the shop to see a new project I'm working on?"

"Sure. I'll take a little time to look around." Raymond couldn't help but notice the scowl on Abe's face.

The pair walked through the shop as Tobe explained his work projects and future possibilities. Their voices dropped for a few minutes as they talked about Tobe's debt.

When Abe left, Tobe walked over to Raymond Yutzy with a broad grin on his face. "He just promised to loan me some more money," Tobe whispered. "What do you think of that for a Christmas present?" Raymond just shook his head.

With New Year's Day 1950 came the annual coyote hunt that drew men from several communities, even surrounding states. Tobe walked to the shop, his breath showing in the cold air. He looked at the thermometer by the shop window. Twenty-five degrees. It was just cold enough to freeze the ground, but not too cold to hunt.

Tobe didn't especially like hunting, and he had work to do. How could he justify taking off a whole day to chase after coyotes? He'd been along a time or two—enough to visualize the game plan. First thing in the morning, a large group of men would form a giant ring and gradually tighten the circle until it closed in on a coyote. The animal would be hemmed in, a good target at close range. Then someone would shoot and claim the prize. There were always many hunting stories.

The morning passed quickly in the shop. Around mid-afternoon, John Mast came by. He was known as one of the best hunters in the community.

Tobe greeted him from the back of the shop, "Hey John. How was the hunt?"

"Real good. We got eight coyotes and thirty jackrabbits."

"How many did *you* get?"

John grinned. "I got lucky. I got a coyote and two jackrabbits." Then he changed the subject, "I hear you're planning to build a new shop."

Tobe stepped back from his work. "Yeah, we need it since we're getting into metal working. Aluminum products are more and more popular all the time. I just found out that Sears and Roebuck is making metal wagon boxes to take the place of the wooden ones we've been making for them.

John nodded. "What material will you use?"

"I'm going to lay block. It will be forty-two by sixty feet."

"Who's building it for you?"

"I'll do most of it myself. I might get a mason to help me with part of it."

John stroked his beard as he turned to leave. "That sounds good. I guess you'll have plenty of help."

Tobe watched John walk to his buggy. John was a successful farmer and businessman. What did he really think about the new shop? You couldn't easily read John's mind.

Not long after, Tobe talked with Clarence about hiring people to work in the metal working end of the business. Clarence showed Tobe a copy of a newspaper he'd gotten in town. "Here it says there's a new law that you must pay a minimum wage of seventy-five cents an hour."

Tobe read the article. "You mean the government is telling us what to pay our employees?" His voice dripped disgust.

"Yeah. They don't want employers to take advantage of their workers."

Tobe brushed some sawdust off his pant legs. "I guess we don't have anything to worry about. We already pay that much for most of our help.

"Oh, I almost forgot to tell you," Tobe continued, "I found someone who'll do some of the masonry work on the new shop in exchange for a set of stock racks."

•   •   •   •

Around the first of February, the Stutzman brothers poured the footer for the new shop and started to lay block. Tobe divided his time between shop work and the new building. He put in long hours, often working by lantern light to stretch out the day.

One evening in March as Tobe put the finishing touches on the building, he noticed an unusual tint in the northern sky. It glowed and flickered a deep red-orange. Was there a fire somewhere to the north? The wind was from the south so he couldn't detect any smoke. Twice during the night, he got out of bed and walked to the window to gaze at the strange light in the sky.

The next morning a customer told Tobe that the strange sight was a prairie fire burning out of control in the sand hills north of Hutchinson. A Santa Fe locomotive had thrown a spark that ignited the dry grass nearby. Fed by a stiff breeze, the flames quickly spread, burning cattle and leaping over highways in its path. The next day, the newspaper reported that 3,600 acres had been burned. It took firefighters more then twenty-four hours to bring the fire under control.

When the new shop was done, both Ervin and Clarence agreed to give more time to the business. They often talked about new products. One afternoon Tobe called to Ervin as he opened the double doors to unload some lumber. "*Ervin, kumm do riwwer. Ich will dir ebbes weise.* Ervin, come over here. I want to show you something." Tobe stepped toward the workbench and picked up a decorative concrete frog. He handed it to Ervin to see. "I found this thing in someone's yard. I wire brushed it so it looks pretty good. We could make these things to sell."

Ervin drew back. "Who would want them?"

"Lots of people like this kind of thing in their yard. We could make a lot of money."

Ervin still wasn't convinced. "I wouldn't want it in my yard."

Tobe shrugged and set it back on the workbench. There must be a market for concrete products. Not everyone thought like Ervin.

Flying sand stung their faces as they unloaded the stack of lumber. The heat was drying out the fields. A strange circle of light surrounded the sun as it shone through the dust in the atmosphere.

Tobe looked up to greet Fred Yutzy as he jumped out of his pickup. "Pretty windy out there, isn't it?" Tobe said.

"No kidding. I heard on the radio that it's the worst dust storm in ten years." Since Fred was Mennonite, he had access to radio news.

"Is that right? I remember it was pretty bad back in '42."

"It's impossible to keep a vehicle clean in this weather," Fred complained. He traced a circle in the layer of dust on the hood of the truck he used to haul products for Tobe. "And look at that wheel." A yellow trail streaked the rim where a farm dog had left its mark.

"I can imagine," Tobe empathized. "If you come back tomorrow, I'll have a load of things for you to haul. There's a set of kitchen cabinets that need to go to town."

"All right, I'll stop by tomorrow," Fred said, as he climbed into his truck. He pulled a rag from his pocket and wiped the dashboard clean. Then he pressed the starter pedal and was off.

When Fred got home, he parked by the shop and rummaged around in a box on the workbench. He grinned broadly as he pulled out an old Model T ignition coil. That afternoon he mounted it under the hood of his truck. He wired the input side to the wiring harness and the output side to the frame of his vehicle. A push button on the inside of the cab completed the circuit.

Fred put away his tools and drove to a neighboring farm yard. A farm dog came exploring, circling, sniffing. Fred stayed in the driver's seat, surveying the two sides of his truck through his rearview mirrors. When the dog lifted its leg to make his mark, Fred pressed the button. Zing! The dog yipped across the farm yard, seared by the liquid fire. The coil made the metal surfaces as hot as the farmer's electric fencer.

The next morning Fred drove to the Stutzman shop and cranked down the window. Tobe sauntered over and leaned against the dark green cab. Fred reached down and pushed the button for his coil. Tobe jumped back and exclaimed, "*Du sell net widder!* Don't do that again!" He hated being shocked. It reminded him of Ervin's battery-operated ParMac electric fencer at their Sand Hill farm.

Fred apologized. "I was just trying out my invention to keep dogs away from my wheels."

"Dogs? Well then why are you using it on people? Don't ever use it on me again," Tobe warned as they walked into the shop to load the kitchen cabinets.

That evening at the supper table, Tobe told his family about Fred's strange invention.

Mary Edna reacted, "That wasn't very kind of him."

Perry piped up. "You should get him back."

"Yeah," Glenn echoed, "you should take him down and sit on him."

Tobe laughed. "I don't think he'd like that. It's okay. I'm sure he won't do it again."

Emma changed the subject. "John and Elizabeth Bender are coming back here next week. Their term of Voluntary Service in Gulfport, Mississippi, is over."

"I wonder if John might want to work for me," Tobe mused. "He can help start the window business. And I'm going to try to get Eli Yutzy to let Raymond work for me full-time. He can help me make windows too."

Tobe liked Raymond Yutzy. The young man was perceptive—quick with words and actions. He would do well at making windows, and Raymond might make a good manager some day. But Raymond had just told Tobe that he needed to help his dad with a large cabinet-finishing job. Eli was a cabinet-maker and wood finisher. Somehow Tobe would have to convince him that it was better to have Raymond work full-time at the Stutzman shop.

Tobe helped carry the dirty dishes to the sink. "Maybe I'll go see Eli tomorrow," he told Emma. "I want to get started with those windows."

The next evening Tobe rode toward the Yutzy homestead. What would convince Eli to release his son to work for Tobe full-time in the shop? He rehearsed his request as he guided his horse into the Yutzy farmhouse lane and tied it at the hitching post. Walking up to the door, he knocked. Mrs. Yutzy came to the door.

"Is Eli home?"

Eli called from the other room, "Come on in." He showed Tobe to a rocking chair. Tobe shook Eli's hand warmly and sat down. They chatted about the recent dust storm and Eli's work as a carpenter.

Then Eli commented, "I hear you're getting into metal manufacturing." It was the opportunity that Tobe was looking for.

"Yes, there's a big demand for aluminum storm windows these days. I'm planning to start manufacturing them. But I'm going to need some help. In fact, I was thinking that maybe Raymond could help me. He's a good worker."

"Yeah, he does well, but I'm going to need him before long to help me with some cabinets."

"Maybe we could work it out so he could help both of us."

"Well, maybe. How would that work?"

"How about if he starts to work with me now? He could help make windows. Then he can take time off to help you later. That way we could both get our jobs done, and you'd end up with some extra cash to do your cabinet work."

Eli stroked his chin. "Well, let me think about it." He glanced toward his wife then back to Tobe. "We'll let you know."

As he stood to leave, Tobe stepped toward the cabinets Eli had built in his kitchen. He commented, "You and Raymond do very good work. It'll be good to have Raymond work for me. Maybe I'll learn things from him." He picked up his hat and headed for home.

Early the next week, Tobe called on Eli again. Eli agreed that Raymond could work full-time for Tobe. He could start the next morning.

The other shop workers soon found out that Raymond Yutzy always enjoyed a good debate. One day he and Clarence sparred about the American role in the growing war in Korea. "I bet President Truman declares war in Korea in the next few months. He's not going to let the North Koreans take over the country," Clarence declared.

"We just got out of a war. Why would we want another one?" Raymond retorted.

"They say the Communists will take over southeast Asia if we don't stop them," Clarence countered.

"If another war starts, we might both have to go into the service," Raymond suggested.

Clarence nodded. "That's true. If we do, we'll go into CPS or something."

A week later Clarence brought the newspaper to show Raymond. "See, what did I tell you? Truman sent troops to Korea. The first thing you know, he'll declare war. You would have thought we've had enough war lately. I wonder what a war would do for our aluminum supply. The last time we had a war, it was hard to get some of these materials."

Although Tobe was starting to make aluminum windows, he wasn't ready to quit making truck beds and other wooden products. He was more familiar with wood, and he like experimenting with different products.

• • • •

One hot summer day young Edwin Yoder was hanging around the shop, starting nails for Tobe and putting nuts and washers on the bolts for the truck beds. As Tobe paid the youngster his usual dime and nickel for helping, their conversation turned to softball. Tobe asked, "So Edwin, who's the best batter in your family?"

"Oh, I don't know. Right now, we don't have a bat. Dad says we can't afford it." Tobe detected sadness in Edwin's voice. Hadn't Menny mentioned something about buying a bat sometime?

"You really should have a bat. I'll make you one on the lathe. We'll do it this evening after the men go home from work. Do you want to watch me?"

"Sure. I'll tell Dad."

"I'll see you after supper.

That evening Edwin and his older brother Emery came to get their bat. They watched as Tobe picked a suitable piece of oak and cut it to the proper length. Then he put a small mark on each end where the sharp points of the lathe would pierce the wooden stock. He placed the long piece in the lathe, cranking the assembly against the end grain. The sharp tip penetrated the wood, squeezing the piece solidly into the machine. Tobe turned on the power.

The square piece of oak turned into a blur. Tobe picked a cutting tool with a straight edge. He laid it on the tool rest and gently engaged the spinning oak piece. Edwin watched as the rough edges whacked against the chisel in rhythm. Chips flew. The chisel quieted as the oak piece grew rounder.

Tobe fashioned the handle end first, forming a knob to keep the bat from flying out of the batter's hands. Then he moved up toward the business end of the bat. After finishing with the chisel, he ran sandpaper up and down the barrel. Then he took the bat off the lathe, trimmed the ends, and gave it to Edwin. He grinned as the brothers raced for home. Making things for pleasure relieved some of the pressure Tobe was feeling that summer. Even practical jokes didn't seem funny.

One afternoon Paul Yutzy drove up to the shop with his cousin Fred's truck. He turned off the engine and set a ripe red tomato on the rounded hood. Then he stepped back into the truck as Tobe strolled over to reach for the tomato. Just as he touched it, Paul pushed the button for the Model T coil. The jolt shook Tobe's arm.

Tobe's face turned dark. To be shocked twice by the same truck was too much. The shop workers looked on as he yelled at Paul never to do it again. One of the men commented, "Something's bothering Tobe."

Tobe's brother Perry said it had to do with money. A few days earlier, he'd overheard a conversation between Tobe and Jack Davis from the lumber company.

After Jack had stormed out and sped out of the driveway, Perry asked Tobe about it. "He looked really upset. What's going on?"

"He wants his money."

"Can you pay him?"

"I told him I couldn't pay him now, but he would get his money if he's just patient."

"Aren't you worried about what he'll do to you?"

Tobe laughed. "*Nee, ich kennt ihn nunnah nemme und uff ihn hocke.* Naw, I could take him down and sit on him."

Tobe couldn't understand why people got so upset when he owed them money. Couldn't they be more patient? The window business was making a profit, and it was only a matter of time before all of their debts would be paid. Besides there were surely some new ways of making money that he hadn't discovered yet.

17

New Horizons

Tobe glanced out the window as the Santa Fe Express roared past. He motioned to his brother Ervin, then pointed to the rail cars with lettering on the side. "We could advertise on the side of one of those cars."

"What?" Ervin looked puzzled.

Behind them Raymond Yutzy started up the large table saw. Tobe shouted over the sound of the train and the saw. "We could advertise on the side of those cars. We'd soon be selling products all over the Midwest."

Ervin shook his head. "That would never work."

Tobe stood there listening to the rumble of the cars and the whine of the saw. He liked the idea even if Ervin didn't care for it. There were some products around the shop waiting to be sold. But perhaps it would be best to concentrate on the new window franchise. He was making 15% profit on windows. That was better than truck beds or other wood products. The two salesmen, Vern Ortner and Hugh Self, kept new orders coming in. But they didn't have quite the knack for persuading people that Tobe would have liked.

Sometimes the salesmen thought Tobe pushed too hard. Eddie confided to Tobe that someone in the shop once commented to him that his boss was trying to be a millionaire. "What did you tell him?" Tobe asked.

"Well," Eddie quipped, "I told him that if you earned a million dollars, you'd probably give it all away."

Tobe laughed. Eddie knew it was hard for him to see someone in need without offering something.

Tobe considered going on the road to make sales himself. Of course, he'd have to hire a driver. Or maybe he could use Clarence's car now that Clarence had joined the Conservative Church. Or maybe the Amish church would allow cars before too long. Many people Tobe's age wished they would. There wasn't enough farm land for everyone so many of them were taking jobs off the farm. A horse and buggy was too slow for them. Some were driving small Ford tractors for week-day transportation. A few pulled trailers behind them with room for their families. To make his passengers less conspicuous, Willie Wagler made a covered trailer with a vent and a door. Others soon borrowed it for their own use.

One Friday evening near dusk, Tobe heard a buggy pull into the gravel driveway. It was Amos Nisly. Tobe strolled out to meet him, the screen door slamming behind him.

"*Wie geht's, Amos? Was kann ich duh fer dich?* How's it going, Amos? What can I do for you?"

"Hi Tobe. We're having church this Sunday and we need a new outhouse. The one we have is just not suitable for company any more. Can you build us one?"

"For this Sunday? That's the day after tomorrow."

"I know it's short notice, but could you do it for us?"

"I'll try. I'll have to run in to Davis Lumber to order the lumber. We'll nail it together in no time. It won't be painted though."

"That's okay."

"What size are we talking about?"

"I want a two-holer."

"I'll get some measurements together, and we'll deliver it tomorrow evening."

"Good enough, what will it cost?"

"I'll charge you time and material."

"It's a deal."

On Sunday some of the men gathered around the new outdoor toilet. When Amos explained that it had been built on short notice, one of them commented, "Tobe can really put out the work."

"He's always willing to help if he can," another commented.

"He doesn't keep shop hours," a third chimed in, "so people come expecting to get help at all hours. Did you hear about the time a customer came early one morning?"

"No."

"Tobe told me he woke up pretty early one morning and went to the outhouse without getting dressed. A car pulled into the yard while he was sitting inside the toilet. The headlights shone right on the door."

The men laughed. "What did he do?"

"He figured it must be a customer who could come back later. He just sat there shivering and waited for the car to leave. Finally, the man gave up and left."

"I bet he hated to see him go. He needs all of the income he can get these days. He still owes a lot of money, I hear."

"They say Clarence is helping him work out a plan to pay back some of his debts."

"Yeah, I heard that too."

The group stepped back from the new outhouse as an older woman made her way toward them from the house. They walked toward the barn to look at Amos's cows.

Some Amish wanted to sell Grade A milk but couldn't because they needed electricity to cool the milk to Grade A standards. Being able to get their dairies up to Grade A was one reason some joined the Conservative Church. Tobe's brother Ervin worked it out by going into partnership with his in-laws who had already joined the Conservatives. The Helmuths milked the cows while he and Emma farmed the land.

Rather than force change in the Amish church, Ervin and others looked for spiritual nurture and expression beyond the *Ordnung*. Sometimes they went to Conservative Church meetings. That summer, for example, William McGrath and Roy Schlabach conducted a series of evening services. Their English sermons coupled with an evangelistic appeal provided hope for young families and fueled further discontent with the Old Order way.

Tobe wasn't ready to spend his time going to church meetings, but he watched with interest as Ervin got involved in the spiritual life meetings. Maybe it would lead the church to allow electricity, as well as cars. Tobe was becoming more and more convinced that his business needed cars and electricity to survive.

In the summer of 1950 Ervin and Emma, along with several other young couples from the Partridge church district, attended a three-day missions conference in Kalona, Iowa. News about the innovative gathering buzzed around the Partridge community. Ervin came back to work full of enthusiasm.

"How was the conference?" Tobe asked.

"We liked it. There were some good speakers."

"Did they use German or English?"

"Both. Some of the older ministers thought it should all be in German, like our regular church services."

"Was everyone Amish?"

"No, there were some there who couldn't understand German. It fact the man who organized the meeting was a converted Catholic. His name was Russell Maniaci, and he's Mennonite now."

"How did he ever become a Mennonite?"

"He read a newspaper article about some Amish here in Yoder, Kansas, who left their farms because oil was discovered in their fields. They didn't want to be tempted by wealth.

Russell was so impressed by their sincerity that he tried to join the Amish church in Michigan."

"I don't suppose that worked too well."

"No, it didn't. They encouraged him to contact the Mennonite Church in Detroit. He visited the church and got saved. He left the Catholic Church and joined the Mennonites. Now he has a burden to help us Amish witness for our faith. He thinks we keep the gospel too much to ourselves."

"That's what mother always says."

"Yeah, she does, doesn't she? Well, it was through Russell that this missions conference was planned. Jonas Gingerich held it on his farm. I understand that Russell asked David L. Miller from Kansas here to be the moderator, but Bishop Will Yoder asked him not to do it. He's planning to get married to Mary Beachy and the church up there wasn't too happy about the meetings."

"Who else was at the conference from around here?"

"Harry Miller was the moderator. Willie Wagler, Ora Nisly, and Eli Helmuth all had devotions. Perry Miller told about their time of service in Puerto Rico. There were people from Iowa and Indiana too, and probably some there from Ohio. J. D. Graber spoke on his mission experiences in India. He's the head of the Mennonite mission board in Elkhart. He gave an invitation and more than thirty people went forward. Emma and I went forward too."

"What do you think will come of this?"

"They're going to start a missions committee to help with evangelistic efforts. And I wouldn't be surprised if we have another missions conference next year."

Tobe saw possibilities in the new mission movement. It was always good to see people who were open to new ideas. Maybe Iowa would be a good place to market his storm windows or other new products.

Shortly after, Emma mentioned that Edith might need to go to a special doctor. She'd heard of one in Iowa who treated children with developmental challenges. Some Amish friends from Kalona had taken their children there. They claimed this doctor was able to help where other doctors couldn't.

It was the opportunity Tobe had been waiting for. This could be the occasion to get to know the folks in Iowa a bit better. In late winter Tobe and Emma hired a driver to take them to Davenport, Iowa, to see Dr. Huls. He was a chiropractor who used unusual treatment techniques.

Tobe paced the waiting room of Dr. Huls's office as Emma sat with their four-year-old daughter on her lap. "Do you think we should ask him about Edith's eyes?" he asked Emma. Edith had difficulty focusing one eye.

"It wouldn't hurt. But we have an appointment with the specialist in March."

"Oh, that's coming up before long."

A nurse appeared at the door. "Dr. Huls is ready to see you." They walked into the examining room. The doctor seated Edith on the examining table then turned to Tobe and Emma, "Let me take a moment to explain my procedures. I do cranial treatments to help heal the brain. With young children, I often make adjustments from inside the mouth."

He examined the young girl's skull carefully, then cradled her head in his left hand. With the fingers of his right hand, he gently explored the inside of her mouth. "I'm working with her palate to relieve the pressure from the brain," he explained to Tobe and Emma, who stood nearby.

Emma turned away as Edith coughed and gagged. The doctor took a moment to comfort the young girl, then resumed his work. Edith began to wail. Emma stood nearby, wringing her hands. Tobe cleared his throat.

When the doctor finished, he explained his work. "She had a blood clot close to her brain. This treatment should really help. We'll give her some time to heal before the next treatment." Gently swabbing the young girl's mouth with a wet cloth, he handed her to Emma.

Emma tossed a diaper onto her shoulder and laid her daughter's head against it. Edith sobbed as her mother swayed and stroked her trembling body.

The doctor showed them to the door. "I'd like to see her again in three weeks. You can schedule it with the lady at the front desk." Tobe made an appointment, then paid for the visit.

Edith fell asleep soon after the driver pulled onto the main road toward Kalona. The next morning after Tobe made a few contacts, they headed for Kansas. They arrived home late that evening, and Emma put the child right to bed. The next morning she commented, "Edith hasn't slept this well in months."

"The treatment must have helped," Tobe said. "Maybe she'll start to talk before long, too."

Emma worried aloud that they wouldn't have enough money to pay the doctor. With the new shop, things were really tight again, but as always Tobe was optimistic. "We'll be doing better in a few weeks. We've just sold a few truck beds."

"Are we making any money on them?"

"Not as much as I would like. I still have to pay Ed royalties."

"What royalty is that?"

"I'm paying Ed Nisly $35 for each truck bed we sell these days. It was one of the conditions for borrowing money. I agreed to pay that amount instead of interest."

Emma's face fell. "That seems like a lot of money."

"It is. But I didn't see any other way around. We needed the money."

"I don't like to borrow money. Grandpa lost a piece of land once because he couldn't make the loan payments. He always told us grandchildren to avoid borrowing if possible."

"Well, I paid Willie Wagler back. I couldn't pay the ten percent interest but at least he got the principal back. With a little luck, I'll be able to give him his interest too."

Indeed, Tobe needed luck that week. Late one afternoon, Ervin refueled the cutoff saw they used to cut window parts. It was chilly, so he was wearing reversible jersey gloves. In the dark shop, it was hard to tell how much gas was in the tank. When he saw gas overflowing the tank, he grabbed for the funnel. As he jerked the funnel away from the hot motor, the unused thumb of his reversible jersey glove caught the engine's starter switch. The spark exploded the fumes into flame.

"Fire!" Ervin yelled and ran to the front doors where Tobe was talking to a customer near the hitching post. Tobe turned and dashed inside to find the blaze leaping up around the saw. Black smoke from burning window parts billowed against the ceiling and spread toward the four corners of the shop.

"Somebody call the fire department. Now!" Tobe yelled. "We gotta get this stuff out." Everyone scrambled to carry wood and tools from the path of the fire.

Tobe's eyes lighted on the gasoline drum along the wall. If the flames reached that barrel, they'd never save the building. He raced toward the fifty-gallon fuel drum. It was nearly three-quarters full.

He jerked the barrel by its flanges and lugged it toward the door. Raymond Yutzy ran to help as Tobe emerged from the shop hefting the container. They set the container down a safe distance from the shop and ran back inside. The fire licked against the ceiling, charring the rafters and sheathing.

After most things were out, Tobe and his employees closed the doors and windows and stood outside, praying for the fire company to arrive. They watched through the windows with dismay as the black smoke dropped lower and lower from the ceiling. When the fire engines arrived, the fire fighters broke a window on the side near the fire. It took only a few minutes to tame the fire. Tobe breathed a sigh of relief that no extensive damage was done. He could live with charred rafters and roof sheeting.

Tobe's creditors observed that it was the second fire in one of Tobe's shops. Neither occasion brought great loss, but they wondered aloud if Tobe couldn't improve on his fire safety. He might not be so lucky the next time. Several church members got their heads together and asked to meet with Tobe.

Tobe greeted the group politely. He listened respectfully to their suggestions and promised to warn his employees to be more careful. He didn't want to offend his investors. That would be as serious as losing the shop to a fire.

As his debts grew, Tobe chafed under the watchful eye of his investors. He got tired of all the advice, especially when it came from close relatives like Emma's family. Even the agreements his brother Clarence made for paying back loans bothered Tobe. He didn't like being told what to do.

After all, Tobe kept thinking to himself, I'm trying to break new ground. What do all these busybodies know about manufacturing? Nothing. Maybe he and Emma would just have to find another place to live. A place where the church would get less involved in his business. Iowa?

That week at work Clarence told Tobe he was engaged. Tobe's first thought was maybe Clarence could take over the Kansas shop. That way Tobe and Emma could move.

• • • •

By late spring 1951, Tobe had made several sales trips to Kalona, Iowa, coordinating them with Edith's appointments with Dr. Huls. He dreamed of starting a business branch in Kalona. Many Amish lived there, so labor would be relatively cheap and easy to find. And it would be close to Davenport, where Edith could get regular treatments. If Emma could be persuaded, the family could move before summer.

Tobe waited for the right moment to share his idea with Emma. He broached the subject one evening after she had put Edith to bed. "Edith seemed a bit fussy tonight."

"She's nearly always fussy. I don't know what she wants."

"Do you think we should take her to the doctor in Davenport more often?" Tobe wondered.

"How could we afford it? It's expensive to be driving back and forth to Iowa."

"Maybe we should just move up there."

"No. Why would we want to move up there? Our families are here."

"It might be easier to make a living up there than here."

Emma was quiet. She would have to be convinced.

Tobe continued. "It would be better to live closer to the doctor for Edith, and we really can't afford to make the trip to Davenport as often as she needs it. We'll just stay a couple months, just long enough to see if he can help Edith."

Still Emma stayed silent.

"I can sell aluminum storm windows and other products up there. People in Kalona have more money than we do here. I'd like to give Clarence a chance to manage this shop. He's doing a good job, and we're getting our bills paid off. Uncle Fred lives up there, so we'd still have some family close by."

"Let me think about it," Emma finally said. The late spring air seemed to grow colder as they went to bed.

The next morning Tobe made another attempt as Emma set the table for breakfast. "Why don't we just try it for the summer? Someone told me about a family in Kalona that's going to be away from their house all summer. They would let us live almost rent-free for taking care of their place. Okay?"

"I guess we could try it if you think we could get out of debt that way."

"Good, we'll plan to move as soon as I can get everything worked out."

18

Iowa

Young Perry Lee Stutzman sat up in his seat as the conductor walked through the passenger car. "Washington station is next. Everyone for Washington, Iowa, this is your stop." Mary Edna and Glenn Wayne sniffed the air. The smell of hot asbestos wafted through the open window as the brakes slowed the train. "*Was schmacke mir?* What do we smell?"

"It's the brakes," Emma explained. She motioned for the children to pick up their luggage. The train screeched to a halt.

"Are you the Stutzman family?" A stranger with plain clothes and a black hat stepped forward to greet them as they disembarked. Emma nodded and smiled.

"I'm Eli Yoder. I'll be taking you out to your new place. I heard Tobe's coming with the truck, right?"

"Yes. He should be in Kalona by the time we get there."

The children climbed into the back seat of the old Nash. Emma joined Eli and his wife in the front seat. As they drove toward Kalona, Perry Lee peered over the seat at the instrument panel. He stared at the gauges as the needle of the speedometer rose above the 60 mark. Eli casually put one hand in front of the speedometer and steered with the other. Perry sat back and watched the landscape.

In less than half an hour, the snub-nosed car pulled into the lane of the Omar Rhodes residence on Sixth Street. The children jumped out ready to explore their new environment.

They ran squealing from room to room in the house. The Rhodes family was gone for the summer and had left their home fully furnished for the Stutzmans.

"Look, Mom. Toys!" little Edith squealed. They emptied the closet onto the floor just as Tobe pulled into the driveway.

"Come on, children, I need help to unload everything. We'll have to store some of our things in the garage."

By suppertime the next day, the family was settled in. As they sat down to eat, Tobe turned to the children: "How do you think you're going to like living in town?" His voice reflected his own optimism.

Glenn spoke first. "It seems so different in town. We can look right out our windows at the neighbors. I could hear them talking today."

Mary Edna chimed in, "I like the electric lights. Will the church mind?"

Tobe shook his head. "They shouldn't mind, since we're only staying for a few months. If we moved here permanently, we'd have to disconnect the electricity."

"Can the neighbors see us at night when we have our lights on?" Glenn was curious.

Mary Edna answered, "Yes. I was outside last night. I could see right into our house."

"Is that why the neighbors have their blinds shut?" Perry asked.

Emma spoke up. "Yes. Since we have close neighbors, we need to close our curtains at night, too."

Tobe turned to Emma. "But there are good things about living in town. We can walk to the store. And Fred Nisly told me that the guy down at the general store, Emil Hesselschwerdt—how about that name—lets you buy food on a charge account."

Emma nodded. "That's good."

A few weeks later on a Sunday evening, the family talked about their new Amish church district. They had been to church twice since moving to Iowa.

Mary Edna dipped into a dish of popcorn and said, "The girls dress different here than back home."

Tobe looked up with interest. "I didn't notice."

"The capes are different, aren't they, Mom?"

Emma nodded.

"The girls here have three pleats in the back where the cape fastens. We have only two."

"That's pretty important," Tobe joked as he munched on a mouthful of popcorn.

"The married women wear organdy capes with ribbons underneath. And they wear bows in the back. Mom just pins hers."

Tobe laughed. "Yeah, I did notice that. The women here dress a little fancier."

Emma objected. "I think it's more strict to wear the organdy cape. They think we're being fancy by wearing the same material."

"I know," Tobe acknowledged. "I was just trying to have a little fun." He hoped Emma wouldn't go to the work of making new capes, even though she stood out as a visitor every Sunday.

"It's nice that they let you lead singing, Dad," Mary Edna said. "That other song leader just couldn't seem to get the song started right."

Tobe laughed. "After three tries, it was time for him to give up." By the Stutzman family's second Sunday, the congregation looked to Tobe to start the songs. His clear tenor voice got the songs off to a good start.

Over the next few weeks, Emma and Tobe observed other differences between the Amish in Iowa and Kansas. In Iowa they were surprised to discover a stronger emphasis on keeping the *Ordnung*. They were accustomed to the growing tolerance in the church at home. Willie Wagler and some of the other young preachers had experienced new vitality in their faith, and they weren't as rigid about the *Ordnung*.

Although the Amish leaders in Kalona had not embraced the revival movement, people still talked a lot about what was happening in other communities. Beginning June 3, 1951, two brothers named George and Lawrence Brunk conducted a series of popular tent meetings in Lancaster County, Pennsylvania. By mid-July 15,000 people had attended the meetings. More than a thousand people made public confessions or rededicated their lives to Jesus Christ. The Brunks took their tent and their message to several other Mennonite communities over the next few months. The words on the side of their truck proclaimed, "The Whole Gospel for the Whole World."

Only a few Amish people attended the meetings, but young Amish leaders followed the campaign reports with keen interest. Tobe's uncle David Miller from Oklahoma was particularly moved by the reports of revival among the Mennonites in the eastern states. That fall the young minister with the booming voice began to travel as an evangelist in several Amish communities.

• • • •

Shortly after they arrived in Kalona, Tobe rented a retail space beside Reiff's General Store, a town landmark. He also ordered some advertising materials. When the package arrived, he eagerly tore it open. "Ah, these look great," he said aloud even though no one was in the room. "Now, whenever someone stops by, I can give them one of my specially made pencils." He rolled one between his fingers. The aluminum-colored barrel sported a message in blue ink:

ALUMINUM STORM WINDOWS
T. J. Stutzman—Kalona, Iowa
World Famous "Calanda" Sewing Machines

Sewing machines were a new venture for Tobe. He convinced himself they would be a good way to get his business off the ground in Iowa, giving him time to develop the window manufacturing business. He pulled one of his newly printed advertising leaflets out of the box and read it.

STOP AND THINK!

Aluminum combination windows are usually pretty high priced. This window sells for much less than competitive windows for these are sold direct from the factory to the user. There are no wholesalers or dealers.
All openings are measured and each window is tailored to fit the opening. The same factory representative who measures your openings will install your windows. If you are building, or have built a new house, these windows are nearly as cheap as a wooden screen and storm sash. The finish on these windows is permanent, therefore needs no repainting.
Order now for Fall Delivery—Ask for a representative to come to your house and give you a free estimate, or call at our local office at East Barnes Street in Kalona, Iowa.
YOU ARE UNDER NO OBLIGATION—
ACT TODAY
T. J. STUTZMAN
Telephone 175 P.O. Box 177
KALONA, IOWA

Tobe liked the printer's work. The sheets looked good and the wording sounded professional. This leaflet would soon be bringing in lots of business. He was sure of it.

He was smiling broadly when Perry and Glenn burst through the door. "Hey, Dad. Guess what!"

"What?"

"We found a place to make some money!"

"Where?"

"You know that Dick White who lives in a brooder house. He doesn't have running water so he said he would pay us to carry it to him. We can earn a lot if we carry it every day."

"That's good, boys. Maybe you'll find other people who will give you work, too."

The door slammed as the boys ran back outside. Tobe looked with pleasure at the phone number on the advertisement sheet. He'd never owned a phone before, but he needed one to get the business going. Would the Iowa district bishop approve? Tobe wondered to himself. Then he remembered that as long as they kept their church membership in Kansas, they probably wouldn't be approached by the bishop.

The next Sunday the Stutzman family joined Emma's Uncle Fred and his family for dinner. After the meal, Emma stood at the sink with her Aunt Katie. All the children except Edith ran out to play. The four-year-old sat on Tobe's lap in the adjoining room. Emma pulled a plate from the rinse water and wiped it dry.

Katie broke the silence, "How is Edith doing?"

"She still doesn't walk right. We're going to Dr. Huls over at Davenport about every two weeks. It seems to help."

"Do they think she'll be able to care for herself when she gets older?" Katie asked.

"I'm afraid not. The doctor said she'll probably not live to be twenty years old."

"Oh my." Katie's head dropped. She scrubbed a pan vigorously. "At least you don't have so far to drive now. It was pretty far to drive from Kansas."

"That's true," Emma sighed. "But I miss my family."

"I can understand that," Katie said. "How long will you stay here in Iowa?"

"Tobe says probably until the end of the summer. Then he'll have the window sales going and someone else can take over the business. But everything usually takes longer than Tobe thinks." Katie laughed but didn't comment as she washed the last dish and handed it to Emma to dry.

That night Tobe and Emma lay in bed, covered only by a sheet. "It's more humid here than back home in Kansas," Tobe complained. "It makes you sweat more."

Emma agreed. "And I miss the breeze at night."

Tobe fanned the sheet up and down to move the air. "The people are different, too. They don't seem as friendly as we are in Kansas."

"Uh huh," Emma said.

"They're more concerned about money, too. It might be a little harder to borrow here than it was back home."

Emma turned toward her husband. "Do we have to borrow money already?"

"No, it's just that if I did need it, it might be a little harder to get."

"Well, I hope we don't have to."

"Me too. But you never know." Tobe turned over and soon dozed off despite the heat.

The next morning Tobe showed window samples to a prospective customer who had called as a result of the new ad. Together they surveyed the man's old frame house.

Tobe stood by a south window and pointed out how loosely the sash fit against the frame. "You could use storm windows all right. How do you heat your house?"

"Heating oil."

"Then you could save a bundle on your heating bill. You lose a lot of heat through those windows."

They walked around the house to the place where Tobe's buggy stood. "Here, let me show you how these windows work. You should have your wife here to watch this."

The man motioned toward the house. "She's inside."

Tobe held up a half-sized window. "We'll take this sample inside."

Tobe greeted the slight gray-haired woman who came to the door. He set the sample on the floor and showed them its features.

After a few questions from the older couple, Tobe knew he was about to make a sale. "We can get these installed in less than two weeks," he promised. "I can measure and order them today and they'll be here next week. I'll install them myself. Satisfaction guaranteed."

The couple looked at each other. She nodded. The man turned back to Tobe. "It's a deal. We'll take them." They shook hands, and Tobe climbed into his buggy. Clucking to the horse, he waved good-bye.

••••

Arvilla Weaver was sitting at the office desk when Tobe returned. He handed his new secretary the order. "Let's put this order in the mail to the Kansas shop today. I'd like to install them by the end of next week. Ervin can send these windows up with the other orders."

Arvilla nodded and took the paper.

Tobe liked Arvilla's work. As partial pay, he allowed her to stay in the little brooder house behind the shop. On weekends she went home to stay with her parents, who lived several miles away.

Tobe reached for a handful of peanuts as he lingered near the cluttered desk. "Maybe by fall we can turn a profit here. But I haven't quite got you Iowa people figured out yet."

"I'm not really from Iowa."

"Oh, where are you from?"

"Indiana."

"Why did you move here?"

"My sister Lulu didn't like the church in Indiana. My folks thought if we moved to Iowa, she'd feel better about joining the church."

"Does she?"

"No. She didn't even move here with us."

"That's too bad."

Tobe paused, then changed the subject. "You seem to have taken a liking to Edith."

"Yes, I like children. But sometimes I wonder if I'll ever have any of my own."

Tobe felt a bit awkward as they talked. At 31 years of age, Arvilla was past the usual age for Amish women to be married.

She continued, "So I think maybe God has called me to take care of other people's children. Children with special needs. If you ever need someone to take care of Edith, I'll be glad to watch her for you."

"Thanks. I'll say something to Emma about that." He paused. "I'm going now. You can lock up when you're ready to go home."

The next week Fred Yutzy delivered the windows. Tobe stepped outside and waved as he rolled down the window of his green Chevrolet truck. "Come on in and see our office."

Fred hopped out of his truck and followed Tobe inside. "*Ich hab gute Zeit gemacht.* I made pretty good time."

"Good. How many windows have you got on there?"

"Fifty-one."

"After you've had a little rest why don't we take them right out to the customer? That way I won't have to handle them twice."

"Whatever you say."

Fred leaned back in his chair. "How's it going up here?"

"Well, I installed the windows you brought up here the last time. And I've been selling sewing machines."

"What kind?"

"Calanda. They're the best. Do you want one for Susan? I can trade you for window delivery."

"No, she already has a Singer."

Tobe held out an advertising pencil. "Here, have one."

Fred looked at the pencil. "Calanda. I never heard of it. At least the pencil looks nice."

Tobe got up from his chair. "Let's get those windows delivered before dark." He dug through a stack of papers on his desk. "Where did I put those orders? Oh, here they are."

The two men walked toward the truck. As Tobe jumped in, he asked, "Your wheels look nice and clean. Do you still have the coil hooked up to shock dogs?"

Fred grinned. "Yeah. It works pretty good."

"That's okay," Tobe replied. "Just don't use it on people."

"Don't worry," Fred laughed as he started the truck and headed north out of Kalona to drop off the windows. By late afternoon, they were finished.

"Hope to see you again soon," Tobe told Fred as he prepared to leave. "We should have another big window order before too long."

The next Sunday at church, several men talked about Tobe's business as the crowd dispersed from the Sunday meal. They watched as Tobe pulled up to the house with the buggy. Emma handed Edith up to Tobe then climbed in and pulled Edith onto her lap. The three older children climbed into the back of the two-seated buggy and Tobe tapped Bess with the reins. The horse took off at a rapid trot.

One of the men commented, "He sure is a go-getter."

"The horse?" a second asked.

"No, Tobe," countered the first. They laughed.

A third man chimed in. "They say he's quite the salesman. Someone said he could sell just about anything to just about anybody."

"I bet he could sell you something you don't want," the first replied. They all laughed.

"I heard that a few of our people bought windows from him already. I wonder how they like them."

"Well, if they like his products, he'll do okay."

The group broke up as their wives walked from the house. It was time to go home.

The next day Eli Bontrager tied his horse and stepped into Tobe's office. As his eyes adjusted to the dim lighting, he heard a child coughing. Arvilla was wiping up the floor. Edith stood nearby, wringing her hands. The smell of vomit hung in the air.

Arvilla looked up. "I'm sorry. I'll be with you in a minute."

Edith coughed into her handkerchief and laughed nervously.

Eli glanced around the room as Arvilla finished her task. She reappeared in a moment at the front desk.

"How may I help you?"

"I need a belt for my wife's Singer. I was told this is the place to get it."

"Yes, we have them." Arvilla stepped to a nearby shelf and picked a belt. "I'm sorry you had to see the mess Edith made." Her voice lowered to a whisper. "We're waiting for someone to take us to Washington to see Dr. Fray. She gets terribly nervous when she's going to the doctor. That's why she threw up."

"I see." Eli cleared his throat. "You know our son Ellis has spastic paralysis."

"Yes." Arvilla remembered having seen the young boy.

"We took him to Dr. Huls in Davenport for a couple of years. Maybe Dr. Huls could help Edith too." He laid a five-dollar bill on the desk and waited as she made change.

"They've been taking her to Dr. Huls but she sees another doctor in Washington as well."

• • • •

The summer went by quickly for Tobe. By the end of August, he knew he wouldn't be ready to move back to Kansas in the fall. He brought it up to Emma one Sunday afternoon.

"How do you like it here in Iowa?" he asked, munching on a handful of popcorn.

"It's okay. I'm looking forward to going back to Kansas though."

"I wonder if it might not be good to stay here for another few months. Maybe a year. It's taking a little longer than I thought to get the sales going here. I'm not ready yet to hand it over to someone else."

Emma bit her lip.

Tobe continued. "If we're going to stay, we need to find another place soon. The Rhodes are coming back you know."

She listened in silence.

"Jason Boller owns a place north of Kalona, just up from the Prairie Dale school. He keeps hogs there. He said he'd let us live there rent-free if we keep up the place. Shall I tell him we want it?"

A tear slipped down Emma's cheek. "I guess."

Tobe used his most reassuring voice, "We probably won't stay there long."

She nodded wordlessly.

A week or so after the Stutzman family was settled at the Boller place, Edith came screaming into the house. Blood dripped from her face. Emma snatched a wet cloth and pressed it against the ugly gashes on the child's cheeks. "What happened?"

Edith wailed as the coarse cloth touched her raw flesh. She waved her hand toward the pig pen.

"Did the sow bite you?"

Edith nodded.

Emma yelled to Perry Lee, who came running. "Go hitch the horse." Soon they were on the way to Dr. Sattler's office in Kalona. Along the way, they stopped at a neighbor's house to call Tobe. He met them at the doctor's office.

By evening Edith had settled down enough to fall asleep. But for the next few days, she was restless. It was hard to keep her facial bandages in place.

By Thanksgiving when Tobe's brothers came up from Hutchinson, Edith's face was almost completely healed. Emma spent the morning preparing a holiday meal while the men discussed business. The mantel clock struck twelve as she called out, "Dinner's ready."

The grace ended and Tobe looked at Ervin and Clarence, "Just reach in and help yourselves."

"I understand that your dad is laid up with heart trouble," Clarence commented to Emma.

"Yes, and he has an awful cough. Raymond is doing the farming now," she replied.

"And you've got some new workers at the shop, too," Tobe said to Ervin.

"Yep. Leander Mast, Samuel Nisly, and Menno Nisly are all there." Tobe smiled. He remembered the time when Samuel had visited his shop as a young boy.

"*Es iss gut fer zammer sei.* It's good for us to be together. It's almost like being back in Kansas," Tobe declared.

"Yeah, there's nothing like getting a bunch of Stutzman brothers together." Clarence grinned. They all laughed.

Tobe looked at Clarence. "So how's it going at EMC?" He could hardly imagine a member of the Stutzman family going to college, but Clarence had enrolled at Eastern Mennonite College in Harrisonburg, Virginia. He began classes that fall.

"Well it's pretty tough. Since I didn't have high school, I really have to hit the books."

"How did they let you in without high school?"

"I took my GED."

"What's that?"

"It stands for General Educational Development. It's a test to prove you know enough to go to college. I guess I proved myself because the pre-med courses at EMC are not easy. I have to go four years to EMC; then four years of medical school. I'm hoping to be a missionary doctor, like our cousin Walter Schlabach. Maybe I'll work in Africa."

"How in the world can you afford it?" It was Ervin speaking this time.

"Bunny's working. I'll work in the shop during the summer and do some sales work during the school year. It's expensive but we'll make it somehow. Bunny and I, we'll hang together. This is the first time we've been apart from each other since we're married."

Tobe felt a twinge of envy mixed with disappointment. "I guess if you're going to be a doctor you won't have anything more to do with the shop."

Ervin chimed in. "It looks as though I'll have to manage the business in Kansas by myself. Of course, Perry helps sometimes."

In early December, Tobe and Emma learned that Bishop Jake Miller had died. Since the bishop led the church district, it would be an important time of transition in the church back home.

A few days later, Emma got a letter from her mother. She sat on the rocking chair and read aloud, "*Da Chek hot en grosse Leicht ghat.* Jake had a big funeral. It was so big they had to hold it in three different houses. They counted 560 people."

Tobe spoke without looking up from his paper, "He had a lot of relatives."

Emma nodded.

"I wonder how things will change now that Jake is gone?" Tobe said aloud.

"I doubt they'll change too much."

"Maybe they'll allow electricity. If they don't, more people will go over to the Conservatives."

"Maybe."

"It would help in the shop."

"Yes," Emma conceded. She moved to the cupboard and pulled out a pan as she prepared to fix supper. Shivering, she watched as flakes of snow fluttered against the windowpane. The Boller house was drafty and cold. The heat from the pot-bellied stove in the living room barely reached to the other rooms. On windy days snow slipped through the loose fitting windows and lay on the beds. Especially at night, the family heard rats and squirrels running through the walls and above the ceiling. As she brought water to a boil on the gas stove, Emma gingerly asked Tobe how much longer they'd need to put up with this house.

"It all depends on whether or not I can get a good loan here. There are a couple of men who are really interested in my business. If I can get a loan, we'll start manufacturing here. Then we can make a really good living and get a better place."

"Edith needs eyeglasses."

"We'll try to get the money. Maybe Ananias Beachy will give us a loan." Ananias, often called A. J., was one of the most influential farmers in the Iowa Amish church. Tobe reasoned that if A. J. loaned him money, others might invest too.

Although A. J. Beachy was more than sixty years old, he identified with the efforts of the younger generation to strengthen the spiritual life of the church. A supporter of the growing mission thrust in the church, he gave considerable money to fund the new missions committee.

Tobe felt excitement mixed with apprehension as he guided his rig into the Beachy farm lane. It wouldn't be easy to talk A. J. into parting with his hard-earned cash. If A. J. refused to loan him money, other prospective investors might get cold feet.

Tobe tied his horse and walked toward the door. A. J. saw him coming and opened the door before Tobe could knock. Tobe surveyed the man's countenance. Would he make a loan?

19

Pushing the Edges

Tobe's heart pounded as he said good-bye to A. J. and walked to the hitching post. *Er lehnt mir Geld! He's giving me a loan*! He untied the horse and sprang into the buggy seat, then guided the team onto the macadam road. Coming to Iowa was going to pay off big. This was going to be a great place to live and work!

Emma didn't say much when Tobe burst into the house with the news. It just seemed like more of the same. And it was bound to stretch out their stay in Iowa. She longed to go home and kept in close touch with the Kansas news.

Already, they were missing out on an important event. Because her father's health was failing, the church had decided to hold an ordination. Emma wondered what the new preacher would be like. Would he be like her father? Or would he be more open to new things like electricity and cars? The ordination took place in May 1952, around the time Tobe and Emma's children finished their first year at the Prairie Dale school. Tobe read about it in the *Budget*. He turned to Emma, who was just waking up from a nap. "It says here that Amos Nisly was ordained."

Tobe read aloud, "'The Lord's Supper was held at the Enos Miller house the eleventh where an ordination took place. The lot fell on Brother Amos Nisly, son of Noah Nisly.'" Tobe looked up from the paper. "Amos is pretty young to be a preacher, isn't he?"

"Maybe two years older than my brother Raymond. Probably about 28."

Images of Amos Nisly's younger days flashed through Tobe's mind. "He doesn't seem like the preacher type. Maybe he's settled down now."

"I think so."

· · · ·

Each evening when school let out, Tobe's three oldest children walked to the shop. Nine-year-old Perry Lee was particularly fascinated by the machines. One day when Tobe was out, the boy stood spellbound by the rotating gears on the punch press. He pressed his index finger against the gear edges, watching them make circles. Suddenly his little finger fell between the gears, nearly pinching it off at the top knuckle.

Arvilla came running when she heard him scream. She wiped the blood off the injured finger. The tip fell away, hanging by a thread of skin. Arvilla grabbed paper towels and clean linens and hollered at Glenn, "We're going to the doctor."

Perry Lee's wound dripped blood on the sidewalk as they walked to the doctor's office a few blocks away. Dr. Beckman stitched the finger back on. "I believe it'll heal," he said.

When Tobe returned to the shop, Glenn told him what had happened. Tobe quickly called the doctor's office to see how his son was doing. Grateful to learn that the finger could be saved, he went back to his work. He was content to leave the situation in Arvilla's hands. Arvilla took Perry Lee back to the doctor a couple of times over the next weeks. The wound healed well, but a visible scar and malformed fingernail left evidence of the trauma.

· · · ·

Over the next several years, a storm brewed in the Kalona Amish church. The new mission committee pushed the edges of the *Ordnung* by supporting and placing evangelistic workers in Gulfport, Mississippi. Among them were Emma's sister Elizabeth and her husband John Bender.

But how were the workers to go about their ministry? The Gulfport mission unit was located in a rural area with scattered residents. Horse and buggy transportation was impractical, and it seemed quaint to drive tractors in the place of cars. But owning a car would have put the workers in jeopardy with church discipline.

After some discussion, the Amish mission committee negotiated with The Wayside Mission, operated by local Mennonites, to purchase a car on the mission committee's behalf. Unrest occurred because the bishops weren't happy about sending out mission workers whose evangelistic methods undermined the convictions of the church at home.

Church leaders also opposed the mission movement because of its close association with the mission conference held the previous summer. For one thing, they reminded each other, the movement was spearheaded by Russell Maniaci, who was not Amish. Maniaci could not even speak German so his newsletter and most of the mission meetings used English.

Furthermore, the meetings were open to people of other denominations. They even had a Mennonite speaker. One needed only to look at neighboring Mennonite churches to see that if the church quit speaking German, it would soon succumb to the ways of the world.

The Missions Interest Committee, as it was by then being called, responded to the criticism by asking Maniaci to bow out of leadership. He reluctantly agreed, handing over his mailing list to the committee. The group carried on where Maniaci left off. They began their own newsletter called *Witnessing*. Tobe's friend Willie Wagler from Kansas was a contributing editor. They set out to provide places of service for the many young people who had consecrated their lives to Christian service in the summer missions conference.

Tension in the church grew, and the controversy reached a climax when A. J. Beachy was asked by his bishop to make a public confession. He admitted that as secretary/treasurer of the mission committee, he had disregarded the ministers and the church. He also agreed to leave his post. But shortly after his resignation, his son-in-law, David L. Miller of Kansas, took over the role.

The mission meetings weren't the only cause for controversy. Amish leaders also looked askance at the growing interest in tent revivals. The Brunk brothers were on the road again, preaching at protracted meetings in communities from Lancaster, Pennsylvania, to Waterloo, Ontario. In Ohio a group of laymen formed the Christian Laymen's Tent Evangelism, Inc. Was it attendance at these meetings that caused members to be discontented with church traditions? Or was it discontent that fueled their interest in the meetings? The bishops weren't sure. But revival preaching often threatened the church with its fanaticism and emotional excess.

Tobe's uncle David followed the path of the Brunk revival preachers to Lancaster, Pennsylvania. While there, he preached to large crowds of Amish believers. His booming voice and fervent manner attracted eager hearers to services every day of the week. Sometimes he began his sermons by introducing himself, "I'm Dave Miller." Such an introduction stood in stark contrast to the humble reserve of most Amish preachers, who simply referred to themselves as God's servants.

Word of Dave's preaching spread quickly, attracting record numbers to a Sunday morning service near New Holland, Pennsylvania. The hosts scurried to borrow extra benches from the neighboring church district. When they still ran short, extra seats were provided by spanning planks across hay bales. The crowd was so large that they had to go to several nearby homes for the noon meal. That afternoon David spoke to a group of two hundred young people. Tears coursed down his cheeks as he pled for spiritual repentance and a Holy Ghost revival.

Many of David's hearers that week were reform-minded Amish. But opposing ministers and deacons also sat in the crowd. Some insisted that the enthusiastic guest preacher was losing his mind. They worried that his emphasis on spiritual life and witness would undermine the church. After a few days of deliberation, church leaders wrote Dave a letter asking him not to return to the area.

Undaunted, David traveled through Delaware and other states with large Amish settlements. Particularly in Ohio, he found eager followers. There he preached for thirteen days straight, addressing record numbers in barns, chicken houses, and open lawns. For weeks afterward, children played "Dave Miller" games. Young boys imitated his energetic preaching while their playmates served patiently as parishioners.

Around the time Uncle Dave was traveling around the country, Tobe's brother Perry moved to Iowa to live with the Stutzman family. Tobe told his children, "Your Uncle Perry is going to stay with us. He'll work in the shop with me."

"Oh good. When is he coming?" Glenn was enthusiastic about the prospects of a live-in guest.

"Tomorrow. We'll pick him up at the train station."

Perry Lee piped up. "How are we going to know which Perry you're talking to, since we both have the same name?"

Tobe thought for a moment. "How about if we call you Perry Lee and just call him Perry? His real name is L. Perry."

"What does the 'L' stand for?" Glenn was curious.

"Levi. That's his grandpa's name."

"Why don't we call him Levi?" Mary Edna inquired.

"I don't think he likes that name. Let's just call him Perry."

The family quickly adjusted to Perry's presence. They especially enjoyed his dry sense of humor, and Perry enjoyed working with his older brother.

Soon after he got to Iowa, Perry and Tobe took a train to Chicago on a business trip. Perry appreciated the opportunity to explore the world beyond the small community back home, and Tobe was glad for the company. On the trip, Perry asked Tobe why he and Emma had not moved their church membership from Kansas to Iowa.

"We're not ready to join the church here yet. They're just a bit too strict for me. I'm sure they wouldn't let us have electricity at the shop. We'll be going home to Kansas for the fall communion. You can go along if you want."

As October 1952 turned into November, the country was alive with election fever. The Stutzman family was back in Iowa after the quick trip home for communion, and the children came home from school each day full of news about the upcoming presidential election. Tobe didn't usually pay much attention to politics, but he hoped that the young general, Dwight Eisenhower, would win.

At the supper table on November 5, the family talked about the vote. Tobe asked, "Did you learn who our new President is going to be?"

"Yes. Dwight D. Eisenhower," Mary Edna burst out.

"Right. He was a general in World War II. Now he's going to try to keep us from getting into trouble in Korea. The Communists are trying to take over."

"Will the Communists come here?" Glenn was troubled.

"No, I don't think we have anything to worry about." Tobe assured him. "But the draft is taking our young men into service."

"What's a draft?"

"A draft is where the army calls you to go and fight. Our people don't believe in fighting so we go to work in camps or hospitals. Remember, Uncle John served in CPS for several years. When you're drafted, you have to go to the service or you'll be put in jail."

A sober mood settled over the family. "Will Uncle Perry have to go?"

Tobe glanced at his brother. "Probably so, if they keep calling men the way they are now."

Perry replied, "If I'm called, I'd go into I-W service somewhere."

"What is I-W?" Mary Edna asked.

"I-W is the new program that President Truman started," Tobe responded. "The COs don't have to go to camps any more. Now they work in hospitals or other places where the government puts them. The draft classifies them as I-W, so we call it the I-W program."

"Isn't that what John and Lizzie are doing in Gulfport?" Perry Lee asked.

"Yes," Emma replied. "They are serving with the Mission Interest Committee."

"When the shop gets going," Tobe said, "we'll have lots of money for missions. Maybe we can support a missionary family by ourselves."

It wasn't long before the draft reached into the Stutzman family. The very next week they learned that Clarence had been drafted along with six other young men from Hutchinson. Tobe brought the news announcement from the *Budget* to the supper table. "Children, do you remember what I said last week about the draft? The *Budget* says that fifty COs were called to Topeka, Kansas, in the past two months. Uncle Clarence is one of them."

"So he has to go back into service?" Perry Lee asked.

"Yes, I'm afraid so," Tobe responded. "He's going to work at a mental hospital."

"Can he still be a doctor?" Mary Edna asked.

"We'll have to wait and see. He had to leave school."

Not long after, Clarence and Bunny invited Tobe's family to Topeka for Thanksgiving dinner. As they served turkey and dressing, the young couple told about their first two weeks of I-W service in the mental hospital.

"You wouldn't believe it, but 130 new guys reported here for work at the same time," Clarence exclaimed. "Most of us came from Kansas and Nebraska."

"We only had one nurse on our floor," Bunny went on. "With just three months of training, the men are going to do nurse's work, giving IVs and so forth."

"We had to read a book called *Snakepit*," Clarence said. "It tells about the problems with mental hospitals. At one hospital, they would beat the patients by swinging a piece of soap inside a sock. That's how they kept them in line."

"The men here are determined to make a difference in the way people get treated," Bunny said.

Tobe listened attentively. He couldn't imagine himself working in a hospital. The day passed quickly, ending with a short tour around the city.

At the same time Clarence was stepping into a new venture in Topeka, Tobe set out on a bold one of his own. With borrowed money, he decided to set up a manufacturing shop in Kalona. He had been right that A. J. Beachy's investment in his company would attract other people.

As Tobe moved into his second full year in Iowa, he could count numerous investors. Most were members of nearby Amish and Mennonite churches who loaned thousands of dollars in unsecured promissory notes. Brothers Ray, Glen, and Earl Beachy, along with several others, formed an informal advisory board. They saw great potential for generous returns on their investment dollars.

As winter neared, Emma again pled with Tobe to move back to Kansas. She was expecting another child in April or

May, and last winter in the Boller house had been so uncomfortable. Instead of agreeing to move home, Tobe promised to find a better place.

The winter solstice had just passed when he announced good news at the supper table. "*Mir tsehle weckziehe.* We're going to move."

"Where are we going?" Mary Edna and Glenn asked at the same time.

"To the Irvin Gingerich farm. Ezra Brennemans are moving out this week. We can move in as soon as they're gone. We can pay the rent there by milking the cows and feeding the hogs."

"Well at least I'll be glad to get out of this drafty old house," Emma sighed. "And we'll be much closer to Arvilla and her parents." Tobe and Emma felt free to leave Edith in their care.

"Okay, we'll move on Tuesday," Tobe said. "That's two days before Christmas."

The move worked out as Tobe had planned, and moving boxes were still in evidence when the children opened their Christmas gifts. Mary Edna squealed with delight at her gift. "Oh, thank you. A five-year diary. Just what I always wanted."

Tobe apologized for the small number of gifts. "We're low in cash," he explained.

"Can't you just write a check?" Glenn suggested.

Tobe grinned. "No, you have to have money in the bank to write checks."

The gray skies in January mirrored Emma's demeanor as the next months passed. Tobe tried to sympathize. She had gained more weight with this pregnancy than with the previous four. The family news from Kansas told about many changes. Her brother Rufus had been drafted into 1-W service. Dad Nisly's heart condition was worsening, and he and Emma's mother were moving into a "Dawdy house" beside the farmhouse. Fred and his family would move into the main house. The farm sale was scheduled for March. Tobe agreed that they would attend the sale even though it would be late in her pregnancy.

About the time that Emma's folks moved into their new "Dawdy" house, Tobe's mother fell on the ice and broke her arm. Tobe told the children about it at the supper table.

Mary Edna asked, "How long will Grandma have to wear a cast on her arm, Dad?"

"At least several weeks."

"Can she work with a cast on her arm?" Perry Lee asked.

Emma answered. "It's hard to work with one arm. They're moving in with Dan Mattie. She's a widow. She's moving all her furniture to the two upstairs rooms. Grandpas will have the rest of the house."

"You mean their own house will just sit empty?" Perry Lee asked.

"I guess so. Mattie doesn't want to live by herself," Emma replied.

Mary Edna spoke up. "Grandma can use help with the housework because she still has bad arthritis. It will be nice for her to live over there."

As the family conversed, Tobe's mind drifted to his plans to unveil his latest invention. He had made plans to show it to the advisory committee the next day.

Tobe's primary investors gathered around a table in the manufacturing shop. Tobe held up a metal box with a glass front. Four numbers were printed on the glass. Inside the box was a light bulb. He plugged the cord into a nearby electrical outlet. The numbers on the box glowed.

"What is it?" one of the men inquired.

"An address lamp," Tobe explained. "People can put their street number on it."

"You're going to make those here at the shop?"

"Yes. They'll sell like hotcakes."

"Where will you market them?"

"Chicago, New York, Kansas City. All the big cities."

"Do you have the equipment to make them?"

"For the most part. I may need to get a bake oven."

By the time Tobe had finished his demonstration, the group promised to back the project. Tobe was exuberant.

He was even more excited to learn that the doctor thought Emma was carrying twins.

"Mom, if you have twins, what are we going to name them?" Glenn asked.

Emma and Tobe glanced at each other. "We've thought of the names Reuben and Rachel," Tobe volunteered.

Mary Edna began singing, "Reuben, Reuben I've been thinking what a grand world this would be, if the boys were all transported far beyond the Northern Sea." Perry Lee echoed, "Rachel, Rachel, I've been thinking. . . ."

"That's enough," Tobe interrupted. "I don't want people to sing silly songs about my children. Maybe we better think of other names."

After supper Tobe took the three oldest children to a German spelling bee. When they returned home, Emma was putting Edith to bed. Edith whined and tossed as Emma tried to comfort her. Tobe sternly told the child to be quiet. She lay still. Tobe knew that Emma couldn't bring herself to be that stern. She pitied her daughter too much.

The older children got ready for bed as Tobe and Emma moved to the living room. Emma sank into a chair. "Did you enjoy the bee?"

"Everyone had a good time. Lester Beachy got the floor."

"I'm glad you took them. It will help them read German better."

Over the next weeks, Tobe concentrated on the production of the new address lamps. In early April, he ordered metal stamping dies from a company at Durant, Iowa, not far from Davenport. Tobe often made his own dies for metal products, but this one had proven too complex. He waited impatiently for the dies to stamp out the main housing.

Soon Tobe's inventory expanded to include chicken catchers, feed scoops, and tomato racks. One Saturday a number of neighborhood children gathered around Tobe as he demonstrated still another recent invention, a self-watering flower pot. The pot was eight inches in diameter and stood about six inches high. He removed the top half of the pot, the part that would hold a plant. In its curved bottom was a small hole. Tobe picked up a bunch of string wick as he spoke to the children. "This bunch of string goes through the hole. It draws water out of the base like the wick in your kerosene lantern. It waters your soil from the roots up instead of from the top down."

"How often do you have to put water in it?" young Wilma Beachy asked.

"Oh, probably about once a month. It depends what plant you have and how warm it is."

"Why can't you just pour water from the top?" one of the other children asked.

"Two things make this better. First, you don't have to water this as often. Second, it's better for the water to come to the roots from the bottom. It pulls up just the right amount for the soil to be moist. It's good for starting new plants."

"I bet my Mom would want one." Wilma suggested.

"Why don't you tell her about it? She can get one here anytime."

Wilma ran up the street to tell her mother. She burst into the house. "Hey, Mom, guess what Tobe Stutzman's up to now."

Her mother shook her head as Wilma described Tobe's invention. "You never know what he'll come up with next."

••••

On April 27, 1953, Emma felt the first twinge of a contraction. A few minutes later it came again, only stronger. She put her hand on her middle. She could feel her distended womb forming into a knot.

Emma walked to the neighbors to get help. They agreed to pick up Tobe at the shop. She lay down to wait for his arrival as the contractions came more quickly now. The children would be home from school soon.

Tobe made a call to Dr. Beckman, who agreed to meet them at the hospital in Iowa City. Tobe arranged for a ride. Then he dropped by to speak to Aunt Katie Nisly, who had offered to keep the children when they got out of school.

Dr. Beckman met them at the hospital. Emma soon settled into regular labor. Tobe paced the father's waiting room. Would it really be twins?

20

Going for Broke

Tobe was pacing the hallway when a nurse came with the news. "Mr. Stutzman, your wife has given birth to twins."

"So it was twins!"

"Yes, a boy and a girl. The boy was born first. The girl came along fifteen minutes later."

Tobe followed the nurse down the hall. He peered through the glass as another nurse wheeled two small bassinets up to the window. They looked so tiny. The tags read, "Ervin Ray Stutzman and Erma Mae Stutzman.

Tobe called his brother Ervin in Kansas to let him know he now had a namesake. Ervin's wife Emma answered the phone. Tobe said, "We have three boys and three girls."

"So the baby came. Congratulations!"

"Yes, but did you hear me? We have *three* boys and *three* girls."

"Oh. You must have twins!"

"Yes, a boy and girl. We named the boy Ervin Ray after Ervin. And the girl Erma Mae. Ervin weighed five pounds, three ounces. Erma weighed five pounds, eight ounces."

Emma handed Tobe's brother the receiver so he could hear the news for himself. After a brief chat, Tobe instructed Ervin to tell Vera Mae Nisly the twins had been born. She had agreed to help Emma for several weeks after the birth.

Vera Mae boarded the next train for Iowa and arrived the next day. That evening she prepared the family meal. They all sat down together and bowed for silent prayer. As the children helped themselves to mashed potatoes and beans, Tobe asked Mary Edna, "Did you know that Mother helped Vera Mae's folks when they had a new baby?"

"No," Mary Edna said.

"That's right," Vera Mae said. "She was just about my age. And I was about your age."

"Oh, that's interesting," Mary replied.

Tobe watched with appreciation as Vera Mae worked around the house. Over the next weeks, she made meals, cleaned the house, and cared for the twins. Mary Edna helped too, particularly with the twins. Perry Lee and Glenn begged to take turns with her to hold the newborns.

"Why does Ervin Ray have a half-dollar taped to his belly button?" Glenn asked.

"Because it sticks out," Vera Mae replied. "We'll probably have to leave it on for a while."

Tobe loved the twins too. One morning Vera Mae heard him talking softly to the babies, "Maybe one of these days we'll do what your mother wants. We'll move back to Kansas. We'll build a greenhouse and build a tunnel under the road so you children can cross the road and not get hit by cars." Tobe loved to talk to children about big ideas.

One day Tobe overheard Vera Mae tell Emma that she was able to make do with less than most people. Tobe hoped it was a compliment. Or was it a statement about Tobe's inability to provide a nice home? Like most of the Nislys, Vera Mae admired people who knew how to make money stretch. After all, Vera Mae was Ed Nisly's daughter. Would he loan more money if Tobe needed it?

Vera Mae also voiced her admiration for Emma's patience with Edith. Although she was over five years old, Edith learned slowly. She had a short attention span. She spoke only in words, not sentences. It was hard to understand what she was saying. Particularly when visitors showered attention on the twins, she whined and gestured for recognition.

Tobe didn't put up with it. One evening at mealtime, Vera Mae watched as Edith whined and picked at her food. Tobe spoke sternly, "Edith, be quiet and eat." The whole table fell silent for a time under his rebuke. Then the conversation turned to matters back home in Kansas. Since Vera Mae was Emma's cousin, she caught them up on the news from the Nisly family.

"Your dad's doing poorly," she said to Emma. "He has such a terrible cough. They say the family is getting tired of hearing it."

Emma sighed. "He doesn't seem to be getting better, does he?"

"No. They moved him from Halstead Hospital back to Wichita. I'm afraid he may not be with us much longer."

Emma looked at Tobe. "I wish we could go visit them."

"We were just home on Memorial Day for the Mast reunion."

"I know. But we didn't get to spend much time with the folks alone. I wish we could all go."

Tobe shrugged and reached for a second helping of mashed potatoes. Nothing more was said about it.

The next Sunday Vera Mae accompanied Tobe and the older children to church while Emma stayed home with the twins. Tobe took the reins of their two-seater buggy with Perry Lee and Glenn Wayne on each side of him. Vera, Mary Edna, and Edith rode in the back seat. It nearly bottomed out on the lateral springs. With the addition of the twins, the buggy would really be full.

"We have a balky horse," Glenn said to Vera Mae.

"Yeah, Bess just won't go sometimes," Perry Lee echoed. "And she kicks so hard that she breaks the shafts. She broke them four times."

Tobe cleared his throat. "You boys just don't know how to handle her." With that, he guided Bess into the farm lane where the church was meeting.

• • • •

Around the end of June, Vera Mae went home to Kansas. Her leaving led Emma to comment about how much she wanted to pay her ailing father a visit. This time Tobe agreed. Shortly after that conversation, they packed up and made the trip to Kansas.

Tobe suspected that it was only a matter of time before they would need to make another trip back to Kansas for Levi's funeral. Then there would be an estate settlement. Might there be money to help with the business? He needed the cash to purchase some big equipment.

Meanwhile, Tobe devised an oven to bake paint onto metal. It was housed in a lean-to that he built at the rear length of the shop. A 100-foot chain with suspended hangers carried fabricated steel pieces through the oven. The parts were dipped in a paint pot before entering the heated tunnel. They emerged with dry, baked enamel.

When Tobe fired up the oven to demonstrate it for his employees, a thought popped into his mind. *If the oven could bake paint, why couldn't it roast peanuts?* As the wet parts began moving slowly through the hot chamber, Tobe motioned for the boys to watch. He hung a bag of raw peanuts on the moving chain as it entered the oven. They all walked over to the other end and waited. In a few minutes, the nuts emerged on the far end. They were perfectly roasted.

Later that week, Arvilla observed that Tobe skipped his usual peanut snack. When she said something about it, Tobe explained that whenever his weight went over 220 pounds, he skipped his favorite snack. After a day or two of hard work and disciplined eating, Tobe stepped onto the scale again. This time the needle was below 220. Arvilla grinned as he reached for a handful of peanuts.

Emma's father died on August third, 1953. The Stutzmans left Edith and the twins with Arvilla and her parents. With their three older children, they traveled home to Kansas. For Emma's family, it meant the loss of a father. But for the Kansas Amish community, it was the loss of a longtime leader.

It was less than a year since the district had ordained Amos Nisly to take his place. People were still not certain how Amos compared to Levi. Would Amos be a man inclined toward change? Or would he try to hold the line on electricity and cars? Already, Amos had openly supported Willie Wagler in the reforms championed by David Miller from Oklahoma.

Tobe didn't have time to worry about what was happening in the church. He was growing more concerned about the time it was taking to get the new address lamps off the assembly line. He waited for months for the metal dies from Durant. His pent-up feelings tied his stomach into a knot. More than once, Arvilla observed him step outside the back of the shop to vomit. He told her it was nervous tension.

In August Durant told Tobe they'd given up on the project. They weren't able to cast dies that worked well enough for Tobe's project. Tobe was heartsick. He'd promised a large order of address lamps to a Canadian firm, and it now seemed impossible to fill their order. Every month that production was delayed, the shop went deeper into debt.

Tobe determined to find a new die maker. The Twain Manufacturing Company promised a relatively short turnaround time so he placed the same order with them. He chafed at the delay, but what could he do? He tried not to let his concern show. There was no use getting Emma worried and upset.

The estate settlement from Emma's father brought some relief from the financial pressure. Emma's brother Raymond delivered a number of appliances with his brand new truck.

Tobe motioned for him to back it up to the porch. "*Sell iss gut!* That's good!" Tobe hollered just before it hit the porch post. Raymond shut off the engine and stepped out of the cab.

Together Raymond and Tobe lifted the end gate off the bed of the new Chevrolet Apache. "Let's take the refrigerator first," Tobe directed.

They lowered the appliance unto the ground and wheeled a cart under it. As Tobe moved toward the door, Perry Lee ran to open it.

In less than an hour, the truck was empty. Just as the men washed up, Emma announced, "Let's eat. "There was the sound of scraping chairs as everyone pulled up to the table.

Tobe looked to Raymond. "*Deedscht du bede?* Would you say a prayer?"

Everyone bowed their heads as Raymond prayed aloud. The conversation soon turned to changes back home. Raymond assured them that things were going well.

"Thank you for bringing the furniture up to us," Emma said to him.

"You're very welcome," Raymond replied, "you just let me know whenever I can help."

"We could use the help right now because we're a little stretched with getting ready to make the address lamps," Tobe said. He rose from the table. "I really should get over to the shop to see how the men are doing."

Raymond scooted back his chair. "I'd like to see what you're up to these days."

After a brief visit to the shop, Raymond headed back to Kansas.

Despite the delays with getting dies cast, Tobe continued to be confident that things would turn around very soon. He entered into an agreement to purchase a property from Dave Hochstetler just east of the Kalona city limits. After making a small payment to seal the agreement, he promised to pay off the balance just after New Year's Day 1954. About a month after the children started school, the family moved from the Irvin Gingerich farm to the three-acre Hochstetler property. The new location was in a different school district and church district. What would the new bishop be like?

It was not immediately apparent what the church would say about the electricity and phone in Tobe's shop, but the children quickly adjusted to the Pleasant Hill School. Teacher Ezra Shenk kept good order in the one-room school. Unlike other small schools, this one had excellent shop equipment and a competitive softball team. The Stutzman boys practiced by having Tobe hit fly balls for them.

In November the Twain Manufacturing Company finally came through with the promised dies. The shop swung into production, stamping out the shells and back pieces for the address lamps. Several women from the church joined Tobe's children in painting, sorting and packing the numbered glass pieces in packages.

As the supply of lamps grew so did the expectations. The bills for the dies and new machinery were due. As Tobe had feared, the Canadian firm grew tired of waiting and withdrew their large order for lamps. Tobe's advisory committee felt cheated and misled when they learned that no papers had been signed in the proposed Canadian deal. They also soon learned that urban home owners were reluctant to buy the lamps because of the high costs of engaging an electrician to install them. It was a problem no one had anticipated.

Tobe's creditors became more uneasy as boxes filled up faster than they were shipped out. As Christmas drew near, they finally convinced Tobe to slack off production until sales improved. But by year's end, the shop had 16,000 completed lamps on hand with 28,000 partly done. After the production of lamps slowed down, Tobe used the new equipment to mass produce decorative products like Christmas bells and flower pots.

The stress at the shop was compounded by new developments at home. Near Christmas time, Edith experienced a grand mal epileptic seizure. From then on, she had occasional seizures. Because the seizures came with little warning, Emma had to watch her more closely to protect her from injury. Dr. Huls showed interest, but he couldn't seem to prevent the seizures.

Emma told Tobe she was worried about the twins. Might there be something wrong with them too? Ervin Ray cried often. Emma tried to comfort him with a bottle, but he didn't seem to like the milk. Arvilla insisted that it was too hard for the infant to digest cow's milk. At Arvilla's suggestion, Emma consented to try milk from the Weaver's goats. It seemed to help. From then on, she fed the boy goat's milk. But to make sure the problem wasn't something more serious, Tobe and Emma took the baby to see Dr. Huls.

The doctor held Ervin Ray in his big hands. With his thumb, he explored the inside of the baby's tiny mouth. The boy gagged and howled as he applied pressure to his palate. When he was finished with his examination, the doctor handed him back to Emma. "I'm so glad you brought him here. I was able to make an adjustment. Otherwise, he would have had the same problem as Edith."

Tobe and Emma left relieved. How could they handle another child with a handicap?

In the midst of their new stress, Emma's mother came for a visit. Now that her husband was gone, Mary was free to travel.

Mary confided to Emma that widower Noah Nisly had been speaking to her about the prospects of marriage. Because Levi had died so recently, Noah's interest in Mary was even more sensitive to her children than it might otherwise have been. Some of the children in Kansas found out about it very early.

Smiling a bit, Mary recounted the story to her daughter. Noah, who was Levi's first cousin, first came to see her under the cover of darkness. He parked his buggy behind the barn. However on one of his first visits, he forgot to extinguish his buggy lantern. Suspecting a fire near the barn, Emma's brother Fred ran out to investigate. The secret soon spread around the family circle.

Tobe laughed when Emma told him the story. They weren't opposed to the prospective marriage although it did seem a bit early for Mother to be courting seriously.

It was more difficult to discuss the inheritance. Shortly before his death, Emma's father had given each child the choice of forty acres of land or its value in cash. Emma and Tobe had opted for the acreage. Now Emma learned that the land would not be deeded to her. Afraid that Tobe would sell the land to finance his projects, Levi had put it in trusteeship under Raymond's name. Emma couldn't get the land unless Raymond signed off. Given Raymond's frugality, that wasn't likely to happen. Emma knew the matter couldn't be negotiated. It was simply a decision to be accepted.

Tobe was under pressure to put the shop under trusteeship as well. By early January, several of Tobe's unsecured creditors pressed for a legal agreement to protect their investments. In the spirit of brotherhood, they voiced hope to work out an agreement without using the law. After several rounds of negotiation, Tobe and Emma signed over most of their possessions to Weldon Yoder in trust. Weldon was a redhead who carried the nickname "Red." Tobe believed that Red had the business savvy to rescue Kalona Products and satisfy the creditors. The agreement left Tobe in charge of production while placing the overall management in Red's hands. Although it wasn't his first choice, Tobe hoped that all of the creditors would agree to the deal. It would allow a year or more for the business to turn a profit. Optimistic that the address lamps would be sold within the year, Tobe believed that all of the creditors could be paid off and the trust agreement ended.

In the middle of January, Tobe and Emma accompanied her mother on a short trip to visit relatives in Buchanan County, Iowa, an Amish settlement not far from Kalona. They didn't tell her that the balloon payment to David Hochstetler for their new house was past due with the money nowhere in sight. After a pleasant visit with family and relatives, Emma's mother left for Gulfport, Mississippi, to see her daughter Elizabeth, who was expecting a second child.

After the setback with the address lamps, Tobe's dreams became even grander. He hired Ray Beachy, son of A. J., to drive him around to different manufacturing plants looking for ideas. Ray belonged to the Conservative Church, and he and Tobe made most of their trips in his brand new 1954 Plymouth. Wherever they went, Tobe prided himself in making friends. He even got along with the cops.

After a long search for a parking place in Kansas City, Ray gave up and pulled into a "No Parking" zone. He volunteered to stay in the car while Tobe went inside. Sure enough, it wasn't long before a policeman sidled up to the back of the car and wrote down his license plate number.

Striding to the driver's side door, the officer asked Ray, "What are you doing here? You're in a 'No Parking' zone."

"My friend is doing business inside. He should be out any minute now."

"What kind of business does he do?"

"Metal fabricating. He's looking at products here."

"I'll talk to him when he comes out." The officer walked around the car. He peered into the rear of the vehicle. On the floor between the sedan seats lay several long metal rods. They had a crook on one end and a wooden handle on the other.

When Tobe returned to the car, the traffic policeman asked, "What are those pieces of metal between the seats, sir?"

"Those are chicken catchers. We make them."

"Who do you sell them to?"

Tobe paused momentarily, then remarked, "We sell them to thieves."

The officer grinned and waved the two men out of the space. As they drove away, Tobe and Ray broke into relieved laughter. No parking ticket!

A month later, Ray took Tobe to Detroit. Already they'd been to Toronto, Chicago, Kansas City, New York, and Louisville. It was past midnight when Ray pulled onto the open highway heading out of Detroit. A car in the thinning late-night traffic began crowding Ray off the road. Ray kept his eyes on the road. The other driver swept toward him several times on the four-lane road.

As the other driver swerved toward him again, Ray leaned on his newly installed cow horn. The eerie reverberations of Ray's novelty horn pierced the darkness. The other driver turned and sped away, exiting at the next intersection. By now Tobe was wide awake. They burst into relieved laughter.

Back home, Emma learned that her sister Elizabeth had given birth to their second daughter, Dorothy Fern. John and Elizabeth were serving in voluntary service. Emma's mother went from Kansas to visit. Shortly afterward, Amos and Anne Nisly, with their little daughter Rosetta, traveled by bus to Mississippi and accompanied Mary Nisly back home. As the progressive new minister, Amos was appointed by the new missions committee to visit the workers at Gulfport. Because Amos was Noah's son, Emma wondered aloud to Tobe if the traveling group would discuss Mary's possible marriage.

Her questions were answered when Noah and Mary announced a May 16 wedding date. Tobe and Emma went to Kansas for the event. Despite a few wagging tongues, it was a happy occasion. On their visit, Tobe also learned that his brother Ervin and his sister-in-law Emma had filed adoption papers. After having prayed and longed for a child for several years, they eagerly awaited the baby's birth, due any day.

Tobe and Emma were back in Iowa only a week when Ervin called to announce the birth of the awaited child, a son they named Mahlon. He was Tobe's first nephew on the Stutzman side.

Tobe reported the adoption to Arvilla at the shop. He knew the subject of childbearing was sensitive, particularly since Arvilla was unmarried. But Arvilla didn't seem to mind. She even allowed Tobe to tease her at times.

A few days later, Tobe smiled as Arvilla came into the shop to work. "I read in the *Budget* about the Old Maids' gathering at Ruth Hershberger's house. I saw your name on the list."

"Yes, I was there," Arvilla acknowledged.

"The *Budget* says it was a success," Tobe continued. "Did you have a good time?"

"Yes," Arvilla said, "it was nice to visit without feeling like you're only half there because you don't have a husband. Most of the time when you go anywhere you don't fit in because everyone else is married."

"That must be hard," Tobe said sympathetically. "I'm glad you can do things together sometimes."

• • • •

As Tobe's plans became more and more grand, Emma squeezed every penny that came her way. She kept a big garden and voiced her worry that they might lose their new place to the creditors. "The payment was due six months ago. I don't see how Dave will be patient much longer."

"Don't worry about it. The trust agreement we made with Red should keep that from happening. Besides Dave's not going to push us out of the house."

Although Tobe was in dire straits, he figured there were others who were less fortunate. Men like Demas Troyer who found it difficult to get a job. So even though Demas had a speech impediment and lacked social grace, Tobe hired him.

Tobe's sons teased the man. They asked him to pronounce words they knew would pose particular difficulty. Their favorite question was, "Who are Dad's brothers?"

He would respond, "Ehvin, Peyah, and Tayah." Hardly the way the boys would have pronounced Ervin, Perry, and Clarence. They laughed behind his back at his struggle.

Demas was irked by the boys' teasing and horseplay in the shop. He told Tobe, "I'll take a cut in pay if I can be responsible for disciplining the boys."

"No, I'll take care of my own boys." There was an edge to Tobe's voice.

Tobe wondered if he should keep Demas as an employee. His limited abilities sometimes made it difficult for other employees. One company had returned defective products to the shop because of shoddy workmanship that Tobe traced back to Demas.

After further thought, Tobe kept Demas on the payroll. Who else would hire him?

Unfortunately, Tobe's creditors weren't as considerate as Tobe himself. Although some of the Amish and Mennonite creditors showed sympathy for Tobe's plight, the big urban companies were concerned solely about their own interests. Tobe feared they might press him into bankruptcy. In May his fears were confirmed. Tobe read the legal notice from the attorney's office with disgust and fear. "Your petitioners . . . represent unto your Honors that the said T. J. Stutzman is insolvent, that his liabilities are in excess of his assets. . . ."

The petitioners were the big corporations—Twain Manufacturing, The Meyercord Company, B. L. Robinson. The first two were from Illinois; the last one was from Iowa.

His eye swept down to the last paragraph: "WHERE-FORE, your petitioners pray that the service of this petition with subpoena may be had upon T. J. STUTZMAN, as provided in the Acts of Congress relating to bankruptcy, and that he may be adjudicated by the Court to be bankrupt with the purview of such acts."

His stomach tightened. The only path forward led to the lawyer's office. Since attorney John C. Owen was on vacation during the declared deadline for filing, Tobe won an initial extension. He also pled for an arrangement to keep the company in business. The judge agreed. The triumph of the moment was soon overshadowed by another development.

In mid July Tobe came home from work to find Emma crying. She handed him a paper, then buried her face in her hands.

A shadow crossed his face as he glanced at the paper. "When did this come?"

"The sheriff brought it today."

Tobe pursed his lips. "I guess Dave means business. We're going to lose our house."

"Will we have to leave right away? Where would we go?"

"I don't know. Maybe we can pay monthly rent to stay here."

He didn't look forward to moving again. It was the fourth place they'd lived in as many years.

Just then the screen door slammed as the boys came running into the house. Tobe folded the paper and tucked it into his pocket. "I'll work something out with Dave tomorrow," he said quietly, "Don't worry about it."

21

Picking up the Pieces

Dave wasn't ready to budge on his commitments, so Tobe approached Chris Miller about an old abandoned house next to the railroad. Chris agreed that if and when the Stutzmans had to vacate their current house, they could move into the property.

That summer the court ruled to honor Tobe's request for an arrangement under Chapter XI. It meant that Tobe could continue his business but had to submit monthly financial reports to the court. As part of the plan, Tobe was required to list all of his creditors and the amount he owed each one. Further, he had to take an inventory of all his supplies and equipment.

The judge sent out a notice to all creditors with a summary of the arrangement. No creditor could demand payment. All were put on equal footing. Church members were listed along with secular corporations.

Some of Tobe's creditors refused to sign on with the bankruptcy or participate in the hearings. They believed that Tobe was obligated to pay back his debts regardless what was said by the courts. The church found no place in the Scriptures for bankruptcy proceedings. Church members should not get tangled up in the affairs of state. Instead, the Scriptures admonished church members to settle their disputes among themselves without going to court. How could they worship together if they argued with each other before a judge?

Tobe's list of his company's assets and liabilities painted a dismal picture, with total assets of $76,729.36 against liabilities of $143,536.45. But Tobe remained optimistic. The machinery that he bought to make address lamps could surely be used to make other products that would sell.

By the end of August, hope dawned on the horizon. Tobe worked out an agreement to make garment bag hangers for the Universal Producing Company based in Fairfield, a small town about forty miles away. Tobe's shop would fabricate the steel wire frames for garment bags. The hanger company would provide all of the raw materials and the cartons to store the finished product. The products would be shipped on a weekly basis.

The court reviewed the agreement with Tobe's creditors then granted him the right to proceed with the venture. For Tobe it was clearly a win-win situation. The deal required no capital outlay except for the creation of dies to bend the raw materials into hanger units. The Stutzman children and other unskilled workers could help with the labor.

Tobe agreed to produce fifty-four thousand units within five weeks. The company promised Tobe that if he delivered the goods, they were prepared to cancel their current contracts with wire frame manufacturers in or near Chicago. They would then provide business for an indefinite period of time, beginning around the middle of September 1955. Tobe was ecstatic.

Over the next few weeks, he worked intensely to gear up for the production of the wire hangers. To his chagrin, it took much longer to cast the dies than he had hoped. September came and went with Tobe still working feverishly to get the shop ready.

He begrudged the time it took to write up monthly financial reports for the court. His first report included the months from May to September with a full listing of receipts and expenses. Because little new was going out the door of the shop, the income was only $11.00 above expenses. To keep bread on the table, Tobe withdrew cash from the accounts and recorded them as expenses.

Tobe opted not to attend the first official meeting of creditors at the bankruptcy court in Davenport. Rationalizing that he needed the time to get the shop back into production, he left it to his attorney, John Owen, to answer any questions. Besides, he wasn't eager to face the angry queries that might arise in the meeting. Mr. Owen agreed to present a request to the court that Tobe be allowed to draw a weekly allowance from the proceeds of the company to support his family.

Although all of the creditors had been notified, only six showed up in court. David Hostetler was there in the interest of claiming back his house and land. All the rest had made cash loans or claimed unpaid wages. They proposed the formation of a creditors committee but left the matter hanging.

A few days later the judge ruled that Tobe had forfeited all rights to the Hostetler property. The Stutzman family would need to vacate it as soon as possible.

Tobe moved his family into the house owned by Chris Miller. Chris was an easygoing man who helped his neighbors any way he could. He charged Tobe very little rent.

Even with the low rent, Emma complained about the lack of cash. The bill for the birth of the twins was not yet fully paid. And not long after the family moved, Glenn cut his finger badly on a barbed wire fence. Emma "doctored it up" herself. There was no money to see Dr. Sattler.

Tobe appealed to the judge for mercy. The judge ruled that Tobe could withdraw a $30.00 weekly allowance from the company for his personal living expenses. Small as it was, the allowance provided some security for the family's needs.

Even with the new contract for wire hangers, Tobe wondered if he could satisfy his creditors. All of his inventory was locked up in bankruptcy proceedings, and he still had to pay monthly rent on the use of the shop. Might there be a way to start over?

Maybe Harvey Bender would let him build a new shop on his land. He could use sand from the river and lumber from the woods. Harvey farmed next to the English River, just a mile south of Kalona. Some of the ground lay low, so it readily flooded during a wet season. More than once, Tobe had watched farmers go fishing in the puddles that remained when the water receded. They stabbed the marooned carp and buffalo fish with pitchforks. Since the land wasn't good for farming, it seemed like the right place to build a shop.

Tobe knew it wouldn't be easy to swing the deal, but he felt he needed an escape hatch if he lost the shop in Kalona. Lying in bed one night, his mind raced with possibilities. He tossed for a time in the darkness then decided it wasn't worth trying to go back to sleep. After getting dressed quietly, he followed the railroad tracks to Kalona. Once in town, he walked the dark streets to the shop. As he turned on the shop lights, he glanced at the clock. It was three forty-five. With such an early start, he could catch up with some things before going to see Harvey about his new idea.

Tobe was delighted when Harvey showed some interest in Tobe's plan. Harvey had an entrepreneurial spirit, especially when it had to do with mission. Some years earlier, he'd started a Sunday school in the small town of Richmond, Iowa. Because such outreach was forbidden, the Amish ministers removed him from fellowship for a time. Now Harvey was closely associated with the new mission movement.

Harvey recognized Tobe's potential. He believed the new shop could eventually provide income for mission ventures. He asked for a bit of time to think about the project.

While Harvey gave it some thought, the Stutzman family made a trip to Kansas to take part in the biannual communion service. The Kansas church had also decided it was time to hold another ordination. David L. Miller, the young man who had helped Tobe's brother Clarence with mid-week Bible study meetings, was chosen by lot. David was an active supporter in the Amish missions movement. He had also attended Eastern Mennonite College for a year. He was about three years younger than Amos Nisly. Tobe mused that with the advent of a new generation of preachers, there would likely be some changes in the church rules.

• • • •

Back home in Iowa, Tobe determined to get the first order out to Universal by the middle of October. But on October 18, he caught his left hand in the punch press. The doctor initially determined that three mangled fingers should be removed, then decided they could be saved if Tobe spent some time in the hospital. The accident shut down all preparations for several days. As soon as the hospital released him, Tobe went back to work with his bandaged hand. He finally got the first order, for 9,700 wire hangers, out by November 5.

A second shipment left the shop on November 18. The gross profit from those two shipments was a little more than $300.00. Tobe's greatest satisfaction was to learn that the Universal Company was canceling its contracts with other companies. They asked Tobe to produce 10,800 frames each week for an indefinite period.

This contract alone would probably have staved off bankruptcy, but Tobe couldn't seem to keep himself from dreaming up other projects. After reaching an agreement with Harvey Bender, he began to lay block for a new shop in mid-November. Harvey ran the saw to cut lumber into planks, and Tobe and his two oldest sons hauled sand from the river, mixing concrete on site. By early January, the new shop was complete enough to move much of the equipment into it from the old shop. This reduced the rent to $65 a month. Further, it enabled Tobe to work more closely with Harvey, his friend and ally.

In late January, Arvilla announced that it was her last day of work. She said she had too many things to do at home; her parents needed her help. At the root of her decision, she told Tobe, was the fact that Tobe was often delinquent with her wages. She wasn't willing to work without pay, but she promised to care for Edith whenever they needed her.

Tobe hired Harvey's daughter, Elva, to take Arvilla's place. Like Arvilla, she was single and lived with her parents, not far from the new shop. She walked across the fields to work. Elva worked quickly and steadily. She helped to spot weld the frames for garment hangers. Together she and Mary Edna put hooks on the hangers and boxed them.

As young Mary Edna scrubbed the black oil off her hands with liquid soap one evening, she bragged to her family, "I and Elva filled 71 boxes, most ever filled in one day. I guess it was just Bender and Stutzman ambition."

Elva told her father that she liked to work with Mary Edna and her brothers. They always respected Tobe's authority, and he never used harsh words to correct them or make them work. She could see why her father went out of his way to help the Stutzman family.

To keep the production going, Tobe's three oldest children worked after school and Saturdays. Emma helped too, mostly threading washers onto garment hangers in preparation for fabrication in the press. It was something she could do while watching the younger children at home.

One Saturday evening in the middle of March, Tobe and the older children were out later than usual. Emma waited impatiently. She wanted all to get their weekly baths before going to bed. As the clock struck 9:30, the weary children marched into the house. Tobe followed a minute later.

"*Memm, mir hen hatt gschafft heit*. Mom, we worked hard today." Mary Edna's eyes sparkled despite her tiredness.

"I guess you must have. What did you work on?"

"We did tomato racks. More than 69 dozen."

As they lay in bed, Emma told Tobe her brother Raymond and his family were moving to the home farm in Kansas. If Tobe had taken up farming, she might be the one moving there. Tobe said he'd rather be running a shop.

At the breakfast table on Monday morning, Glenn said, "We only have two more weeks of school."

"I'm glad," Perry Lee said. "I'm tired of school."

"Me, too," Mary Edna agreed.

"I let you sleep in this morning," Emma said. "I was going to ask you to help wash before school, but the motor didn't start. We'll have to ask Dad to look at the machine."

Tobe wasn't happy to take time off to work on the washing machine, but it had to be done. After some tinkering, he got the motor running again.

The next Sunday, they had just finished breakfast when Edith fell to the floor. The seizure did not last long, and Edith lay still, her body spent. She blinked her eyes as Emma gently stroked her cheek. She shook her head in bewilderment, then stood to her feet when Emma offered her hand.

Tobe said, "I think one of us should stay home with her. It's probably best not to take her to Sunday school."

Emma agreed. "I'll stay home with Edith and the twins. You can take the others and go."

That evening Arvilla's family joined them for supper. They empathized with the family's plight. The two couples talked in the living room while Edith played in an adjoining room.

Arvilla asked, "When did Edith first get her spells?"

Emma walked to the desk and pulled out a notepad. "I believe I have it written in here somewhere. November 25, 1953. The doctor calls them epileptic seizures."

"Are you treating for them?" Sarah inquired.

"We take her to the doctor but he can't seem to do much. And we buy pills from the mineral man when he comes around."

Edith's prognosis seemed as dismal as the shop's prospects for profit. In May Tobe gave up the struggle to meet the court's demands. The income from Universal didn't yield enough cash to pay back creditors. The rise of sales on other products was too flat, and the mountain of debt too high. Like hawks circling above a defenseless mouse on the Oklahoma prairie, the large companies were about to put an end to Tobe's small business.

On May 24, 1955 Tobe signed a form consenting to straight bankruptcy. The court appointed L. E. Dunlap to be the temporary receiver of the assets. It was his responsibility to make an inventory of the assets and to protect them until they could be distributed among the creditors. Dunlap chose Tobe's attorney to continue representing Kalona Products.

It was not easy for Tobe to face his fellow members at church. Some people avoided his gaze. Others whispered in small groups. When everyone stood to pray the Lord's prayer, Tobe took special notice of the words. "Forgive us our debts, as we forgive our debtors." *Could God ever forgive my debts? Could the church? Some of my creditors are paying mission workers to tell people about God's forgiveness. Can they forgive me?*

Tobe pondered the questions that afternoon as he lay down for his afternoon nap. When he woke, Emma asked, "Did you read the Hutchinson piece in the *Budget*?"

"No," Tobe yawned.

"Delilah says they had a lot of hail. She says it made the sweet corn look sick. Then she says the grasshoppers are quite numerous. I imagine the farmers are having a hard time."

Tobe thought about the forty acres Emma had gotten through the inheritance. He had hoped to get some income from the property. Raymond was farming it. At least they wouldn't lose it to bankruptcy.

To supplement his meager income at the shop, Tobe took up carpentry work and other jobs in the neighborhood. One day he laid a tile floor at the Ezra Shenk place. Mose Yoder and his young son were responsible to get the tiles to the basement where Tobe laid them in mortar. The boy began tossing the tiles without looking. A stray tile struck Tobe on the head. Blood trickled from the gash and trailed down Tobe's nose. He wiped it with his handkerchief as he worked. Mose apologized profusely. Although the wound kept bleeding, Tobe assured him that everything was all right. Finally Tobe agreed to see a doctor. It took five stitches to close the wound.

Emma was hoeing weeds in the garden when Tobe came home for supper. He looked over the tomato racks. "I'm going to need to take these to the shop," he said, pulling a rack off the plant.

"Why?" Emma asked, "Don't you have enough at work?"

"No, I need six more for a customer. I'll replace these next week," he promised.

Emma sighed and laid down her hoe.

In mid-July a young man named Walter Beachy came to work for Tobe. Since he'd recently broken his leg, he couldn't work well on the farm. Tobe soon noticed Walter had a keen eye for mechanical detail. After some days at the shop, Walter talked Tobe into letting him improve one of the homemade dies that crimped the ends of the cross wires for the garment hangers. With some adjustment, Walter eliminated one machine operation for the hangers. In the long run, it would save a good deal of time. Tobe took a liking to young Walter.

Together with Earl Beachy, Walter talked to Tobe about the way he figured his prices. A customer had just left the shop after getting an estimate for a new product. Tobe had made a prototype out of steel.

"Tobe, you priced that thing out too cheap," Walter said.

"How's that?"

"You weighed the metal after you had it all cut out."

"That's how much it takes."

Earl chimed in. "But *you* have to pay for the whole piece, including the scrap."

Tobe scratched his head. "I hadn't thought of that."

A few days after Walter began work, Emma welcomed her mother and her new stepfather, Mary and Noah Nisly, into their home for a few days. When they arrived, Noah handed Tobe a paper sack, "A gift for you and Emma."

Tobe opened the bag. "A book. *Salvation Full and Free.* Thank you."

"We wanted you to have a copy of Dawdy Mast's book. Originally, he wrote articles for the *Herold der Wahrheit*. Now they have been put into this English book. It's good food for the soul."

The author was Daniel E. Mast, Emma's great-grandfather. Daniel had moved to Kansas just three years after the first Amish settlers. After years as a preacher, he was remembered as a patriarch in the community. His spiritual shadow loomed large, even years after his death.

As Tobe leafed through the book, Noah asked, "Did you hear about the time that Dawdy Mast went to see an erring brother?"

"No."

"The man attacked him, accusing him of many things he had done wrong. When the man was through, Dawdy asked him, 'Are you finished now?' He said 'Yes.' Then Dawdy told him, 'I have many other faults that you did not name.'"

Tobe laughed. "That was a good answer."

Noah kept going. "You're an inventor. Did you know that Dawdy Mast was an inventor too?"

"No."

"He had a creative mind. He was the first to have a paved feeding area for his cattle. One day, driving to church in his buggy, he passed a wind-powered grain grinder and started thinking how to add that improvement to his farm. Suddenly he realized he was doing all this work on the Lord's Day. He decided if the idea was so strong it took his mind off of spiritual things on the way to church, he should abandon it. So he dropped it right there. He never made his invention."

To himself Tobe thought that riding in the buggy was a good time to get ideas, but he didn't say it aloud.

"Dawdy Mast was a good preacher. He taught our young people against smoking, drinking, and carousing like the Amish do at Haven and Yoder. He taught us to read the Scriptures and live holy lives. The book you have in your hand has many great spiritual lessons. I trust that you will read it."

Tobe looked at the book, "I'll try."

Tobe changed the subject. "Would you like to see the new shop?"

"Yes."

They climbed into a buggy and rode toward the shop. When they arrived, Tobe tied the horse and led Noah into the facility. "This is our main business right here," Tobe said, pointing to the stack of garment hangers. "The company in Fairfield buys them as fast as we can make them."

Perry Lee, who had ridden in the buggy with them, stepped in to explain the manufacturing process. "We start by bending this wire into a frame, then we butt-weld the ends with this machine. We use a spot welder." He fingered the joint on a sample.

Tobe pointed to a large press. "Then we use this machine to crimp this wire and put loops on the ends. It gets put on the frame as a cross-piece."

"The company makes pink or blue bags to hang on these frames." Tobe said, pointing to samples. "We make three different widths. The different sizes hold different amounts of clothing.

They moved around the shop as Tobe demonstrated his machines and the products they manufactured.

"It takes a lot of supplies to make all of these things," Noah observed. "Where do you get them?"

"We get the wire from the steel company in Chicago," Perry Lee explained, "They bring it in on a tractor trailer. It comes in rolls. We use a machine to straighten the wires before we use them."

Noah seemed impressed until Tobe showed him several samples of wall mottoes. "Do you make these?" Noah asked.

"Yes, we print them with a silk screen." Tobe pointed to the frame with its various screens. But Noah was still gazing at one of the mottoes. "Who would want to buy one of these?" he asked. "It has a man smoking a pipe."

"It's the message that's important," Tobe said, not caring to be scolded. He held up the motto as he read it aloud: "No man has as much to learn as he who thinks he knows it all."

"The message is true," Noah agreed. "But the pipe is a bad example. Our people should always set a good example for others."

"That's true," Tobe acknowledged. He picked up another motto. "What do you think of this one?"

Noah looked it over. It had a picture of bills and coins with the slogan: "If mistakes were money, I'd be rich. By Toby."

Noah cleared his throat. "Is that Toby you?"

"Yes." Tobe laughed and glanced at the wall clock as he put the motto back on the shelf. "Maybe we better go now. We promised the womenfolk we'd be back by 12:30."

• • • •

Back in the kitchen, Emma and her mother were canning sweet corn, the first of the season. Mary quietly confided that she'd been going through some adjustments. By marrying Noah, Mary had agreed to move off the farm that she had called home for decades. And she was learning to relate to her step-children.

The financial arrangement demanded an adjustment as well. Since all of the children in their two families were grown and gone from home, Noah and Mary had decided not to merge their estates. Both would keep their own land. Raymond had agreed to farm Mary's place. Amos was farming Noah's land. Noah provided for Mary's living expenses.

After dinner the Stutzman family sat in the living room with their guests. The children listened respectfully as Noah launched into a detailed account of their wedding trip. He first explained that his former wife Rosa had died of cancer. Following her death, Noah was a widower for eight years. He had often prayed, asking God for another companion. God had brought Mary his way. Now some fourteen months after the wedding, they had hired drivers to take them on a five-month wedding trip to visit friends and relatives. The first leg of the trip was to visit the Stutzmans in Kalona, Iowa.

Tobe knew all of this but listened patiently. "And where all do you plan to go from here?" he asked, trying hard not to yawn.

"Lord willing, we're going to Indiana from here, then on to Pennsylvania," Noah explained, "then up through Canada and out to the west coast. We won't need to stay in hotels more than one or two nights along the way."

Shortly after Noah and Mary left, Tobe's brother Perry got married. Several of Tobe's relatives stopped by Kalona to take the family along to the wedding in Indiana. The driver was Eldon Miller, Tobe's cousin from Kansas. Tobe's parents accompanied him, along with Ervin, Emma, and Mahlon.

The next morning, Tobe and his brother Ervin picked up the sofa in the living room and hoisted it into the back of the

Chevrolet truck with a tarpaulin over the bed. "Everybody into the truck," Tobe yelled, "We're leaving for Indiana!" It would be about a six-hour drive.

Eldon got behind the wheel. Several others joined him in the front seat. The rest climbed into the back of the truck. Several sat on the sofa. The rest sat on chairs or on the floor.

The truck pulled out of Kalona onto Route 22. The tarpaulin on top flapped a steady rhythm as the vehicle gained speed. The flapping sound was a nuisance, but the cover would provide shelter in case of rain. Within a couple of hours, the overcast skies began to drop rain. Water found its way under the tarpaulin. Soon everyone got wet. Tobe was relieved when the truck pulled into the town of Kokomo where Perry's fiancé, Sylvia Hostetler, lived.

Perry came out to the truck as Eldon pulled into the Hostetler yard. The noisy children hopped out of the back of the truck.

Perry laughed, "You guys would fit right into a gypsy camp."

"Is that what this is?" Tobe was quick with a retort.

"No, you'd have to go farther down the road."

Tobe watched as Perry greeted his parents with a handshake. "Welcome to Indiana." He knew it was hard on his mother that Perry was marrying a Mennonite girl. Anna was fiercely loyal to the Old Order Amish church.

Tobe could still hear her words after Clarence left to join the Conservative Church: "*Es muss ebber Amish bleiwe.* Someone needs to stay Amish." He knew Mother feared her sons might follow the examples of her brother Johnny and John's brother Jerry. He remembered his Uncle Jerry telling him about the letter he'd gotten from Grandpa Levi Stutzman when he was stationed in the Philippines at the height of the war. Levi was afraid either one of them might die before they'd see each other again. He told Jerry he didn't have to be Amish to be a good Christian. He couldn't imagine Dad saying that to him, even if he thought it. Jerry had never joined the Amish Church. Despite it, Grandpa Levi had been lenient with him. He had even invited him to manage the home farm.

Tobe's mind snapped back to the scene as Sylvia and her parents came to greet them. After a few greetings, the guests dried off from the rain and helped prepare for the wedding. Tobe observed the wedding festivities with some reserve. The large wedding cake seemed extravagant. Half seriously, he asked Perry what the cake cost. He figured that money could have been used more productively somewhere else. The wedding dress, too, looked like it could only be worn for this one occasion. How much better to have a dress one could wear for many occasions. But Mennonites did things in a more fancy way than the Amish.

The trip back to Iowa on Monday afternoon was uneventful. Although they had no drivers' licenses, Tobe and Ervin shared the driving with Eldon. Tobe enjoyed driving. As they motored along, he thought about buying his own car. It only seemed practical. He would talk to Emma about it.

The following Tuesday, Tobe made arrangements with Walter Beachy and Doug Stanley to accompany him to Chicago to buy equipment. While there, Tobe showed them the city from the top of the Board of Trade building.

On the way home, Walter asked Tobe, "Are you satisfied with what we were able to find in Chicago?"

"You bet," responded Tobe, "we got just what we needed. $101 is a good price for a roller and four sets of dies. You could hardly buy a splitter at home for $50 and I've never heard of selling a break and a spot welder for $25. It's just what we need to make those pig feeders for Harlan Stubbs."

The next week Tobe went back to Chicago again. Harvey Bender and Walter stayed home to work in the shop. Both punched in with the new time clock Walter had just installed.

At mid-morning Walter heard a cry of anguish, "*Ken noch eemol.*" It was Harvey Bender's voice. Walter cocked his head when he heard a second anguished cry, "*Der Schinner!*"

Walter realized that something serious must have happened. Harvey was holding his left hand with a pained expression on his face. He ran to Harvey's side. Blood was oozing from Harvey's hand.

"I smashed my hand in the press," Harvey moaned.

"We'd better get you to the hospital," Walter volunteered. "Maybe Mose Coblentz can drive." They wrapped Harvey's hand in a spare rag to stop the bleeding.

"I'm afraid he's going to lose the ends of those fingers," Walter told one of the boys after Mose had taken Harvey to the hospital. "They looked pretty bad to me."

Walter spent the next several hours building a safety guard around the press. Then he started on Harvey's pile of work.

Walter's fears about Harvey's injuries were confirmed the next day. The doctor had amputated the ends of several fingers. It took weeks to heal. Through it all, Harvey kept his commitment to help Tobe make it in the new shop. Things seemed to be moving ahead.

Harlan Stubbs intended to market the pig feeders along with hog feed. Tobe designed a couple of prototypes, then Walter made a wooden jig to speed up production.

Tobe was making galvanized feed scoops when Harlan dropped by to check on progress. Harlan was upset because Tobe had promised to get his feeders done. Tobe agreed to work on the feeders and get them out soon.

Ray Beachy was upset with Tobe too. Tobe owed him money for the car trips they had made together. Ray told his wife Anna May, who worked at their watch shop, that she was not to give Tobe any more rides until he had paid up.

The very next day, Tobe showed up at the watch shop. "I need to go to Iowa City."

"Ray says you're not paid up."

"But this is an important trip." Tobe went on to explain his errand.

Before long Anna May reached for her keys and said, "Let's go."

When Ray wouldn't take Tobe where he wanted to go, his brother Jonas provided rides. Jonas also belonged to the Conservative Church so he had a car. Along with his wife, he took Tobe and the three oldest children on a day trip to see the sights in Chicago. They started out at 3:00 o'clock in the morning and arrived at the Board of Trade building at 9:30 a.m. The boys gazed in wonder at the skyscraper, the tallest structure in Chicago. They all went up the elevator and out onto the observation deck.

Although it was nearly the middle of August, the morning gusts made it feel cool. Mary Edna shivered as her dress flapped around her legs.

"Hey, Dad, now I understand why my teacher called Chicago the Windy City."

Tobe nodded. "The breeze comes off the Great Lakes."

Perry exclaimed, "*Daed! Gucke eemol datt! Die Autos gucke wie Schpielsache!* Dad, look over there! The cars look like toys!"

"Yes," chimed in Glenn, "you can watch the lights change colors up and down the street all at once.

Tobe pointed toward a residential section. "Imagine how many address lamps we could sell for all those houses."

"Yeah," Mary Edna agreed, "we'd get rid of all those boxes in the old shop."

The group soon left the Board of Trade and visited the Museum of Science and Industry display. From there they went to the waterfront for a little while, then on to the Brookfield Zoo. Finally, they visited the airport.

At 7:00 p.m. they began the journey back to Kalona. Emma was still up when the family got home. She listened attentively as the children recounted the day's exploits. Tobe wished she'd have come along, but Emma said she didn't regret staying home. Unlike Tobe, she didn't care for the big city.

Tobe wished he had his own car to travel to places like Chicago. It would be possible if they'd change their church membership. He brought it up to Emma one night after the children had gone to bed.

Tobe glanced at Emma, who was mending a sock. "I've been thinking."

"Yes."

"I'm wondering what you would think about us joining the Beachy church. We've been here four years and we still haven't brought our membership to Iowa."

"We had been planning to stay here for a few months or a year," Emma reminded Tobe.

"I know. But it seems the Lord would have us stay here indefinitely, and the Amish here are more strict than back home. I don't really want to join here. If we went to Sharon Bethel, we'd still be Amish, just not Old Order. They preach and sing in German."

The Sharon Bethel church appealed to Tobe since they allowed members to own cars and to have telephones in their homes. It seemed like the best place for them.

Emma hesitated. "Do we need to decide tonight?"

"No, let's give it more thought. But communion is coming up before too long. We should make a decision before then."

22

Parting Ways

The last Saturday in August dawned warm and humid. After a prayer of grace before breakfast, the family enjoyed a few moments of silence.

Tobe broke the reverie. "*Mir gehn mariye zue en nei Gemee.* We're going to a new church tomorrow."

"Which one?" Mary Edna was curious.

"The Beachy church, Sharon Bethel. Some people call it the Borkholder church."

"How will we get there?" Glenn wondered aloud.

"We'll take Bess."

Mary Edna frowned. "The Beachy people drive cars. Won't it look silly for us to have our horse and buggy there?"

"For now we can take our buggy or have someone pick us up. We'll get a car soon."

"Oh, goody," the three older children answered.

That evening after a full day at the shop, the family took their weekly baths. Everyone looked forward to attending a new church. Mary Edna asked her father: "Dad, are you going to start parting your hair in the middle?"

"I don't know. Does it make a difference to you?"

Tobe glanced at Emma. "It doesn't make much difference to me. I can try it the other way."

The boys chimed in. "Sure Dad, go ahead."

The next morning, Tobe appeared at the breakfast table, his hair parted in the middle.

Mary Edna laughed. "It doesn't seem to want to part quite in the middle."

Tobe explained. "My cowlick kinda gets in the way."

Emma consoled him. "I think it looks just fine."

They went to Sunday school that morning and to the church service in the evening. One of the ministers came by to fetch them in his pickup truck. The older children sat in the pickup bed, reveling in the open-air ride. The two-year-old twins rode in front with Tobe and Emma.

Tobe's decision to change churches was prompted partly by his desire for modern convenience. But because of the business pressures, it was also a time to look anew to God as a source of strength. A vibrant personal faith seemed more important now than keeping the traditions, even if Mother and Dad would be disappointed. Uncle David would certainly approve. His fervent preaching helped pave the way from the old church to a new fellowship.

Emma's brother Rufus dropped by to visit them that week. Accompanying him was his girl friend, Emma Eash from Indiana. They too were leaving the Amish church. Although neither couple talked about it, Tobe was quite aware that their choice would have saddened his father-in-law, Preacher Levi Nisly. At least his untimely death had spared him the grief of seeing two more children leave his beloved church.

Rufus laughed as he watched Ervin and Erma take turns riding the brightly painted rocking horse Tobe had made. Both rocked hard, small feet barely reaching the foot rests.

"Are you making many wooden things?" he asked Tobe.

"No. I'm mostly concentrating on metal products."

"Where do you get all your equipment?"

"Mostly Chicago, but other places too." Tobe tried to sound casual as Rufus shook his head in apparent admiration.

The next week Tobe took a day trip to Chicago, the first with his own car. It was exhilarating to think that he could go wherever he wanted without needing to call for a driver. The sun had just dropped behind the hills when he pulled up to the house. The children ran to greet him. Emma appeared from the kitchen.

"I brought you something," Tobe said with a grin.

"What is it?"

"Come and see. It's in the car." Tobe opened the trunk.

"Peaches!" She counted the baskets. "Five bushels."

"They're a little overripe," Tobe confessed. "But I got them at a good price."

Emma picked up peaches and squeezed. "Oh, my, these must be put up right away. I'll have to can them tomorrow."

Emma spent the next day canning the bargain fruit. The children helped at lunch time, stuffing peaches into jars on the noon break from school.

Two days later, Tobe took some time off from the shop to help pick apples at Mark Hershberger's home. With the help of several others, the family picked 30 bushels. At least they would have applesauce and peaches when there was no cash to buy groceries.

Back at the shop, Walter worked toward production of the pig feeders and waterers. Harlan Stubbs came by to voice his disappointment that it was taking so long to get his hog feeders off the line. Walter promised to talk to Tobe about it.

Tobe wanted to make the feeders, but there were too many other irons in the fire. With the onset of cooler weather, he needed to set up a furnace into his new facilities. Meanwhile, the wheels turned slowly in the bankruptcy process. L. E. Dunlap established a value on the assets and began selling them. He sold about 7000 of the address lamps that had been stored at the Mid-Continent Screw Company warehouse in Chicago. Tobe hated to see them go for only a few cents on the dollar. He desperately wished that a buyer would come forward to purchase them at wholesale value.

Ray Beachy, Tobe's friend and partner, offered to buy the remaining assets for $1550. Along with the assets, Ray claimed that he had the right to make the garment hangers for Universal. Tobe disagreed, arguing that he should be able to keep making the hangers along with chicken catchers and other products. The contention threatened their friendship.

Since Tobe had his own car, he made arrangements to get a permanent driver's license. Walter Beachy took him to Iowa City for the required exam. Tobe and Walter chatted as they rode toward the city. Halloween decorations were everywhere in evidence. Walter fidgeted with the wheel: "I almost forgot it's Halloween. I imagine there'll be some mischief in town tonight. Have you had trick or treaters in Kalona?"

"We've had a few. I give them my business pencil when they come to the door. It's better than candy. It's good advertising too."

Walter pulled up to the highway patrol building. Tobe took a deep breath as he walked through the double doors. Walter did a bit of reading while Tobe was inside.

Tobe emerged with a big grin. "I passed with flying colors!" He yanked open the passenger door and slid into the seat.

That evening the sun was setting as the Stutzman family sat down for supper. Tobe gulped down his food. Edith whined. "I'm not hungry."

Tobe glared at her with arched eyebrows. "Have you been snacking?" He looked at Emma, a question in his eyes.

"She had a little applesauce," Emma admitted.

"I don't like it when she complains at supper," Tobe told her.

The family fell silent. Edith picked at her food.

Tobe pushed back his chair. "I'd like the children to go to the shop with me. We have lamps to pack. The feed scoops order is finished now."

In a few minutes the children put on their coats and headed toward the door. "We should be done in a couple of hours," Tobe said as they got into the buggy. True to his word, they finished the task and got back by 9:00 p.m.

The next day Harlan Stubbs dropped by with a representative of Yoder Feeds. The feed company was interested in purchasing the new pig feeders. With a potential customer in the wings, Tobe redoubled his efforts to get the new stock into production.

At the same time, Tobe kept his eyes open for a more reliable car. Emma felt a bit guilty about them owning a car, so she wasn't eager to get a newer one. She knew the church in Kansas would frown on it, but Tobe said he needed a car for his business. At least there wouldn't be a problem until fall communion time. Perhaps if they made a trip to Kansas over that time, John D. Yoder would serve them communion.

True to their prediction, Bishop Yoder agreed to serve them communion if they made a public confession. It seemed that there was nothing else they could do. That Sunday the congregation listened wide-eyed as the bishop explained the charge. Tobe and Emma stood to acknowledge their error. It wasn't easy to do with parents and siblings watching. Tobe was philosophical about it. At least they had gotten communion.

That fall Tobe's three oldest children worked in the shop most evenings after school. Sometimes he held them out of school during the day, particularly when shop production was running behind schedule. One Wednesday morning in early November, Mary Edna was nearly ready for school when Tobe called her name. "Mary Edna, wait a minute"

"Yes, Dad."

"I'd like for you to stay home from school today. There's a lot of work in the shop."

"I'll miss my geography test."

"You can make it up later. Which is more important?"

"Okay, Dad."

Mary Edna worked with Elva Bender all day, putting hooks on garment bags. By the end of the day, fifty packed boxes stood as testimony to their hard work. On the way home, Tobe praised Mary Edna for her hard work.

When they got home, the family rushed to get ready for prayer meeting. Tobe was still adjusting to the new routine of a Wednesday evening prayer meeting. "Who'll stay with Edith?" He asked.

"I will." Perry Lee spoke up.

"All right. You finish the dishes, too. The rest of us need to get ready."

Tobe enjoyed worship at Sharon Bethel. The Wednesday evening meetings appealed to him, as did the weekly Sunday worship, occasional four-part singing and the emphasis on missions. He felt new faith grow inside as he followed the preachers' expositions of Bible texts. He followed the Bible reading with interest in his German-English edition. It was a new thing to carry his Bible to the service.

The business at the new shop also seemed to be gaining ground. Tobe dreamed of building a house next to the shop. That way, he could oversee the business without having to drive to work. And he was tired of renting. But would Harvey Bender approve?

With Harvey's support, Tobe poured a footer and in November began laying concrete block for a new house. Eager to get the building under roof before winter, he kept the boys out of school to help lay block. Each evening at supper they reported the number of blocks they had laid that day, and Mary Edna wrote the number in her diary. The whole family was excited about the prospects of living in a new house.

Tobe was grateful for the boys' assistance. It saved labor costs and sped up the project. Their school teacher was less enthusiastic. Just before Thanksgiving vacation, she spoke to Glenn about his absenteeism. "You've missed several days at school. Have you been sick?"

"No, I was helping my dad to lay block on our new house. Yesterday we got the south wall finished. Dad laid 219 blocks."

"I just hope you don't get too far behind in your work."

Keeping the teacher happy wasn't Tobe's main concern. But he was worried about losing his friendship with Ray Beachy. The shop workers weren't always sure who was in charge. Tobe thought Ray seemed sullen and quiet.

Walter talked to Tobe about the problem during the lunch hour. "Ray's tide was way out this morning," Walter commented. "What's the problem?"

"He's upset that Henry Bender didn't let him keep the lumber from the bake oven shed. He thought he was getting the lumber when he bought the shop inventory. I think he deserved to get it. Henry never paid a penny for that shed. I put all the money into it."

"So Henry got to keep it?" Walter mused. "I figured too that Ray would get it, since 'lumber in shed construction' was listed in Dunlap's inventory list."

Tobe shrugged his shoulders. "Henry argued that the shed was fastened to the side of the shop building. That means it was considered part of the structure. You can't take something with you that was attached to the building."

Because of Ray's disappointment, Tobe went out of his way to smooth things out. Even so, things seemed to grow colder between them. Meanwhile, Tobe worked hard to finish his house before winter. With Walter's help, Tobe got the roof on the building by the middle of December. Walter complained that he nearly froze when they put the sheeting on the rafters. It was even colder the following Sunday.

"I'm glad we have a car instead of a buggy when it's so cold," Perry Lee commented as they headed out the door for church. They all got into the old Ford and slammed the doors as Tobe pumped the accelerator. He turned the switch and pushed the starter button. The engine cranked but wouldn't start.

Perry Lee leaned forward. "*Was iss letzt, Daed?* What's wrong, Dad?"

Tobe paused, then hit the starter button again. "It doesn't seem to be getting its gas."

"We're going to be late for church," Glenn announced. Tobe got out and lifted the hood. The boys joined him as he surveyed the engine. "Perry Lee, you get inside and push the starter while I look at the carburetor."

Perry Lee got inside and cranked the engine. It barely turned over.

Finally Tobe announced: "Let's give up. We'll just have to miss church today. We don't even have a horse."

As they made their way back into the house, Emma mumbled to Tobe, "We'd better get the car fixed before we take it to Kansas this Friday. We don't want trouble along the way."

Tobe nodded but didn't comment. The problem probably wasn't too serious.

The next morning, Tobe got the car started with little difficulty. "Perhaps it was just too cold," he commented to Emma.

The week flew by as Tobe filled orders for feed scoops, flower pots, and hanger frames. Walter Beachy made a bending jig for Tobe's newest product, a retail glove display rack for the Fairfield Glove Company. Tobe worked on the advertising boards with his silk screen. Tobe intended to promote them after New Year's Day. But first, the family wanted to visit their kin back home.

It was 2:45 on Friday morning when the Stutzman family headed toward Kansas for a few days of Christmas vacation. Tobe, Edith, and Emma rode in the front seat of the old

Ford; the other three children rode in the back. The twins took turns sitting on the others' laps. They all arrived at the Stutzman Brothers shop at 5 p.m. The three children in the back seat hopped out of the car, their legs cramped from the long ride.

"We're going down to Mennys." Mary Edna's announcement was also a request. Emma glanced at Tobe, a question in her eyes.

"That's okay. I'll pick you up before long. We're going to Dawdy Stutzmans for supper."

That evening Tobe and the family sat around the table with his parents. Tobe was glad that Mother didn't comment on their having arrived in a car. She surely couldn't be happy that he and Emma were leaving the Old Order church. Perhaps she kept her tongue because they were all in a hurry to get to the Christmas program at the Elmhirst School.

Sunday was Christmas Day. The extended Stutzman family gathered at John and Anna's home for Christmas dinner. Now that Perry was married, the circle included spouses for all four of the Stutzman boys.

Tobe spoke to his youngest brother, just released from service. "Well, Perry, are you glad to be out of I-W?"

"Man, am I ever."

"Would you rather work in a hospital or in the Stutzman Brothers shop?"

Perry replied with dry humor. "Well I wouldn't have found Sylvia in the shop."

All of his brothers laughed.

Ervin's son Mahlon came toddling up to his grandmother. Anna showed Tobe where the end of the child's little finger had been pinched off in the irrigation motor.

Tobe looked at the finger then told Mahlon, "You're a pretty young man to be working on engines." The boy nodded and went off to his toys.

Bunny watched Tobe pace the room.

She looked up at him with a smile. "*Du kaanscht anne-hocke.* You can sit down."

"*Nee, Ich wett liewer schteh.* No, I would rather stand."

Tobe valued the chance to walk off some of his nervous energy.

That evening Tobe and the family joined Emma's extended family at Noah Nisly's house for their Christmas celebration. He felt a bit self-conscious as he drove his Ford into the yard. What would Emma's folks think?

The next day he stopped by to chat at the Fairview Service Station. The proprietor, Dan Yutzy, sold used cars. Might he have a more reliable car that Tobe could afford? Tobe looked over the row of cars for sale. He liked the looks of the '47 Plymouth sedan parked near the road.

In conversation with Dan, Tobe learned that the car had been owned by several Amish boys in Denver, Colorado. They were COs serving in I-W service. Since they needed the car to commute to work, they were given special dispensation by the church. On one of their trips to Kansas, the car broke down. Engine trouble. Since they needed a car for the return trip to Colorado, they make a quick trade with Dan for a '49 Chevy. Dan repaired the engine and put the car up for sale.

Tobe liked the '47 Plymouth. It was six years newer than his Ford and would probably be more dependable. He talked to Emma about it. She didn't seem happy about the added cost, but she agreed they needed a dependable car. Tobe bought it.

The children loved it. They felt proud to ride in it back to Kalona.

Although Tobe had been released from all debts in October, the settlement of the bankruptcy case stretched out for months. For one thing, it took time to dispose of the Kansas property. The trustee in the bankruptcy case engaged a Hutchinson, Kansas, attorney to put the property up for sale. Since he managed the shop, Ervin hoped very much to buy it. As marriage partners, Tobe and Emma each owned half of the Stutzman Brothers shop.

The attorney made it easy for Ervin, informing prospective buyers that only Tobe's half of the property was for sale. In the end the court agreed to sell Tobe's share to Ervin. Emma retained her share.

Back in the shop at Kalona, Tobe increased Walter Beachy's responsibilities. In addition to having Walter work at design and development, Tobe pulled him out of the shop to help him catch up with the account books.

Walter showed Tobe the work he'd done on the monthly statement.

Tobe was pleased: "You do good work. It looks like we're making profits now."

Walter smiled. "If we keep earning the way we are now, we'll surprise some people around here."

"Maybe I should let you do the books all the time. You would make a good manager."

"I'd have to think about that."

"For now you can weld steel bars onto those glove racks. I'm trying to get an order out."

"I think there's promise in glove racks," Walter said. "We have orders coming in for twenty or thirty racks at a time. At $100 apiece, we can make some profit."

A few weeks later Walter remarked that if the company did well, perhaps people would give him credit again. After that Tobe, went back to doing his own accounting. But he relied on Walter for other tasks. In early January, he took time off to cut firewood to heat the shop. With Walter's help, they cut ten big loads.

Tobe was pleased, "That should be sufficient for the rest of the winter. Now we can concentrate on work in the shop."

From New Year to Easter, Tobe didn't spend much time working on the house. The shop took most of his attention. Besides, the ground was frozen. But in early April, he made arrangements to dig a partial basement. It wasn't easy, since the walls and roof were already in place. Walter joined Tobe at the site of the excavation. A dirt elevator ran from the opening into a waiting truck.

Walter scooped dirt from the site. He worked all day, picking at the gumbo soil. "This is like picking against a tractor tire," he grumbled. "The pick just bounces right back at you."

While Tobe was working on the basement, he learned that Ray Beachy had convinced the hanger company to give him their business. Hoping to regain both the business and peace with his partner, Tobe and several others went to the company headquarters at Fairfield. After the meeting, Tobe knew he had to talk to Ray.

Several days later after a conversation with Ray and Anna May, Tobe and Ray decided to part ways. Ray took part of the business, and Tobe took the rest. Some of the employees stayed with Tobe; others went with Ray. The next Saturday, Walter decided to quit working for Tobe. As he was leaving for the day, he told Tobe he wouldn't be back.

"Well, that's up to you." Tobe sounded disappointed.

"That's what I've decided."

"If you change your mind, you're welcome to come back," Tobe responded. Walter didn't say it, but Tobe suspected Walter wasn't happy that pay from Tobe was running late.

Despite this setback Tobe was determined to finish their new house. By the third week in April, the project was far enough along that the family prepared to move in. They made the move on the last Monday of the month.

After he had carried in the last of the boxes, Glenn stood outside gazing at the long square building with a flat roof. "It looks like the Alamo," he declared.

Tobe laughed. "We won't fight any wars here."

The next day Walter dropped by the shop while in Kalona for an errand. He chatted with Tobe and took a brief look at the new house. "I'm glad to see you were able to move in."

When Walter didn't seem in a hurry to leave, Tobe said, "I really could use your help. Why don't you come back?"

Walter pondered the question. When Tobe sensed that he was wavering, he expressed strong appreciation for Walter's past work.

Finally Walter shook his head. "No, I really am quitting. But I'll come down to finish figuring up Harvey Bender's time cards next Monday."

They shook hands and parted. Tobe was deeply disappointed. He should have been able to talk Walter into coming back. What could he have done differently?

• • • •

Three weeks after they had moved into their new home, the children came home from school early in the afternoon. Mary Edna ran into the house waving her report card. "Mom, Mom! I passed! Now I'm free. I never have to go to school again!" She handed the card to her mother.

Emma smiled as she looked over Mary Edna's grades. "You did really well. Now you can work at home."

"Don't forget. We have Vacation Bible School coming up."

A few days later Tobe pored over the month's financial records. He hoped to get the books up to date before leaving for prayer meeting that evening. He smiled as he saw the bank balance. He could pay off some debts. He looked over the list. Perhaps he should pay Ray first.

The next morning dawned bright; it was a beautiful day to kick off Vacation Bible School. Tobe dropped off the children at the church house. He stopped by the shop to see how production was going. About that time, Harlan Stubbs came by. They conversed briefly. As Harlan turned to leave, Tobe commented, "If I don't see you again, I'll see you in heaven." Harlan nodded and walked away.

Then Tobe drove over to Mose Yoder's home to discuss a deal on hog feeders.

"How are things going at the shop?" Mose asked.

"I've gotten a terrific contract just recently. I'm going over to Wapello today to work on some sales."

"That's good." Mose stroked his chin.

Tobe thought Mose sounded a bit skeptical. "If this comes through, we'll be able to give to missions," he said. "Now, how about taking some of these hog feeders?"

Mose stroked his chin. "Yes, I'll take them."

Tobe shook Mose's hand to close the deal. Then Tobe headed for Ray's home.

Ray met him at the door. After a few pleasantries, Tobe reached into his pocket. "I have something for you." He pulled out $200 in cash. "This should make things current."

Ray smiled as he took the cash. "Thank you."

Tobe bid Ray good-bye and headed toward Wapello on Highway 1. The breeze through his open window provided some relief from the heat. He rehearsed his sales pitch for the new glove racks. He surveyed the countryside, observing that the corn was sprouting nicely. Taking a right onto Route 61, he headed south. His head ached as he struggled to stay awake. Several times he caught himself starting to doze. He glanced at the road sign on the outskirts of Wapello.

Heading north out of Wapello, John Ibbitson shifted down a gear in his concrete truck as he approached the bridge project where he would unload. He saw Tobe's Plymouth sedan approach, veering off course toward his truck. Tobe slumped as his car drifted across the center lane. The vehicle was traveling fast. Unless the car straightened out immediately, a crash was imminent. John yanked his steering wheel.

23

The End of Ambition

John swerved hard to the right but not in time to avoid Tobe's Plymouth. It smashed into the left side of his large concrete truck and knocked it off the road. The concrete drum lay smashed against the grass as the rig's tandem wheels turned lazily on the frame that lay on its side.

John pushed open the door and crawled out the top of his truck. He wiped sweat from his face with his arm as he surveyed the scene. Tobe's sedan lay 200 feet away in the side of a bridge abutment. The roof of the car had been ripped off along with the left front door. Pieces of sheared-off metal and rubber lay strewn on the highway and roadside. The front seat angled crazily toward the rear.

John walked slowly toward the mangled car. All was still as he approached. Tobe's body lay limp, his muscular neck nearly severed by the impact of ripping metal. His left arm hung by a thread. Blood seeped down his cotton shirt and onto his denim trousers.

A passing motorist volunteered to call for help. Neighbors gathered around the scene. A few minutes later a sheriff arrived, then an ambulance. They loaded Tobe's lifeless body onto a stretcher and headed for town. The sheriff helped clean off the highway and directed traffic around the wreck.

Late that afternoon Preacher Mose Yoder and his wife Cora came by the Stutzman home. They were dressed in their Sunday best. Mary Edna answered their knock at the door.

338

"*Iss dei Memm daheem?* Is your mother home?" Mose asked, a deep soberness in his voice.

"*Nee, sie un der Glenn sin in die Schtadt gange.* No, she and Glenn went to town." Mary Edna cleared her throat. "Is something wrong?"

"We came with very sad news. Your dad was killed in a car accident this afternoon. We want to find your mother to tell her."

Mary Edna took a deep breath. "I hope you find her right away." She closed the door slowly as the pair left.

The news was making its way around Kalona so several people went looking for Emma. A van driver found her walking on the sidewalk a few blocks from home. Glenn was with her as she had promised to buy him a hat. She paused as the driver pulled alongside. "Have you heard the news?"

"No." Emma sucked in her breath.

"You should go down to the funeral home. The man there has a message for you."

Emma's face blanched as she walked into the funeral home and identified herself.

The director asked her to sit down. Then he informed her of Tobe's death.

She buried her face in her hands.

"We'll do all we can to help. The ministers are making arrangements. I believe Mose Yoder is trying to find you."

Emma nodded, then made her way outside to where Glenn was waiting for her.

She burst out, "Oh the big debt!"

Glenn clung to her and asked what was wrong. Emma mumbled a few words of explanation as she took his hand and headed for home.

Preacher Fred Nisly soon came by the house. He assured Emma that he would take care of all necessary arrangements. They talked briefly about her wishes for the services and burial. All evening people dropped by to express their sympathy. Most brought food to serve the many visitors who would drop by in the next two days. A few pressed money into her hand.

Emma wanted desperately to call her relatives in Kansas. Fred thought it better to wait until all the funeral arrangements were made to make the long-distance phone call. It was late that evening when the men finally called Emma's brother Raymond. He immediately relayed the news to other relatives who had telephones. Then he drove to Mattie Miller's house to inform Tobe's parents.

Bunny was at home alone when she answered Raymond's phone call. She kept thinking the news couldn't be true. When Clarence got home, they tried going to bed. No sleep came. Bunny voiced her thoughts to Clarence, "It just doesn't seem real. Maybe it's Harmon Yoder's dog Toby that got killed." They got out of bed and drove to Clarence's folks, then called on several other relatives. A group decided to leave for Iowa that evening. Clarence volunteered to drive his car.

It was past midnight when Clarence decided that his tires were too worn for the trip. He called up Dan Yutzy to explain their plight. Dan agreed to meet them at the Fairview Station to mount new tires right away.

The group finally got off in the wee hours of the morning. Mourners on both sides of the family rode together— Emma's mother Mary, her sister Barbara, and Tobe's brothers, Perry, Ervin, and Clarence. The engine began to sputter as they approached Cottonwood Falls, barely two hours from home. They limped up to a garage in the small town.

Clarence explained their predicament to the sleepy owner. "We're on the way to my brother's funeral. He was killed in a car accident yesterday."

The owner surveyed the women with their bonnets. "Are you folks Amish?"

"Yes. Amish and Mennonite."

"I see." He scratched his head. "I don't usually do this, but I'll loan you a car. You can pick yours up on the way back. I'll have it fixed."

The group got into the car and headed back out toward Route 50. Ervin shook his head as they turned onto the main road. "He didn't even say anything about rent for the car."

"No, I believe he's giving it to us free," Clarence said as he shifted into third gear.

Emma's mother spoke up from the back seat, "That was really kind of him."

Clarence cranked down the window and breathed in the cool morning air. His passengers settled back to sleep.

As the car moved toward Iowa, people came and went from Emma's home in a virtual stream. Walter Beachy and Mose Yoder stayed for a time, then left for the print shop in Kalona to place the order for memory cards. George Ropp agreed to make the casket, extending his sympathy by offering it free of charge.

Ray Beachy worked at the shop. There were customer orders to be filled before the funeral. He turned on the big crimping machine and began to feed in the wires. The wire seemed to stick. He wiggled it with his left hand. It worked a bit better. He pushed harder.

The machine made a crunching noise. Ray yanked back his hand to see blood spurt from four mangled fingers.

Later that day Ray lay on his hospital bed. He moaned to the attending nurse, "Yesterday, I lost a friend, today I lost four fingers. I won't even be able to attend Tobe's funeral."

In the hallway she whispered to other nurses that it would be hard for a watch repairman to work with fingers missing.

The undertaker brought Tobe's body to the house late that evening. As visitors came and went, members of the family accompanied them to the casket. "He doesn't look natural," several of them commented.

"The undertaker did the best he could," Clarence volunteered. "But the accident really messed up his face. The undertaker wouldn't let us see the body when we stopped by the funeral home today."

Arvilla spoke to Clarence, "I held up Ervin Ray to see into the casket. He said he doesn't want to look at Tobe. He said his face is too crumbly."

"Clarence, Ervin, and I drove over to Wapello to see the car," Tobe's brother Perry told Mose Yoder. "It's really a sight. It's no wonder his face is messed up."

At a moment when no one was close to the casket, Perry Lee reached inside to stroke his father's lifeless arm. He squeezed it. He hesitated, then told Clarence. "It feels like crumpled paper."

Emma put the children to bed and lay down to catch a few hours of sleep. Friends came and went from the wake, alternately singing and quietly conversing. Some stayed all night.

Saturday morning dawned bright and clear. Cars and buggies found their way into the parking lot of the Sharon Bethel Mennonite Church. By 9:30 a.m. a congregation of nearly five hundred mourners had crowded into the newly remodeled church building. A trustee was heard to say that he was glad they had just installed double doors as part of the remodeling project. It made it much easier to handle caskets during funeral services. He had not envisioned that the church would need them so soon.

People sat quietly, waiting for the service to begin. Emma's family sat in the first row on the right hand side. Perry Lee glanced at the memory card in his hand. He scanned the information about his father. He nudged Mary Edna and pointed to the mistake, "Dad's birth date is printed wrong!" It was printed as 1938, just four years before hers. At least the age was correct. 37 years, 7 months, 10 days.

The clock's hand had moved past the half hour when several ministers emerged together from the prayer room. They walked onto the platform and sat down together. Mose Yoder was the minister in charge, assisted by Jonathan Miller, John C. Helmuth, and Tobe's uncle David A. Miller. He opened the service and called for some singing. The audience sang both German and English. Then an octet of four men and four women sang from the rear of the audience. The sermon and eulogy were in English, favoring attendees who could not understand German.

Following the service, Emma sat quietly as the long line of mourners filed past the open casket. Some nodded and greeted her with words of condolence. A few whispered to each other about the way Tobe looked. After the long line had filed by, Emma got up and walked to the casket. She reached in and tenderly stroked Tobe's body.

Then the undertaker loaded the body into the waiting hearse and took it to the train station for shipment to Kansas. Not long after, Emma and the family climbed into Mose and Cora Yoder's car as they left for the second service to be held the next day in Hutchinson.

Tobe's uncle Henry Miller met the casket when it arrived in Hutchinson. The train rumbled into the station as he stood waiting on the platform. He saw the casket right away, visible through the open doors of the baggage car. They had been open for the last leg of the journey—the thirty miles from Newton to Hutchinson. Henry put the casket in his truck and took it to Mattie Miller's house. Tobe's body lay there overnight, right next to the room where Tobe and Emma had been married fifteen years earlier.

The sun rose hot the next morning. By noon, it burned like a furnace in the prairie sky.

After lunch several attendants picked up the body and drove it to the Albert Yoder residence, less than three miles away. They placed it inside the tin farm shed known to locals as a round top.

The host had made careful preparations. The concrete floor was swept clean. Most of the farm machinery had been moved outside, leaving room for several dozen rows of back-less gray benches. Mourners began to arrive in cars as well as buggies. They parked on the sandy surface of the farm yard or on the browning grass. They huddled in small groups or made their way quietly to the round top.

Emma stood outside under a shade tree, her Aunt Lizzie nearby. "Raising children alone is such a responsibility," Emma said to Lizzie.

Lizzie nodded. A tear slipped down her cheek. Then both of them began to make their way to the round top. Ervin Ray wiggled in Emma's arms, begging to walk on his own. His small white shirt was soaked with sweat. Cora Yoder stepped forward. "I'll take him inside the house."

Emma breathed a sigh. "Thank you. He needs a nap."

She walked to the front and sat near the handcrafted ma-hogany casket in the bare shed. There were no flowers. Several ministers walked to the front and sat down on a backless bench. They watched as Bishop John D. Yoder rose to address the congregation. He greeted the congregation in German, acknowledging the solemnity of the occasion. He then read a portion of Scripture and made a number of comments in English. Unlike the Beachy Amish congregation in Iowa, the Kansas Amish did not sing at the funeral. While singing at the wake was customary, funerals were a time of mourning without song.

The heat was sweltering. A baby cried in its mother's arms, exhausted by the heat. Boys and girls squirmed in their seats, tired from the unforgiving surface of wooden benches. Women fanned themselves with their handkerchiefs. Sweat beaded on the men's bearded faces and wet their broad backs.

Provoked by a breeze, the branches of the elm trees outside scratched rudely against the tin roof of the round top. A train whistled its warning as it approached the nearby crossing on the railroad that angled out of Hutchinson, carrying passengers and freight into the Southwest. The long train rumbled by a few hundred yards to the north of the homestead, making it hard to hear the sermon. A tractor-trailer truck roared by on Highway 61, paralleling the railroad track. The lid of a wooden feeder dropped in the farmyard nearby, accompanied by the squeal of a hog that was being pushed away from the feed.

David A. Miller rose to preach the main sermon. He quoted several verses from the Bible, then began to expound the Scriptures. He assured the congregation of a better life beyond the grave for those who came to God through Jesus Christ. He explained that it was not through personal merit or good works that one found salvation and eternal life. Only God's grace made it possible to enter heaven.

David spoke favorably about his deceased nephew. He lauded Tobe's natural abilities, his high energy level, and his willingness to help people. Then he posed a question to the congregation, "If Tobias had put that same kind of energy into spiritual work and preaching, would he have been accepted among his people?" It seemed to be a reminder of David's own ministry. Detractors sometimes responded to his enthusiastic preaching with caustic criticism.

David also praised Tobe's unique ability to work and design products. He extolled Tobe's care for others and asserted, "I have never seen him angry." Then he dropped his voice and admitted that Tobe had some difficulty managing money in his business. But in a bold voice he proclaimed, "If Tobe had lived, he would likely have become a millionaire."

When the preaching service ended, people paid their last respects. An attendant lifted the lid of the casket and braced it open. Ushers released the congregants row by row to file by the coffin. The family silently observed from the front rows. Young and old paused by the bier, each paying silent respect. Several men plunged their calloused hands into the pockets of their handmade trousers to pull out huge white handkerchiefs. They blew their noses and wiped the tears off their weather-beaten faces as they stepped outside the building. Women dabbed at tears with handkerchiefs as they greeted Emma with a handshake.

After the crowd of 625 mourners had filed by, the family gathered around for a final farewell before the ushers closed the lid. John B. Yoder stepped forward, pulled out a Yankee screwdriver, and put several screws in the wooden top. Then six pallbearers lifted the casket and gently carried it to a wooden wagon. The spring wagon would need to go slowly, lest the ride be too bumpy. The horse switched its tail at some pesky flies.

Some members of the family had suggested that an automotive hearse be employed. Tobe's mother wouldn't hear of it. She said it wouldn't do to have a hearse at an Old Order Amish funeral, even if her son had recently joined the Beachy Amish church. John B. Yoder's spring wagon would have to do for this occasion. It was made so that a casket could slide under the raised seat. And so it was that a horse and wagon led the train of mourners through the heat to Tobe's grave at the West Center Amish Cemetery.

Epilogue

Soon after Dad died, our family moved back to Kansas. That is, all of us but Edith. Arvilla Weaver had become quite attached to Edith and offered to care for her in the Weaver home for the rest of her life. Mom agonized over the decision, then reluctantly agreed.

A few years later, the Weaver family moved from Iowa to Indiana. Eventually Noah and Sarah both died, leaving Arvilla to take care of Edith alone. At the time of this writing, Edith has lived with Arvilla for forty-five years. Edith far outlived the doctors' predictions.

When we first moved to Kansas, we lived in Grandpa Stutzman's house that was standing empty while they lived with Mattie Miller. By selling her share in the Stutzman shop to my Uncle Ervin, Mother gathered enough cash to buy materials to build an inexpensive new home. Grandma Mary Nisly offered an acre of land for a building site at the front edge of the shelter belt Mother helped to plant as a teenager.

Family members and community volunteers built our house in fall 1956. Fourteen-year-old Mary Edna went to work. Perry Lee and Glenn helped Uncle Raymond Nisly on the farm next door until they finished grade school, then each took full-time jobs in the neighborhood. Only Erma and I, as twins, had the luxury of going to high school.

About the time we children left home, Mother moved into a basement home next door to the main house. Perry

Lee's family was living in the main house when Mother succumbed to cancer in June 1989.

Mother worked hard and rarely complained about being widowed, at least not in my hearing. She never remarried. As I was growing up, we milked a cow, raised a few pigs, tended a small flock of chickens, and grew most of our own vegetables in the sandy Kansas soil. Mother cleaned houses to earn a bit of cash. Until the end of her life at age seventy-three, she lived very frugally and left a small estate.

After spending more than a decade in the researching and writing that produced this book, I find myself asking several questions. How has this journey changed my life? What difference does knowing Dad make? Have the results been worth the effort?

Yes, I'm convinced the journey has been well worth undertaking. First of all, I've learned a good deal besides family history. Writing a family narrative has helped me hone new skills. I watch more carefully for the small details that add distinctiveness and flavor to family stories. I observe individuals and families with more care and listen with greater concentration. I am more alert to the influence of family systems, the web of relationships that shapes generational behavior in nearly inexplicable ways.

More importantly, delving into the history of my family and church community has given me a deeper appreciation for my faith heritage. I understand more fully the challenges my ancestors faced in their generation and I have gained a greater determination to face the challenges in mine. I respect the way Amish church leaders adapted to the pressures of modernization while implementing a new vision for mission. As I have come to recognize their deep longing to do what was right, I have become a more empathetic person.

Most of all, I've learned a good deal about myself. Gazing into my father's face has helped me see my own. Like my father, I wake up most days with energy, enthusiasm, and unflagging optimism. My head, like his, is filled with innovative ideas I can hardly wait to put into shoe leather. And like him, I sometimes underestimate how long a new endeavor will take, then work long hours to prove to skeptics that the daunting task can be indeed be accomplished. Finally, like my father, I readily enlist other people to invest in my dreams, believing that what matters for me also matters for them. While I'm awed by the way Dad broke new ground, I'm humbled by his mistakes. I tremble when I see how easily I could make similar ones.

Thank you for staying with me to the end of this book. Perhaps now you can understand most fully what prompted me to choose the subtitle to this book. It is borrowed from a song written about the time that my father was born. It has become the prayer of my heart as I've traced the tangled strands of ambition in my father's life and reflect on the strands of my own. Perhaps this prayer may become yours as well.

> Dear Lord, take up the tangled strands
> Where we have wrought in vain
> That by the skill of thy dear hands
> Some beauty may remain
> —*Mrs. F. G. Burroughs*

One-room school at Thomas, Okla.
Tobias (Tobe) Stutzman is third from left in front row.

Young people at Hutchinson, Kan. Tobias is second from left.

Young people in Hutchinson, Kan., after church service, 1940. Tobias is fourth from left. Emma Nisly, his future bride, is sixth from left.

Tobias Stutzman's wrecked automobile.
Used by permission of the Kalona News

The Author

Ervin Stutzman was born into an Amish home as a twin in Kalona, Iowa. After his father's death a few years later, his mother moved her family to her home community in Hutchinson, Kansas. Ervin was baptized in the Center Amish Mennonite Church near Partridge, Kansas. Later, he joined the Yoder Mennonite Church, near Yoder, Kansas.

Ervin married Bonita Haldeman of Manheim, Pennsylvania. Together, they served five years with Rosedale Mennonite Missions in Cincinnati, Ohio. In 1982, they moved to Lancaster, Pennsylvania, to serve with Eastern Mennonite Board of Missions. Ervin was Moderator of Lancaster Mennonite Conference from 1991 to 2000, when he moved to Harrisonburg, Virginia, to serve as Dean of Eastern Mennonite Seminary.

Ervin has a B.A. from Cincinnati Bible College, an M.A. from the University of Cincinnati, a Ph.D. from Temple University, and an M.A.R. from Eastern Mennonite Seminary. He is a preacher, a teacher, and a writer: *Being God's People* (1998); *Creating Communities of the Kingdom* (co-authored with David Shenk, 1985); and *Welcome!* (1990), all published by Herald Press. Ervin and Bonita have three children, Emma (1978), Daniel (1981), and Benjamin (1983).